PRAISE FOR *UNSHACKLED*

"Every page felt like Amanda took on the struggles I've gone through straight from my soul. This story is heart wrenching, beautiful, and suspenseful. Camille Delaney is the attorney every incarcerated mom prays for. She experiences and uncovers the magnitude of challenges that we incarcerated moms endure trying to be in our children's lives while also attempting to navigate a judicial system that has set us up to fail. Thank you for bringing to light our dark situations."

—Kaylee Knudson, currently incarcerated mom

"As a formerly incarcerated mom who was shackled in the hospital when I gave birth, this story speaks to my heart. The experiences of the thousands of mothers in prison are stories that need to be told. I pray that readers recognize the devastating impact of incarceration on moms and their children. We need to do better."

—Cynthia Brady, formerly incarcerated mom, grandmother of twenty-five, and a substance use–disorder professional

"I'm a formerly incarcerated mother who experienced the issues that Camille Delaney struggles to remedy in *Unshackled*. Separation during incarceration causes emotional damage to both mothers and their children. Being in prison alongside so many mothers was heartbreaking. And the challenges they face when they are released are inexcusable. I appreciate how this story brings all these inequities to light."

—Deb Sheehan, formerly incarcerated mom and current program operations manager for Freedom Education Project, Puget Sound

"Amanda DuBois writes from her experience as a family law attorney and her lived experience working closely with people who are justice impacted. In *Unshackled*, she highlights the inequities experienced by incarcerated moms, and the strains it causes on familial ties. These stories are important to bring to light in a society that cautions on the side of silencing women in general but silencing even more the women that have been deemed 'bad.' I value Amanda for being able to use her position of power and privilege to tell these important stories."

—Carolina Landa, formerly incarcerated mother, current equity and policy analyst, Washington State House Democratic Caucus

"It was a full circle moment for me to provide feedback for this novel from my perspective as a mom with young kids when I was locked up. This story about moms in prison highlights the profound impact of incarceration on families and the gaps in justice for our communities. Stories like *Unshackled* foster greater understanding and ensure that the voices of these moms are heard and their struggles recognized. It is my hope that by telling our stories, readers will be moved to more deeply consider the collateral impacts of incarceration. So many of us who served prison time are striving to implement effective strategies that promote healing in our communities."

—Carolyn Presnell, formerly incarcerated mom and director of community engagement at WELD Seattle

"I spent over thirty years as a Seattle police officer, and during that time I also cofounded The IF Project, an organization that works with incarcerated women, many of whom are mothers. Through their stories, I have learned about the trauma they and their children have experienced because of women's incarceration. *Unshackled* weaves a story of sadness and hope into a compelling page turner that illuminates the huge challenges our criminal legal system places on women and their families. It was an honor to provide Amanda my unique perspective and experience not from just a police lens but from my many years working with moms and their children both in and out of prison."

—Kim Bogucki, retired Seattle Police detective and founder of The IF Project

"*Unshackled* is more than just a good read. The book continues the tradition of the Camille Delaney series—readable, entertaining, and tackling important issues. As an addiction policy professional, I was drawn to this compelling story about the criminal legal system and our societal failures to deal with untreated addiction."

"As a criminologist, I am not easily impressed with fiction in the crime and justice space. What a refreshing gem DuBois has given us in Camille Delaney! She did her homework to create characters and narratives that portray the actual lives of justice-involved women and the people who serve them. I'm now a fan!"

"Amanda DuBois has done it again. So vivid and engrossing that it is downright cinematic, *Unshackled* uncovers injustices in how our criminal legal system relates to victims of domestic violence. It exposes the irrationality of imposing criminal punishment, and specifically dehumanizing confinement, on domestic violence victims principally in need of mental health treatment and rehabilitation from trauma-spurred addiction. It gets to the heart of how family reunification is an imperative to healing. It is nothing short of a tour de force and required reading for all those who are passionate about criminal law reform."

UNSHACKLED

ALSO BY AMANDA DUBOIS

UNSHACKLED

AMANDA DuBOIS

A CAMILLE DELANEY MYSTERY

FLASH
POINT

This is a work of fiction. Names, characters, organizations, places, events, and incidents are either products of the author's imagination or are used fictitiously.

Copyright © 2025 by Amanda DuBois

Published by Flashpoint™, Seattle
www.flashpointbooks.com

Produced by Girl Friday Productions

Cover design: Emily Weigel
Production editorial: Katherine Richards
Project management: Sara Spees Addicott

Image credits: cover © Christopher Poulos

ISBN (paperback): 978-1-959411-74-1
ISBN (ebook): 978-1-959411-75-8

Library of Congress Control Number: 2024911274

First edition

To every mom who's ever been incarcerated. And to their kids.

CHAPTER ONE

The click of the handcuffs echoed across the antiseptic room. Charli's contractions were coming hard and fast. Straining against the steel cutting into her wrist, she locked eyes with the labor and delivery nurse hovering over the prison guard's shoulder. Charli blinked back tears as the guard roughly shackled her ankle to the bed rail. In prison you never let a guard see you show weakness.

"Stop!" the nurse snapped. "Do you really think this patient is going to escape while she's in active labor?"

A doctor, who had apparently been just outside the door, entered the room authoritatively. She glared at the woman clad in a blue prison guard uniform, complete with a gun on her hip. "Take them off," the doctor instructed the guard, gesturing to the cuffs. She removed her bright-red reading glasses and let them hang on the colorful beaded chain around her neck, then put her hands on her hips. "Now."

"Sorry, ma'am—DOC policy. There's nothing I can do." The guard's tone was polite, but she positioned herself so that only Charli could see the sarcastic, snarly glare directed solely at her. It wasn't often that Charli saw a guard apologize to anyone, let alone treat them with respect. But then, there was no way this guard would ever let the outside world actually see how inhumanely she treated prisoners. Charli strained unsuccessfully to read the doctor's name embroidered on the breast pocket of her white jacket and silently hoped the doctor had noticed the face the guard had made. *Sometimes you just need to be seen.*

The doctor wasn't buying the guard's act. "Seriously? You expect a patient to labor while shackled to the bed?"

The guard turned to the doctor with a forced smile. "Nothin' either of us can do, ma'am." Her southern drawl creeped Charli out.

"This is my patient." The doctor's voice was firm. "Department of Corrections is not in charge of this unit. I am. And I'm writing an order to remove the shackles. This is barbaric."

The guard flashed a genuine look of concern at a male guard who stood outside the door, watching the whole exchange. He was obviously senior to the woman assigned to stay in the room with Charli.

The male guard spoke up. "If we have a problem, we can call the hospital legal department. They should have the protocol for patients admitted from the prison." He sauntered into the room and stood behind the doctor, craning his head to look Charli up and down. Her hospital gown had fallen off her shoulder, and her breast was nearly exposed. She felt naked and vulnerable, and he knew it. Charli had never felt so humiliated. She set her jaw. This guy would never see her squirm.

The female guard sat down on the vinyl chair used by families of laboring patients. She settled in, grabbed the TV remote, and turned on the TV.

"Turn it off." The doctor could barely hide her contempt for the guard, who quietly complied.

Charli groaned as another contraction enveloped her in an all-consuming pain she'd never imagined possible.

The doctor pulled the privacy curtain so the guard couldn't see her performing a vaginal exam. Just as she snapped on her glove, the female guard pushed the curtain aside tentatively. "I'm sorry, ma'am, but DOC protocol says this patient can't leave my line of sight."

The doctor sized up the guard, holding her sterile gloved hand up in front of her, considering her options. Then she moved her body between Charli and the guard to try to provide as much privacy as possible.

The nurse seemed to sense what the doctor was doing. She held Charli's gaze as she moved over next to the doctor, to help protect her patient's privacy.

Another contraction. Charli closed her eyes and tried to erase the face of the guard, who had perched herself just in Charli's line of sight, with her hand on the edge of the curtain. It was obvious to Charli that this woman wanted her to remember that she was DOC property and that the guards were in charge and no one else.

Charli held her breath as the doctor swiveled around and said firmly to the guard, "There is no *protocol* that allows you to invade my patient's privacy." She emphasized the word "protocol." "Now sit." She glared as the guard backed away and sat down on the edge of her chair as if she might have to take off and chase down a runaway prisoner—never mind that the prisoner was currently in active labor and shackled to the bed.

Then, like magic, the doctor's visage softened entirely as she directed her attention to Charli for the examination. She pulled off her glove, smiled, and rubbed Charli's thigh. "You're four centimeters, just getting into active labor." She squeezed Charli's hand. "Everything's going to be fine. I can't imagine what this is like for you. I promise we'll do what we can to make this easier for you."

The nurse caught the doctor's gaze and nodded, then grabbed the phone. "We have a DOC patient up here, and we need someone from legal to interpret some policy questions. Room 605. Thanks."

The nurse turned away and spoke curtly on the phone before quickly resuming her position next to the doctor, between Charli and the guard, who was clearly struggling to appear compliant to the doctor while staying within DOC policy.

Charli's eyes grabbed the nurse's again.

The nurse leaned in close and spoke gently to Charli. "My name is Jayne, and I'm going to take good care of you." She stroked Charli's hair.

Charli was beyond relieved when she realized this Black sister with a deep Haitian accent was her assigned nurse. *Maybe it's an omen.*

Jayne turned to a colleague, who had appeared out of nowhere with a preheated blanket. Jayne tucked its folds around Charli with a gentle touch. She whispered, "I'll be here with you. I promise I won't leave you."

Charli tried to find a smile but was overtaken with another contraction. Her attempts to move to a comfortable position were barred by the shackles.

"Breathe with me, hon." Her nurse was inches from her face, taking one deep breath after another.

Charli stared intently into her nurse's hazel eyes and breathed with her.

"Big exhale." The nurse held Charli's hand and gave it a squeeze. Charli couldn't let go. She knew that as a Black woman, she had a higher risk of a poor outcome in childbirth. Being pregnant in prison had caused her unrelenting fear. If Serena Williams had trouble getting good maternity care, what were the chances that a nameless prisoner would mean anything to the prison medical staff? In the past several months, since she'd been incarcerated, she'd gone from being a successful business owner to just another Black woman with a long DOC number. Having Jayne as her nurse went a long way to easing her fear, and while she reveled in their immediate connection, she remained on high alert. Trust didn't come easy to Charli anymore.

"I'm so scared," Charli whispered, torn between sharing her true feelings with her nurse and not letting the guard see her vulnerability. "Please don't let the guard see me."

"I'm here for you, sis," Jayne whispered back. Her smile reminded Charli of her mom. "You're safe here, I promise. I can't imagine what you've been through. But right now, right here, you are safe with me. Okay?" She squeezed Charli's fingers with one hand and cupped the other under Charli's chin, looking her straight in the eye. "I won't leave you."

Charli wasn't sure she would ever let go of this woman. It had been months since Charli had had physical contact with another human being. Prison policy forbade any of the prisoners from touching each other. She basked in the nurse's soft, dry skin. And finally let loose a tear. The harsh exterior she'd built up the last several months in prison was beginning to crack. But just for a moment. And only with Jayne.

Jayne put a warm washcloth on Charli's forehead and helped her get ready for another contraction. "Look right at me."

Charli locked on to her nurse's eyes.

"Okay, let's breathe together. One . . ." Jayne inhaled deeply and loudly exhaled. "Two." Another deep inhale, and an exhale with a *whoosh*. "Three . . ."

Charli's uterus turned against her. The pain was relentless.

Jayne's voice came from the end of a long tunnel. "You're doing great—it'll just last a few more seconds."

Charli now had Jayne's hand in a death grip. She tried in vain to relax.

The doctor came back in and again stood shoulder to shoulder with the nurse to protect Charli from the guard's line of vision.

Charli startled at a knock on the door.

Jayne looked up. "Who's there?"

"Hospital legal."

Jayne turned to the doctor. "Can you ask Terri, the charge nurse, to talk with legal about these shackles and . . . the other issues?" She cocked her head at the guard.

"I'm on it." The doctor opened the door just wide enough to slide out and called for the charge nurse.

Charli squeezed Jayne's hand to grab her attention from whatever was going on outside the door as another contraction slammed her body. *Where are those eyes?*

It felt like Jayne was looking deeply into Charli's soul. Jayne nodded as Charli let out a deep, exaggerated breath.

The next thing Charli knew, a brigade of nurses entered the room and stood in front of the guard, in an obvious attempt to block her view. "Dr. Downey said you need some help in here." The tallest folded her arms and puffed herself up as she took her place in the wall of nurses. "Thankfully, we're not that busy tonight."

Another nurse stepped forward and took Charli's foot in her hand and began to massage it. She looked at one of her colleagues, who gently took the foot with the shackle on it. She wrapped Charli's ankle in a washcloth so the metal wouldn't chafe her.

Charli had never expected to feel this kind of care from a medical team in her entire life. As a Black woman, she'd long ago shied away from traditional medicine. She knew the system wasn't set up to address the health needs of women of color. But here she was, surrounded by a bevy of caring white women. And while she appreciated their concern, she never diverted her gaze from Jayne's. She needed a sister now, more than ever.

The doctor came back and told the prison guard that legal had advised her the hospital had to comply with DOC policy and keep the shackles on, but they were allowed to use a privacy curtain because the patient was restrained. The guard looked slightly embarrassed as the doctor officiously pulled the curtain, enclosing Charli in a cocoon of nurses. One of them turned down the lights.

Charli looked back into the sea of white faces, searching for the blessing that was her nurse, Jayne.

Jayne leaned over her and emphatically closed her eyes, demonstrating a deep, relaxing breath. The sides of her nostrils flared out. Charli closed her eyes and mirrored Jayne's exhalation.

After a couple of hours of early labor, Charli was beginning to get the hang of the breathing. She forced her mind to ignore the shackles, but every contraction jolted her back to reality. Jayne never left her side. Ever since she had gone to prison, Charli hadn't allowed herself to trust anyone. But now, she had let Jayne in. And she had a fleeting feeling of safety.

The next vaginal exam showed she was dilated enough to get an epidural. A nurse pulled the curtain open to allow the anesthesiologist to set up his tray and help Charli roll onto her side. This time, the guard—duly chastised—tried to look nonchalant, staring straight ahead as Charli rolled over and bared her naked backside to the medical team.

Jayne reached for the call bell. "We need some help in here again."

The anesthesiologist looked curiously at Jayne. "I think we're good here. You and I can handle this."

Jayne pointed at the guard and shook her head. "No—no, we're not good. That woman there is not a family member, nor has she been invited in here by the patient. She's a prison guard, and this patient deserves privacy from her." She raised an eyebrow and cocked her head to the side.

Three nurses filed in and stood again between the anesthesiologist and the guard. The anesthesiologist understood what was happening and immediately got to work. One of the nurses held Charli's leg so she couldn't fully feel the shackle.

"Wait a minute, she's shackled? What the hell?" the anesthesiologist shouted. "You're expecting me to do an epidural on a woman who can't properly position herself?" He turned and stared down the guard, who looked like she wanted to climb out the window at this point. "This patient needs to curl up so her lumbar spine is in the right position to safely place this needle." He held up a four-inch-long needle as though he was planning to joust with the guard.

A huge contraction built quickly, and Charli felt herself having to bear down. She grunted loudly and let loose a scream.

The OB flew into the room as Jayne yelled, "She's pushing—can you check her, Rene?"

The doctor hopped up on the side of the bed and slid on a pair of gloves just as water gushed all over everything. Charli felt an intense pressure building.

"Well, that happened fast," the doctor said. "She's ten centimeters and ready to go."

Charli felt like her insides were being torn out. Yet at the same time, she felt a wave of calm as she watched a ballet of seasoned nurses flying around the room, opening sterile packs and handing a suction device to the doctor, who gently welcomed her baby into the world. She placed the slippery little being onto Charli's abdomen and put Charli's hand on the baby. "Here's your mommy, sweet one."

The doctor had transformed right in front of Charli from her guardian into her angel. Charli blinked to see if the halo around the doctor's head was real. But then, in a split second, there was no one else in the room—all Charli could see were the gorgeous, big brown eyes looking up at her. She burst into tears. "Her name is Willow." She smiled up at her newfound friends. *Is it strange that a few of the nurses and even the doctor are wiping away tears?*

Charli couldn't tell if she lay there for two minutes or two hours. She felt only the bliss of motherhood washing over her.

At some point in her reverie, Charli handed little Willow off to Jayne, who took her to the nursery to be cleaned up. And much to Charli's surprise, one of the nurses—the one who had been massaging her feet—returned with a big plate of homemade ravioli. "Here, it's my grandma's special ravioli—I brought it for my dinner tonight, but I don't expect you get any home-cooked food in prison." She smiled and set up a tray so Charli could eat.

"Oh my God. This is amazing." Charli was beyond touched by the generosity. "Thank you so much."

Dr. Downey appeared next, with a bowl of fresh strawberries. "From my garden—I brought them in for the nurses tonight."

"Thank you," Charli said softly.

"Speaking of gardens, how about some fresh-grown romaine salad from mine?" Jayne reappeared with a bowl of fresh greens.

"I feel like I'm in a dream of some kind." Charli smiled. "You all are so kind. I can't thank you enough."

Charli inhaled the home-cooked meal and was about to lie back in bed when she jolted up. She could hear a familiar voice yelling in the hallway. *What the hell is he doing here?* She suppressed a gasp as her estranged husband crashed through the doorway, brandishing what looked like a pile of legal paperwork. "I have a court order that says I can see my baby!" he announced brashly.

Jayne looked at Charli. "Do you know this guy?"

Charli froze.

Jayne moved quickly to the door and grabbed the guy by the arm, ushering him out into the hall. "I'm sorry, sir, this is a private patient room. I need to ask you to leave."

Charli could see through the half-open door. "Oh no, you don't." He thrust the paperwork into Jayne's face. "I'm her husband—and this is my kid."

"Your kid? Really?" Jayne put her hands on her hips and looked across the hall at the ward clerk. "Looks like we'll need security up here."

"Security? You're calling security on me for coming to see my wife? And my *child*?" He hovered over the nurse menacingly.

Jayne ignored him. She went back into the room and shut the door firmly.

"Do you know him?"

Charli nodded like a terrified child.

"Is he your husband?"

"He was," Charli whispered. "Well, I guess he still is, but he set me up and got me thrown in prison, so . . . I wouldn't say we're close."

A young hospital security guard opened the door a crack and said, "Jayne, can I see you out in the hallway?"

Jayne returned with a handful of signed court orders. "It looks like he went to court last week and got an order allowing him to come to the hospital to see the baby when you gave birth."

Charli considered her options for a minute. She reached up and pulled Jayne close so the guard couldn't hear her. "It's not his baby and he knows it."

Jayne stood up and took her cell phone out of her pocket. "Hang on, my husband's a lawyer—I'm going to call him. Is that okay with you?"

"Well, I can't say I'm a fan of lawyers, but I do think we need some kind of legal advice here," Charli agreed.

Jayne put the papers down on Charli's bed and began methodically taking pictures of them one at a time. "I'm going to text these to my husband. I'll be right back."

Before Jayne could return, a nurse appeared with Willow in a polka-dot beanie cap, tightly rolled in a fuzzy pink blanket. Her thick black curls crept out around her face. The nurse looked at the prison guard, who almost cracked a smile at the sight of the angelic baby. The nurse pulled the curtain. "Excuse me, the patient is going to breastfeed now."

The guard shrugged. It looked like she'd been chastised enough for one evening.

Charli was lost in love again as the tiny baby latched on to her breast. She was completely unprepared for the rush of openhearted adoration that almost burst out of her chest every time she saw those amazing big brown eyes.

When Charli came back to reality, Jayne was standing at the foot of her bed, taking pictures of Charli and Willow, who was still dreamily nursing. "Can you keep her with you in prison?" she asked, with genuine concern.

Charli shook her head as the tears ran down her face. "No. I can't qualify for the mothers-and-babies program. It's only available for mothers who will be released within three years. And I don't get out for twelve." She hugged Willow close.

The doctor, who was standing by the bedside and overheard Charli, chimed in. "Well, jeez, I'm concerned about your blood loss. We're going to need to keep you here for a few days to observe your hematocrit."

Charli understood the magnitude of the doctor's gift to her and sobbed quietly. "Oh my God. Thank you so much. You are an angel."

Jayne reappeared. "Okay, I called my husband, and the judge ordered that your ex *can* hold the baby and take her to see his family in the waiting room."

"But it's not his baby!" Charli almost shouted.

"Well, here's the weird thing. According to my husband, under the law, since you're still married, he's considered the father. They call it a presumed father. So until some kind of genetic testing, he has all the rights of a father."

"You've got to be kidding me." Charli moved the baby to her other breast with the help of a nurse.

Jayne lowered her voice. "I think you need to let him hold the baby and let his family see her."

"Wait—what? He has no family—his mother is in Taiwan, and he got his brother thrown in prison, just like he did to me."

Jayne looked again at the court order, then put it down. "Well, it says he can take the baby to the waiting room to meet the family. The hospital legal team reviewed the court order and says we have to let him take her. Just for a few minutes." Right on cue, Willow's mouth opened, and she unlatched, sound asleep and sated.

Charli wasn't going to let this asshole ruin her bliss. "Well, let's get it over with so you can kick him out. Tell him to come in here." She adjusted her hospital gown and pulled the covers up over herself with her nonshackled hand, glaring at the guard, who was lost in her phone, playing a video game.

Jayne opened the door and ushered Charli's ex into the room. "You can take her to the waiting room, but a nurse is going with you."

As Charli stoically handed him the baby, he leaned over and whispered to Charli, "You be good now."

Charli narrowed her eyes. "You have five minutes. Asshole."

The guard looked up for a second, then went back to her game.

Charli watched a petite blond nurse nearly run to keep up as Charli's ex whisked the baby down the hallway.

Charli looked at the clock: five minutes after ten. She grabbed a chocolate chip cookie one of the nurses had offered her and watched the second hand sweep around the clock.

Ten minutes after ten came and went. As did ten fifteen. Then ten twenty. At ten thirty, Charli could sense a bustle of activity outside her room. *There must be some kind of OB emergency happening.* She could hear people yelling. Finally, Jayne came into her room. This time she wasn't just crying—she was sobbing.

She sat on Charli's bed and held her free hand. "He took her. He just cut off her security band and took her."

Charli couldn't breathe. The room was turning black, and the walls were closing in on her. She opened her mouth, but nothing came out.

Just then, the bedside phone rang. Jayne picked it up. "It's him," she whispered.

Charli grabbed the phone. "You bring her back this minute!"

The line was silent for a few seconds, and then he spoke. "You've got my computer—I've got your baby. Better keep quiet, bitch." He hung up.

Charli began to cry. And then she screamed, wailing as if her heart had been ripped from her chest.

CHAPTER TWO

Camille Delaney had been a lawyer for fifteen years but had never seen the inside of a prison. She stood shakily at the front desk of the Washington Corrections Center for Women and handed the officer the letter from Northwest Women's Law Center that explained she was there to review child-custody cases for some of the women inside. It was just like the Law Center to approach her to represent one woman and then casually mention that it would actually be more like a legal clinic for several women all trying to gain access to their children. And, as usual, Camille couldn't say no. So here she was, standing in the drab, low-ceilinged prison lobby, wondering what the next few hours would hold. Camille was grateful that her legal assistant, Lucia, who had served sixteen months at WCCW, had tried to prepare her. But still, this place was a little scary.

As she handed her driver's license to a guard, it struck Camille that the only spot of color in the monochromatic beige lobby was the pair of flags hanging limply on metal stanchions—the green Washington State flag and the Stars and Stripes. Camille looked blankly at the guard, who gestured to a bank of small lockers on the wall behind her. "Put your keys and personal belongings in one of those lockers. You can take a pad of paper in with you." He handed her a visitor's pass to clip to her jacket.

Camille smiled. The guard didn't.

The metal detector was similar to the one at the courthouse. But at the courthouse they didn't have the green-light, red-light style, like the kind at customs in some airports. Everyone here had to walk through the metal detector, but the limp sign hanging next to the magnetometer stated that only those who got a red light had to undergo a pat-down. As she stepped through the metal detector, grateful for the green light, she gave up the idea of engaging with the prison staff—they clearly had absolutely no interest in small talk.

"Over there." The guard cocked his head toward a wooden bench next to a glass door leading to an outside courtyard. She walked tentatively toward the door and sat down. The wall in front of her was filled with pictures of prison officers surrounding a couple of plaques congratulating the volunteer of the year and employee of the year. The smiles on their faces were a sharp contrast to the oppressive vibe of the prison lobby.

No one was in a hurry around this place. It took about twenty minutes for her escort, the law librarian, to arrive. The librarian was friendly, but businesslike. Camille waited as the woman ushered her through a big door that magically buzzed. When the door opened, it made a very loud click that made Camille jump. The courtyard was chilly, so the twosome walked quickly to a gate that had yet another imposing mechanical lock on it. Huge coils of barbed wire hovered over the sturdy chain-link fence that encircled the next enclosure. The gate buzzed, the click echoed, and then they were through. If there hadn't been so much barbed wire, the place might have been a typical suburban high school. Off to her right was what looked like a portable classroom, but with no sign of life. It seemed a bit misplaced. Not quite inside the actual prison complex, but for sure not outside the barbed wire.

Another gate. Another loud buzz. And another scary click. They were getting closer to the low-slung buildings Camille had seen from the parking lot. Camille crossed her arms for warmth as the wind picked up. They hurried across another small courtyard.

At last, they reached the end of their trek, and the librarian pulled open the heavy entrance door to the building. This time, buzzing filled the cramped entryway as they entered. It hit Camille that she was on the precipice of entering into the heart of the complex, where she'd soon be meeting women whose stories were likely as varied as the women themselves.

Camille startled as an intense-looking gray-haired guard spoke through a tinny-sounding speaker from behind thick plexiglass. It was apparent that the floor where he was standing was a few feet higher than where Camille and the librarian stood. His presence even behind the glass was imposing. "Badge." No eye contact. No indication of any humanity.

"I'm sorry?" Camille stammered.

"Your badge." He pointed at the plastic badge she'd clipped on her lapel.

She looked at him blankly.

His impatience was apparent. "Show me your badge, ma'am."

Camille noticed her hand trembling as she unclipped the badge and held it up for the guard to see. He cocked his head to the side as if to tell her to move along.

Camille followed the librarian, who had turned away from the guard toward yet another serious-looking metal door. This one was the scariest yet. It slid slowly open, as if it were giving visitors one last chance to back out. As metal grated on metal, Camille took a deep breath and stepped across the threshold.

Now she was in a short colorless hallway that ended in yet another heavy metal door. Now that they were out of the wind, the twosome slowed their pace as they walked down the hall and waited as the giant sliding door behind them clanged shut. They were trapped now between the two doors—one on either end of the hallway—clearly intentional so that no one could get through one door if the other was open. Camille reminded herself to breathe and wondered how many more of these locking doors they'd have to traverse.

Another buzz. Another click. And she was in.

This was the heart of the prison. Camille stood in a huge cement courtyard landscaped with intermittent skeletons of emaciated rhododendrons that surrounded classroom-like buildings. Oddly, despite the openness of the giant space, there was no place to sit. There were big planters filled with actual color—the prolific purple cabbage looked totally out of place in the oppressive courtyard. She'd heard about the horticulture project inside the prison. *This must be one of their crops.*

For the first time since she'd been buzzed inside, the next door they went through simply opened. No buzz. No click. It was temporarily disorienting. The librarian smiled at a guard sitting at a desk on a pedestal—this one with no plexiglass. But still, the guard's facial expression was deadly serious even as she acknowledged the librarian.

"Hey, Tina. I saw your daughter's robotics team is heading to the finals. Congrats!"

"Don't congratulate me; her team worked hard on their project. But I'll pass on your kind words to Lexi."

The librarian pointed Camille down another hallway. "Law library straight ahead. Follow me."

Camille felt like she was in a community college or a high school as she looked down the hallway lined with classrooms.

Everything was some shade of gray or beige. Even down to the concrete floors. The librarian seemed to be warming up, and she actually smiled again as Camille surveyed the medium-size room lined with shelves sparsely populated with a mishmash of worn books.

The woman finally introduced herself. "I'm Tina." She gestured to a plastic chair at a government-issued metal table, where a can of pens had been placed. "It's not fancy, but this place sometimes feels like a lifeline to the women in here."

Camille put her purple legal pad on the table and looked around the room as she watched a group of khaki-clad women and others in gray sweatpants hurrying to and fro in the hallway outside the library. It reminded Camille of the chaos in a high school between classes—but not exactly. She couldn't help but wonder what had brought these women here.

Camille had only recently returned to the world of family law, when she had realized that she missed helping families transition to their new lives. These cases would obviously be different, but still she hoped she could provide some hope to the women trying to reunite with their children after their release.

As she turned around in her chair, Camille caught her breath, surprised to see a young woman dressed in baggy khakis and a dingy gray sweatshirt standing in front of her. Her brown hair was pulled up in a ponytail, revealing an intricate tattoo curling around her neck. She looked intently at Camille with gray eyes. *Where did she come from?* Camille looked around curiously.

"You the lawyer?" The woman's voice was quiet yet harsh.

Camille stood up. She had been advised not to have any physical contact with the women, and she stopped herself from reaching out to shake the woman's hand. "I'm Camille."

The woman smiled and said, "I'm Lizbeth. Thanks for coming."

It was hard to put an age on her new client—maybe midthirties? "Please." Camille pointed to the chair opposite hers at the table. "Have a seat."

What the woman said next surprised Camille. "I work in the law library here, and I help the women fill out the paperwork to get started on custody issues for when they're released." She went to the desk by the doorway and pulled out a stack of files.

So this wasn't a potential client; this was her new assistant: a jail-house lawyer, according to Lucia, who had explained to Camille about her own foray into the world of law during her time in prison.

"I'm really hoping you can help us here." Lizbeth plopped down the file folders. "I thought it would make sense for us to just meet alone, since it's your first visit. That way I can get you up to speed on the cases I've been working on. Sometimes I get in a bit over my head." She took a handful of files and held them out to Camille.

Camille went on autopilot now. Hand a lawyer a stack of files and . . . She flipped her glasses down from their usual perch on her head and began skimming.

Lizbeth narrated the cases as Camille nodded.

"And Veronica's mom has her kid, but she won't let Veronica have visitation when she gets released. I filed a petition to modify the parenting plan, but I'm not sure the court will allow it until Veronica fulfills her drug-treatment requirements."

"What are the requirements?" Camille turned to the relevant section of the form parenting plan. "Okay, so she has to go to Allied Drug Treatment Center and finish the program there." She paused to think for a second. "I think that's a twelve-month program."

Lizbeth interrupted. "But check this out. The judgment and sentence in her criminal case says she has to complete treatment at behavioral care, and if she doesn't, she goes back to prison. So, she has to do this one first. But that doesn't qualify for the requirements in the family law parenting plan."

Camille reached out her hand. "Can I see that?"

Lizbeth handed her the paperwork.

"So, you're telling me that in order to stay in compliance with the terms of her release, the judge in her criminal case ordered her to go to one treatment center, but the judge in the family law case ordered her to go to treatment at a completely different place?"

Lizbeth nodded. "Yup. It happens all the time, and the judges aren't all that keen on reconsidering these orders. So moms can't even get back with their kids until they do both treatment plans, which takes about two years—one year for each program. It sucks."

Camille put her hand on the stack of file folders. "What's up with all the drug-treatment orders? Almost every single case has a variation of this."

"Mostly opioid related," Lizbeth explained. "Lots of the women here ended up on meth because of some kind of trauma or domestic violence in childhood. The drugs are the only way they can numb the pain. Others got hooked on legal pain meds, like for an accident or surgery or something, and then the doc doesn't reorder the meds. So they hit the street for heroin and, more recently, fentanyl." She looked at Camille. "The people in our community can't afford to run to a therapist, like you or your friends can. They have no way to process their DV, or maybe it was a childhood rape, or their moms sent them out onto the street to sell crack, or to sell their bodies so the mom can buy meth. Whatever it was, they self-medicated with what was available."

Camille felt embarrassed that she had never considered actual psychological trauma could be what might precipitate someone to turn to heavy street drugs. Somehow, she'd had the idea people made a conscious decision to use street drugs and then things just spiraled out of hand. "That's awful. But I guess it makes sense." She thought about her wealthy divorce clients who sent their kids to see a therapist at the first sign of family discord. "Of course these women couldn't access mental health services," she said out loud to no one in particular.

Lizbeth interrupted her. "So they get on drugs, and then they can't afford them. And they end up committing property crimes or robbery to fund their habit—usually encouraged by their boyfriends, who are often their dealers. Then the women take the fall. It's a screwed-up mess. We aren't bad people in here. We're traumatized people who society doesn't care about."

Camille was silent for a few minutes. *Traumatized women taken away from their kids and thrown into this place to allegedly protect society.* She'd never given much thought to the plight of women in prison, and certainly hadn't really considered the effect on their children and therefore society as a whole. Her mind started to race as she imagined the lives of these forgotten and ignored innocent children, who, without their mothers, were likely to reenact the same family trauma and end up in prison in a never-ending generational cycle.

Returning her attention to Lizbeth, Camille wondered what had caused her to be locked up—but remembered Lucia telling her that it was invasive to inquire about a conviction. *Let them decide if, and when, to disclose it,* Lucia had advised her.

"Okay, I need to figure this out." Camille was feeling pissed. "I'm going to get this issue in front of our judges—this isn't doing much to help kids get back with their moms—and we all know that being removed from their parents is one of the main predictors of kids who fall into the prison pipeline."

"You would do that for us?" Lizbeth looked like she was about to cry. "Present this to a judge?"

"Of course." Camille smiled. "But I need a case to argue this issue to the court."

"Okay, I get it. We find a case that has these issues and you go to court on that case."

"Exactly." Her new associate jailhouse lawyer was growing on her. "Your legal work is really amazing, Lizbeth. When you get out of here, you should consider law school."

Lizbeth beamed. "I really love this law library. And I love working with the women. It's the only thing that keeps me sane in here." She hesitated for a second. "And I'm not getting out of here for a pretty long time," she said quietly.

Camille wasn't sure how to respond. She offered, "Well, I mean it. You're doing great work."

"Here's a really interesting one, and it's way beyond my pay grade." Lizbeth held up a thick file folder. "This woman gave birth at Puget

Sound General, and her ex kidnapped the baby. She has no idea where the baby is now. She wants to get an order placing the kid with the actual bio dad."

"Oh my God. The father took the baby? And there's a different bio dad?"

"Yeah. The guy who took the kid is technically her husband—not really her ex, because they never actually got a divorce. But he's not the father. I learned through research that there's something called a presumed parent." Lizbeth spoke like a first-year law student. "It's when a married person has a baby, their husband—or wife—is considered the legal parent when the baby is born."

"You're exactly right." Camille was impressed.

"Anyway, the asshole 'presumed father' kidnapped the baby from the hospital."

"So, if he's not the father, who is?"

Lizbeth leaned forward. "Get this. Charli's husband set her up on a drug charge because she was having an affair with his twin brother."

"And she ended up in prison?"

"Yep. It was a big amount of heroin she was caught with. And to be sure she got a long sentence, he planted a gun under her driver's seat. So her sentence is way longer than you'd usually see for someone with no record. Her husband really hates her. He also did the same thing to his brother—but a much smaller amount, and no gun, so his sentence is shorter."

"Jeez."

"Can you help her find the baby?"

"When did this happen?"

"Like, about seven years ago."

"Seven years ago? I'm not so sure. But even if we could find the baby, we'd have to get a DNA test because he's still the presumed parent. Like you said, the baby was born while they were married."

"I know, but here's the thing. The husband and brother are identical twins, so they'd have the same DNA. That's what Charli told me. So she's not sure what would happen even if she finds the baby. And the real bio dad is getting out of prison soon, and Charli wants him to have custody of the kid."

"Wow. What a mess. And so sad."

"Charli's new bunkie is a nurse or something. She just got down about a month ago. She's been helping on the medical end."

"The bunkie got down where?" Camille asked.

"Down. Here. In prison. When you go to prison, it's called 'going down.'"

"Lots of lingo to learn." Camille tried not to look too embarrassed.

"Charli's bunkie's been helping brainstorm how to genetically prove that the husband's brother is actually the father. Charli wants to file a motion to give custody to the bio dad after he's released, even if they can't find the baby yet. She wants him to have a court order so, in case the baby turns up, he can get custody."

"Well, first we'd need to get a DNA test to prove who the dad is before we even try to get a court order giving him custody. We'd need to find the child, get a court order for the dad and child to get DNA tests. Get the tests interpreted. And then we could ask for a custody order."

"This is so fucked up—Charli couldn't even qualify for the mothers-and-babies program, so all she had were those few hours in the hospital, and he stole those from her. And now no one can even find the kid."

"I didn't know moms could have their newborns in prison."

"Just moms who are three years from the gate. Moms with longer sentences have to give up their babies in the hospital. It also depends on the crime they were charged with. But it definitely sucks that they take babies from their moms."

"Oh my God, that's awful that they limit who can keep their babies in prison."

"Can we get a court order giving the baby to the bio dad? If we can find her and get the DNA testing done?"

"I can't say. This is complicated. I'm not sure if the court would even give the baby back to the bio dad now that the presumed father has apparently had her for seven years. The court doesn't like to disrupt an established parent-child bond."

"That might not be the case. Charli is pretty sure her ex dumped the kid with his mother. That kid probably couldn't pick the ex out of a lineup. I can't imagine there's going to be a bonding issue."

Camille nodded. "If we could prove that, it might help."

"Well, that's why we need your help. But first we need to find the baby. Lucia sent me a JPay prison email message that you have a kick-ass PI who might be able to find the baby."

Camille smiled. Of course Lucia had reached out to Lizbeth, the jailhouse lawyer, via the antiquated prison email system. "Gotta love Lucia."

"Best bunkie I ever had. Love that girl. Turns out she was a helluva writer—she helped me on a bunch of legal briefs. Seems like she was in and out of here in a flash. Her family has money, so she had a real live private lawyer. Private lawyers negotiate the best sentences. They have connections."

"Didn't you have access to public defenders?"

Lizbeth rolled her eyes. "I can't believe you even said that." She smiled. "In here we call them public pretenders." She laughed. "Actually, some of them are okay, but they're all so busy. All they usually do is convince us to plead guilty and take a lesser sentence. If we don't, the prosecutor threatens us with all kinds of additional charges. And if we go to trial on those charges and lose, we're fucked. So, we plead out and end up here. It sucks."

"I hear you." Camille relented. "Let me see the file."

Lizbeth handed the last folder to Camille. "Thanks."

Camille was hooked and completely lost track of time, talking with her new colleague about the facts of some of the most complicated and interesting cases she'd heard about in years.

The PA system shattered her concentration. "Movement." Prisoners were only allowed to move between the buildings at twenty past the hour during a time called "movement." Lizbeth stood up dutifully.

A stocky gray-haired middle-aged woman in a blue prison guard uniform stood in the doorway and pointed at the clock. "Time to wrap it up, Trujillo. Let's go."

Lizbeth looked at Camille as she headed for the door. "I'm hoping you can come back next week and meet with the women; they're on the list to come to the family law legal clinic. I kinda told them you'd run it." She ducked sideways as if she were expecting a blow.

Camille laughed as the guard guided Lizbeth down the hall. "I'll be here!" she shouted.

Lizbeth turned and threw her hands in the air and gave a touchdown sign. "Appreciate you!" she hollered back as she merged into the sea of khaki-clad women out in the hallway.

CHAPTER THREE

Camille sat in her car in the prison parking lot. She looked up at the tall fir trees surrounding the barbed wire enclosure and began to formulate a possible plan to find the missing baby. *How the hell did the husband manage to dodge security at the hospital?* She plugged in her phone and dialed her private investigator, Trish Seaholm, who picked up on the first ring.

"I've been trying to reach you!" Trish nearly shouted. "I followed the husband of that new divorce client of yours, and you're right—the jackass just walked out of the bank with a huge wad of cash. I stood right behind him in line and watched him pocket the dough."

Camille ignored Trish's jackpot. "We have a new case." She tripped over her words. "Our client's husband kidnapped her newborn baby from the hospital. We have to find her." She pulled out of the parking lot and headed down the country road that wound through the forest toward State Route 3 on the Kitsap Peninsula.

"Holy shit! When did it happen, and at what hospital?" Trish was all business.

"About seven years ago."

"Wait. What?" Trish was clearly deflated. "You want me to find a missing kid on a cold case from more than half a decade ago?"

"Yep. This is so screwed up. Since the mom was a prisoner, she could only stay with her baby for a day or so. But hours after she gave birth, the baby disappeared. The baby's name is Willow."

"Prison? What are you talking about?"

Camille pulled up to a stop sign and noticed that a string of client texts was downloading. "Can you and Gigi meet me at my place for dinner? There's an issue of DNA involved in this, so I'm hoping your doctor girlfriend can help. I gotta hop off and answer some calls."

"Sure. Prison? Really? Can't wait. See you around six-ish?"

Camille looked at her watch. "Better make it seven—I'm heading toward the Narrows Bridge, and traffic might be tight this time of day."

The usually one-hour drive back to Seattle from Gig Harbor during rush hour took about two and a half that night. But it gave Camille time to check in with her paralegal, Amy, and call a handful of clients, who peppered her with questions about their cases—all of them anxious to be in and out of the legal system as quickly as possible. Camille was grateful to exit the congested freeway and head down toward the urban houseboat where she lived with her three girls and her husband, Sam.

Late fall ebbed and flowed its way into winter in the Pacific Northwest. And at nighttime, Lake Union kicked up shades of dark and light gray, along with shimmers of silver and gold reflected from the downtown high-rises and the houses and apartments peppering the hillside across the lake from Camille's houseboat community. Camille loved living on the busy lake in the middle of the rapidly growing metropolis.

Houseboats only really pitch and sway when there's a serious storm. Nevertheless, Camille marveled at the distinct transition as she stepped from the solid cement dock onto the wooden entry deck of the large, boxy floating home. She stopped for a beat at her own front door and reflected on the fact that there would be no buzz. No loud click. What must it be like to live behind all that barbed wire? She pushed open the door and hollered up the stairs to the living area. "I'm home!"

Camille's heart did a little flip of gratitude when the three separate disembodied voices responded together, yet separately. "Hi, Mom!"

"Is Daddy home yet?"

Camille's friend and private investigator, Trish Seaholm, looked over the balcony at the top of the stairs. "Not yet! But since I beat you here, I saw your note on the counter about having chicken for dinner, so I preheated the oven!"

Camille smiled. Trish was more adept at calling Uber Eats than she was at actually cooking, but Camille appreciated the effort. "I'm going to change—I'll be up in a minute." She dropped her black Tumi backpack on the entryway floor and opened her bedroom door. The cozy espresso-brown room enveloped her, and she exhaled deeply as she sat for a moment on the bed, wondering where Lizbeth went for a moment of peace.

Slipping out of her work clothes and pulling on her yoga pants, Camille zipped up her hoodie and stopped to watch the drizzle on the glassy water outside her bedroom. A colorful male mallard paddled by aimlessly. She wondered if father ducks ever kidnapped their babies. The case was coming alive inside her head now.

"Mo-om!" Camille's fourteen-year-old daughter, Libby, crashed through the door. "I got an A on my Chinese test!"

Camille gave Libby a hug. "You have such a language brain! I can't believe you can make sense out of all these different characters." She took the paper from her daughter's outstretched hand and admired the complex Chinese words scattered across the page—the symbols could have been Egyptian hieroglyphs for all she knew. "Unbelievable." Her admiration was sincere. "Did you get a hundred percent? I don't see any red marks anywhere." She kissed Libby's head.

"Top grade in the class." Libby giggled. "And I'm teaching Gracie too! She's way ahead of her class in Chinese." She grabbed her test paper from Camille's hand and put on Camille's glasses. Standing tall, she announced, "I might be a teacher someday." She reconsidered. "Or maybe a professor, like Daddy. I'm gonna learn, like, a hundred languages."

"You can be anything you set your mind to, my little language prodigy." Camille grabbed Libby's hand, and together they bounded up the stairway to the living area on the second floor of the floating home, where Trish was helping Camille's older daughter, Angela, with another of her famous art projects. Camille would never have guessed that the girls would be so different, even though they were biological sisters whom she and Sam had adopted from Korea when they were four and seven.

Angela didn't look up from her position on the floor at the top of the stairs where she was pouring paint on a large canvas. "Shh . . . I need to concentrate."

Camille smiled at her darling teen in her paint-spattered overalls, her long black hair up in a bun, peeking out from under a red bandanna scarf. Angela pushed a tendril of hair off her forehead with her wrist and bumped Jake, the family greyhound, away with her hip.

Camille held her breath, hoping that none of the bright-pink paint would spill on her newly refinished hardwood floors. She looked at Trish and rolled her eyes.

"Genius at work here," Trish whispered as she handed Camille a glass of white wine. "Angela just learned that a group of flamingos is called a 'flamboyance,' so she decided she had to come home and paint one."

Camille tiptoed over to the open kitchen and began unwrapping the chicken that had been marinating in the harissa sauce she'd made the day before. No matter how intense her work as a lawyer was, she loved to decompress by making her family a home-cooked meal nearly every night. Thankfully, her girls were experts at cleanup. It seemed like a fair deal.

The girls shared about their day at school as Camille chopped the cauliflower and threw it on a sheet pan to roast along with a scattering of mushrooms, while Jake sat calmly at her feet, waiting for the core of the cauliflower—his favorite part.

"Okay, Picasso, time to clean up your studio." Camille faked a stern look at Angela as she shook the marinade from the chicken and plopped it in the sauté pan. "Down," she commanded Jake, and tossed him his veggie treat when he complied.

"I do need a real studio," Angela whined. "And I'll clean up after dinner. I'm not at a good stopping place right now."

Camille looked around at the open floor plan that took up the entire top story of the houseboat. Cushy oversize cream slipcovered couches faced each other next to the sliding glass windows that opened onto the deck. Between the living area and the kitchen was a long modern walnut slab dining table with eight woven-leather chairs. Angela's art project was set up on the only open floor space, at the top of the stairs that led down to the first-floor entry.

"Not exactly sure where we'd have space for an art studio, sweetheart." Camille shook her head as she filled the pot with water for the pasta. "But your painting is lovely."

No one had heard Trish's girlfriend, Gigi, arrive at the front door. The striking Black woman, wearing a bright orange-yellow Gore-Tex jacket, stopped herself from stepping onto Angela's painting at the top of the stairs. "Hey, guys!" She held up a bouquet of purple and yellow pansies. "Best winter flowers ever!"

Libby looked up from her laptop. The screen was filled with Chinese characters. "Nice. Wonder how you say 'pansy' in Chinese." She clicked her mouse.

"Whatever happened to learning French and Spanish?" Gigi peered over Libby's shoulder at the incomprehensible content on the screen.

Libby looked up at Gigi. "Do you have any idea of how many more people in the world speak Chinese than almost any other language?"

"Good point."

Libby was googling. "Twice as many people speak Chinese as Spanish. And let's not even waste time on French." She clicked back to her Chinese homework.

"You're right. I guess I'm just jealous," Gigi said as Trish helped her out of her jacket, kissed her on the cheek, and gazed for a few seconds into her eyes.

"Busy day?" Trish handed Gigi a glass of wine.

Gigi rolled her neck to get the kinks out. "Ugh. Sometimes I wish I'd chosen some specialty other than pathology. My neck gets frozen when I lose track of time in my lab, staring into a microscope."

Trish pulled a chair out for Gigi and began to massage her neck. "Camille has a new case and needs some doctor advice."

"Well, where's Sam? Last time I checked, Camille was married to a hunk of a doctor. Epidemiologists are smarter than us pathologists. He can probably help." Gigi laughed. "Not sure a pathologist is what you need."

"He's finishing up his paper for the *Journal of Epidemiology*." Camille smiled as she turned the chicken breasts over in the sauté pan. "Deadlines, deadlines—you university professors are all the same."

"I hear you." Gigi smiled. "So, what's your case about?" She leaned forward.

Camille started to explain about the kidnapped baby but thought better of it as her seven-year-old foster daughter danced into the room in her turquoise leotard and pink tights. She pirouetted across the floor. Sometimes Camille's clients' stories gave Gracie nightmares.

"Mom. I'm doing this flamingo piece as interpretive, but which pink looks best for shading in the feathering?" Angela pointed to several slashes of pink on the leg of her white overalls.

Camille stood back and framed her hands over the slashes of pink. "Come stand over the painting." She pulled Angela gently.

Angela balanced on one leg so the leg with the color samples hovered over the artwork.

"That one." Camille steadied Angela by holding her elbow and pointed thoughtfully to the middle pink paint sample.

"I was thinking the top one." Angela looked at the paint colors intently.

Camille nodded. "Well, that was my second choice. So . . ."

"Thanks, Mom!" Angela grabbed her painting knife and was immediately lost in the color she was creating on her palette.

Camille returned to the stove and dumped the penne pasta into the roiling water, checked the chicken, and then pulled the roasted cauliflower and mushrooms out of the oven while Gracie hovered over Libby's shoulder. Libby was pointing at pictures of cars and boats and planes and colors and animals while Gracie answered in Chinese. Camille felt a surge of love for her kids and friends as she looked over the busy family scene unfolding in her kitchen.

Gigi turned to Camille as Gracie and Libby spoke to each other with a sense of bravado using words none of the adults in the room could ever imagine speaking. "Now, about your case?" Gigi asked quietly.

"Super-sad story, but without all the details, the question is—do identical twins have the same DNA such that it would be impossible to tell which one is the father of a child?"

Gigi looked up at Camille and paused for a beat.

What was that flash in Gigi's eyes?

Gigi took a sip of wine. "Identical twins share *almost* identical DNA," she said slowly. "So a standard DNA test wouldn't be able to tell which one is the dad."

"Is there any testing at all that would distinguish between them?" Trish prodded.

"I'd have to research it; actually, there may be some kind of more detailed test," Gigi said.

"When is Daddy going to get home?" Libby interrupted. "I totally forgot I have biology homework I need help with."

Camille looked at the clock. "Hopefully before bedtime, but who knows? He's on a deadline for a paper he's submitting this week."

Libby scrunched her face. "I know what you're gonna say—he's helping keep everyone healthy by studying those crazy diseases. But I seriously need some help with my homework."

Camille turned to Gigi. "Well, Gigi's a doctor. She probably knows something about biology." She took off her reading glasses so they didn't steam up as she drained the pasta in the sink.

Gigi got up and sat next to Libby and leaned to see her laptop screen where the Chinese characters had been replaced by an image of a giant cell. "Here, let me take a look." She felt her head, looking for her glasses. "Now, this for sure I know something about!"

Camille grabbed the glasses on the counter and handed them to Gracie, who pirouetted her way over to Gigi, singing, "Glasses, at your service!" She curtsied.

Over the past year, Gigi and Gracie had developed a special friendship, which Camille especially appreciated, because she knew how important it was for Gracie, who was mixed race, to have a Black role model in her life. Gigi held out both of her hands for the glasses and bowed to Gracie's curtsy. "Why, thank you, miss." She reached over and placed a gentle kiss on Gracie's head.

Gracie sat down on Gigi's lap and hung her arm around Gigi's neck as Gigi leaned toward Libby to explain how the parts of the cell work together as she traced the image on the screen.

"Do you know how to say 'dinner' in Chinese?" Gracie asked Gigi, who somehow managed to both answer Libby's biology queries and converse with Gracie at the same time.

"I do not."

"It sounds like 'wonton,' but not really." Gracie spoke the word in a singsong voice.

"You moms have some kind of uncanny ability to multitask in a way I'm not sure I could ever do." Trish marveled at the scene in front of her.

Gracie looked at Trish. "I can teach you to say hello in Chinese."

Trish laughed. "Please do."

"*Ni hao.*" Gracie smiled proudly. "Say it after me."

"*Ni hao.*" Trish bowed toward Gracie.

"Don't bow so deep." Libby got up from her computer and demonstrated a slight bow, which Trish copied.

"Show them how you can count," Libby instructed Gracie, who rattled off her Chinese numbers to no one in particular, while Libby and Gigi went deeper into the intricacies of the plasma membrane of the cell.

The kitchen had become more of a learning lab than a place where she could get some answers to her case-related questions, so Camille settled in and pulled out a stack of plates before combining the chicken and veggies in with the pasta along with some goat cheese, toasted pecans, and olive oil.

Libby turned from her computer to Gracie. "Now do the colors!"

Gracie rattled off another litany of words. Libby nodded as she and Gigi explored the properties of the cell nucleus.

As she was setting the table, it struck Camille that her new clients had only memories of their children to keep them going. Would the women in prison ever share this kind of loving family chaos at the end of their workdays? Would they help with their daughters' biology homework, listen to second-grade Chinese, and help choose the right shade of pink for an art project? *What is it about our society that compels us to lock up mothers? And why do we even consider keeping them from their children?* She leaned over and gave Gracie a hug as Gracie continued her singsong Chinese monologue while folding the dinner napkins in her own special way.

CHAPTER FOUR

The Law Office of Camille Delaney took up half a floor of a wood-frame waterfront building in the Fremont neighborhood of Seattle. Years earlier, Fremont had been an alternative neighborhood where Birkenstocks and tie-dye ruled. Now, Google and Tableau had moved in, and it was overrun with young techies who hung out at the year-round outdoor patio at the nearby Fremont Brewing. Still, it was home for Camille and her two-person office crew.

Amy Hutchins slammed the front door behind her as she precariously balanced three lattes and a small bowl of fruit and yogurt. Camille looked up at her longtime paralegal, relieved that she'd recently returned to the office after a short-lived stint at a stuffy downtown firm.

"What? Where's the chocolate éclair?" Camille teased her chocoholic friend.

Amy winked. "Ten more pounds and I can reward myself." She twirled around, clearly proud of her recent weight loss. "Not sure I'm going to go with the éclair, though," she said thoughtfully. "Might be more like a giant fudge brownie."

Camille hopped up from her office chair and grabbed two of the lattes, handing one to their assistant, Lucia. The striking young Asian woman with multiple piercings was growing out her formerly blue-streaked hair—it was in the awkward phase, but it didn't seem to bother her a bit. She took the latte and plopped down on Camille's lavender leather couch.

Lucia had shown up in Camille's office a little over a month ago, when Amy had taken the short-lived higher-paying paralegal job downtown. Camille had hardly believed her luck when the blue-haired messenger who had arrived at her door one day had offered to provide some desperately needed admin support while Camille prepared for a huge trial. Lucia turned out to be smart, savvy, and responsible— the perfect legal assistant. Camille had been surprised to discover that Lucia had served sixteen months in prison on a drug charge, but she'd embraced Lucia, along with her background. It hadn't taken much for Camille to realize that she had a lot to learn about how the world really worked for a huge swath of marginalized people, and she found herself drawn in by Lucia's stories of the women she had left behind inside. It had been a no-brainer when the Women's Law Center had asked Camille to take a pro bono case at the women's prison. Camille suspected Lucia was somehow behind that request, since she had become a fairly well-known activist for women returning from prison and had volunteered on several committees at the Law Center that addressed issues around mothers in prison.

"Thanks for the latte, Amy!" Lucia hollered to the outer office, where Amy was unloading her backpack and hanging up her coat.

Camille grabbed a pad and turned to Lucia. "So, when you were in prison, how many of the women there would you say had problems with custody issues? I'm just trying to get an idea of the scope of the situation I'm walking into."

"Well, way over half of them. I'd say about eighty percent are moms, and most of them were dealing with some kind of custody problem. It was super sad."

"Any idea of the main issues?"

"Mostly they were either trying to keep the state from terminating their rights, or they were trying to maintain contact and fighting with the foster care system, or with family members and exes who had taken over custody of their kids."

"So, while the moms are in prison, someone in their family takes in the kids and won't let the moms see them?"

"Yeah. Or if the moms' rights aren't terminated, which happens all the time, the kid ends up in foster care. Either way, it's a huge struggle for the moms inside to stay in touch with their kids, and then it's an uphill battle for them to get custody back when they get out."

Camille pointed at a book on her desk. "I've been reading about the school-to-prison pipeline, which I've now learned is actually the trauma-to-prison pipeline, and it turns out that one of the biggest risk factors for a child ending up in prison is having lost a parent to the system."

Lucia nodded. "Exactly. From the kids' perspective, they feel that their moms abandoned them. So if any kids need contact with their moms, it's these kids. I have a story for you about a friend inside. Imagine a little seven-year-old girl." Lucia pointed to the mélange of family pictures in mismatched frames scattered across the corner of Camille's big desk. "My friend Iris's daughter, Abby, was just about Gracie's age. She comes home on the bus from school and the apartment door is locked. Mom isn't home. The little girl, Abby, sits down in the hallway outside the apartment, but her mom never comes home because she was arrested for a personal amount of meth. At some point one of the neighbors comes home and finds Abby crying on the floor in the hallway. The neighbor has no idea what to do, so she calls the cops. They take Abby, and she gets thrown into a foster home." Lucia softens her tone. "Abby was a happy little second grader. Yes, her mom took drugs, but she was an okay mom—she had a job and an apartment filled with lots of love. From Abby's point of view, one day her mother went to work and never came home. Abby is alone and terrified in some foster home, even though the people seem nice enough. She wants her mom. I was in prison with so many women who had, themselves, been lost in the foster system. They became so hopeless as little kids that they cried themselves to sleep every night. There's even a group in the men's prison called the state-raised group. All the men in the group came out of foster care. And their stories of abuse in the system are heartbreaking."

Camille had never thought about foster care from the perspective of the child. She felt tears welling up.

Lucia continued. "Meanwhile, Abby's mom can't make bail, so she's sitting there in county jail. She has no way to communicate with her daughter to tell her what's going on. And no one in the foster system explains any of this to Abby. All she knows is her mother left her alone and afraid. Abby starts to think she must have done something wrong for her mother to just take off and leave her alone."

Camille shook her head in disbelief.

"So, Mom never makes bail—she goes to court and takes a plea and is sent directly to prison. *And she never gets to say goodbye to Abby.* Abby is ultimately placed with her maternal grandmother, who is overwhelmed with her own issues, not the least of which are financial and also drug related." Lucia leaned forward. "I'm not here to justify what the mom or grandma could have done differently, but no one is looking out for Abby. She's now lost in the system. And while Mom is inside, Mom gets drug-free. She gets her GED, and then she goes to college in prison. But do you think the court gives Abby back to her mom on release?"

"Oh God. They don't give her back to her mom?"

"Not only do they not give her back, but now Grandma is relying on the extra state assistance, so she blocks every attempt Iris makes to reunite with Abby, who is now nine years old and can't even read because no one cares about her academics, never mind her psychological well-being."

Camille was speechless. This was exactly what she needed to understand before going inside to run the family law clinic. "Thanks for sharing this with me."

"I'll introduce you to my friend Iris sometime soon. She could use your help, even though she's on the outside now. Can you even imagine how hard it is for her to stay optimistic and hopeful when every door is slammed in her face?"

"I can't."

"She's managed to stay drug-free and has a good job at a pizza chain where they hire people like us, with backgrounds. But she needs Abby, and Abby needs her mom." Lucia was almost shouting. She slammed her latte on the coffee table. "I'm so sick of how our criminal legal system treats families!"

"I honestly had no idea." Camille felt embarrassed by her privilege. "This is heartbreaking. And of course I'll help Iris."

Lucia smiled. "Sorry, I didn't mean to go off. But I get so pissed about the whole school-to-prison pipeline. The answer to the problem seems so obvious: families need each other. They just need support. Treatment, not prison."

Camille let the moment pass. "They now call it the trauma-to-prison pipeline. Makes more sense, doesn't it?"

Lucia nodded. "It does."

"Does your friend Lizbeth have kids of her own?" Camille had been curious about Lizbeth's background and what had motivated her to become a jailhouse family law lawyer.

Lucia took a sip of her latte and put it down slowly. "Like I told you before you went inside, we try to respect each other's privacy as much as possible, since nothing about prison offers any of us anything close to personal privacy. The only thing we have control over is our own story, so most of us guard our story from invasion by people we don't know well." She looked intensely at Camille. "You have to honor that if you're going inside to help, Camille."

Camille was slightly shaken by the deep well of passion she'd inadvertently opened up in her assistant.

"Understood." Camille nodded.

"I don't think it's my place to tell Lizbeth's story. She'll tell you what she's comfortable telling you when—and if—she's ready." Lucia looked at her phone. "You need to leave in ten minutes if you're going to get to the prison on time." She got up. "Let's get you packed up."

"Well, there's not much to pack since all they let me take in is a legal pad."

"This time you're coming in to run the clinic, so you're going to need your intake forms at least." Lucia pulled a stack of preprinted forms off the printer. "Hope you don't mind, I altered your forms a bit—you need to know what county each woman is from, where their kids are, who has custody, if there's a court-ordered parenting plan. Stuff like that." She handed Camille a newly edited intake form.

Camille skimmed it, marveling at the insight and depth of understanding Lucia had about prison custody cases. She looked over her reading glasses at Lucia. "Where did you come up with these questions?"

Lucia grinned. "Who do you think was Lizbeth's legal assistant inside?" She winked.

CHAPTER FIVE

Camille wondered if it ever became routine to go through the multi-step process to get inside the prison. It was a soulless place. The guards looked disconnected and bored. Camille knew that most prisons were located in small towns, where the pool of available workers was limited. But still, it bothered her how heartless most guards seemed. But at the same time, she'd read that many guards' stories weren't all that different from those they had been charged with "guarding." Many prison guards came from lives of similar trauma as the women inside. Most were uneducated, and many had witnessed family and community violence as children.

Maybe it's psychological self-defense from their own trauma—imagine if they actually connected with the pain and trauma of those in their care. Then again, how could anyone with a heart ignore the pain of the women inside—even if they committed crimes? They are mothers and sisters and daughters, most likely living traumatic lives before ending up here.

This was a complicated place, for sure.

The guard pointed Camille to the door and nearly shoved her aside to open it as it buzzed. Another trip with the librarian across the courtyard and through the series of gates in the enclosure heavily laced with barbed wire. A guard was heading through the gate at the same time that Camille and Tina, the librarian, were passing through. Camille had learned during her visit the prior week that there was no point making an effort at small talk with the stoic woman in the blue uniform. But she did ponder how all that garb, like the bulletproof vest and the holster with the gun and various other accoutrements, could weigh a person down.

Lizbeth jumped up and greeted Camille when she arrived at the law library. She had a table all set up for interviewing the women, who sat laughing and giggling in the mismatched chairs lining the room. It struck Camille that there was more camaraderie among the prisoners than the guards, who ostensibly should be happier because of their freedom, unlike the women caged inside this barbed wire campus. Camille looked at her prospective clients and smiled.

They're so young.

Lizbeth stood up and pointed at Camille. "This here is attorney Camille Delaney. Let's all give her a round of applause for her willingness to captain our new family law clinic!" Lizbeth's rough edges cracked a bit when she threw her arm in the air as though throwing a lasso.

There was some hooting and hollering along with clapping, finger snapping, and high fives. A chorus of thank-yous filled the room.

Camille turned to the group of ten women, who looked to her more like a class of community college students than a roomful of prisoners, and said, "I'm happy to be here, and I certainly hope I can offer you some chance at reuniting with your children." She felt a chill of excitement as she turned to Lizbeth. "Shall we get to work?"

"Here's your first client. Her name is Raven, and she lost her kids to her ex. She was in on a drug charge. Her doc refused to refill her oxy script for back pain after a car accident. That sent her off into the world of street drugs. She fell off probation, so she had to come back in. She's in our recovery group here and doing great. And now she's only a few months to the gate, so we need to file a motion to modify her parenting plan."

Raven was quiet as Camille reviewed her current plan. Sure enough, her ex had cut her out of her kids' lives by entering a parenting plan by default while Raven was in prison. And so the onetime stay-at-home mom was about to find herself having to jump through impossible hoops just to get a court to order supervised visits with her three boys. Camille took a deep breath and explained to her client the challenges ahead. It was clear Raven was up to the task. She had strong support from her family, especially her sister, who was a social worker. She would do whatever it took to get her children back.

The next few hours went by in a blur. There were tears and smiles and dejection and hopefulness. And most of all there was intense gratitude. In all the years Camille had been practicing law, she'd never felt so appreciated. By the end of the session, she felt honored to have been trusted with the stories of these brave mothers. Nearly every one of them had a story of unimaginable trauma and heartbreak. It was one thing when these facts were explained to her by Lucia and Lizbeth, but it was another thing entirely for her to hear them firsthand from the mothers themselves. And exactly as Lucia had explained, most of the women had turned to street drugs because they had absolutely no access to psychological treatment for their trauma. There was something seriously wrong with the system.

Just as Camille was beginning to close up shop, Lizbeth spoke up. "Oh, wait! There's Charli! We have one more client." She pointed to a poised Black woman who had been reading a thick law book, her chair turned toward the book stack.

"Charli! You're up!" Lizbeth hollered.

The woman replaced the book and turned toward Camille and Lizbeth. Camille caught her breath and froze. The woman coming toward her was the spitting image of her friend Gigi. Camille struggled to speak. It was Gigi, herself a Jennifer Hudson look-alike, but with a super-short, natural haircut and no makeup.

Does Gigi have a twin she's never mentioned?

"Camille? You okay?" Lizbeth grabbed a chair and put it behind Camille. "You need to sit down?"

Camille remained standing, unable to move. Her mind was racing.

"You're probably hungry. You haven't eaten all day, and you've been working nonstop," Lizbeth offered.

The new client stood perfectly still, not exactly sure what to do, as Camille tried to gather her composure.

"I—I'm sorry, you look exactly like a very good friend of mine." She blinked, trying to focus and see if she could find anything other than the haircut that distinguished this woman from Gigi.

The woman smiled sheepishly. "Should I come back next time?"

"No!" Lizbeth almost shouted. She turned to Camille. "This is Charli. She's the mother I told you about who had her baby kidnapped out of the hospital."

Camille gasped. "Oh my God, I'm so sorry about what happened." She reached out to shake Charli's hand, or hug her, but quickly remembered the prohibition against contact with prisoners. "Please . . . sit." She pointed to the chair across the table.

Charli sat on the edge of the chair and gave Camille a huge smile. "I'm so grateful that you're here to help."

Camille felt behind her for the chair before she sat down, her head in a fog. She looked awkwardly at her client. "Before we start, can I ask you a question? You look astonishingly like a good friend of mine, Gigi Roberts—Dr. Gigi Roberts. Are you by any chance somehow related?"

Camille struggled to interpret the way Charli sat back in her chair, almost defiantly. "No, I'm sorry. I don't know anyone by that name."

Fumbling with her paperwork, Camille looked up and into the woman's eyes. Without breaking her gaze, she handed Charli a form to fill out. There was a heavy knowing silence between Camille and Charli. It was impossible that this woman wasn't somehow related to Gigi. If Camille didn't know better, she would say this was Gigi's long-lost twin sister. She tried to recall where Gigi had grown up and whether there was any chance she had been adopted. She felt like she was on one of those shows where they reunite twins separated at birth. Just as she was about to ask Charli if she was adopted, she remembered Lucia's warning about how the women guard their life stories in prison, so she let it go. For now.

Camille pulled the top off her turquoise felt-tip pen and wrote Charli's name at the top of the page. "Your last name?"

"Zhao. Z-H-A-O."

"I heard a bit about your case from Lizbeth. Do you have any idea where your daughter is or could be? Or is there any information at all that would help my investigator, if she even has time to take on a pro bono case?"

Charli appeared to be considering her options. "Actually, I have access to money. My husband and I own a chain of pharmacies. And since we're not actually divorced yet, I assume I still have the right to our money. Correct?"

Camille blinked back her implicit bias as she realized the assumption she'd made about this Black woman sitting in front of her. "Well, technically yes. But as a practical matter, is your name still on any account?"

"I have a . . . a relative," she stammered, "who has power of attorney for me. So that person can access my funds."

Camille noticed for the first time that Lizbeth was leaning forward, her chin in her hands, elbows perched on the table between the lawyer and client. Her eyes were darting back and forth.

Charli looked at her friend. "Tru, this is confidential, okay?"

Lizbeth nodded. She didn't speak.

"I can pay you and your investigator if you can help us find Willow." Charli started to cry. She pulled a picture out of her pocket. Camille smiled at the image of a gorgeous baby with huge brown eyes wrapped in pink with a polka-dot hat, a blissful Charli kissing the baby's forehead. "My nurse took this picture. She sent it to me." Charli looked at Camille. "I hear you used to be a nurse. My nurse was sent to me from God. That's one thing I know for sure."

Camille held the photo with the respect it deserved. This was the only thing Charli had that connected her to Willow. "She's gorgeous."

Camille carefully perched the picture up against the pencil can and turned to the issue at hand. "So, tell me anything you know about where your ex could have taken Willow. And first of all, what's his name?"

"Martin. Martin Zhao."

Camille caught her breath. "Martin Zhao, the former professor at the UW pharmacy school?"

"You know him?" Charli drew back.

"My husband is on the staff at the med center. We know lots of the docs there."

"Well, then you probably know that he left the U and opened a chain of pharmacies." Charli paused. "Actually, *we* opened a chain of pharmacies. I have an MBA, and I was the finance director."

Lizbeth leaned in farther. She obviously hadn't heard this part of Charli's story before.

Charli looked at her friend. "I'm trusting you with this, Tru."

Lizbeth nodded silently.

"There's a lot more to this story. But for now, all that matters is that Brian is getting out soon, and I want him to have Willow. If we can find her."

"Brian?" Camille asked.

"Willow's bio father, my boyfriend. I haven't discussed Willow and this whole situation for several years, but now that Brian is about to get out, I'm ready to take a chance and talk." Charli paused and took a deep breath. "Brian and my ex, Martin, are identical twins. My new bunkie was in the medical profession before she got thrown in here. I think she's a nurse, but she hasn't really said yet. It takes a while for us to build up enough trust to share our stories with each other. Anyway, she says it will be hard to do DNA testing to prove that Brian is the father since he's Martin's identical twin."

Camille was grateful to have Gigi on her team—she'd figure out the medical end of things. Then it would be up to Camille to make the most medically sound and persuasive argument to the court.

Lizbeth weighed in. "Brian got a lighter sentence than Charli, since his jackass brother planted a smaller amount of heroin on him. And there was no gun enhancement added to his sentence, like there was for Charli."

"All I really need now is some kind of court order that will take effect if we can find Willow once Brian is released. I just want him to get custody of Willow."

"Do you even know where Willow is?" Camille was genuinely curious.

"I'm pretty sure she's still with Brian's mom—maybe overseas, but also maybe back in the States."

"What do you know about the grandma?"

Charli closed her eyes as though channeling her past. "She's a tiny, frail-looking woman who's much stronger than she appears. And she's fancy. Always impeccably well dressed and not a hair out of place. She's Taiwanese, and that's how they roll."

Camille scribbled some notes.

"Oh, and her English is getting better, but it wasn't perfect the last time I saw her."

"Are you still trying to find her?"

"My sister knows a PI, but I'd rather get a referral from a lawyer who has firsthand knowledge of his work."

Camille smiled and was about to tell Charli all about Trish when the guard shouted, "Zhao and Trujillo, let's go!"

The two women quickly got up and joined the line of other women in baggy khakis. Something about the power the guards had over the women inside irked Camille. It was as if their sense of self disappeared somewhere between getting up from their chairs in front of her and reaching the doorway. Their posture changed, and they looked blankly off into the distance as though they were disassociating themselves from their circumstances. It was probably a survival skill. Camille stood and waved goodbye to her associate and her new clients.

Sitting back down and staring at her pile of notes, Camille bit the end of her pen. It was completely up to her to find a way to explain the trauma these mothers had experienced, trauma that had led them to prison in the first place. And Camille knew that, above all else, these kids needed their moms. She cradled her chin in her hand and watched the women outside the window as they laughed with each other. How could they be so optimistic in light of all the pain they had faced in their lives? She turned to the last page of her notes. And how on earth could she convince a judge to place a seven-year-old little girl with a father she'd never known? And what were the chances of them even finding her in the first place? All she knew was that Willow might be with her frail, fancy, Chinese-speaking grandmother somewhere in the world. Tina, the librarian, gestured to her from the door, and she grabbed her papers and followed her escort back across the cold, empty courtyard.

CHAPTER SIX

It was surprising to Camille that so many people were coming into and going out of the prison. She turned the prison-issued key in the lock of the tiny locker next to the front door, smiling at a South Asian woman with tiny bright-blue hexagonal-framed glasses. She was carrying a box of paperwork. They each extracted their car keys from the lockers and left the locker keys protruding from the locks, where the key would wait for the next person to bring their own brand of hopes and dreams to the women inside. Camille followed the woman and held the lobby door open for her to carry her box through.

The woman smiled. "Thank you."

As they headed toward their cars, Camille introduced herself, curious about what had brought this woman to the prison.

"I'm Camille. I'm volunteering here."

"I'm Viyja. I teach college statistics here every Thursday." Viyja held up the box. "Homework. I'm going to have a busy weekend!"

Camille didn't know what she had expected her to say, but it certainly wasn't that she was teaching statistics to the women. "Wow. I heard that there are some kind of college classes here, but stats? That's serious."

"Some of my best students live behind these walls. I had no idea of the potential inside a prison until I started teaching here three years ago."

"I'm new around here, and I've been blown away by the women I've met. I honestly never had the world of prison on my radar before." Camille turned and looked at the low brick structure surrounded by rolls of barbed wire. "I'm kind of ashamed I didn't know anything about these women before now."

Viyja nodded. "Me too. I'm a professor at University of Puget Sound in Tacoma, and a colleague suggested I sign up to teach a class here. I'm pretty sure I'll never leave. My students here are more motivated and serious about their studies than any other students I've ever taught." She opened her car trunk and hoisted the box into it. "And don't feel bad. I had no idea about the exploding population of women in prison either, until I started teaching here." She closed her trunk. "Did you know that between 1980 and 2019, the number of incarcerated women in the US increased by more than seven hundred percent?"

"What?!"

"I know, I'm a numbers geek." Viyja smiled. "And more than sixty percent of them have a child under eighteen."

"Well, that's why I'm here. I'm running a family law clinic to try and get the moms connected with their kids when they get released."

"Oh my gosh, I'm so happy to meet you! I've heard from my students about your program. They're over the moon that someone is here to help them." She looked directly at Camille. "Thank you so much. You have no idea the difference you're about to make in these women's lives—and more importantly, the lives of their kids."

Camille leaned against her new friend's car. "You know, I've been in both family law and personal injury law, so I guess you could say I'm a people's lawyer. And what makes me crazy about the so-called justice system is how little we seem to value people's lives. I hope I can at least make a difference for a few of these families."

Viyja opened her car door. "Believe me when I tell you that you already have. Just giving these moms hope is an amazing gift to them. They've been working hard to overcome so much tragedy and trauma. And now many of them are getting associate's degrees, and even bachelor's degrees inside. And then the courts tell them they're not good enough to be moms. It's just so wrong."

Camille took a step back from the car and held out her hand to her new friend.

"I'm a hugger." Viyja smiled and gave Camille a hug. "Welcome to WCCW. We're so grateful to have you here."

Lost in thought on her drive home, Camille turned her focus to the pristine scene surrounding her—the steel blue water, framed by the greenery on the banks jutting up on either side of the single-span Narrows Bridge, high above the South Sound. In that moment, crossing above the water swirling furiously two hundred feet below her, Camille knew she would find Willow. She called Trish.

"Where will you be tonight? We need to talk," she said, without so much as a hello.

"We'll be at the swim meet—Kaitlin and Angela would be a little disappointed if you missed it." Gigi's daughter, Kaitlin, was one of Angela's best friends.

Camille looked at her watch. "Shit. I forgot there was a meet tonight." She did some mental calculations. "I should be there on time, traffic permitting."

"Traffic never *permits* between Tacoma and Seattle, but you'll mostly be going against the commuters, so you'll probably be there with no time to spare. What's up?"

"That kidnapped baby. We're going to find her. I just met with her mom—and you're not going to believe what I'm going to tell you."

Trish interrupted. "I'm on a stakeout, and the guy I'm following just came out of his place. Gotta go!"

Camille dropped her phone on the passenger's seat. How was she going to approach Gigi about her doppelgänger? She merged onto northbound I-5 and breathed a sigh of relief to see the traffic moving along nicely. Then she called Amy to see if there was anything pressing that needed her attention. As always, Amy was full of chatter about this client and that, and before she knew it, Camille was pulling into the school parking lot. It didn't escape Camille's attention how similar the building looked to the prison, absent a few hundred rolls of barbed wire.

A rush of chlorine-infused steam greeted Camille as she entered the natatorium at the girls' rival high school. Sam had offered to stay home with Libby and Gracie to help with Gracie's science project, so, although she'd be disappointed, Angela would have to make do with just a one-person cheering section tonight. Well, three, if she counted Trish and Gigi, who were almost family.

It didn't take long for Camille to find Gigi and Trish on the top row of the bleachers, sharing a grilled panini. Trish smiled and held out a neatly wrapped sandwich for Camille.

"I know they don't let you have any food with you in prison, so I bet you're hungry." Gigi winked.

Camille smiled and tore open the white deli wrapper and took a huge bite of the previously melted mozzarella, basil, and tomato panini. "Oh my gosh, this is so good," she garbled, her mouth full. "You're right, I'm starving." She paused. *How did Gigi know that you can't bring food into prison?* she wondered as she wiped her mouth with a crumpled-up paper napkin.

Gigi popped up and cupped her hands around her mouth. "Go, Kaitlin!" she yelled to her daughter, who was climbing up onto the starting block.

Trish let out an earsplitting whistle and laughed as Kaitlin waved her off so she could concentrate on her race.

Camille stood and let out a whoop just as the gun went off, and the girls sprinted off the blocks for their fifty-yard butterfly.

As usual, Kaitlin won by a full body length. She pulled off her goggles and reached over to shake hands with her opponent in the next lane. Then she turned and waved at her personal cheering section as Camille's daughter Angela grabbed Kaitlin's hand to pull her up out of the pool. Camille studied the leaderboard and figured out that both Kaitlin and Angela had no more races until the final medley relay, which wouldn't occur for at least thirty minutes. She turned to Gigi.

"They forgot to give us the ranch dip. Dang." Gigi held up a naked piece of celery.

"I met someone in prison today who looks exactly like you. It was astonishing." Camille held her breath to see what kind of reaction she'd get from Gigi.

Gigi didn't look up from her food.

Trish piped up. "What do you mean, someone in prison looks like Gigi? There is only one Gigi!" She gave her girlfriend a huge kiss on the cheek.

But Gigi froze.

"Gigi?" Trish put her arm around the hunched-over woman, who had suddenly lost interest in the ranch dressing. And the celery.

"I'm not sure I want to talk about this," Gigi whispered.

Camille was sensitive to Gigi's sudden change in mood, but she couldn't help herself. She turned to Trish. "I met with a woman in WCCW. Her name is Charli. Her baby was kidnapped out of the labor and delivery suite at Puget Sound General about seven years ago. Charli is the spitting image of Gigi. If they're not related, they should be on one of those Facebook pages where they put images of identical people that don't know each other."

Gigi's shoulders began to shake, first slowly and then full on.

Trish leaned over and rubbed Gigi's back. "You okay, hon?"

Gigi was nearly sobbing. Trish got up and squatted down on the bleacher in front of Gigi in an effort to give her some privacy from any curious onlookers. She stroked her cheek. Gigi took a wobbly breath, looked up, and exhaled slowly a few times.

Camille put her hand on Gigi's arm. "If you and Charli are somehow related, just tell us. We can help you find Willow."

Gigi buried her head into Trish's shoulder and held her tightly. Trish looked quizzically at Camille and turned to comfort her partner. "It's okay, babe." She stroked Gigi's hair.

Camille knew when to be quiet. She gently rubbed Gigi's back.

After several minutes, Gigi spoke softly. "He stole Willow. Right out of the fucking hospital." She wiped her nose with the sleeve of her hoodie. "I was in my fellowship in California, and I couldn't get here in time to find her." She took another vibrating breath.

Trish pulled back ever so slightly. "So, who is Charli?"

Gigi took a deep breath. "She's my identical twin sister."

Camille focused on her best friend's face, wondering how Trish would react to the fact that her girlfriend had held this back for so long. To her credit, Trish enveloped Gigi in a hug and whispered in her ear.

After a minute, Gigi pulled back. "Well, I guess I might as well fess up. It looks like you two can probably help us find Willow. God, I hope it's not too late."

Trish leaned forward and rested her hands on her knees. "Tell us what happened."

Camille scooted up close so she could hear Gigi's uncharacteristically soft voice.

"My sister was—or I guess I should say *is*—married to the world's biggest asshole." She looked knowingly at her friends. "I mean it. He's unparalleled." She shook her head slowly.

Camille started to say she knew him but thought better of it.

Gigi continued. "They own a chain of pharmacies. He was a professor at the U, but he left to become an entrepreneur. And my sis has an MBA, so she was the CFO." She paused. "But then she fell in love with her husband's twin brother—that happens often with identical twins: we end up marrying other identical twins. It's so weird. Anyway, Charli and Brian figured out that there were lots of irregularities in the way Martin was running the pharmacies. When they confronted him, he denied it. And before we knew it, Charli and Brian were both separately arrested on drug charges. Charli was discovered to have a kilo of heroin in her car. And to be sure she went down for as long as possible, her asshole husband planted a gun under her driver's seat so she got a horribly long sentence. Brian was caught with heroin too, but there was no gun, so his sentence is shorter. Obviously, the drugs and gun were planted by Martin, who was handing out opioids like candy and had recently gotten into dealing hard drugs. And for reasons I will never understand, Martin wasn't charged. But both Charli and Brian got sentenced to prison. She's served seven years of a twelve-year sentence. And Brian is about to get out after serving his own seven-year sentence."

Camille waited for a pause, then asked, "What about Willow? She's Brian's baby, right?"

Gigi nodded, covered her mouth, and started to cry again.

The announcement of the final medley relay pierced the momentary silence in their conversation. Gigi wiped her face and stood up to wave at Kaitlin, who blew her mother a kiss. Angela was right behind Kaitlin, as the freestyle anchor on the relay. She waved at her mom and friends in the stands, then turned her attention to stuffing her long ponytail up into her swim cap.

After the race, Gigi sat down slowly.

Trish leaned in and took Gigi's hands in hers. "Tell us what happened. We can help." Her voice was almost a whisper.

"Willow is seven now, and she's never met her family." Gigi's eyes narrowed. "I hate him for what he did—not just to Charli, but to all of us."

"Just start from the beginning," Trish prompted.

Gigi's eyes welled with tears. "The police were useless." She paused and took a shaky breath. "They said since she was his baby, he had every right to take her."

Trish whipped her head around to look at Camille.

Camille nodded slowly. "Technically, she's right. If there's no parenting plan or court order, either parent can take control over their child."

"We consulted with a family law lawyer, who said that even if we went to court, the court would be likely to place Willow with her father since Charli was in prison."

"But he wasn't even the dad!" Trish interrupted.

"There's a legal presumption that when a person gives birth, their spouse is the parent," Camille interjected.

"Right." Gigi nodded. "So we learned. So, we hired a PI." She smiled forlornly at Trish. "Sadly, he wasn't exactly in your league. But we had no idea what else to do."

Trish looked all business. "Did he track her? Find anything?"

"Actually, he discovered that, as we expected, Martin, the asshole husband, had taken Willow to his mother. They holed up at his place on Lopez Island, in the San Juans, for a few weeks. Then Jing—the grandma—and Martin took off with Willow for Taiwan, which is what we were terrified of."

"So did the PI follow them?"

Gigi almost smiled. "Didn't have a passport."

"You hired a PI who didn't even have a passport?" Trish almost yelled.

Gigi put her hand on Trish's arm. "We were doing our best."

"So, did you lose track of them once they left the country?" Camille asked.

"Thankfully, Charli had been to the family compound outside of Taipei, so we were able to hire a PI over there and have them stake out the place."

"Did he see Willow?"

"Oh yes. Jing was showing her pride and joy off all over their little community."

"Then how'd you lose track of her?" Trish asked.

"That's where it got really scary." Gigi cupped her hands over her mouth. "And it's pretty much why we stopped having Jing followed. We figured that Jing was probably as good a person as any to watch over Willow at that point. And Martin was long gone. He didn't even stay overnight when he took them to Taipei."

"So what happened?" Camille asked quietly.

"Well, the PI disappeared. Like totally disappeared. No one ever heard from him again."

Trish raised her eyebrows. "You think he's dead?"

Gigi continued. "Well, around the time he stopped communicating with us, a stranger showed up in the visitors' room at the prison, asking for Charli."

"And . . ."

"And she was full of scary news and unbelievable threats." Gigi paused. "She had pictures someone had taken of the Taiwanese PI we'd hired. Apparently, Martin had found out about the PI and was having him followed. The woman had pics of Jing getting on a plane in Taipei and made it very clear that Martin was making sure no one would ever find the baby. And if we tried, he'd kill Willow, just like he killed the PI. She said that Willow and Jing left Taipei, so it was pointless to even try looking there. The woman said Martin would put Willow and Jing in a place where he could have complete control over who had access to them so there was no hope she'd ever find them."

"Oh my God. How did Charli react to that?" Camille couldn't imagine what she'd do if someone kidnapped one of her kids.

"She's a cool customer. She had the presence of mind to ask the woman what Martin wanted, to which the woman replied casually, 'He'll be in touch.' And then she left."

"Holy crap. So then what?" Trish was all business.

"So, then Charli called me for a meeting where she made it crystal clear that no one was to ever know anything about what happened to Willow. She took Martin at his word. I was forbidden from ever telling anyone about Willow. I was forbidden from even telling anyone that Charli was in prison. Nothing." Gigi began to cry. "And I honored her wish. I can't tell you how hard it's been keeping this from you guys. Especially since I know you might actually be able to do something about it. I even asked her, and she said absolutely not. Until the past month or so. Now that Brian's about to get out of prison, he'll probably be able to find Jing, and then maybe we could restart the search."

"Didn't he stay in touch with his mom while he's been inside?"

"He did for a while, but then she stopped communicating with him. We figured Martin was somehow preventing her from reaching out to him. It was super sad for him to be cut off from her."

"That's awful," Camille whispered.

"It was. But like I said, even though they lost touch with Jing, Charli felt that if Willow was with Jing, she'd be safe until Brian could get out. And that's why she agreed to meet with you, Camille. She was told that some high-end lawyer was coming into the prison to help the mothers there. Charli has access to money and could hire any lawyer she wants. But she was interested to meet with what she understood to be a highly regarded lawyer who was compassionate enough to come inside and help the women. I just didn't put two and two together to realize that it was you."

"Well, this is a huge challenge. Finding Willow after seven years isn't going to be easy," Camille said as her stomach churned.

"We'll find her." Trish left no room for doubt. "We will absolutely find her." She extended her hand to Gigi and pulled her gently up from the bleachers as Kaitlin and Angela signaled from the door of the locker room that they'd be out in ten minutes.

Gigi stood straight in front of Camille and Trish. "If anyone can find her, it's going to be you two."

CHAPTER SEVEN

Camille finished brushing her teeth and climbed into bed next to Sam. She wasn't ready to share what she'd heard from Gigi that evening. That would be a much longer conversation. And besides, her head was still swimming with all she'd been learning about her new clients in prison. "All these women have such sad stories, and mostly they end up in prison for drug-related crimes. I've heard of opioid addiction issues, but I had no idea how this crisis impacts women, especially mothers."

Sam put down his medical journal. "It's just another unacknowledged aspect of the opioid epidemic."

Camille sat up and looked at Sam. "Leave it to an epidemiologist to view everything from an epidemiological perspective." She stopped to think. "But you're right, it certainly could be called an epidemic."

"It totally is. In fact, there's a PhD candidate at the nursing school who wants me as her research supervisor. Her dissertation is on this exact issue."

"Really? This is a thing? An opioid epidemic sending women to prison?"

"It's a thing, and the science of epidemiology applies to it." Sam paused. "I'm meeting with the student this week. I'll let you know what she's proposing. We could all learn something from someone who's interested in this issue."

"Huh. Calling it an epidemic seems to take some of the responsibility off the women who've become addicted." It wasn't often that Sam took an active interest in one of Camille's cases. This might even be a first. "You're right, it's for sure a disease and shouldn't be considered a moral failure for someone to become addicted to opioids." Camille cocked her head, lost in thought as Sam picked up the journal he'd been reading. After a few minutes, she continued. "I wonder if I could use this as an argument in court when I ask the judge to reunite mothers and their children."

Sam peered over his journal. "I don't see why not. There's some good science being done on this issue."

"Do you know any experts who could sign a declaration for me?"

"Saying what?"

"Not sure yet . . ." Camille pondered as she turned to face her husband. "If I could convince the judges that these women aren't criminals but more like collateral damage of the opioid crisis, or at least people with a serious disease of addiction, maybe there would be less criticism of them and more compassion."

Sam put down his journal and turned to Camille. "Maybe this is what happens when a nurse becomes a lawyer." He touched her cheek. "I'm serious. You have a unique perspective on science and the law. The medical disease model is exactly how this whole addiction mess should be viewed. But that's not exactly compatible with your justice system."

"Wait a minute. *My* justice system? Seriously?" She playfully slapped Sam's journal out of his hands.

"Okay, *the* justice system. You know what I mean. In the legal system it's all about being responsible for your actions. But what if your actions are due to forces beyond your control?"

Camille shot up. "Like addiction!"

Sam smiled. "Well, you certainly have your work cut out for you. All you need to do is convince the court to completely upend its entire approach to criminal law. No more rights and responsibilities. That sounds simple." He picked up his journal.

Camille flopped back down on her pillow. "I know nothing about the criminal legal system. I think I have lots of reading to do."

"Actually, sometimes the system needs an outsider to shake it up. And I can't believe I'm saying this, but after the way you took down those two doctors this past year, I have a feeling your dual degrees in nursing and law might make you exactly the right person to champion this issue in court."

"Well, maybe I could start with your nursing PhD candidate. I hope she has an open mind and at least a moderate interest in the intersection between law and medicine. I could use some help with research, for sure."

"We'll know this week." Sam leaned over and turned off his bedside light, then kissed Camille. "I have a sneaking feeling we're about to become opioid experts."

—

Christmastime on Lake Union came with all kinds of water-related special events, and the highlight of the season was the boat parade. Camille loved celebrating this annual tradition at home on their houseboat. But when Lucia had surprised Camille by asking if her friend Iris could come to the office after work to discuss her custody situation with her daughter, Camille was so caught up with the whole concept of reframing addiction in the family law system that she completely forgot about the boat parade. She cursed herself for agreeing to a meeting with Iris on the opening night of festivities, but there was no way she was going to let down a mom who was trying to get her kid back.

So there she sat, in her waterfront office, watching the windows on the west side of Capitol Hill light up with an indescribable copper color reflecting the light of the 4:30 sunset. She was lost in an online article about opioids when Lucia ushered in a tall Black woman dressed in dark pants and a collared T-shirt with a pizza logo on it.

"Camille, this is my friend Iris."

Camille stood and shook Iris's hand. "Have a seat." She gestured to the purple leather couch.

Iris's eyes darted around the room nervously. "Thanks so much for meeting with me."

Camille smiled. "It's my pleasure. I understand you're working hard to regain custody of your daughter."

"I'm trying so hard, but everything I do just backfires. And my mom refuses to even let me see Abby." The tears started. Slowly at first.

Camille handed Iris her handy box of tissues and waited a few minutes for Iris to compose herself.

"I admit I wasn't such a great mom. My ex was horrible. But for some reason I kept going back to him. I can't explain it. Maybe it was the drugs. But I've been clean and sober for four years now, and I've been able to get my life back on track. I did everything they told me to do after I got out, and still the family law judges won't let me have my daughter back." She stopped to blow her nose.

Camille grabbed a purple legal pad. "Can you tell me what you've done since your release? Judges need to be educated about the fact that people can be rehabilitated."

Iris sat up and looked Camille straight in the eye. "It started for me inside. And then I've been involved in a very special group on the outside. We meet in the wilderness and learn to do hard stuff like mountain hiking and a little rock climbing. The leader is amazing, and the group helps me stay in recovery, especially with all my struggles trying to get my daughter back. I'm proud not just of my recovery but of my education and the possibilities for my future."

Camille was intrigued. "It sounds like you have a lot to be proud of. Tell me more."

"Well, I'm the first person ever in my family to go to college. I graduated with my AA inside, and I just got accepted at UW Tacoma in the BA program." She was on a roll. "And I attended recovery groups the whole time I was down, and by the end, I was leading the group. I even trained the new group leader. She's a nurse or something, and she told me I have an excellent understanding of the physiology of addiction. I'm thinking of going to nursing school, but my background might prevent me from getting my nursing license, so I'm considering getting an MSW. I did especially well in my statistics class, so I might have a good chance in social sciences."

Camille smiled as she recalled her encounter with the stats prof in the parking lot. It hit her that something as simple as doing well in a stats class could change the trajectory of someone's life. She turned her attention to the issue at hand. "The family law judge knows about your degree and your recovery, and they still won't let you see Abby?"

Iris shook her head and bit her lip. "Nope."

"Did they tell you why?"

"Yeah. My mom went to court while I was locked up and got a custody order that has all kinds of requirements for me to fulfill in order to even get supervised visits with Abby. So, I'm basically screwed because the judge explained that the parenting plan is a court order that they have to follow unless I modify it. Which I understand is pretty complicated, legally."

Camille nodded. "You're right, there are lots of legal hurdles to jump through to modify your parenting plan. I can help you with that, but it's going to take a while to litigate. Do you have the parenting plan with you?"

Iris rummaged around in her messenger bag and pulled out a neatly organized file folder. "Here it is." She handed it to Camille, who grabbed a pair of glasses and began skimming the court document.

"Okay, I see the problem. This plan says you have to complete an inpatient program for substance-use disorder. And then you need to take a parenting class." She flipped the page. "Then you need to show six months of weekly random UAs. And after all that, you can only get professionally supervised visits once a month for six months. Then once a week for another six months. And then you can petition the court for weekend visits once a month." Camille threw down the paperwork. "This is so fucked up. You don't need to jump through all of these hoops. And you certainly don't need inpatient treatment if you've been clean and sober for years. You just need your daughter. And she needs you." She shot up out of her chair. "I'm going to help you get Abby back, but it's not going to be easy. The legal system is not exactly user friendly. Especially for people coming out of the system."

Iris stood up and held out her hand. "Oh my gosh! Thank you so much!"

Camille ignored the outstretched hand and gave Iris a hug. "I'm so sorry you have to deal with all of this on top of all the other challenges of reentry."

"Well, honestly, everything else about reentry—finding a job and housing—doesn't really matter if I can't get my little girl back."

"I understand, and you're totally right. And it makes me wonder how many other women are fighting this same battle."

"Most of us, to one degree or another. The one thing I have going for me is that I have a really supportive probation officer. Lots of women haven't been so lucky, but mine actually wants to see me succeed, so that's something I'm very grateful for."

"Well, that's one bit of a silver lining in this mess. I'll read through your paperwork and come up with a plan. Let's circle back after the holidays." She looked at the stack of papers and realized that this was the case she'd been waiting for. It was way past time for the judiciary to take notice of the challenges facing moms coming out of prison and the risk to society if they didn't find a way to reunite kids with their bio moms and dads. The lawyer in her felt the familiar rush of taking on a challenging case. This was important. Really important.

"Oh wow! Look!" Iris pointed out the window at the line of boats of all shapes and sizes motoring slowly along where the ship canal spilled into the urban lake in front of Camille's waterfront office, facing south toward Queen Anne Hill, with downtown just beyond. Each boat had been carefully decorated for the holidays. One had a mechanical Santa all lit up and waving from the boat's flying bridge. Another had a giant Star of David in silver and blue lights on its hull. And most of the sailboats had some configuration of lights twisted all the way to the top of their masts. Even the little pontoon boats were decorated with lights and Christmas trees. The Christmas ship parade was a true Seattle tradition.

Lucia heard the commotion and popped open the door. "So cool!" She came in and stood next to Camille and Iris.

"Grab your coats—let's go out on the deck!" Camille beckoned as she pulled open the sliding door. The two women followed her out onto the small wooden deck. "Listen: you can hear the Christmas carols coming from that big tour boat." She pointed. "They have different musical groups and choirs every week. It sounds like the Seattle gospel choir is performing tonight."

Iris stood totally still. "I've never seen anything like this. Ever," she whispered, clearly awestruck. "I wish Abby was here . . ."

Camille put her arm around Iris as one festively lit boat after another cruised by, right in front of Camille's deck. "Let's make that our goal. Next year at this same time, we'll have a party, and Abby will be the guest of honor."

"That would be awesome." Iris turned to Camille. "But let's see if we can make it a bigger party and have a bunch of moms and their kids all reunited here, celebrating the holidays all together for once."

"That sounds like an awesome goal." Camille squeezed Iris around her shoulders.

The three women stood silently and slowly began to sing along with an upbeat gospel version of "Silent Night" as music blasted across the lake.

Camille closed her eyes and imagined Iris and Abby and Charli and Willow along with other mothers and their children all standing on her deck, belting out Christmas carols. And then her vision expanded to moms and kids across the country finally getting their first postprison holiday with each other. The task was overwhelming. But so very necessary.

CHAPTER EIGHT

The following morning, Camille rolled over in bed and looked past the sleeping heap of dog trying to take over her bed. On her bedside table was a cup of hot coffee and a note in Gracie's familiar handwriting.

She reached over Jake and read the note. "Daddy and me are gonna get a Christmas tree all by ourselves. Daddy says you should have coffee and read a book until we get back. I love you. And Daddy says he's sorry he got home so late last night after you went to bed."

Camille smiled and wrapped her hands around the hot mug. She took a deep breath and enjoyed the moment of solitude. It was a typical Seattle December morning, dark and misty. Now, if she just had a book to read, she thought as she watched the drizzle scattering across the glass-like water outside her bedroom on the first floor of their houseboat. She grabbed a book from Sam's pile of reading material on his bedside stand: *The Epidemiology of Opioid Addiction*. It wasn't exactly pleasure reading, but it was necessary for her to gain an understanding of the magnitude of the problem. She flipped it open and got lost in the sad facts of the crisis sweeping the country. No demographic was spared; the effects were chilling.

Camille wondered how many mothers, if left alone for a morning, would willingly choose to immerse themselves in a scholarly treatise on opioid addiction. But she was hooked. There had to be some solutions being proposed for this epidemiologic catastrophe. She closed the book to look at the front cover and remind herself of the author,

Reginald Latrell. She wondered if Sam knew him and could get her in touch.

"Mom." Libby gently knocked on the door. "Dad said not to bother you, but he also left some bagels and lox on the counter for you, so I thought we could have breakfast in bed!" She held out a cutting board with freshly toasted bagels, lox, and cream cheese.

Camille put down the book and held out her arms to hug Libby, who jumped into bed with her and handed Camille a black-and-white-checkered cotton napkin. Libby grabbed the book and flipped it open.

"You're reading about oxy? That drug people used to take for pain, but now it's just a party drug?" Her eyes narrowed as she spread cream cheese on a half a bagel. "Why are you reading this?" She held up the book.

"I have a new case where some of the people got addicted to oxy and other similar drugs. And it's not just a party drug. You're right, opioids were invented to treat pain, but some really bad drug companies convinced doctors that it wasn't addicting, so the doctors started prescribing it to their patients. And then they discovered that it was in fact very addictive, and thousands of people can't stop using it."

"It's kinda scary to think about." Libby paused. "And drug companies shouldn't lie."

"You're exactly right." Camille took a bite of the bagel Libby had stacked with Camille's favorites—lox, cream cheese, tomatoes, and capers. "Yum!" She licked a wayward streak of cream cheese from the side of her mouth.

"So, what happened to the people who all got addicted?" Libby ignored her own heavily buttered bagel for the moment.

"Well, they couldn't stop taking the drugs, so a lot of them lost their jobs and their families. And lots of them lost their children and ended up in prison."

"Why prison? Shouldn't they be in some kind of drug treatment?"

"They absolutely should." Camille nodded. "But they end up in prison because once they're addicted, they can't always get more prescriptions from their doctors. And so they turn to street drugs, like heroin or fentanyl, to feed their addiction."

"And then what happens to them when they're locked up? They get therapy and stuff to help them?"

"Nope, but they usually try to get off the drugs while they're in prison. And lots of them are able to beat their addiction. And some even go to college inside prison, and others get their GED or learn a trade. But most importantly, when they get out, they try to get their children back."

"And do they get their kids back? Because I bet those kids are a mess without their moms."

"Not always. That's the big issue; it's not easy for them to get their kids back. Sometimes judges don't look very favorably on people who got addicted to drugs."

"But it wasn't even their fault! You said their doctors gave them the drugs!"

"It's a totally messed-up system for sure, Libs."

"But the drug companies got in big trouble for lying, right?" Libby turned the book over to read the back jacket cover. "Did they go to prison? They're worse than the patients, right?"

"Actually, they didn't. The drug companies have lots of high-paid lawyers who help keep them out of trouble."

Libby threw the book down. "So, you're telling me that the drug companies lie to the doctors, then sell people drugs that are really bad for them, and the people who took the drugs get in trouble, but not the drug companies?"

Camille put down her bagel and finished off her coffee. "Yep, that's exactly how it works." It wasn't lost on Camille how something so simple could be understood by a fourteen-year-old but not by most judges. They were either clueless or just didn't care. Or maybe the fact that so many judges started their careers as prosecutors clouded their judgment.

"This is so messed up, Mom. What if *you* got addicted and they took you away from us?" Libby sat up on her knees and gesticulated intensely.

"I'm not going to get addicted, but there are lots of moms and kids who are really lonely for each other, and they need lots of help."

"Well, you're a lawyer. What are you doing about all this?" Libby's gaze was penetrating.

"I'm going to help the women in prison get their children back." Camille sat straight up in bed and ran her fingers through her shortly cropped hair. "Let's get up. I have lots to do."

"You need to tell Trish about this, Mom—she's calling now." Libby pointed at Camille's cell phone, which was muffled by the brown chenille comforter.

Camille grabbed the phone. "We have fresh bagels over here. Wanna stop by?"

"Sure. I'm on my way back from the Braeburn in Bellevue. It's where Zhao's mother lived, last Charli knew. Turns out the concierge is a former cop friend of mine from SPD. Who knew that a concierge at one of these fancy-ass places makes more than a Seattle cop? And the tips are insane."

"What'd ya find out?"

"Actually, lots. I'm just heading across the 520 Bridge now. I'll be at your place in twenty minutes. Coffee would be fantastic."

Camille hopped up. "On it! I'm going to take a quick shower. See you in a few."

—

"Mo-o-o-o-m!" Gracie blasted into the bathroom where Camille was towel drying her hair. "We bought the biggest, bestest tree of 'em all!" Her missing front tooth made for a pretty cute smile.

Gracie could barely keep up with her own words. "We went to the place on the corner, and Daddy said they don't have good trees. But I told him I had the feeling that our tree would be there. And Daddy said, 'No, let's go to another lot.' And I said no." Gracie put her hand out in front of her as if she was a traffic cop ordering a car to stop. "And Daddy said, 'Well, okay,' and he drove right into the lot, and there it was. *Right in front of us.* It was just standing there waiting for us! And Daddy said you wouldn't even have time to drink your coffee before we got home. And I said Mommy wants us to hurry back with a tree. And so Daddy asked the woman to help him turn the tree all the way around! And I said perfect." Gracie stopped for a quick breath. "And then they put the tree into some kind of net so we could put it in the car. And Daddy brought it right in and took it up to the living room."

She pointed at the stairs. "It's right up there." Her voice was urgent. "Can you even believe it?" She grabbed Camille's hand and dragged her out of the bathroom just as Trish was poking her head through the front door.

Trish looked at the foyer covered in pine needles and hugged Gracie. "Merry Christmas! Where's the tree?" The urgency in Trish's voice echoed Grace's.

Grace didn't miss a beat. "Upstairs. C'mon! You're just in time to decorate!"

Camille turned and looked longingly at her empty bed and grabbed her half-drunk coffee and partially eaten bagel. "I'm coming, I'm coming."

All that could be seen of Sam were his legs as he directed Libby to hold the tree while he cranked the trunk into the stand. Camille took charge. "A little more toward the wall, Libby." She gestured. "No . . . to the left." She leaned her head. "To the right just a tick." She paused to assess the angle of the trunk of the tree. "Perfect." She knelt down to open the well-worn cardboard box of ornaments and reminded herself to try to remember to get one of those plastic storage tubs this year.

Sam extricated himself from the bowels of the Christmas tree and hugged his knees. He looked up at Camille. "You're not going to believe my meeting with the grad student yesterday. I got home so late last night, I didn't want to wake you."

Camille leaned forward to help Sam up from the floor. "Tell me!"

Gracie put her hands on her hips and interrupted. "No work talk. We gotta decorate the tree."

"Let's practice your Chinese," Libby interjected. "Say 'red' and 'green.'" She looked at her parents. "For Christmas."

Gracie sang the Chinese words for red and green.

Camille pulled a string of lights out of the box and handed them to Sam, who handed the plug end to Trish.

"How about 'tree'?" Libby instructed.

Gracie complied.

"How do we say 'Christmas'?" Gracie asked.

"Huh." Libby pulled out her phone translator.

"Ugh. Do these lights ever last more than one season?" Camille lamented as she noted that half the string had failed to light up. She took out another. "Damn."

"How about this one? It's in a new and unopened box," Trish suggested.

Camille congratulated herself for having remembered to buy brand-new lights on sale the week after Christmas last year. "Good idea." She tore open the box and handed the string to Trish.

"Bingo! This one looks good." Trish nodded. "Hand me the other one." Camille unwound the second string, which, to everyone's delight, also worked. And then the third.

Camille turned back to the box and gingerly began unwrapping the ornaments. Some glass balls and some family mementos handmade by their girls, as well as some ancient artwork from her and Sam's childhoods. One by one she handed them to Trish, who distributed them to Libby and Grace, who thoughtfully placed them around the tree.

"Put the fragile ones up high so Jake doesn't get them." Camille pointed to the branches high up on the tree.

Sam squatted down next to Camille and Trish. He spoke quietly so Grace wouldn't admonish them for mixing Christmas with work. "You two remember the nurse who's been dating Tony?" He referred to their longtime friend who owned and operated the floatplane service from Seattle to the San Juan Islands and other communities along the Salish Sea.

"Of course." Camille paused. "Sally, right? I like her. And I'm pretty sure they're still together. So happy for Tony. Why do you ask?"

"Turns out, she's the nursing grad student who wants me to be her dissertation sponsor. She's a PhD student at the U, studying opioid addiction in mothers in prison."

Camille's eyes popped wide open. "What? Are you kidding? I thought she was an OR nurse. She was the circulating nurse in the OR when Dallas died."

"And who kept such good track of the blood loss in the OR that night that you were able to successfully sue that asshole surgeon, Willcox," Trish added.

Sam jumped back in. "Well, remember how she took to the women at the shelter, the one Gloria opened on San Juan Island with the money she got from the lawsuit against Willcox?"

Camille thought back to the opening-day picnic for the shelter, where women coming out of prison could be reunited with their children. "Yeah, she really did seem to have a special interest in those women."

"Did you ever wonder why?" Sam asked.

"Not really. She just seemed like a really sweet, loving person who likes to help."

"Why?" Trish asked. "What do you know?" She looked at Sam quizzically.

"Hey! Where are the beads that we put around the tree last?" Gracie demanded.

"Here, let me do it." Camille loved the glass beads her mother had given her, which had been in her Greek family for a couple of generations. "Be careful. These are breakable."

Gracie and Libby dutifully stepped back and let Camille do the honors.

"Too much on the left," Angela commented from the doorway. "Put more beads over toward the wall." She gestured.

Camille complied, and the entire group stood back to admire the heavily decorated tree.

"Lights, Daddy! Lights!" Gracie yelled.

With a theatrical flourish, Sam plugged in the lights, and the tree spread its Christmas cheer across the dimly lit room. Always the professor, he explained, "Now you know why the early Christians co-opted the festival of lights for their winter holiday. It hardly gets fully light in the northern latitudes this time of year, so we all need some colorful, twinkling lights to get us through the dark winter."

Camille smiled at her husband. "Thank you very much, Professor."

Grace pirouetted across the living room, singing. "Festival of lights! Festival of lights!"

Camille hugged Gracie and suggested that she and Libby go find the wrapping paper in the storage closet so they could get started on their gifts. She turned to Sam and beckoned him and Trish to the kitchen island, where she began another pot of coffee and reorganized the mess of bagels Libby had left strewn across the counter.

"Okay. Now, about Sally." She popped a bagel into the toaster for Sam. "You were saying something about why she was interested in moms in prison."

Sam pulled the half-and-half out of the fridge and grabbed three coffee cups off the open kitchen shelving. "Turns out her sister got into a car accident and ended up addicted to OxyContin. And you can guess what happened from there." He held out his cup for Camille to refill. "Street drugs. Lost her kids to her ex. Got arrested for stealing credit cards and identity theft." Sam tipped his head back and snaked a long piece of lox into his mouth.

"Did she end up in prison?" Trish asked as she stirred half-and-half into her coffee.

Sam nodded. "She did time at WCCW."

"And . . . ," Camille pressed.

"And when she got released, she ended up overdosing."

"Oh no."

"So tragic." Sam paused. "Sally was explaining how the system is set up for these women to fail, and they're so hopeless. You're doing the right thing, helping these mothers."

"So are you going to sponsor her research?" Trish was all business.

"Actually, I am. Turns out she's very smart, and her dissertation idea is pretty compelling. She's going to do a study of moms coming out of prison and their likelihood of relapsing if they're reunited with their kids."

Camille stirred her coffee thoughtfully. "Do PhD students need research assistants?"

"Usually," Sam responded. "Why do you ask? I have a handful of students looking to join projects to get experience, but do you have someone in mind?"

"Actually, I do. I have a new client, Iris Thomas, who got her AA inside WCCW and is at UW Tacoma. She's a wiz at statistics, and I think she'd love an opportunity to get involved. And she has a kid she's trying to reunite with, so she'd be very interested in the issue."

Trish weighed in. "Here's one thing I'm learning from Gigi about this whole mothers-in-prison issue. The people who should be finding the solutions to these problems are the ones who are directly impacted, so I'd say your friend Iris would be perfect. Who would better understand what the women are going through?"

"Exactly." Camille changed the subject. "Now, what did you dig up over at that fancy-ass condo in Bellevue? Any leads on Grandma Jing?"

"Actually, yes." Trish stood and stretched her knee, which was still a bit sticky after she'd been laid up earlier in the year with a broken leg. "I'm pretty sure Willow was with Jing at the Braeburn for a while, a few years back. My buddy Johnny said that the grandma had a little baby at her place, and a nanny who cared for the baby. Then the nanny and the baby disappeared after about a year, when Jing became bedridden due to some kind of health issue. He and the nanny were friends."

"Holy crap!" Camille sat up straight. "We have a lead on Jing?!"

"Yup! And Gigi and I are going down to the prison to meet with Charli tomorrow to update her and get her thoughts on next steps."

"You can't just pop into the prison. You need to go through their crazy process to get a visitor's pass."

"Unless you're a former cop who's been going down there for various events over the years." Trish smiled. "I couldn't believe I got a pass so quickly. But a friend at SPD helped me pull some strings."

"As usual, you're amazing. I'm heading down tomorrow as well. Lizbeth invited me to attend a recovery group inside. Maybe we can ride down together. It'll give us some time to brainstorm."

"You mean time when we aren't in the middle of all this Christmas bliss?" Trish pointed to the old newspaper turned ornament wrapping strewn across the living room floor.

"Exactly." Camille got up and began to stuff the papers back into the box. She unwrinkled yellowing old pages from the *New York Times* and read aloud. "Kamala Harris and Elizabeth Warren shifting into high gear for the presidential nomination." She crumpled it up and dropped it on the floor with a flourish. "Those were the good old days— when we actually believed that women had a chance to lead."

"Let's not even go there. I gotta split—wanna meet here in the morning?" Trish put on her bright-blue puffy coat.

"Perfect." Camille ducked as Sam threw a wadded-up piece of old newspaper at her, which Jake caught in midair. "Let's leave at seven thirty. I'll bring a thermos of coffee and some of these bagels for the drive." She turned toward Sam, snatched the ball of paper out of Jake's mouth, and returned fire.

CHAPTER NINE

Camille showed her newly received yellow volunteer badge to the expressionless guard. Trish and Gigi signed in and waited for their visitors' passes, after surrendering their driver's licenses to the guard at the desk. Now that she was a full-fledged prison volunteer, she didn't have to go through the drill of handing over her driver's license every time she entered WCCW. But this was the first time Camille had been to the prison with Gigi, and she tried to imagine what it must feel like to have your sister locked up in this hellhole.

Gigi passed through the metal detector and stood for a moment with her eyes closed and her hands clasped, as if she were saying a quick prayer. The large glass door buzzed open, and another guard ushered the three women through, along with an assortment of other family members and friends there for a visit.

It was going to be Trish's first time meeting Charli. She turned to Camille. "I can't decide if I'm more nervous or excited to finally meet Charli," she whispered.

Camille gave Trish a quick sideways hug, unsure if the prohibition against touching prisoners applied to visitors as well. So many rules.

The visitors followed the guard across the now-familiar courtyard and were buzzed through the barbed wire fence into the next courtyard. When they got inside the building, a staff member met up with them and took Camille down a different hallway to the recovery-meeting room.

—

Trish gently took Gigi's hand. Nervous. She was definitely nervous. She was mildly surprised that her cop persona had kicked in, and she stopped herself from swaggering across the courtyard. This time she was just a family member coming for a visit. It felt a little destabilizing.

The guard waited for another door to buzz open, and suddenly they were in a large room that reminded Trish of a small school cafeteria, with several tables and chairs placed haphazardly around. Half-filled vending machines lined the back wall, and several homemade plastic Christmas wreaths, a Star of David, and a Kwanzaa poster adorned the walls and were surrounded by a few glittery angels. But actual holiday joy was nowhere to be found. Trish realized that she'd never been inside WCCW as a visitor. All her trips inside had been as a volunteer for holiday events, back when she'd been on the force, working with children of prisoners when they came for Christmas or Easter visits.

Trish's inspection of the room was interrupted by Gigi grabbing her arm and pointing. "There she is!"

Trish caught her breath. Identical was an understatement. It could have been Gigi nearly running toward their table. Well, Gigi with her hair short and natural. And no makeup.

The twins entwined themselves in each other's arms. The no-physical-contact rule didn't apply in the visitors' room.

Gigi didn't take her eyes off Charli as she spoke. "Trish, this is my sister, Charli."

Everything was surreal. Gigi's smile emanated from the woman in prison garb.

"I've heard so much about you. Thank you so much for coming."

It was Gigi's voice too.

"I feel the same way. I feel like I already know you." Trish tried not to stare too much.

The sisters lost no time catching up. Gigi told Charli about the progress of her current research grant. As the sisters bantered back and forth about research statistics and the slog of working in white men's academia, Trish was surprised at how much Charli seemed to know about her sister's work.

"How do you follow Gigi's work so closely?" Trish asked.

"She sends me her draft journal submissions in the mail, and I send back comments. It keeps me busy. And I'm taking some advanced math and stats classes here, so I've been learning about medical research."

"That's awesome."

"Yeah. They can shackle my body, but not my mind. I'm a bit of a math nut—I have a CPA and an MBA, so it's fun to apply my business math to Gigi's research."

"She's being too modest. Charli's input is immensely helpful. She got the math gene, and I got the science gene." Gigi's smile enveloped the threesome.

Charli leaned forward and changed the subject. "Okay, speaking of math and my former career, let's get down to business. I have some information that might help find Willow—or at least get my ex worried for his future."

Trish perked up. "I'm all ears." She looked around the room. "I can't believe they won't let us bring in paper and pens. I'm a note-taker." She looked at Gigi. "Listen up, we need to remember everything Charli tells us."

Charli paused. "You know, Camille is my lawyer in here for my family law issue. So I'll tell this all to you, but I can repeat it to her, and she can write stuff down."

Gigi nodded. "Good point. And you've already given me the high-level download, so let's get Trish up to speed."

"Okay, but first, I was so anxious about meeting you, I totally forgot to thank you for your willingness to help us find Willow. For the first time in years, I actually feel a glimmer of hope."

Trish smiled. "I hope you're right. Cold cases are challenging, for sure, but all we need are a couple of breakthroughs. Let's start at the beginning."

Charli explained to Trish how she had been shackled in labor and how her nurse, Jayne, had created a safe space for her and Willow by protecting her from the degradation of being a prisoner in labor. Then she took her through the catastrophic way Martin had shown up and kidnapped Willow.

It was almost too hard to bear. Trish had been a cop for a decade and a PI for almost as long, but somehow people's stories seemed to feel more compelling and emotional as the years passed. And this one was especially heartbreaking, since it was family.

Charli had obviously told the story many times, but still she broke down in tears as she relived the humiliation of that night in the hospital, the deep love she had experienced when she held Willow, and the devastation of her loss when Martin absconded with the thing she loved most in the world.

"And the last thing he said to me was that I had better not snitch on him, now that he had my baby." Charli wiped her nose with her sleeve.

Trish waited a beat and asked, "Snitch on him about what?"

"Well, that's why you're here." Charli stopped to compose herself. She trembled just slightly as she continued. "I think Gigi probably told you that Martin was a professor at the University of Washington School of Pharmacy. And then we decided that he should leave the U so we could open a chain of pharmacies. All on the up-and-up." She stopped and looked away for a minute. "But then along came OxyContin, and everything changed."

Trish waited as Charli paused again. "What happened?" she asked quietly.

"Martin got intoxicated by the money he started to see flowing after the docs, especially in smaller towns, started prescribing oxy."

Trish nodded.

"Everyone thinks I landed in here because Martin found out I was in love with his brother, Brian. But that's only the beginning of the story." Charli looked at Gigi. "You sure it's okay to talk about this?"

"Yes. You need to come completely clean with Trish so she can help you. I trust her with my life, and yours. And Willow's."

Charli took a deep breath. "So . . . Brian and I got suspicious about how much money Martin was spending—way beyond our means—and we for sure made really good money. But not enough to be chartering private jets to Cabo and buying a three-million-dollar penthouse in downtown Seattle. And I was the business manager and CFO, so I knew everything about our income." She paused. "It just didn't add up."

"So, what'd you find out?" Trish was mesmerized. Not just by the fact that she was spellbound by Gigi's twin, but by the story she was weaving.

"I finally found a set of shadow books where he was keeping track of a hugely illegal drug operation. He was methodically documenting how he calculated the kickbacks he was giving to small-town docs who were prescribing astonishing amounts of oxy. There was no way those prescriptions could have been valid. There were some towns with, like, five thousand residents, and Martin was running something like a hundred thousand pills a year out of one of his pharmacies in a town that size. Multiply that by as many as twenty little towns. He has to have millions stashed somewhere."

Trish shook her head. It had been over a decade since she'd investigated one of these ventures where pharmacists teamed up with prescribing docs to addict entire towns. "I'm familiar with this kind of operation." Her cop voice caught her by surprise.

"I'm sure you dealt with this when you were on the force. But then it got even worse," Charli explained. "Turns out that once people get hooked on oxy, they often can't keep getting prescriptions, so they move on to street drugs like heroin—and now fentanyl, which is even more dangerous."

Gigi couldn't stop herself. "And so that asshole started a whole illegal drug operation, selling heroin and then meth right out in the open behind some of their pharmacies!"

This was a new twist. The pharmacist teaming up with illegal drug dealers. Trish chided herself as she reached for her nonexistent notepad.

Charli continued. "And when I figured it out after downloading his computer files, he had a kilo of heroin planted in my car, along with a handgun, and I got arrested."

Gigi jumped in again. "Not only did he plant drugs and a gun in her car, but he had apparently been putting heroin into Charli's food, so when she took a tox screen, it came back positive."

"Wait, how'd they get a warrant to search your car?"

Gigi smiled. "I told you she's a cop through and through." She turned to Trish. "Our lawyer made all kinds of motions about illegal searches, but the cops said there was something called exigent circumstances because Charli's car matched the description of a car that was the subject of an Amber Alert, so the search was apparently legal."

"Oh my God. That's awful." Trish leaned back in her chair. She changed the subject back to the issue at hand. "So, where's the data you downloaded from his computer? That's evidence!"

"Brian and I took the laptop and the hard drive that I had downloaded all the data on. That's what set Martin off in the first place. I was going to turn him in—but I was so naive. I had no idea how the legal system worked. So before I knew it, I was in handcuffs, and so was Brian."

"And the laptop?" Trish almost demanded.

"Brian was a high school girls' soccer coach, and he also had a group where he took girls hiking and taught them climbing in an after-school program. He put the computer in the trunk with all of his mountain climbing gear, in the locker room. It was just for the weekend, but that's when we got arrested, so Brian got fired and couldn't get back into the gym to retrieve the laptop. I thought maybe I could use it as a plea bargain, but we lost track of it. I don't think Martin has it, but none of us knows where it went."

Trish held back on asking the obvious question—*Why the hell would they hide evidence in a trunk filled with school athletic equipment?* But that question was all over her face.

"I know it sounds so stupid, but when I told my ex what I'd found, Brian told me to give him the computer and he'd hide it in his locker room. No one would think to look for it in the trunk with all the ropes and stuff because he knew none of the other coaches were involved in the hiking group." Charli paused. "And he was right. No one ever considered looking there, and I can tell you for sure that Martin had people looking everywhere. And he was pissed and threatening me and Brian, so in a way I felt safe when I got arrested and put in jail. Martin couldn't get to me in there."

Trish picked up the storyline. "So when you were in the hospital, it was Martin's only chance to get to you. He took Willow to keep you from turning over the data."

Charli nodded. "But he doesn't know that we can't find the laptop. So not only do we need to find Willow, but we need to find that laptop and the hard drive. My lawyer told me that I might be able to get my sentence reduced or even vacated if I can turn in Martin."

Gigi smiled. "So that's your mission: Find the baby. And the laptop."

Trish looked at both women. "Okay, but I'm going to have a lot of questions."

———

Lizbeth was waiting in the hallway outside the recovery-meeting room.

"I can't wait for you to meet Charli's new bunkie, Red," Lizbeth said excitedly. "She has some kind of medical or nursing background, and she's an addict, so she's real helpful to the women here who are working on their addiction issues. She leads the recovery group now, even though she's only been here a few months."

Camille wondered if Red would have any actual credentials that might be useful in helping her explain the challenges of beating an addiction here in prison. Camille was looking forward to learning more about Red's background and her thoughts on how she might be able to frame the whole issue of substance-use disorder in her upcoming family law motions.

When they entered the classroom where the recovery meeting was happening, Camille found herself at the front of a roomful of khaki-clad women listening intently to a tall woman who stood directly in front of Camille, facing the crowd. From behind the woman, all Camille could see was the loose pile of auburn hair on the top of her head. *Pretty clear where she got her nickname.* Red was so focused on an older woman with several missing teeth, telling her tearful story of domestic violence that had led to her addiction, that she didn't seem to notice Lizbeth and Camille's entrance.

"Hey, everyone!" Lizbeth waited for the woman to finish her story before interrupting the meeting. "We have a guest observer today: our new family law clinic lawyer."

Before Lizbeth could finish her sentence, Red turned to greet the twosome. Both she and Camille froze. Camille struggled to catch her breath as she stared into the green eyes of Dr. Jessica Kensington, the ob-gyn whom she had recently sued, and who had ended up pleading guilty to several felonies that were intricately related to Camille's malpractice case. It was the first time in her career that Camille had had a person arrested right in the courtroom.

After a heart-stopping beat, Red turned to the group and announced, "Ladies, this here is the absolute best lawyer in Seattle. I heard there was a new family law clinic here, but I had no idea that Camille Delaney was our volunteer lawyer. Any of you who have cases being handled by Camille are in excellent hands." Kensington smiled sincerely at Camille. "On behalf of the women here at WCCW, we can't thank you enough for helping the women here reunite with their children."

Camille tried to breathe and slow down her racing heartbeat. She opened her mouth but couldn't speak.

Kensington sensed Camille's awkwardness and asked Lizbeth to get Camille a chair. "We're delighted to have you join our recovery meeting today, Camille." The doctor's welcome was genuine.

"Thanks for having me." Camille regrouped. "I'm so inspired by you all that I thought it would be helpful for me to better understand the depth of your work here, so that I can best represent you all in court."

Kensington nodded. "There is no reason that these women can't take back custody of their children upon their release. And I'm happy to help you explain this to judges in any way I can."

Jessica Kensington's demeanor hadn't changed since Camille had last seen her. She looked just as peaceful and serene here at the front of the room of recovering women in prison as she had when she was shackled and led off that day in the King County Courthouse.

Kensington passed out some worksheets and explained the instructions to the women. Then she beckoned Camille to stand next to her at the back of the room as the women busied themselves with their assignment.

It was Camille who broke the heavy silence. "How *are* you?"

Jessica turned to face her former adversary. "Actually, I know I belong here, so I'm settling in. I discovered that I can help these women. They're poor, so they've never had access to any kind of treatment for their addiction. And God knows I've had plenty of real-life training in treatment, after being in and out of some of the best facilities in the country. So I find that I can really make a difference for women in here. In a way, I guess you could say I've found my calling."

Camille's reaction to Jessica Kensington always surprised her. "You're a mystery to me. Just when I think I know what drives you, you turn everything upside down."

"These women need me. They need you. You know my story, and to be completely honest, if you take away all of my education and privilege, my story and my internal wounds are the same as these women's. And I don't mean to minimize all of their poverty-related intergenerational trauma. But at the base of it all, we are all abused broken people who need the help and support of the community to heal."

Camille recognized the same sense of confusion she'd felt the first time Kensington had told her the story of how her family trauma had led her to a life of addiction, duplicity, and crime.

"I'm glad you're here, Camille. You have the capacity to make such a huge difference in these women's lives. I'll be in here for decades, so I'm not going to personally benefit from the work we do in here. But most of these women will be getting out in the next few years, or even sooner, and they desperately need your help getting their children back. And I'm here to help make that happen."

———

The rest of the recovery meeting went by in a blur, and before she knew it, Camille was at the front desk in the prison lobby, waiting impatiently for Trish and Gigi.

As soon as they got outside, they ran through the driving rain to the car. It was a typical late-December day in the Northwest—dark at 4:30. And raining sideways. It was impossible to talk until they were safely inside the car and slithering out of their soaked Gore-Tex rain jackets.

"You're not going to believe who runs the recovery group inside." Camille couldn't wait to tell her friends all about her afternoon.

"Charli's new bunkie, right?" Trish turned up the heater and blasted the defroster.

"Want to take a guess who her bunkie is?" Camille pulled out of the prison parking lot onto the country road. She barely noticed the high fences topped with barbed wire now.

Gigi spoke up. "She's a nurse or something."

"Nope. She's a doctor. And you guys will not believe it."

"Okay, we give up." Trish rummaged in her backpack for a package of smoked almonds and tore it open with her teeth. She shook a handful into Camille's outstretched hand.

"It's the good doctor Kensington!"

Trish snapped her head toward Camille and twisted to look at Gigi in the back seat. "What?! Gigi, your sis is bunkies with Jessica Kensington?"

Gigi leaned forward. "Oh my God."

Camille almost had to yell to be heard over the sleet hitting the windshield as they wound their way toward the highway. "And you know how Kensington always has that serene look when the world is falling down around her? She's exactly the same. That woman fascinates me."

"Well, that's one way to describe her," Trish offered.

Camille continued. "There's something about her sense of peace and serenity that we could all learn from. And she offered to help me with my family law motions to get the moms in my prison law clinic back with their kids. I'm not going to turn away that kind of help from a medical doctor." Camille craned her head to the left to look for traffic as she merged onto the highway. "And how about you two? What did you learn from Charli today?"

Trish spoke first. "Turns out Charli's husband was running an opioid ring—supplying drugs to small-town patients whose docs were overprescribing oxy."

"I wouldn't have pegged Martin Zhao as a drug dealer."

"And that's not all. He ended up running a drug operation selling illegal drugs to the folks who got addicted to oxy. Happens all the time. Local docs get bamboozled by the drug company into prescribing OxyContin—the drug reps convinced the docs that the drug wasn't addictive. So, they prescribed the drug for pain management, and before you know it, all their patients are addicted."

By the time the three women were crossing over the terrifyingly tall Narrows Bridge, they had finished debriefing their respective afternoon visits. Then they fell silent as the sinister driving rain buffeted the car as it crawled across the bridge in the heavy traffic.

Camille's eyes were glued to the road as she loudly announced, "So now, in addition to finding Willow, we need to get that laptop. I imagine that a prosecutor would be willing to consider a reduced sentence or even vacate the conviction if we can find the nanny and, better yet, the computer. I don't know much about criminal law, but I can start by reaching out to my friend Trent Conway, the prosecutor."

"What are the next steps?" Gigi asked.

Camille got down to business. "I'd say Trish needs to go back and talk with her pal Johnny, to see if he's been able to track down the nanny who was working for Jing. And I'll start doing research on how one can overturn a conviction, or at least get a sentence reduced. Let's see what Trent says about our chances—that is, if we can find the laptop."

"And how do we find the laptop?" Gigi inquired.

Trish and Camille looked at each other and shrugged.

"No idea," Camille admitted. "But Trish is an honest-to-God investigative genius, so I'm sure she'll think of something."

Trish smiled sheepishly. "I was just going to say the same thing about you."

"I hope you two have some fucking clue about what to do next. I've been living this nightmare for way too many years. There's gotta be some way to get Willow back and get Charli out of that hellhole."

CHAPTER TEN

The cramped security office at the Braeburn condo building in Bellevue was down a narrow hall, hidden behind an opulent concierge desk next to a tastefully decorated Christmas tree. On one side of the room was a bank of security monitors, and on the other, a bulletin board with weekly schedules posted alongside several mandatory workers' comp notices that hung in every business across the state.

Trish took a seat on a wobbly swivel chair next to her old police buddy, Johnny Jenkins. He pointed the remote at the small TV that was perched on the crowded desk and turned down the volume on the Monday-night Seahawks game. But both Trish and Johnny kept an eye on the screen—just in case there was a big play.

"So, you knew the nanny who worked for Jing Zhao?" Trish pulled out her small spiral notepad—this one had a glittery image of Nemo on the front. She flipped it open.

Johnny grinned. "Once a detective, always a detective. Nice pad." He gave Trish a thumbs-up.

Trish shot Johnny a serious look that was almost comical. "Thank you very much. It comes in handy when I'm interviewing a potential witness." She smiled sarcastically.

"Whoa, nobody said anything about a witness. I left my witness credentials back at the east precinct a decade ago."

"C'mon, Johnny, what do you know about that nanny—and the kid?"

"You looking for the nanny or the kid—or both?"

"Ultimately the kid, but I expect the nanny has info that could help us find the baby."

"Shit! Interception! Goddamn it!" Johnny slammed his Red Bull on the desk.

Trish grabbed the remote and hit rewind. "It's gonna get called back—the Rams were offside," she said as the yellow flag showed up in the live feed and the referee called back the play.

"You know, Malika was a wiz at football rules too."

Trish grabbed her pad. "Malika?"

"Yep. That was her name. We spent most Sundays, and some Monday and Thursday nights, down here watching the Hawks. Went to some Hawks games—that girl was really all about women's basketball, though. Loved hitting the Seattle Storm with her."

"How'd you two become friends?"

"Well, look around. I think we were the only two Black people in the building most of the time, so it was inevitable that we'd become friends. I had her back whenever the residents made innuendos about her."

"So, you two were sports buddies. Did she ever bring the baby down here?"

"All the time—she was so cute. We used to grab her little hands and raise her arms whenever the Hawks made a touchdown." He smiled genuinely. "She had the best giggle I've ever heard."

"Did you know her name? The baby, I mean."

"Her name was Ju, but Malika learned that Ju was Chinese for Daisy, so we called her Daisy."

"Okay, so what happened to Malika and Daisy?"

"Jing—that was the woman Malika worked for—fell and broke her hip, which she'd previously had surgery on. So she couldn't take care of Daisy, even with help. And man, she loved that baby."

"So . . ." Trish raised her eyebrows.

"So, you won't believe this, but the old lady ended up on boatloads of oxy for hip pain after her surgery, and she went downhill fast."

Trish perked up. "Oxy? Where did she get it?"

"According to Malika, her son was a pharmacist and he seemed to have a never-ending supply of it. You'n me used to see it all the time back in the day. Person gets hurt and needs pain meds, and before you know it"—he held his hands out—"they're hooked." He rummaged around in the overflowing drawer. "Even that sweet little super-rich old lady, totally strung out."

"What are you looking for?"

"Malika grabbed a bottle of the oxy just in case Jing ever OD'd. She wanted to be able to show the medics what she was on."

"Why couldn't they just get the pills from her condo?"

"Her son was weird about his mom taking oxy, so he always put them into some kind of fancy Chinese glass pill bottle."

"Strange," Trish said absentmindedly.

"Yeah. No one wants to admit their mom is a junkie. Especially in this place."

"So what happened to Malika and Daisy?"

"It all happened really fast." Johnny paused. "This is between you and me, right?" He took the pad gently from Trish's hand and put it on the desk.

"Right. Just between us." She left the pad where it was in an unspoken acknowledgment that this was off the record.

"Okay, thanks."

Trish refocused on Johnny. "What happened really fast?"

"Her leaving. It happened in a big rush."

Trish raised an eyebrow.

"One night Malika came down here and told me that she was going to set off the fire alarm. She said something about the son hiring a security guard of some kind that she had to get away from."

Trish looked at him. "Go on."

"And she needed a car."

"So . . ."

"So I gave her my car. I even signed the title over to her."

"Jeez."

"It was an old Jeep, no big deal."

"Tell me exactly what you remember." Trish wished she could pick up her notepad but thought better of it.

"Malika was panicking. Something had happened. As far as I could tell, there was a fight between Jing and her son. I got the impression that things might have gotten physical, and Jing wanted Malika to take the baby and get away. Malika showed me this huge wad of cash and said that Jing gave it to her to care for Daisy. Malika told me she had to split. And fast."

"So, what was up with the fire alarm?"

"She had to distract the security guard who'd allegedly been protecting Jing, but Malika was convinced that he was there to keep an eye on the baby. So she decided to set off the alarm and grab the baby and escape in the chaos that followed."

"Did it work?"

"You bet it did. She started an oil fire in the kitchen. On the stove. The whole building had to be evacuated, and the guard got stuck trying to help Jing get out of the building. She was awfully frail, but it was pretty clear that Jing was the mastermind of the escape, and she probably kept the guard busy while Malika got away."

"Did you see Malika leave?"

Johnny nodded. "I gave her my Richard Sherman jersey and helped her buckle Daisy into the car seat Malika and I had put in my car that afternoon. She carried that baby down fifteen flights before any of the other residents even knew what was happening."

"Sounds like it was a pretty well-orchestrated escape."

Johnny suddenly jumped up. "Touchdown!" He did a little end zone move along with Seahawks wide receiver Tyler Lockett.

Trish grabbed the remote and rewound a bit so they could watch the play. She reached out, high-fived Johnny, and did a little dance of her own.

Still standing and waiting for the extra point, she asked, "So, do you know where Malika ended up? Seems like you two were pretty close."

"Hell yes! We was tight. She was my girl, man." Johnny pulled out his phone and showed Trish a string of pictures of Malika, one of which was her in the Sherman jersey and full Seahawks gear at a game.

"Nice seats! Where'd you get those? What were you? Forty-yard line?"

"Row eight. Jing got 'em from her rich pharmacy son and gave them to Malika once in a while."

Trish held her breath. "Do you know where Malika is now?" She closed her eyes in a moment of silent hope.

Johnny shook his head. "Man, I wish I did." He scrolled through his phone and showed Trish the pictures. Malika and Daisy walking down by Lake Washington in Kirkland. Malika and Johnny in a selfie at the iconic Dick's Drive-In before a Seattle Storm game. Malika helping Daisy walk in the main lobby of the Braeburn.

"Tell me a bit about her."

"Not too much to tell. She was pretty quiet about her past. She made some innuendos about an old boyfriend who sounded like a first-class asshole."

"How so?"

"Just some of her comments. And how she acted. Seemed a little skittish at times. Like she was expecting something bad to happen."

"Did he hit her?"

"I wouldn't be surprised. But I don't know for sure."

"Well, it seems unlikely she'd go back to him. Any idea where her family is?"

"Who knows? After Malika took off with Daisy, I have no idea what happened to either of them. And to tell the truth, I miss them. We were a thing for a while there. I sure hope she didn't end up going back to that asshole."

"I need to find her."

Johnny smiled. "You and me both."

"You gotta help me."

"I'm down. Just let me know how I can help. To be honest, I feel kinda bad for not reaching out after they took off. But at the same time, I knew Malika didn't want to be found."

"Why do you say that?"

"Jing loved that kid more than life itself. If there wasn't something serious going on, she never would have bankrolled Malika to take off with her. I kinda wanted to honor their privacy, if that makes any sense."

"Actually, it does. But I'm looking for Daisy now, so I need your help. First we need to figure out where they went. What do you know about Jing?"

"Mostly just that she was a rich little ball of fire."

"Did Malika give you any idea of where she was headed when she took off in your car—which I can't believe you just gave her?"

Johnny paused. "My gut tells me she would have taken Daisy home to her family. She talked about her sisters and her mom a lot."

"Well, that's a start. Any idea where she lived?"

Johnny shook his head. "I know it was a small town. She was a high school basketball player, and from what she told me, it was one of those towns where the high school athletes were a pretty big deal. She often mentioned that she liked the anonymity of Seattle, where everyone didn't know her business."

"Anything else?"

"She complained about having to run for the ferry, and how expensive it was getting. Not sure if she had friends on the other side of the water, or maybe family."

Trish held her hand out. "Let me see those pictures again."

Johnny held his phone to his face to unlock it. He opened the Photos app and handed it to Trish.

Trish scrolled slowly through the pictures and stopped at one of Malika holding Daisy up as though she were going to throw her in the air. She enlarged the image with her two fingers and held it up to Johnny. "Any idea what the logo on this sweatshirt is?" She pointed to a green circle with a guy on a horse holding some kind of sword. The letters *P* and *A* were in the lower left of the circle.

Johnny looked closely at the image and back up at Trish. "High school logo?"

"It's a little weird for a high school logo, but that's my guess."

Johnny grabbed his phone out of Trish's hand. "*P-A*—maybe Port Angeles?"

Trish pulled out her own phone and started googling. "That'd be my guess."

"Bam!" Johnny held up his phone to the Port Angeles High School web page. "The famous PA Roughriders!"

"Now, tell me you know Malika's last name. Please," Trish teased her friend.

"She never told me. She was a little mysterious that way."

"Well, how old do you think she is?"

Johnny shrugged. "She was maybe twenty-three or so back then."

"So, she'd have graduated in, like, 2010? Mind if I use your laptop here?" She pointed to the clunky laptop on the cluttered desk.

Johnny leaned over and pressed the power button. "It's a dinosaur. If you can get it to boot up, be my guest."

Johnny typed in the password, and the twosome held their breath as the icon circled around and around, trying to find the internet signal.

"C'mon, baby," Johnny coaxed.

Trish looked at him. "Seriously, this is the best they can do in this fancy-ass place?"

"It's mine. I brought my old machine to work—if it gets stolen, I'm out nothing."

"Okey doke! Here we go. Internet signal located." Trish's fingers flew across the keyboard, and within less than five minutes, she had found a picture of the Port Angeles Roughriders girls' basketball team at the state championships. She turned the screen to Johnny. "Back row, third from the left. Look familiar?"

"That's her." Johnny's smile was a mile wide.

"I'm going to head over to PA, see what I can find out."

"Might not be an impossible task to find Malika, especially since she was a fairly well-known high school athlete. But it's been, like, five years. Lots can happen in that amount of time."

Trish stopped and looked at Johnny. "I'm going to dig into this one. I know what you're gonna say—it's a cold case, and they're impossible to solve. But this one is really important to me personally."

Johnny shrugged. "Cold case or not, I really hope you find them. I felt like it would be weird for me to sleuth around looking for them, so I kinda just let it go. I knew that Jing wanted them gone from Bellevue and somehow hidden. From what, I don't know. But I tried to respect everyone's privacy. So, no, I didn't go looking for them. And now I kinda wish I had."

CHAPTER ELEVEN

The plan to find Willow by tracking down Malika had come together rather quickly. Camille's longtime friend and floatplane pilot, Tony Quarton, had flown Camille, Trish, Gigi, Libby, and Gracie up to San Juan Island, where Camille and Sam kept their forty-two-foot Valiant oceangoing sailboat. Angela and Katlin had way too many social engagements to spend a few days sailing, so they stayed home with Sam. The women planned to sail the boat across the Strait of Juan de Fuca to Port Angeles so Trish would have a place to stay while she was undercover. Camille's friend had taught in nearby Sequim but recently moved to Port Angeles. Robin taught high school there and had become quite well connected in town, so she'd agreed to meet up with the gang to devise a plan to help them find Malika and hopefully get a lead on the whereabouts of Willow—a.k.a. Daisy.

Just as the crew was walking back from grabbing coffee in the early light of dawn in the picturesque town of Friday Harbor, a wiry woman with a brown bob hollered at Camille.

"Hey, you!"

"Sally?" Camille waved back. "Wow. So nice to see you here!" She pointed to Trish and Gigi. "You remember Trish and her partner, Gigi. And these are my daughters Libby and Grace." She pointed at the two girls hopscotching half a block behind them, then turned to Trish and Gigi. "Sally was the OR nurse the day Trish almost got murdered by that asshat Willcox."

Sally grinned as she jogged across the street. "Oh my gosh! I'm so happy to see you up and around, Trish! I'll never forget seeing you on the operating table while we tried to stop Willcox from slicing you wide open." Sally looked at Gigi. "And you're the doc who saved the day in the OR, right? What a total shit show."

Trish gave Sally a hug. "I'm pretty sure you saved my life by preventing Willcox from operating on me, so thank you."

Gigi joined the hug. "That's for sure! You were the real hero that day!"

Sally changed the subject and looked at Camille. "Did Sam tell you that he's agreed to be on my dissertation committee?"

"He did, and I had no idea that you were about to get your nursing PhD. And I for sure didn't know about your interest in studying opioids."

"Yep. It's become a very personal cause for me."

"I heard about your sister. I'm really sorry."

"Thanks. And who knew your next case would be helping moms in prison? What a small world."

"I know, crazy, right?" Camille grabbed Sally by the arm. "So, what brings you back to the Island? I thought you had your fill of Friday Harbor General after that whole Willcox thing went down."

"I did. But just like all other hospitals, they're pretty short staffed here now, so I agreed to take a few shifts. Saving up for grad school. Yesterday was my last shift for a bit."

"Looks like you're headed back to the city." Camille pointed at Sally's bulging backpack.

"I am. Tony has a full flight today, so I'm going to hop on the ferry and take the airporter back to Seattle."

"Your own boyfriend can't even squeeze you onto one of his floatplane flights back to town? How about you grab a ride with us? We're going to sail across to PA, and Tony's going to pick us up there and fly us back to the city tomorrow. Thankfully, the weather is just about perfect, especially for a December day. And the wind is directly from the west, so it's a broad reach all the way."

Sally paused and looked down at her jeans and leather boots. "Hmm, I'm not sure I'm properly attired for cold-weather sailing."

"No worries, we have plenty of fleece and foul-weather gear."

"Okey doke, then. Sounds like an adventure!"

"Perfect!" Camille reached into the bag of coffee shop pastries and handed Sally a scone. "We need to get moving. There's not much light at this time of year, and it's about a five- or six-hour sail." Camille looked at her watch. "If we leave by eight, we'll be on the dock in the marina about an hour before dusk, which should be around four or four thirty." She looked up at the waning dusty-peach morning sky that held the remnants of the colorful winter sunrise over the harbor.

As soon as everyone boarded the boat, Camille and Trish flew into action. They'd clearly done this drill often.

Camille popped open the floorboard and reached for the oil dipstick to check the levels while Trish flipped on several switches on the electric panel to turn on the lights and navigation equipment. Gigi and Sally made themselves busy emptying the bag of sandwiches and snacks into the top-loading refrigerator, and Libby and Grace snuck up to the V berth and pulled out a couple of sleeping bags.

Camille climbed up into the cockpit, uncovered the helm, and removed the sail cover from the boom. She checked the winches while Trish slipped the lines through the blocks so they could control the big genoa sail that would soon hover above the bow of the boat, pulling them out into the open water.

Camille hollered down the companionway to Sally. "The fleece is in a duffel bag in the quarter berth, and there are a pair of sail boots that should fit you in the locker forward. And hats and gloves are in the drawer under the V berth!" Camille turned on the engine.

"Got it, thanks!"

"Ready?" Camille shouted at Trish, who was up on the bow.

"Yep! Let's do it!" Trish jumped onto the dock and untied the lines, which she held in one hand as Camille threw the boat into reverse.

"Hop on!"

Trish grabbed the stay and pulled herself aboard just as Gigi appeared from below with two coffees, handing them to Camille and Trish before returning to the galley to grab the other two.

Camille looked at her watch and held up her cup in a toast. "Record timing, crew!" She guided the big sailboat down the fairway, which held only a scattering of boats at this time of year. In a matter of minutes, they were motoring past Brown Island and heading out into the San Juan Channel just as the sun peeked up over Lopez Island.

Camille and Trish began a well-orchestrated ballet as they hoisted the sails. It didn't take long for Camille to get them on a perfect reach down the channel toward Cattle Pass between San Juan and Lopez Islands.

Camille looked at Sally and gestured for her to sit. "So, tell me about your sis."

Sally closed her eyes quickly and took a breath. "Her name was Kitt."

Camille leaned over to better hear Sally over the slapping of waves against the hull.

"Kitt's situation is what got me interested in this whole issue of moms in prison."

"Want to talk about it?"

Sally nodded and took a sip of coffee. "Like so many women, Kitt got caught up in the whole opioid racket after her doc overprescribed meds for post-op pain following a back surgery for a bulging disc."

Camille nodded.

"Then the doc cut off the script, causing Kitt to spiral—at which point, my sweet, smart, well-educated sister learned that her only real option was to feed her opioid addiction with street drugs. She ended up in prison and had no access to any kind of treatment. Our family tried to be supportive, but we had no idea how hard prison life would be on Kitt."

"Other than the obvious, what was it that Kitt struggled with inside?" Once Camille had opened herself up to learning about women in prison, she was always on the search for a way to make life better for the women inside.

"Well, for starters, did you know that women inside make about fifty-two dollars per month for working?"

Camille shook her head slowly. "Just when I think I have some kind of global idea of what goes on there, I realize it's just the tip of the iceberg."

"How much do you think it costs to watch a movie on their tablet?"

Silence.

"Fifteen ninety-nine. Do the math—that's about thirty percent of their monthly income. So, let's say you make five thousand per month. That would be like having to pay one thousand six hundred and fifty dollars to watch a movie." Sally was on a roll. "And if they want to download music? It's two dollars per song. And they don't even get the original artist—they only have access to covers. And books? Nope. All books available on their tablets are old B-list-type books. Nothing any of us would be looking to read."

"I heard that they need to also buy their own personal products as well," Camille added.

"Don't even get me started. Shampoo, tampons, deodorant, lotion. You name it, DOC charges them a jacked-up, premium price for it."

"How do the women afford any of that on fifty-two dollars per month?"

"If they're lucky, like Kitt was, they have family that puts money on their commissary account."

Camille thought about her legal clinic. "I have a whole new appreciation for what it must take for the women I'm working with just to show up so well put together. They really take pride in their appearance. I had no idea."

"Well, as you can imagine, having access to decent personal care products can make a world of difference when you're living someplace where the goal seems to be to remove most aspects of the innate uniqueness of an individual."

Every time she learned something more about the challenges of prison life, Camille became more committed to doing something about it.

Trish changed the subject. "So, what happened to Kitt?"

"Well, she got sideways with her asshole CCO shortly after her release."

Gigi, who'd been listening intently, interrupted. "CCO?"

Sally looked at Gigi. "Community corrections officer—it's a fancy title for a probation officer. I've heard there are lots of CCOs who are supportive and work hard to make reentry smooth for the women. But like with any other profession, there are some bad eggs. And Kitt's was a total ass." Sally was clearly getting angry just thinking about it. "Kitt got released. But since she had an issue with addiction, part of her probation was that she had to drug test whenever they called her in. *And* she had to show proof of outpatient treatment. *And* she had to meet with her CCO on a very specific schedule. And then she had to show proof that she was searching for a job. And she got some public assistance, which meant that she had to meet with a social worker to prove she needed help."

"So, exactly how was she supposed to work a job when she had all those other obligations?" Gigi asked curiously.

"Excellent question. And the better question is how she was supposed to get to all those appointments when they took her driver's license away from her and she had to take public transportation everywhere."

"I take it all of these agencies weren't located close to each other either." Trish had obviously heard similar stories in her days on the police force.

"Oh my God, it was crazy. At that point, she hadn't lost her kids, and her ex was off in the military, stationed overseas. So, when Kitt was released, she got her two boys back from our mom, who was pretty much done being a full-time grandma after the two years Kitt was locked up. In fact, our mom decided to move to Arizona as soon as Kitt got out. And I was off doing flight nursing, so I was never home."

"So, what happened?"

"She went to do the drug test, two kids in tow. One was two and a half, and the other was almost four. And the drug testing center told her that she couldn't bring her kids in with her—so they failed her on the drug test as a no-show even though she was right there in the hallway trying to get tested."

"What?!" Gigi yelled.

Sally nodded. "And then she had to take the bus across town to the CCO's office at the time he mandated, which was impossible because there was no direct bus route, and she couldn't get from her required appointment at the drug testing site to the CCO's office in time to make her appointment there. So, he wrote her up for being late and refused to see her. Also, once she got there, they told her that the kids couldn't come in."

The three other women were speechless.

"Then, a few days later, she goes through the same drill, except now she has to drag her kids on another bus trip, including something like three transfers to get to the place where she has to apply for food vouchers of some kind—I'm not sure what they call them—but she had to go in person. And once again, she's late, so they cancel her appointment and reschedule it for two weeks later. This means the only way she can get food for her and the kids is to go to the food bank, which of course now means another bus ride. She gets there just as they're closing, but they give her a couple bags of food anyway."

"Unbelievable." Camille's mind was going a mile a minute. These women were totally set up to fail immediately upon their release.

"It gets worse. The same thing happens at the WorkSource place. The one she went to won't let her in with her kids, and she has no one to watch them. So now she's totally out of compliance with her probation—she missed her drug test and her meeting with her CCO, and she barely has any food and can't show the CCO that she's signed up at the job-search place. And the CCO is planning a pop-in home visit to her apartment. She's terrified that he'll report her to CPS for not having enough food for her kids."

"Was she able to reschedule the appointments?" Gigi asked.

"Nope. The CCO insists that the only time he's available is at a time she can't get there, if she's going to get her drug tests at the right time. And now she has to leave her kids with a neighbor she doesn't know, so there's that."

"Crap. She didn't have a snowball's chance in hell." Camille felt anger well up inside her.

"Exactly. And the crappy thing is that Kitt went through a carpentry program inside and was poised to get into a union apprenticeship for HVAC when she was released. But there was no way she could attend the training and still hop on buses from one end of the city to the other just to try and stay in compliance with her probation. And of course, I had no idea this was going on, because she already felt like she'd been a burden on the family by getting herself into so much trouble in the first place. If only she'd reached out to me." Sally shook her head sadly.

"And so they violated her?" Trish asked, already knowing the answer.

Sally nodded. "They took her kids away and sent her to the county jail for six months for failing to comply with the terms of her probation. And by that point her ex showed up and took the kids and got a parenting plan entered, with all kinds of restrictions against her because she looked terrible on paper to the judge, who believed that she was blowing off her drug testing and her CCO. And the judge even put in the order that Kitt refused to even try and get a job. It was awful."

"That's disgusting. But I'm glad for the heads-up. I expect my sister, Charli, will have to deal with those shitty CCOs, if she ever gets out."

Sally looked at Gigi. "Your sister is in prison?"

Gigi nodded. "WCCW. Doing a twelve-year sentence for a bogus drug charge."

"Well, that sucks." Sally stated the obvious. "I wonder if they knew each other?"

"No idea," Gigi said softly.

"So what happened to Kitt?" Camille's concern was genuine.

"When she finally got out of the local jail where she got locked up for her probation violation, she lost it. She'd done everything right." Sally's voice went up an octave. "That asshole CCO wouldn't give her a break. He kept setting appointments all over town for her and seemed to take pleasure in her being unable to stay in compliance. And by this time, she didn't have her kids with her, but she still couldn't get all over town on public transportation to be able to meet his demands. And not seeing her kids was killing her."

"This is heartbreaking." Camille reached out and put her hand on Sally's shoulder.

"So she finally relapsed. And she got some heroin that was laced with fentanyl and OD'd. Never got to see her kids again. So now they have no mom, and their dad refuses to let any of our family see them. And of course, now my mom blames herself. And I blame myself. And our family is completely torn apart knowing that we'll never see the boys again." Sally wiped a tear from her cheek with the back of her gloved hand. She turned to Gigi. "What about your sister—how's she holding up? Prison is just so awful."

"Actually, Charli is the reason we're all here," Trish said. "Her ex kidnapped her baby right out of the hospital when she was incarcerated. They took her to Puget Sound General to deliver her baby, and her ex showed up and took off with Charli's daughter. Camille and I are trying to find Willow."

"Oh my God. He took the baby right out of the hospital? That's terrifying. When did it happen?" Sally asked.

"Seven years ago. So it's a seriously cold case. But we have some leads that point to Port Angeles. Hence our little sailboat adventure today. I'm off to investigate and see what I can find out about where Willow might be." Trish grabbed the line running from the boom and adjusted the sail a bit.

"And then, if we can find her," Camille interjected, "I'm going to take the ex to court to get Charli prison visits. But most importantly, the ex isn't the bio dad, so he has no business keeping Willow from her mom. And so, ultimately, we need to get Willow back with her mom and dad."

"That's crazy." Sally was fully engaged in the mission. "Any idea who the bio dad is?"

Gigi jumped in. "It's her husband's brother." She looked at Camille. "Remember, he isn't officially an ex yet. But hopefully soon."

"Good point," Camille agreed.

"So, what's the plan? Anything I can do to help?" Sally asked.

"Well, once we find Willow, we'll need help convincing a judge to let her see Charli, because she's in on a drug charge, and you know better than anyone how that rolls." Camille rubbed her hands to warm them up inside the thick sailing gloves. "Actually, I was talking to Sam about you. I need help educating the local judges about addiction and why it's important for moms to be reunited with their kids. That's your research, right?"

"Yep. These kids are at such high risk for entering what used to be called the school-to-prison pipeline. It's been renamed based on research—the trauma-to-prison pipeline. You take a high-risk kid and then keep them from their mom—it's a recipe for disaster. And the problem isn't solved just by reuniting them or even getting some amount of custody. The kids need their moms involved in their daily lives. I've interviewed moms who can't even volunteer in their kids' schools. No field trips. No bringing cupcakes for their kids' birthdays. No volunteering to help teach kids to read. These kids start to believe that their moms don't care about them because they don't volunteer like the other moms, even though the moms are trying to jump through every conceivable hoop to be able to get involved in the school. But the schools won't allow the moms on the premises because they're 'felons.'" Sally air quoted the word "felons"—the more appropriate appellation was "formerly incarcerated person," since people didn't want to continue to be identified by the worst thing they ever did.

Sally continued. "And the kids struggle in school because their moms are prevented from volunteering in their classrooms, which compounds the problem. And then our society acts all upset when these kids end up getting into trouble, and ultimately, they end up in the system too. It's our fault. We are not taking care of these poor kids. We deprive them of what everyone can agree is essential for someone to become a responsible adult—their moms. So, when these kids fail—it's on us."

Camille chimed in. "Exactly. This is what I need to teach the judges. It's their responsibility to do what's in the best interest of the child in each family law case. I honestly don't think they have a good understanding of the risk to these kids and to the rest of society when they deny kids their moms. I want to go into family court armed with as much research as possible. And I'm hoping you can help."

"I'm all in." Sally high-fived Camille as they moved through Cattle Pass and out into the twenty-five-mile-wide Strait of Juan de Fuca. Thankfully, conditions were calm, but Camille knew these waters well enough to be prepared for a totally unexpected squall. She surveyed her electronic chart and took a heading straight for Port Angeles on the southern coast of the strait. Trish grabbed the winch handle and cranked in the mainsail while both women silently watched the luff of the sail until it was perfectly trimmed. Then they did the same for the huge genoa sail attached to the foremost stay on the bow of the graceful boat as it gently rode the swells, which gradually grew in size as they got farther from land.

Camille loved the quietness of sailing. The water lapping against the hull. The seagulls squawking overhead and the splash as the boat glided over the rolling waves moving in from the massive Pacific Ocean, about fifty miles to the west.

After a couple of hours of solitude, Gigi appeared with a bag of sandwiches, which caused Libby and Gracie to magically appear.

Camille, as an experienced sailor, always kept her eyes on the water. It wasn't unusual to see a floating log or other piece of detritus, which could prove disastrous for the hull of a boat. On a happier note, there were often pods of orcas that brought hours of joy to sailors in the Salish Sea.

"Mom! Freighter off our port side!" Libby yelled as she put down her binoculars.

Camille could barely make out the silhouette of the huge ship coming out of the haze to their left. She popped down into the cabin and focused navigation software on the icon indicating that a large ship was moving in on them. Camille knew well that even though they looked to be far away, freighters moved quickly through the water and that the blip on the horizon would soon be upon them. And freighters always had the right of way.

"Can I run the nav program?" Libby hung over her mother's shoulder.

"Just a sec, I need to find him first." Camille focused the navigation software onto the ship. "It's about ten miles off to the east!" she shouted up the companionway to Trish.

"I see it!"

"Okay, Lib." Camille moved aside. "See if you can tell me the name of the ship."

"*Colibri Queen*. It's a bulk carrier."

"Which means . . ."

"It's probably carrying grain from the grain terminal in Seattle."

"Daddy would be so proud of you!" Camille clicked on the map and enlarged the icon of the freighter.

"It's going about thirty-five knots." Libby's voice was all business.

"Right. And check this out: since we're out in the strait, we might see the pilot boat coming out to pick up the pilot! Let's go up and see!"

Libby scrambled up into the cockpit. "We might see the pilot coming off the ship, everyone!"

Gigi looked at Trish quizzically.

"Every ship that comes through the Strait of Juan de Fuca has to have a local pilot aboard for safety and ease of navigation," Trish explained. "And they on- and off-load right off Port Angeles. It's quite a sight!"

Trish handed Gigi a pair of binoculars.

"Who knew that sailing twenty-five miles would be so action packed?" Gigi said as she held them up.

"Can I see?" Gracie held her hand out for the binoculars Libby was using to scan the horizon.

Libby, ever the teacher, turned to Gracie and pointed. "If you look over that way, you'll see the red pilot boat coming out to pick up the pilot."

Gracie patiently held her binoculars perfectly still. "Looking for *hong chuan*!" She sang the Chinese words for "red boat" loudly.

Libby nodded approvingly at Gracie's mixed-language sentence.

Camille came over and put her arms around both girls, keeping one eye on the freighter, which was rapidly approaching, and one eye out for the red pilot boat. "There!" She pointed. "See it? It's going pretty fast."

Gracie swiveled in the direction Camille was pointing and sang loudly, "Red boat," first in English and then in Chinese.

Camille turned her attention to the sails and released the line that allowed the mainsail to luff in the wind. "We're gonna have to wait and let the freighter pass." She took the steering off autopilot and turned the boat so that the large genoa sail on the bow was also luffing in the wind, which caused the sailboat to stop all forward movement, pitching lightly in the swells. She turned to the group.

"This is really cool." She pointed to the small red boat that was pulling up against the freighter, which was still going full speed. "Check it out. See that ladder hanging off the freighter? I had a divorce client one time who was a freighter pilot. They have to climb down that ladder about fifty feet and somehow jump into that pilot boat that's keeping the same speed as the freighter. See how the freighter is unaffected by the huge choppy waves, but the little boat is rocking and rolling? So scary."

The cockpit crew stood silently, all of them willing the pilot to make it onto the deck of the pitching pilot boat safely. Camille held her breath as they watched the brave pilot make his way down the ladder and wait at the waterline as the pilot boat edged close enough for him to hop on board. Then, he turned to high-five the men on the bow of his boat. When they noticed the women in the rocking sailboat, the entire crew of the pilot boat turned and waved—which of course made the women wave wildly in return and clap their hands high in the air as the pilot boat turned and did a circle around the sailboat, honking its horn before speeding off toward the small town of Port Angeles, just visible on the shore.

The women turned to each other and did a little dance with Gracie and Libby. Then Camille and Trish set about trimming the sails and pointing the boat toward the marina on the edge of town.

As soon as they reached the breakwater outside the marina, Camille flipped the radio to channel sixteen to call and get a moorage slip. Suddenly, a pod of orcas appeared right off the bow of the boat, and the crew stood up in unison as the whales welcomed them to town. Camille put down the radio and watched the orcas jumping out of the water just a few feet from the boat.

"Every time the whales show up on the bow, something good happens. This is a hopeful omen, team," she said quietly.

Trish nodded. "Yep. This is a very good sign." She put her arm around Gigi and kissed her on the cheek. "We're going to find Willow. I know it."

CHAPTER TWELVE

Camille looked around the cozy dockside restaurant and spotted Robin, her sister-friend, waving from her perch alone at a huge booth.

"Lucky me, the whole dang team reunited here in my crazy little town!" Robin hugged and pecked each woman on the cheek and then pulled Libby and Gracie into the booth, right next to her.

The women took turns peeling off layers of fleece and hanging jackets, hats, and scarves on the coat hooks at the end of the booth. Then each slid in turn into their spot as the server waited to take their drink order.

Robin held her hand out in a gesture of introduction. "Family, meet Brittany. Owner of this illustrious institution."

"Love your place!" Trish gushed. "And love all the sports memorabilia." She pointed to the wall of autographed photos of Seattle athletes—both current and not.

Libby was transfixed. "Especially this one of Sue Bird! Did you get to meet her?"

"I did. She's awesome. And thanks. This place has been in my family for two generations. It's on me to keep it up and running."

There was nothing Camille liked better than supporting women-owned businesses. "No surprise that Robin is a regular here." She cradled her friend's chin in her hand.

"What can I get for y'all?" Brittany got down to work.

Trish looked at the chalkboard on the wall. "Wow. Hard to choose. I'll have your fave microbrew."

Gigi smiled at Brittany. "Same here."

Camille held up a finger to add to the microbrew order but didn't wait for the table to complete their own orders before turning her attention to the reason they had gathered there. She handed Libby her tablet and two sets of headphones so she and Gracie could play a game. Then she turned to Robin. "Like I texted you, we're pretty sure Malika, the nanny, ended up in PA after she took off from Bellevue. And it turns out that she was quite a basketball star here in town several years back, so we're hoping maybe some of your teacher friends might know her and can give us a head start on where to look."

Robin nodded. "About what year are we talking?"

Trish chimed in. "2010. They won the state championship."

"Shouldn't be a problem. Lots of teachers here have been here forever. Let me make some calls."

"Thanks so much." Gigi looked like she was about to cry. "This is the most hopeful I've been in years. You all are amazing." She held up her water glass in a toast to the table just as Camille stood up and waved to a woman sitting at the bar.

"Rose! Hey!" Camille shouted. She turned to the table. "Old friend from my time at the Women's Law Center. Amazingly smart criminal defense lawyer. I'll be right back."

The woman at the bar scanned the room to identify who was calling her name and lit up when she saw Camille walking toward her, arms extended for a hug.

The two women embraced.

"What brings you to my fave hangout right here in PA?" Rose's question was sincere.

"I was kinda wondering the same about you." Camille grabbed a barstool and climbed up on it, right next to Rose, who appeared to be alone.

"Would you believe that this lovely county elected me as their prosecutor a few years ago?"

"What? I didn't even know you lived here! And prosecutor?! Are you freaking kidding me?"

Rose nodded. "Moved up here about twelve years ago to do defense work, then got recruited to be a deputy prosecutor about seven years ago. This is my hometown, so it was time for me to come back and see what I could do to serve my community. Lots of challenges here, with the whole opioid thing blowing up."

"But prosecutor? Damn. You were such a kick-ass defense lawyer. Why on earth did you go to the dark side? How did this even happen?" Camille held up her hands in a questioning gesture.

Rose smiled and took a sip of her beer. "Honestly, after years of defense work, I realized that someone has to work to change how prosecutors charge people. Most prosecutors I worked with couldn't seem to understand that the people they're dealing with are mostly folks who have suffered some kind of trauma. And putting them in jail, where they'll just get out and commit more crimes, isn't the answer to the revolving door of the so-called criminal justice system. It was very clear that we need some progressive prosecutors with new and innovative ideas. So, here I am. Being as progressive and innovative as I can within the confines of a really challenging job in a relatively conservative county."

Camille was duly impressed. "Good for you. I've been doing some work with women down at WCCW and the stories are gut wrenching. I had no idea about the lives of the women who end up behind the walls of our prisons."

Rose looked Camille directly in the eye. "Then you know exactly what I'm talking about. There has to be a better way of dealing with women who've been sexually assaulted and who've suffered childhood trauma, who then go on to make monumentally bad choices in men. And the men in prison are often similarly impacted by traumatic childhoods, and/or addiction. It just doesn't seem to me that locking people up for what are mostly mental health issues is the answer our community needs."

"That's a tough sell as a prosecutor," Camille responded.

"It is, but we have to start somewhere. I started a diversion program here for people who are caught up in the system because of their addiction. There are tons of opioid users up here, so I created a therapeutic program for those who choose to get treatment. One component of the treatment is using medication. That's an important aspect of the overall program here, because some people come in and they're already on treatment meds but are forced to withdraw. We make sure that those who are already on medications can continue their treatment. And so people who need medications for opioid use disorder can receive it."

"Wow. A prosecutor using all the tools in her toolbox. Very cool."

"And now that program I started as a deputy prosecutor is getting some significant funding, and it turns out to really be working. I get to go to the graduations, and it's so heartwarming to see people we used to consider hopeless addicts standing in front of the drug-court judge, with their family members there cheering them on after they complete the treatment. I never imagined I could make this kind of difference in a community. I'm constantly blown away by these folks' bravery and commitment to getting their lives back on track. It's so much better for all of us than throwing them in jail."

"You're amazing. I was just observing a recovery group at WCCW, and it was exactly what you're talking about. But there, they have no families to support them, and they're mostly serving some serious time. But somehow, they're able to dig deep and help each other recover and gain some sense of pride and ownership over their circumstances. Some of them even go to college inside."

"I know. Those prison college programs are life changing. I've visited several classes, and I've been overwhelmed by how brilliant so many of those people in prison are. They work on legislation from inside and stay in close touch with their communities outside in an effort to keep kids from going down the wrong path and ending up in prison. There is so much treasure wasted in our prisons. I got into this work to see if I could make a difference in how we deal with people who break laws, mostly out of addiction and poor life choices. But that's not to say there aren't some really bad people who do horrendous things—those folks need to be kept out of society for a very long time. The challenge is figuring out who can be helped."

Camille reached over and grabbed a few peanuts from the jar on the bar and began to shell them. "You're a goddamn prosecutor." She chuckled quietly. "I don't believe it." Suddenly she perked up. "I gotta tell my mom! She's going to be so proud of you for being brave enough to run for office!"

Rose smiled. "Your mom was the best prof I had at law school. Her crim procedure class was what inspired me to go into criminal law in the first place."

"She's something. That's for sure," Camille agreed. "So, how did you manage to get elected up here in Clallam County? That's a big deal. This isn't the most progressive place in the state, I'm sure." She held her beer up in a salute. "To the voters of Clallam County!"

Rose clinked glasses with Camille and looked around the room. "I know, it feels surreal to me even now. I think everyone is tired of the same old so-called solutions to our public safety concerns. There were so many families in town that were being brought down by addiction that I think they decided to give me their vote and give me a chance. I sure hope I can make a difference, even if it's just in some small ways."

"Well, getting people into treatment is not a small way to make a difference. It's huge. If you can keep even one person from ending up in prison, that's a really big win." Camille grabbed her phone out of her pocket. "Hang on—what time is it in Greece?" She opened her app. "Five a.m. in Greece. I'm going to text my mom."

"Greece? Your mom is in Greece? What, for the holidays? Wait, she's Greek, right? Her accent was iconic at the law school."

Camille was lost on her phone. She looked up. "She lives on her home island of Lesvos now. She started an asylum organization there."

"Wow! So cool! I know she did research on the overlap between immigration and criminal law, but I always thought of her more as a criminal law geek."

"Yeah, she's from Lesvos and she happened to be home for a few months in 2016, when the immigrants started coming across in those inflatable boats. And since you know my mom, you can imagine how she quickly became consumed with seeking justice for those terrified families. She came home briefly to negotiate a sabbatical at the law school, and then moved home to a small town called Mithymna, that looks across the water to Turkey. It's actually not that far from Turkey to Greece—you can see the land about six or seven miles away. But kids and families were drowning because of overflowing boats, and even mild wind waves would capsize them. And then, those who made it were thrown into these horrid camps, where they were told they'd be held until their asylum paperwork was processed. But, as you can imagine, it never happened, so my mom took up their cause and never looked back."

Rose put her hand on Camille's knee. "Of course she did. I'm not one bit surprised."

Just then, Camille's phone lit up with a FaceTime call. "Hey, Mom! You'll never guess who I'm sitting with."

The one thing that had never changed in all the years Camille could remember was the sparkle in her mom's deep-brown eyes. People often commented on how similar her eyes were to her mother's, but she didn't really see it. Her mom always looked like she was going to explode with some new insight or piece of breaking news that she had analyzed and created a unique narrative for. It felt to Camille like most of those sparkly-eyed moments were saved for the plight of her mom's marginalized clients. She'd often wished that one day maybe she'd be the object of her mother's enthusiasm. But for now, she'd have to be satisfied with her mom's excitement about Rose's new career.

"Do tell, my dear."

Camille's stomach did a little flip when she heard her mother's melodious Greek accent, which had deepened after she moved back to Greece.

"Oh, I'm just hangin' out with the prosecutor who was elected over here in Port Angeles." Camille giggled as she grabbed Rose and pulled her into the screen.

Here we go—Mom's about to gush.

"Rose Adams! What fabulous news! I could not be more proud of you!" Pella's smile just about burst through the phone.

"What a happy surprise, Professor Rallis—I just learned that you're over in Greece saving lives and doing asylum work. That's amazing." Rose almost looked starstruck. "You were honestly the best prof I ever had. Your crim procedure class inspired my whole career."

"That's such a sweet compliment, my dear." Even over FaceTime, Pella had a way of making a person feel like there wasn't anyone else in the world she'd rather be talking with. No one would ever have guessed that she had just awakened at 5:00 a.m. on a small Greek island overflowing with terrified refugees. "And, Camille, tell me what fascinating case you're working on now."

"Well, I got kind of roped into running a family law clinic at WCCW. And I'm hooked. I'm horrified that I knew so little about the explosion of women being incarcerated."

Maybe this will impress her.

Pella jumped in. "Last I heard, the number of women being incarcerated in the US, it was something like a seven hundred percent increase."

How on earth did she just happen to pick the exact right number out of thin air?

"That's right," Camille agreed. "And the number of women inside for drug-related crimes is so misleading."

"It's not the drugs, my dear—it's their unspeakably horrible childhoods, usually involving some kind of DV, often including sexual assault that precedes the drug abuse."

"That's what I've been learning. And from a family law perspective, it's almost worse. The women are having a helluva time being reunited with their kids when they get out. So I'm working to change that." At least it gave her a topic of conversation with her mom.

"Have you gone inside yet?" Pella asked.

"I have—and the women I'm working with are so inspiring. So many have suffered so much, and yet they hold out hope that someday they'll get back to their children. I think it's what keeps them going."

"And their children need them just as much as the moms need the kids. The trauma-to-prison pipeline is a real thing."

Of course my mom would stay current on the research and nomenclature. Is there anything she's not an expert on?

"You taught this in law school?"

"I sure did. And I have a few friends who have been working in this space for quite some time. But they struggle to get grants because their data is mostly anecdotal. It's a vicious cycle. They know what needs to be done to help the women, but since it's not evidence based, they can't get funding. And without the funding, they can't prove that their programs work. The nonprofit industrial complex is a beast."

"I don't know if you remember Sally Berwyn, Tony's girlfriend, who was an OR nurse at Friday Harbor, but she's now a grad student in the UW nursing school."

"Well, she must be very smart. That's the top nursing school in the country—maybe even the world." Pella's admiration was palpable.

"I know, and her dissertation is about the intersection of public health and women in prison. She's helping me with the research."

Her mother's tone took on a professorial ring. "Then I expect she can help you to understand the new studies that tell us how women differ from men in terms of why they end up in prison. Are you familiar with those?"

"I'm not." Camille deflated for a hot second, then looked at Rose, who leaned in, clearly enamored at attending her own personal lecture by her favorite professor.

Rose turned toward Camille and mouthed, "Fangirl right here," and pointed at her chest and then at Pella's face on the phone.

Rose and how many others? Camille smiled weakly.

Pella continued. "Turns out that the pathways to prison vary from men to women. The behaviors that serve as precursors to prison for men have to do with antisocial behaviors, antisocial environments, antisocial friends, and a previous criminal history. For women, there are four major typologies we see over and over. One is highly addicted women: most of these women are in prison for the first time, maybe someone who's on her fifth DUI or got hooked on opioids after an injury. The second pathway is made up of lifelong victims and survivors. These women come from poverty, and many have domineering and violent partners. Most have traumatic histories of early sexual abuse. The third group is women who've been socialized from an early age into a life of crime. They use drugs, often sell them, and have lived lives of limited social mobility. These women are under heavy antisocial influence from their families, partners, and communities. Last are the aggressive antisocial women. These poor souls don't stand a chance in life. They've typically been involved in drug and property offenses, and they're usually victims of horrible childhood physical and sexual trauma and frequently suffer from serious mental illness—sometimes even psychosis. They have a high rate of suicide and self-harm and score off the charts for virtually every risk factor."

Once a professor, always a professor—and rarely a mom. "Can you send me links to that literature?" Camille gave up trying to impress her mom and surrendered to her scholarship.

But Pella was on a roll. "And you've probably already learned that eighty-five percent of women in prison are mothers, and ninety-seven percent of all prisoners eventually get out, so it's in everyone's interest to fix this overwhelming problem."

Camille was silent. As usual, her mother made Google look like a second-rate data source.

"I'll send you two girls some articles. And an intro to some judges at the National Association of Women Judges who might be interested in your mission. I'm very proud of you, my darling! And over the moon to hear that you're taking on this issue as a prosecutor, Rose. Our communities need more prosecutors like you."

"I know this is your workout time, Mom, so we won't keep you. I just thought you'd be super excited to hear about Rose's career trajectory." Camille knew that the key to staying in touch with her mom was to keep calls short and frequent, and if the topic of the call involved legal or game-changing challenges, it might even extend the call.

Pella shook her long gray hair and grabbed it into a ponytail. It was clear that Pella took very seriously the lives and futures of her clients and was hyperfocused on the importance of her work. "I need to keep myself in fighting condition—I've got a date with my yoga teacher in fifteen minutes. Gotta run! Very proud of you, Rose! Hug my beautiful granddaughters for me!" She blew Camille and Rose a kiss and hung up.

"Your mom is one of a kind." Rose put her hand on Camille's arm. Perhaps sensing Camille's feelings of inadequacy, she added, "You take after her, you know?"

I wish.

Rose gently changed the subject. "How long are you in town?"

"Just tonight. But I expect I'll be back soon. I'm working on a cold case—trying to find a missing baby—well, she'd be seven now, but we think she was brought over here to PA about five or six years ago. We think her nanny brought her here—she was a basketball star at PA High back around 2010 to 2012. Were you here then?"

"Actually, I was. And like I said, this is my hometown, so I probably either know her or know someone who does. It's a pretty small community. Who are you looking for?"

"Her name is Malika. Malika Franklin."

"The name is familiar, but I can't place it right now," Rose said thoughtfully. "Let me ask around." Rose looked toward the door. "Hey, my husband just arrived." She waved at a man who was unzipping his puffy jacket. He blew her a kiss as she stood up and grabbed her belongings from the back of the barstool.

"I'll let you go." Camille hugged her friend, then grabbed her arm. "Hang on. What's your number? Can you put it into my contacts?" She handed Rose her phone and turned to the crew at her table and mouthed, "One minute." She held up her index finger.

Rose handed Camille back her phone. "Let's stay in touch. Maybe I can help with your cold case. I'll ask around about Franklin." She sounded like a prosecutor now.

"Appreciate any help you can give us," Camille shouted as she headed back to her table.

"Trish ordered for you." Libby pointed at the Caesar salad at Camille's place.

"Jeez. How many people did you say it was for?" Camille asked as she ogled the size of the salad. "My friend Rose over there is the county prosecutor. She was telling me a little bit about the opioid issues around here." She turned to Sally. "I should introduce you to her. I expect she'd be interested in your research—she started a therapeutic diversion program here."

"I'd love to know her. I'm about to start looking for my research site, so maybe this place should be on my list."

The group spent the next hour getting Robin caught up on the status of the investigation while Libby and Grace not-so-quietly worked their way up the challenges of their video game. Around 8:00 p.m., they thanked Brittany for a lovely evening and great food and then headed out into the clear and frosty night. It was about a five-minute walk back to the marina, and everyone snuggled into their parkas to brace against the biting wind that had picked up since the afternoon.

Gigi caught up with Camille. "Any chance you have some tampons on the boat?"

"Shoot. I don't. Angela was up with us a few weeks ago and used them all, then tore the place apart looking for some the day we left."

Trish looked up the street and pointed. "There's a store half a block up."

"Okay. Let's all head up there. I'm not exactly sure of the combination to the lock at the top of the dock, so I don't want y'all locked out." Camille turned and led the group briskly up the empty street.

"At least it's warm in here." Trish held her hands over the heater just inside the entrance while Gigi ran to the back, looking for the feminine hygiene section. Sally and the girls busied themselves in the candy section, carefully considering their options.

Trish, always the cop, stopped and stared at the back of the store. She turned to Camille. "What's up with that dude stocking shelves over there?"

A skinny guy with heavily tattooed sleeves on both arms appeared to have abandoned his stocking duties, his gaze locked on Gigi.

"Racist?" Camille whispered to Trish.

"Probably."

He pulled his phone out of his pocket and was talking quietly. Camille watched Trish pull up her hood and quickly grab a shopping basket, then pretend to be looking at the shelves as she surreptitiously eyed the guy in his bright-blue vest with the drugstore logo on the breast pocket. She plopped a bottle of vitamins in her basket as the clerk watched Gigi head toward the checkout stand.

Trish caught up with Camille, the large bottle of vitamins alone in her shopping basket.

"I think he thinks she's shoplifting," Camille whispered.

Trish shrugged. "Yeah, and he's just waiting to nab some Black woman buying tampons. Let's get out of here. All kinds of shit goes down in these small towns."

"This place is giving me the creeps."

Camille and Trish kept their eyes glued on Gigi as she rummaged through her pockets at the checkout.

Gigi was oblivious to her stalker in the back of the store. She turned to Camille and Trish. "Shoot! I left my credit card on the boat. Do either of you have any money?"

Camille reached past Trish and handed the clerk her credit card, anxious to get Gigi back to the marina.

Gigi reached over and took the vitamins and put them on the counter along with her tampons. She smiled at her friends. "No worries, I've got this," she joked.

It was all Camille could do to stay calm and hope that they could get Gigi out the door without any incident. She held her breath while the clerk handed Gigi the plastic bag. It occurred to Camille that this was something she'd need to begin discussing with Gracie soon. Navigating the world as a Black person was no joke—especially in a small town like this. Camille felt this weight creeping up on her as she imagined someone handcuffing Gigi for no reason other than her skin color.

"This is so fucked up," she said more loudly than she'd realized.

"You okay, lady?" the clerk asked. He seemed genuine.

Camille ignored him and held the door for Gigi and Trish. "Let's go, girls!" Her voice had so much authority that neither Libby nor Grace pushed back. They just scurried through the open doorway, leaving the clerk holding Camille's credit card receipt.

It had never felt so good to get out into a freezing night. Sally ran to catch up with everyone as Camille and Trish nearly dragged Gigi down the street.

CHAPTER THIRTEEN

Trish and Camille spent a night of soul searching on the boat. It wasn't the first time that Camille had shared with Trish how she constantly compared herself to her mom, and how it caused her world to feel impossibly small. They didn't turn out the lights until the wee hours of the morning—after Camille let Trish convince her that helping one person, Charli, could be as world changing as her mother's work. For the umpteenth time in their long friendship, Trish had to remind Camille that she didn't need to run an asylum organization, or any other organization for that matter, in order to make a difference. Change happens one person at a time.

About an hour after dawn, the group found themselves drinking coffee and hot chocolate in the cockpit, watching as Tony circled the marina in his floatplane before coming in for a landing in the gray mist. Camille and Sally grabbed their backpacks and waited on the dock as Trish and Gigi kissed each other goodbye for about the fifth time. Libby and Grace were already halfway to the floatplane. They loved flying with Tony.

Gigi hopped off the boat, grabbed Trish by the arm, and announced to her friends, "My dad was a pastor. He died suddenly, but we often talked about angels in heaven watching over us. In fact, I almost gave Kaitlin the name Gabriella, after the archangel Gabriel, but my ex wouldn't have it. The past few weeks, I've felt my dad's presence more than I have in a very long time. I'm quite sure he brought all of you to me, and that he's going to make sure we find Willow! I just wanted to tell you all that and how much it means to me and Charli that you're helping us. I really appreciate you guys."

Trish wasn't much of a believer in organized religion, but she could hardly fault Gigi for her faith. Especially when it brought her such comfort in a nearly hopeless situation. Cold cases like this were just about impossible to solve. "Good to know, because we'll need all the help we can get!" she shouted up into the sky. "You hear me, Dad? I'mma need you here!" Trish, still shaken up from their experience in the pharmacy, was anxious to get Gigi out of PA. She held her hand and just about dragged her toward the gas dock, where Tony was expertly tying up the plane under Libby's cheerful guidance, with Sally laughingly pitching in comically to direct her boyfriend.

"Got enough cooks in this kitchen?" Tony teased the twosome as he hopped off the plane and embraced Sally while keeping a watchful eye on Libby, who was thoughtfully wrapping the line around the cleat on the dock. "Nice job, Libby! You can be my copilot anytime."

"Hey!" Camille pulled Trish aside while they were heading down the last dock finger before the gas dock. "Check this out." She held her phone up for Trish to see. It was an email from Lizbeth via the JPay prison email system. *Need to talk with you asap. Something's come up. Urgent. Are you coming to the legal clinic today?*

"You are, right?" Trish asked.

Camille nodded as she typed her response. *I'll be there by 6:15.*

Trish stood on the dock next to Camille and watched as Tony made an extra effort to show Camille that he'd checked the fuel level and double checked the instruments before she boarded. It was their ritual.

Even though Camille flew regularly on the small floatplanes, she had never really gotten over her own floatplane accident that had landed her in the Strait of Juan de Fuca many years ago. In a way, Trish admired Camille's bravery. She wasn't sure she'd be all that keen on flying in those tiny planes again if she'd been piloting one that crashed off the coast of Whidbey Island. She squeezed Camille's hand in hers, then handed her off to Tony.

The floatplane bobbled as Tony held Camille by the arm and guided her gently into the copilot seat. He took time to tighten Camille's seat belt and kissed her on the cheek. She smiled at him and gave Trish a thumbs-up.

As the plane taxied away from the dock, Trish knew that Camille would momentarily be closing her eyes and taking her deep breaths in preparation for takeoff. She smiled and waved at Gigi, who was blowing kisses through the foggy window as the plane revved its engine and kicked up a spray of freezing cold water. It headed out into the open water right outside the breakwater. The takeoff was noisy but stable. Trish knew Tony went out of his way to make smooth landings and takeoffs for his longtime friend Camille. He clearly appreciated her trust in him, and Camille reciprocated by flying exclusively with him as the pilot.

As soon as the plane was safely on its way, Trish jogged up the dock to meet Robin at the coffee shop on the main drag in the center of town. She found Robin sitting under a macramé plant hanger that could barely contain the leggy plant nearly touching the table. Robin was deep in conversation with a middle-aged woman in a bright multi-colored striped sweater that was a bit too tight across the midsection. Trish decided it must be homemade. She motioned to Robin that she was going to order at the counter and would be right there.

Latte and croissant in hand, Trish wound her way through the cramped tables and waited while Robin introduced her to her table-mate. Before Robin could say Trish's name, Trish held out her hand and interrupted her. "Patrice. Patrice Swanson." When she was under-cover, Trish always used a variation of her first name, and used the first letter of her last name. Swanson was her go-to last name these days, after she and Camille had solved a big crime up in the San Juans the year before. There, she'd gone by Patsy Swanson, and now she considered Swanson her good-luck name.

Robin didn't miss a beat. "I couldn't believe it when I saw you here this morning." She turned to Trish. "It's just our luck—Norma is the incomparable former basketball coach at Port Angeles High!" Robin turned to the coach. "As I told you, Norma, my friend . . . Patrice here played pickup basketball with Malika back in Seattle, and since she's here for a few weeks, she was asking if anyone knows where Malika is. She'd love to get in touch with her."

The coach leaned forward and looked each woman in the eye briefly. Then she looked around the room, as though she was concerned they'd be overheard. "The whole Franklin family came on some hard times a few years back."

Robin and Trish edged closer to hear the coach, who was speaking barely above a whisper.

"Years ago, the parents got hooked on that damn OxyContin. You heard of that crap? It's deadly." She paused. "They were such a nice family—always at their kids' basketball games. I can't believe what happened to them."

Trish and Robin nodded.

"How about Malika, did she get hooked?"

The coach looked into the distance. "You know, I'm not sure. Malika took off. Heard she ended up in Seattle somewhere."

Trish nodded again, not wanting to break the coach's chain of thought.

The coach continued. "Then a couple of years later, one of the parents got to cooking up some concoction of drugs and blew their trailer up to smithereens."

She looked at Trish. "Maybe that's when you met her. That fire was terrifying for the whole community."

"Was anyone hurt?" Robin was sincere in her question.

The coach stirred her latte. "Yup. It was all over the paper. Both parents died in the fire." She dropped her voice. "Awful. That shit's still ruining so many families around here."

"But not Malika," Trish said almost desperately. "She wasn't a victim in the fire, right?" She held her breath.

"Not Malika." The coach smiled. "I just try to remember her standing at midcourt, ready to pounce on whoever crossed her. She really was an awesome kid. I hope to God she's okay, wherever she is."

Trish thought back to the articles about Malika she'd read in the local paper. "Best damn point guard I ever played with."

"She could have gotten a full ride almost anywhere. But her family had no idea how to support her education." She put down her cup. "Such a pity. I loved that girl. And her sisters—they were all kick-ass basketball players." The coach's face reddened, and she blinked her eyes shut.

Trish waited while the coach collected herself. "Did she come back?"

The coach continued with a far-off look. "Came back from the city with a baby. No idea who the father was. She was pretty quiet about it."

Trish felt her pulse quicken. "Baby? Was it hers?"

The coach scowled at Trish. "Of course it was hers. But her old boyfriend wanted nothing to do with that kid." She dropped her voice an octave. "Quinn was a nice kid in high school. Kind of a chemistry nerd, but then something happened to him. Looking back, maybe he got on those drugs. He became crazy and more than a little violent. I can't understand why Malika went back to him. Maybe she still saw him as her geeky high school crush, but that was a long time ago. Anyway, they taught us coaches that DV victims tend to go back to their abusers. But Malika? Seriously? She coulda kicked his ass to kingdom come."

Trish knew when to tread lightly. "Any idea of where she might be now?"

The coach shrugged. "To be honest, I have no idea. I kinda lost track of the Franklin girls. Then I retired a few years ago. Lots of my players are like daughters to me. They watch over me and my partner—she has early onset MS—so we appreciate all the help we get from the girls."

"And Malika?" Trish asked hopefully.

"Good question. If you'd asked me a decade ago, I'd have bet that the one kid I could count on to stay in touch woulda been Malika. But then again, I never saw it coming that she'd end up with the likes of Quinn Hastings." The coach puckered her lips and blew out a whalelike sound. She looked down at the floor, then looked up slowly. "Heartbreaking, really."

"If I wanted to find Malika, where would I start? She really meant a lot to me."

"Well, Malika's sister is out on Spring Lake Road. I'd start there."

"And Quinn? Where would I find him?"

"His parents own an auto repair out on Fruitport Road. Hastings Auto Shop. I think he lives out there on that property somewhere."

CHAPTER FOURTEEN

The drive to the women's prison was faster than usual that day. Probably because it was Christmas week and lots of people were on vacation. Camille pulled into the parking lot with fifteen minutes to spare before her clinic started. She grabbed her phone and checked her Amazon account to be sure the Christmas gifts she'd ordered would arrive on time—like tomorrow. She couldn't remember ever being more disconnected at Christmastime. Finding Willow was beginning to take over her life. She clicked on her local grocery delivery to order the Cornish game hens and ingredients for the garlic-lemon sauce the girls had requested for Christmas dinner and glanced at her watch— five minutes until she could go in. She scrolled through her email, then threw her phone in her purse, hopped out of the car, and secured her bag in her trunk.

When she walked into the prison library, Camille was surprised to see only Lizbeth and Charli waiting for her. "Where's everyone else?" She grabbed a chair and pulled it up to the table.

"We asked the rest of the women to give us this meeting on our own." Lizbeth was all business. "We need to talk."

A prickly feeling crept up Camille's back, and her heart began to race. "Is everything okay?"

Charli spoke. "You aren't going to believe what we're about to tell you."

Camille looked at Charli and then Lizbeth. "Okay," she said quietly. "I feel like I just finished a trial, and the jury is back and I'm nervous as hell. What's up?"

Lizbeth took charge. "Remember I told you that I'm serving a very long sentence?"

Camille realized the significance of this moment. Lizbeth was about to share what had brought her to prison. "I do," she said gently.

"Well, I killed a guy." Lizbeth waited to let that sink in. "I know I probably don't seem exactly like what you'd expect a killer to be like, but that's the reason I'm here." She didn't wait for a response. "I'm sure you're aware that lots of women who have been abused end up in prison for killing their abuser. And that's me. I killed my high school soccer coach because he'd been molesting me and a bunch of other players on our team. Most of us ended up a mess. Several got hooked on drugs. A few others pretty much dropped out of life, living on welfare or just never moving out of their parents' homes. But some of us tried to get jobs and be self-sufficient. I was in that group. I got a pretty good job as a receptionist at a law firm—I know, that's why I love the law library." She digressed for a moment and then continued. "Then one day I went to pick up my little sister at high school, and I found her in the locker room. That asshole had her pinned down, and his one hand was pulling down her pants, and the other one was holding a dirty sock he had shoved in her mouth."

Camille was struck by how mechanical Lizbeth's voice had become. There didn't seem to be a scintilla of emotion in her as she recited the horror of finding her sister in the clutches of her own abuser.

Lizbeth continued. "I had told her a million times to stay away from that monster, but she loved soccer and was the star of the team, so she wouldn't quit. And our family was poor, so we couldn't move. And besides, my drunk parents didn't believe me—or at least didn't care—when I told them what happened to me."

Camille noticed a small crack in Lizbeth's voice when she mentioned her parents.

"Anyway, I lost it. I grabbed a baseball bat and cracked that motherfucker's head wide open. And I didn't stop. I kept beating him until he was a bloody mess. The rest is a blur. It was police, handcuffs, jail, no money for bail, a shitty public defender, and a quick one-way trip to WCCW, where I'll live for the next ten years."

Camille tried but couldn't keep the tears from coming. The only thing she could think of to say was "I'm so very sorry, Lizbeth. Truly, I am." She reached out to comfort her friend and stopped when Lizbeth pulled away.

"No touching. We'll get written up."

Lizbeth continued. "I told the prosecutor about the abuse, and that that asshole had videos of me, and lots of the girls, on his laptop. Not a fucking thing mattered to that fucking prosecutor. You would have thought I killed Santa Claus. They didn't give a shit about me. All my teammates gave interviews confirming my story. And it didn't make a damn bit of difference. They even took his laptops and found videos of him forcing a girl to give him a blow job, and a bunch of other videos of him raping different girls." Now Lizbeth was getting emotional. "There were also videos of him sodomizing his own wife. She actually came to my sentencing. I remember her looking at me. But I couldn't read her at all. One minute I thought her eyes were telling me 'Thank you.' And the next, she looked as if she was lost in a fog. My sister ended up making friends with her. They're in the same DV support group. Her name is Talulla. Irish."

"She's probably relieved that he's gone for good," Camille agreed.

"She tells my sis that I saved her. And I'm pretty sure I did. Talulla works with other DV victims now. She says I saved all those other girls who would have played on his soccer teams. She keeps telling my sis that I went to prison for saving others. She's become a total activist for battered women who get sentenced to prison for killing their abusers." Lizbeth redirected the conversation. "You do know, don't you, that I'm not the only woman here who's doing time for killing her abuser? This whole thing is just such a fucked-up mess." She took a deep, shaky breath. "Maybe, just maybe, they could help us. Give us therapy or something." She paused to catch her breath. "Instead, they lock us up, which is traumatizing by itself. But then, every time we have contact with anyone from the outside, like you, they force us to undergo a humiliating strip search. As you can imagine, for a woman who has been sexually assaulted—which is like ninety percent of all of us here—having to bend over and spread our butt cheeks and have someone look up our privates is retraumatizing for all of us. And if we're on our period, then we have to remove our tampon and stand there naked with blood running down our legs under the cold, watchful eye of a prison guard." Lizbeth swallowed in an effort not to break down. "It's disgusting how they treat women who have lived lives of sexual assault." Her sadness quickly turned to anger. "Maybe someday someone will convince a court, or a legislator, or someone in a position of power that women who are victims shouldn't just be summarily locked up. I personally won't rest easy until someone does something."

Camille didn't know what to do. There was no comforting Lizbeth. One moment, she seemed resigned to her fate, and the next minute, her anger dissolved into an inkling of hope—if not for herself, then for other women. "I had no idea," Camille said softly. "I can't imagine that level of humiliation. I'm just so very sorry." It was all she could think of to say.

Charli waited a minute and began her part of the story. "Remember when I told you that Brian put Martin's computer in his sports equipment trunk for safekeeping?"

Camille looked at Charli curiously. "Y-yes." She had that creeping feeling up her back again.

"Lizbeth and I had a long talk last night about what brought us here, and we figured out that my Brian was *that* coach's assistant, and he ran the summer program at the high school. Our computer was one of the ones the police took into evidence. I had no idea about the whole situation with the coach being murdered, since all that happened after we were already in prison."

"So, let me get this straight. The computer we can use to bring Martin down, and hopefully get you a new sentence, was taken into evidence after Lizbeth got arrested?" Camille took it in for a second. "I wonder where they store that kind of evidence," she said to no one in particular. "And how long they store it." Her mind was racing.

"Well, we know where it was in 2013," Charli offered seriously. "Trish should know what happens to evidence after law enforcement takes possession of it." She lowered her voice. "This isn't something I feel comfortable talking about with her on the phone or on a JPay email. Everything is listened to and reviewed by DOC."

"Got it." Camille looked at the clock and stood up. "Remind me when movement is," she said, referring to the hourly time when prisoners were able to move about the prison and when the librarian would be able to take her out.

"Twenty after."

Camille sat back down, frustrated at the lack of any agency or power over oneself behind the barbed wire of this lonely place. "Well, okay, then let's go over what we need to do next." She took out the one notepad they let her bring inside and tried to focus. "It sounds like there were at least two computers. One with the videos of the girls, and the one Brian hid in the locker. What kind of computer are we looking for?"

"It was a Dell," Charli said authoritatively. "And there was a Dell external hard drive. It was covered with UW Husky stickers. And tennis-racket brand names. And when I won the divisional championship, Gigi gave me a cool glittery sticker of Lucy from *Charlie Brown* holding a tennis racket. My undergrad tennis teammates started calling me Lucy after that."

"Okay. And last we heard, the police took it into evidence from the locker room, right?"

Lizbeth nodded.

"Are we sure the police have both computers?"

Lizbeth looked at Camille. "Yes. I remember my public pretender"— she used the pejorative often used by people in prison—"telling me that there was only one computer with the videos. The other one had some kind of financial records on it, so she tried to make an argument that the asshole was selling our videos as porn and the computer with the financial records was evidence of that. But, again, the prosecutor really couldn't have cared less. One thing I feel a little relief about is that there probably wasn't a porn business driven by videos of me and my teammates. So there's a tiny silver lining here."

Charli spoke up. "And I'm pretty sure we can all imagine what those financial records were on the other computer." She turned to Lizbeth. "Thank you so much for trusting me with your story. It could change my life." She didn't even try to hold back the tears. "And, Lizbeth, I promise you on a stack of Bibles that if I ever get out of here, I will not rest until I get you out—and all of the women who are in here for assaulting or killing their abusers." She looked at Camille. "You know that ninety-five percent of all women in prison for murder are in for killing their abusers, right?"

Camille used the back of her hand to wipe away the tears now streaking down her cheek. She sniffled and nodded. She held out the pinky of her other hand. "As long as I live, I pinky promise that I will do whatever I can do to get this information out to the public. And of course you'll always have whatever legal help you need from me as well."

The three women sat silently for a couple of minutes, each taking in what had just happened.

Lizbeth spoke first. She turned and grabbed a stack of legal paperwork. "As long as you're stuck with us for another twenty minutes, can you take a look at these motions I drafted for some of the women getting out in the next several months? Lucia sent us a template she created for us to use."

Camille took a shaky breath of admiration and felt tears welling up. The presence of the two women in front of her was astounding. Here they were, locked up for years, trying to get some relief for their own sentences, and at the same time fighting for the other women inside who'd be getting out way sooner than they would ever even hope to. And not only that, but they were working to change the lives of women who had not even been convicted yet. *Where does that kind of strength even come from?*

CHAPTER FIFTEEN

Trish had no idea what to expect as she pulled up to the long, new-looking Airstream trailer parked behind Hastings Auto Shop. She swerved to avoid being T-boned by an old Suburban filled with a group of twentysomethings on their way out of the long driveway. Quinn's trailer looked oddly out of place, surrounded by skeletons of old cars that had obviously been cannibalized for parts over the past decade. Trish wondered if the owners had any idea of the value of the Westfalia parked right next to a string of rusted burn barrels.

Turning her attention to the issue at hand, she pulled the pink hat with the glittery pom-pom down over her ears. It was unseasonably warm and sunny for a late-December day, but the hat was everything, so she decided to go with it. Climbing out of the old truck she'd borrowed from Robin, she cursed the thigh-high spike-heeled boots she'd chosen to go along with the fluffy hat. She swore under her breath as her boots sank into the mud.

Before she could gather herself, the door of the trailer flung open, causing one end of the lonely string of Christmas lights to pull off the thumbtack holding it in place. "What d'ya want?" The man took a long drag on his cigarette. His baggy brown Carhartts and plaid shirt hung awkwardly on his gaunt frame. He ducked to avoid the wayward string of lights now hanging across the doorway.

Trish stopped and searched her memory to figure out where she'd seen this guy before. "You Quinn? I'm an old friend of Malika's. I heard she might be living out . . ." Trish wasn't able to finish her sentence. This was the guy at the pharmacy who'd been watching Gigi. "Here," she added, her voice strong.

Quinn Hastings looked her up and down. "Malika, here? Says who?"

Trish backed up a step, and, not moving her head, she looked to her right and to her left to figure out her possible escape route. She noticed a backhoe moving car parts around the junkyard. Realizing she wasn't alone with Quinn allowed her to regain her internal swagger. "Her sistah said she might be out here." A little accent might soften this guy, but her mind was caught up in trying to figure out the relationship between Malika and the racist drugstore clerk, who, according to Norma, had been a chemistry nerd in high school. It was for sure a small town.

"Nope. She ain't here." He paused, then continued slowly. "Not in a long while."

Sensing Quinn might have more to say, Trish took a few steps forward. "Can I bum a smoke?" She cocked her head to the left and gave him a slight smile. "C'mon, don't be mad at me. I'm just in town for a couple of days and I thought I'd look up my old basketball friend."

Quinn's smile revealed a row of brown-stained teeth. His left incisor was missing, and the tooth next to it was broken at an angle that made it sharp and a little scary. He shook a cigarette out of a pack. Trish didn't recognize the brand.

"Sorry, I thought you were someone else."

Trish took the cigarette and recognized the distinct smell of cloves. "I thought they outlawed clove cigarettes a long time ago."

Quinn's laugh was phlegmy. "I got a source." He held out his lighter.

"Haven't had one of these since high school." Trish leaned in as he cupped his dirt-crusted hand over it and held his lighter. He smelled of sweat mixed with lingering clove-cigarette smoke. She held his wrist to steady the lighter and inhaled just enough to get it lit. She suppressed a cough. "You sure looked like you were expecting me to jump out at you or something." She laughed and gave him a little smirk, trying not to break into a coughing fit from the unfiltered smoke.

"You want to come inside?" Quinn held the door open.

Trish noted the fancy leather couch inside. *Something's off here.* "Nah, I gotta get back."

Quinn reached into a shiny stainless steel cooler right outside the trailer door and held out a can of Rainier beer. He opened the pop top and held it out. "Beer?"

Trish hesitated.

"We can talk about Malika." He winked and set the beer down on the picnic table that looked like it might once have been painted a cheery red but was now just covered with a thin layer of slimy grayish moss. Quinn grabbed another beer and opened a collapsible lawn chair for Trish and one for himself. "Nice afternoon for a picnic." He pulled a pack of beef jerky out of his jacket pocket, opened it with his teeth, and tore off a chunk of meat. He sat.

Trish considered her options, and feeling a bit emboldened by the fact that she was not alone, she picked up the beer and moved the other chair a few feet away from where Quinn had placed it. She sat on the edge of the seat.

Quinn leaned back and took a long drag of his cigarette. "Ya. Malika got pretty fucked up after her family blew up their trailer." He pointed across the field behind him at a charred piece of rubble Trish hadn't noticed before.

Quinn started to chuckle. As he cleared his throat, he turned his head a bit and spat a wad about three feet to his side. "I loved that girl. Loved her ever since high school. It was hard to see her get so totally fucked up, man."

Trish wondered what had happened to turn a nice kid into this dirty, creepy dude. She faked a long drink of the beer. "Yeah, I guess that'd be pretty horrific. Was she in the trailer?"

Quinn turned in the direction of a beat-up Corolla pulling into his driveway. He shook his head and waved the car away.

Trish followed his gaze. "Friend coming to visit?"

"Yeah, he can come back later." Quinn pulled out a small vial and sprinkled some white power on the back of his hand, which he proceeded to snort.

Trish stood up. Nothing good would come from her hanging out with some dude snorting who knew what. She dropped the cigarette she'd been holding and ground it out in the gravel.

"Wait." He reached out to grab her, nearly tipping his chair over. "Don't go."

Trish took a step back. "I gotta get back." She put the beer down.

Quinn leered at her, stood up unsteadily, and lunged her way.

Trish easily sidestepped him and turned to go.

"I didn't get to tell you about her fucking baby." His entire presence changed as soon as the drugs took hold. His eyes half closed. "God, I hated that fucking kid. Cried all the damn time."

Trish froze and judged the distance between her and the stoned lumberjack. Plenty of room to run. And in his condition, there was no way he'd ever catch her, even in these shoes. "What baby?"

"That bitch ran off to Seattle and came back with a kid. She moved it in here with us. Noisy little shit." He nodded and lifted his head, then let out a sinister laugh. "If she hadn'ta took the kid to her parents', I woulda beat the thing to death trying to get it to shut the fuck up." He snorted when he laughed and threw his head back.

Despite her heart pounding in her ears, Trish somehow held steady. She tried to stay cool. "Any idea where she and the baby are now?"

Quinn nodded and jerked his head up. "Baby?"

Trish wanted to reach over and slap the shit out of this asshole. "Her baby." She tried not to scream. "Where did she take the baby?"

Quinn lunged and tried to grab her. "You know what?" He'd started to drool. "You're kinda cute."

Trish backed up, cursing herself for even trying to walk in these ridiculous boots. He was too stoned to care that she was now yelling at him. "Where is the baby? Where is Malika?"

"No idea where Malika is." His speech was slow and slurred as he slumped back into his chair. "I loved her so fucking much." He started to cry. "I shouldn't have kicked her around so much." He gave Trish a forlorn look.

"How about the baby?" Trish tried to calm herself.

Now he looked to be asleep. He was snoring lightly.

Trish grabbed her beer and doused him. "The baby!" she screamed. "Where is the fucking baby?"

Quinn looked at her under heavy eyelids and pointed at the charred hulk of the trailer across the field. "Over there with her granny and gramps. Burned to shit."

Quinn didn't wave off the guy on a motorcycle that was gunning up the driveway. This time he hiked up his drooping Carhartts and gave the cyclist a thumbs-up.

Trish felt the bile creeping up in her throat as she turned and ran, swearing as she twisted her ankle in the mud. She didn't even try to hold back the sobs. She fumbled for her keys and tried not to run over the guy on the motorcycle as she sped away from Quinn Hastings.

CHAPTER SIXTEEN

There was no way Trish was going to tell Gigi what she had just learned. Not until she had confirmed the story. She pulled her laptop out of its bright-orange neoprene sleeve and booted it up while she shoved a slice of sourdough bread into the toaster. Usually, she felt soothed being under the waterline in a sailboat galley—cozy and efficient. But tonight it felt stifling. She knew she should eat something. Out came the peanut butter and locally made strawberry jam.

The boat swayed against its moorings as she logged on. Steadying herself, she reviewed her notes and tried to put the chronology together to see if she could figure out when the trailer fire had occurred. It surely must have made it into the local newspaper. She began to scroll, forgetting for the moment about her dinner, which had just popped out of the toaster.

Trish got lost in the string of local stories about oxy and meth problems that had come to haunt the citizens of this working waterfront town. One story in particular caught her eye. A local doc had been arrested in some kind of drug-related situation. A picture of him being searched, his hands plastered to the hood of his car, looked more like a drug bust in the inner city than a local doctor who might have been overprescribing oxy. She clicked on the story: *Longtime Port Angeles Doctor Caught with a Trunk Full of Heroin.* The doctor had complained loudly that he'd been set up after threatening to expose the local pharmacy for filling bogus oxy prescriptions. But the prosecutor was having none of it. A kilo of heroin was obviously too big to ignore. As Trish paused to consider what seemed off, another story caught her eye. *Trailer Fire Kills Members of Local Family.*

Trish closed her eyes and said a quick prayer before clicking the link.

Just as Norma had said, the Franklin parents had caused an explosion while cooking meth inside their trailer. How the family of a string of local basketball stars had come to be living in such depressing circumstances was further evidence of how meth had ravaged a once-tight middle-class community. She skimmed the story, looking for anything that would confirm Quinn's story about Willow being a victim in the fire. There was a picture of Malika's sister Marlys standing in front of the burned-out skeleton of the trailer. She was surrounded by family and friends and a few members of what must have been the local press. Both parents had succumbed, but there was no mention of a baby, although the investigation was ongoing at the time of the article. Looking at the remnants of the fire, it seemed unlikely that anyone would have survived.

Trish grabbed the cold piece of toast and threw it in the trash. Her stomach turned, and she curled up in the V berth, in the bow of the boat, and closed her eyes, hoping for a bit of inspiration as to how to find out whether Willow had been in the trailer at the time of the fire. In most arson cases, there would be a report of who was missing. But here, Malika had concealed Willow's identity, so it was possible that no one would have even reported her missing. How would she ever discover the fate of a nonexistent toddler in a drug-infested community? Trish couldn't hold it in any longer. She flopped over in the bed and screamed into her pillow.

—

Camille pulled into the houseboat-community parking lot and stopped to gather herself before walking down the dock. She knew that once inside, she'd have to dig deep to find her inner Christmas vibe so she wouldn't ruin everyone's holiday.

She tried Trish again, then threw her phone into her backpack. *Probably on a stakeout with her phone off. No need to worry. She'll for sure check in later.*

The dock was colorfully lit for the holidays, with each houseboat having a bit of a different theme. The Delaney-Taylor place was lined with deep-blue lights interspersed with twinkling white ones. Camille stopped briefly to admire her husband's handiwork, performed under the watchful eye of their oldest, Angela—the artist.

She grabbed her phone back out of her bag and texted Trish to call her. They had lots to discuss.

"Mommy, it's Christmas Eve eve!" Gracie could barely contain her excitement. "I know there's no real Santa, but you said his spirit would be here tomorrow night!" She hugged Camille tightly before Camille could even close the front door.

Sam looked down over the balcony at the top of the stairs. "I got us a pile of fresh crab and a couple of fresh baguettes at the Market today. Crab's out on the deck to stay cold." He blew Camille a kiss and looked at Gracie. "Let Mom change her clothes for a sec. I could use some help up here."

Gracie turned and scurried up the stairs. "Hurry up, Mom! We have to wrap our presents tonight!"

"The oven is ready when you are, hon!"

"Wow. Nice job, team!" Camille yelled up the stairs. She felt just a little of the day's tension run off her shoulders as she walked into their room and sat on the bed, pulling off her boots and kicking them into the dressing room.

Angela popped her head into the doorway and waved. "I'm off to Kaitlin's for movie night with the swim team! I'm going to spend the night, 'kay?"

Camille stood up, hugged her daughter, and kissed her on the cheek. "Okay, but remember, tomorrow is Christmas Eve, and I'm making game hens just for you."

"With the lemon-garlic cream sauce? And homemade pasta?"

Camille could have kicked herself. She had totally forgotten the whole fresh-pasta thing. "Well, we might have to cheat on the fresh-pasta part. But we have some of that really good dried Italian stuff."

Angela was halfway out onto the front entry deck. "It'll be great, whatever you make!" She slammed the door.

Camille brushed her teeth, tousled her short dark hair, and headed up into the world of Christmas, wondering if there would be any kind of peace on earth for the women inside the prison. She'd been so taken with the disclosures she'd heard from Charli and Lizbeth that she'd completely forgotten to ask them about their Christmas plans. Then again, maybe that was for the best. No need to rub it in.

It was nearly impossible to see the floor in the living room under the masses of wrapping paper. Libby quickly grabbed a small box and warned Camille to turn her back. "Stop! Just stop there! You can't see this stuff, Mom!"

Camille turned and backed up toward the kitchen. "No worries. I have some garlic bread to tend to." She gladly took a glass of wine from Sam and gave him a longer kiss than usual.

Sam sat on the stool in front of the kitchen island and held up his wineglass in a toast.

Camille held her glass. "Well, what's the toast?"

"I got a new research grant."

Camille realized that she'd been so distracted by the goings-on in the prison that she hadn't checked in on Sam's career in too long. "Oh, honey! You're amazing!" She turned toward the girls in the living room, then stopped and turned her back on them. She hollered, "Daddy got his grant! How cool is that?"

"Cool!" Libby yelled. "Who are you going to save now?"

"Looks like me'n Mom are going to be working together to save women from going to prison." He clinked Camille's glass.

Camille was dumbfounded. She knew Sam had taken an interest in the epidemiology of addiction but didn't remember him telling her he was applying for a grant to study it. Or maybe he had told her, but she had been too busy to remember. Dang.

Sam smiled widely. "Sally is over the moon. I don't think I've ever gotten a grant approved so quickly."

"Sally's barely started her program. When did you apply for it?"

"Actually, it came up quite suddenly. One of our other research docs had applied last year, and he ended up leaving the U. So when

Sally reached out, I offered to jump in and put my name on his application. Easiest grant ever."

"So, what exactly did they end up agreeing to fund?" Camille put the rice in the rice cooker pot and began rinsing it.

"It has to do with the confluence of women getting addicted to drugs and, rather than being given treatment, they end up in prison. And we're studying the impact of that on mothers and their children. It's a gendered response to the prison industrial complex. Women have different needs in prison than men. They end up there for way different reasons. I'm about to learn all about how messed up the system is."

Camille plugged in the rice cooker and opened a bag of mixed greens. "You're doing it in conjunction with the nursing school, right?"

"I am now. The whole connection with Sally is brilliant. The PhD nurses over there are badass, world-class researchers. I can't wait to work with them on this. Especially now that you're right there on the front line. I'm excited to get started. This seems like it could lead to some cool shit."

"For once, we're on the same side." Camille handed Sam a stack of plates and pointed at the table.

"Yeah, feels good that you're not suing a local doc this time. It gets kinda awkward."

"I know." Camille kissed Sam on the cheek and headed outside into the wind and light rain to grab the bag of crab. She checked her phone one more time. Why hadn't she heard from Trish yet?

CHAPTER SEVENTEEN

Trish woke up at midnight. She spent a few minutes reviewing the events of the day and reached for her phone in the dark, then threw it across the bed when she realized the battery had gone dead. She reached over and plugged it in and watched as a stack of texts downloaded. Mostly from Camille. She hit the Call button.

"You up?" she asked Camille, knowing full well that she'd been sound asleep and had answered the phone because she'd assume the only reason for a late-night call from Trish would be some kind of an emergency. Before Camille could ask, Trish offered, "I'm fine, nothing to worry about. But we may have a really big problem."

She could hear Camille rustling the bedding, probably getting up so as not to wake Sam.

"Give me a minute. I'm going to sit in the bathroom," she whispered.

Trish felt she was about to burst as she waited.

"Okay, what's up? Are you sure you're okay? I've been trying to reach you!"

"Sorry to call so late, but I fell asleep. I had a really bad day today."

There was a pause on the other end of the line. "Well, I had a really interesting day at the prison."

Trish didn't imagine that anything Camille had learned would be as important as her news. She continued. "There's a very good possibility that Willow may have died in a fire here in PA."

Trish waited to let that sink in.

"Are you sure?"

"No. Not sure at all. But last time anyone knew her whereabouts was when she was staying with Malika's parents, and they were both killed in a fire when their trailer blew up in a meth-related explosion."

"Oh my God. Oh my God . . ."

"I know. We can't tell Gigi and Charli until we know for sure."

"I feel sick."

"Me too. I'm going to set up a meeting with your friend Rose and see if she can get me the details of the fire."

"So, all we know is that Willow was living with Malika's parents and they were both killed in the fire?" Camille sounded like a lawyer.

"Exactly. But there was nothing in the newspaper articles about a baby's body being found."

"Thank God."

"Yeah. But remember, Malika was trying to keep Willow's identity a secret, so it's totally possible that no one would confirm that there was a baby in the trailer."

"Except Malika," Camille pointed out. "Are we sure Malika wasn't in the fire?"

"Yep. She wasn't there at the time. But we have absolutely no leads on where she might be now," Trish added and took a drink of the luke-warm iced tea that had been sitting on the shelf over the V berth since the day before. "And one other thing that's been bothering me. There was an article in the local newspaper about a doctor that got busted for having heroin in his car. Says he was set up—someone planted it in his car after he made waves about the pharmacy oversupplying oxy."

"Kind of like Charli . . ."

"Exactly. I'm not sure if I'm overreacting, but it just seems weird."

"Any connections you can determine?"

"Not yet. But it's really bothering me." Trish changed the subject. "How about you? What happened at the prison today?"

Camille launched into the conversation she'd had with Charli and Lizbeth, her words pouring out.

Trish waited until Camille finished. "Wow. So we know that the computer we're looking for was taken into evidence in 2013." She stopped for a minute to think. "I think my old pal Johnny Jenkins, the guy Malika was hanging out with over in Bellevue, did some shifts in the evidence room. I'll head over there tomorrow." She looked at her phone. "Shit. It's almost one. We need to see if we can get some sleep."

"Doubtful," Camille said dryly.

"I know, right? But I do think I'll head over to the city and talk with Johnny tomorrow."

"You do know that tomorrow is Christmas Eve, right?" Camille reminded her.

"Crap. I do now. Shit, I told Gigi I'd be there for dinner. Totally forgot that's tomorrow."

"I know what you mean. I've never been so distracted at Christmas. I gotta find my Mrs. Claus energy." She laughed. "First thing in the morning."

"'Kay. G'night. Let's try to get some sleep."

"G'night."

CHAPTER EIGHTEEN

Trish felt just slightly out of place in the old beater truck Robin had generously loaned her for her escapades in Port Angeles. The terminal where the ferries shuttled cars and walk-ons over to Seattle was in the upscale village of Winslow on Bainbridge Island, and as expected on Christmas Eve, the line was long. The ferries at Christmas were Puget Sound's version of "over the river and through the woods to Grandma's house we go." The ferry holding lot was filled with minivans and SUVs, packed with little girls all decked out in velvet and little boys looking awkward in colorful sweaters. Trish waved at them as she threaded between the parked cars on foot on her way up toward the charming Winslow shopping district, a few blocks from the ferry. She stopped and texted Johnny to see if he was working on Christmas Eve. He wasn't. He told her to meet him at Uptown Espresso on the pier close to Myrtle Edwards Park. Trish was happy not to have to schlep over to Bellevue on a holiday—it would be a madhouse over there near Bellevue Square today. And the wait for the ferry gave her some time to cruise through the shops in Winslow to get some Christmas presents for Gigi and Kaitlin.

As luck would have it, Trish got the coveted ferry parking spot right in the front of the car deck on the boat, with its unparalleled view of the cityscape. It was a glorious day in the Pacific Northwest, and Trish put down her phone and just watched the intermittent whitecaps punctuate the sparkling blue water as the ferry powered its way across

Elliott Bay—the juxtaposition of the powerful body of churning water against the harsh, jagged line of glass skyscrapers never got old.

She let her imagination soar as the rumbling of the engines drummed her into a kind of trance. She searched for some kind of miracle that would let her know Willow had survived the fiery inferno. But hope was hard to find in the onslaught of images of a little baby screaming for her mom. She tried to reassure herself with what she'd read somewhere, that most people who died in fires succumbed to the toxic fumes before the fire got to them. Soon the front engines of the ferry began creating a cauldron-like bubbling as they kicked into gear to slow the boat as it slid into the ferry dock in downtown Seattle. She texted Johnny to let him know she'd be there soon. As she turned the ignition, she decided not to tell Johnny about the meth and the fire and the distinct possibility that the baby he had known as Daisy might very well have succumbed to an awful death.

When she arrived, Johnny was waiting with a hot latte in an over-size ceramic coffee cup across from his seat at the table. She smiled, took off her beanie cap, and sat down.

"Did you find her?" He skipped the pleasantries and pointed at the latte. "Got you a double."

"Thanks." She held the cup to her lips and blew on it. "Nothing yet on Malika. But I have some good leads. It's a small town, and since she was a bit of a celebrity back in her time, it's not too hard to find folks who knew her."

"So, we were right? She did go back there?"

Trish nodded. "And your intuition was right about her having an asshole for a boyfriend. I met the guy. And he's weird—snorts meth and works as a pharmacy clerk."

"I knew it." Johnny put his elbows on the table and blew into his fist. "That asshole better not have hurt her."

Trish thought better of sharing how Quinn had likely abused Malika, and quite possibly baby Willow. That would set them both off and they wouldn't get anything accomplished. She changed the subject. "So, I think I remember that you did some shifts in the evidence room at SPD. Yes?"

"I did."

"I have some questions about how evidence is stored."

"What's your question?"

"Well, as part of our search for Wil—Daisy, we learned that there was a crime that sent Daisy's biological mom to prison."

Johnny perked up. "You know Daisy's bio mom?"

Trish nodded. "And there's evidence that we could use to possibly reduce her sentence, and hopefully get her husband charged. It's in a computer that got taken into evidence in a totally different crime."

"Her husband?"

"Long story, but he planted drugs in her car, to take the focus off of his oxy operation."

"So . . . when did this happen? The evidence getting taken into custody?" Johnny asked slowly.

"2013."

"Do you remember Ernie Dayton? He ran the evidence room."

"The name sounds familiar."

"He was a bit of a legend at the east precinct. Mean motherfucker. Always in trouble for mistreating people he took into custody. So they assigned him to the evidence room. And man, was he pissed."

"You think he might know the whereabouts of the missing computer?" Trish felt her hopes creeping up.

"If he ever did, it'd be long gone."

Well, that bit of hope didn't last too long. "How so?"

"He was a dirty cop all the way. And putting that guy in a department where valuable stuff was held was too tempting for him. It wasn't long before he started selling the drugs and other stuff taken into custody."

"Wouldn't he get caught?"

"He would if he just out-and-out took stuff. But he was a crafty shit. Just skimmed off drugs. Left enough that no one would notice. It took a while for internal investigations to catch up with the scam."

"So, it sounds like Officer Dayton likely sold off the computer we're looking for, yes?"

"Electronics in the evidence room after the perp was sentenced didn't last long when Dayton was in charge."

"Well, shit."

"On the other hand, oftentimes evidence went back to the owner after the litigation. Any idea who owned it?"

"Yeah. My friend did. And she's sitting in WCCW for the next five years if we don't figure out how to bust her out of there."

CHAPTER NINETEEN

The Christmas Eve game hens were, as always, a huge hit. Camille picked up the well-cleaned plates and headed for the kitchen as her phone alerted her that a FaceTime call was coming in.

"Mom!" Camille put down the plates and smiled at her mother, who was sitting erectly on her yoga mat on Christmas morning, on the island of Lesvos in Greece.

"Kala Christougenna!" Pella's Greek Christmas greeting was rich and warm. "How's everyone?"

Camille caught herself before she called for the girls. She wanted a few minutes alone with her mom—hoping for her own personal connection to her mother's never-ending effervescence. Just the two of them.

"I miss you, Mom." Camille felt the familiar pang of mom loneliness.

"Probably not as much as kids who have moms in prison. How are your prison mothers?" Pella reflected with genuine interest. She didn't even respond to the idea of being missed by her own daughter. Maybe it was guilt for prioritizing the migrants over her actual family, or maybe it was because she saw the world a bit differently than most. She had a different experience of time and space and believed that family connections weren't restricted by earthly concepts like distance.

Recognizing that there would be no conversation about sappy family feelings, Camille sat on a barstool and propped her phone against the food processor. Her mom was always up for a deep dive into anything related to justice, in any form. "This case is a little over-whelming. It all started with a mother in prison who had her baby kidnapped from labor and delivery. And now Trish and I are trying to find the missing baby, while I'm running the family law clinic inside WCCW at the same time. And, oh my God! Guess who's running the recovery group inside?"

Pella took a drink of tea from a colorful hand-painted mug. "Do tell."

"Jessica Kensington! That crazy doctor I sued last year."

"Well, well, well." For some reason Pella did not seem surprised in the least. "How do you feel about that? Someone you thought was perhaps irredeemable now helping others inside of the prison walls?"

Camille smiled. "I know. It's complicated. She assaulted a bunch of women and caused them to lose their babies. And now she's this grace-ful, centered leader in prison."

"People are complex," Pella mused. "She's just like all the other women inside. What does Bryan Stevenson say? We are all better than the worst thing we have done."

"Exactly. You'd think that someone who kills someone would be a reprehensible person. But I just learned that my jailhouse-lawyer friend, Lizbeth, killed the guy who molested her and a bunch of other girls when they were young. And to be honest, I can see why she did it. I'm not saying it's right, but the question we need to ask as a society is why someone didn't stop that monster from abusing so many girls in the first place."

Pella's energy pierced right through the internet from her homely little apartment overlooking the Aegean Sea. "You are asking the right questions, my dear. Why don't we allow for the legal defense we used to call the battered woman defense? Why is it okay to shoot people under some stand-your-ground defense but it's not okay when a woman defends herself from her abuser? When the woman finally cracks and attacks the man who abused her for years, we put her in a cage. Not treatment. There are lots more questions than answers in this world of punishment and retribution. Whatever happened to the concept of rehabilitation for those who make life-changing mistakes?"

Camille picked up the thread. "And then there are the women in there because they made poor choices in men, and when they get beaten down, they often get convinced to commit crimes in order to support their drug habit."

"A habit that is typically caused by trying to find a way to treat the trauma of abuse," Pella added.

"So, of course, we put them in prison. Not treatment. I don't think most people ever give a second thought to women in prison. But they sure do complain about the crime rate. And guess how that all gets started?"

"Traumatized children who lose their mothers to addiction and prison."

Camille nodded. "I had no idea the magnitude of this. And now I'm not sure I can ever go back to life as I knew it."

"Well, my darling daughter, that's the exact perfect place to be. Let your mind wander and see if you can envision some solutions. Simply sitting around complaining about rising crime and putting traumatized people into cages certainly hasn't done anyone any good."

Before Camille could answer, Gracie raced into the room. "Yia Yia! Hey, Mom! You didn't tell us Yia Yia was on the phone!" She didn't skip a beat. "Hand me that phone—Yia Yia needs to see our Christmas tree! And all the presents!"

Gracie grabbed the phone and skipped across the living room, holding it up for her grandmother to admire the tree. Camille listened to Gracie with half an ear as she loaded the dishwasher. As always, Gracie's words could barely keep up with her thoughts. The Christmas festivities in the Delaney-Taylor household were in full swing. Camille poured herself another glass of wine, snuggled up in the oversize chair, and looked out at the lights reflecting on the lake as Gracie continued to regale her yia yia with her nonstop narrative of the past few days putting up the tree and wrapping presents, and the ingredients of the family dinner.

Gracie's chatter melted into the background as Camille tried to imagine what the women at WCCW were doing at that moment. Then she let her mind wander to try to imagine the potential reunions between those mothers and their children. If she was successful in reuniting some of the mothers with their kids, the upcoming Christmas celebrations would be epic. She didn't even want to think about the alternative. What if she couldn't convince the judges to give these families a chance?

———

Christmas Day flew by. It was all friends, family, presents, food, movies, games, and a significant amount of champagne. Camille woke up early the next day and headed for the gym to work out and debrief with Trish. Despite their intentions to work out, it had been too long since they'd hit the weights. Years back, Trish had offered to train Camille, and what had once been a regular schedule had drifted, and now they were just glad to find a sliver of time to work out together.

Trish handed Camille a couple of fifteens and pointed at the bench. "Skull crushers. Sixteen of 'em. And . . . go."

Camille dutifully lay back and began her reps while Trish did the same on the next bench over, albeit with heavier weights.

Squats, bench presses, and bicep and triceps curls kept the two women quiet and focused for the next hour. When they were done, they grabbed a table at the juice bar and ordered a couple of smoothies. Finally they had time to catch up.

"You first." Camille pointed at Trish with her straw and then opened it with her teeth and pulled it from its wrapper.

Trish closed her eyes for a second to gather her thoughts. "Okay, here's what we've got so far. We don't know if Willow was in the fire. But if she wasn't, then we need to find Malika, who is probably the only person who might know where she is. Our only real lead so far is some dude who apparently used to be a good kid, until he got hooked on meth and forced Malika to abandon Willow to her parents and ultimately maybe into a fiery inferno. Not so sure how helpful he's gonna be, but he may be our only hope. Oh! And I think I forgot to tell you that he's the creep at the pharmacy who was watching Gigi."

"Wait. What? Malika's meth-head boyfriend works in the pharmacy? Are you sure?"

Trish nodded. "I know, right? The coach, Norma, said that he was a chemistry geek in high school, so maybe it makes sense that he landed in a pharmacy. Not sure it matters, though, since he may have info on how to find Malika. So I'm not writing him off just yet. Also, he lives in a pretty sweet rig—a new-looking Airstream—which doesn't make much sense, given his lifestyle." She paused. "But hiring a meth head as a clerk in a pharmacy doesn't seem to add up."

"What's his name?"

"Quinn. Quinn Hastings."

"Not feeling particularly great about our cast of characters as yet. Who else ya got?"

"Well, Norma suggested I check out Malika's sisters, so that's my next step. I expect the sisters would know Malika's situation and likely knew—let's say 'know'—about Willow."

"You know where to find them?"

"I know where one of them lives. I'll go out to her place tomorrow."

"Perfect. Who else?"

"Then there's the local doc who got sent down for heroin. It hit me that his story was really similar to Charli's. As far as I can tell, and according to that article, he was about to crack open a local pharmacy for overselling opioids. And bam, he gets busted."

"Local pharmacy, as in Port Angeles local?"

Trish stopped and stared at Camille. "Yep."

Camille paused for a beat. "And you think maybe Zhao owns a pharmacy in town over there and set up that doc?"

"Well, that seems like a distinct possibility."

Camille raised her eyebrows. "And if Zhao is in biz over in PA, that puts your buddy Quinn in a whole new light. Zhao hires a meth head to work in his pharmacy—it does kind of go along with the whole idea of Zhao moving into the illegal drug market."

Trish picked up the narrative. "Well, Hastings was absolutely selling some kind of drugs out at his trailer. He could be tangled up with Zhao somehow."

"Okay, let's do a search to see if Martin is doing business over there. It sure fits his MO. Small town. Manufacturing and forestry-type jobs. I think they have a paper mill over there."

"And probably lots of on-the-job-type injuries in those places. That would open patients up to opioid prescriptions," Trish added.

"Well, I'm not sure we're qualified to do a socioeconomic analysis of the peninsula, but Zhao could put up an opioid mill just about anywhere."

"Seems to make sense to take a trip over to whatever prison that doc ended up in," Trish suggested.

"He went to prison? Are you sure?"

Trish nodded. "Seems our new BFF Rose the prosecutor does not go lightly on dealers. She's all about warm-and-fuzzy drug-court treatment for the end users, but she throws the book at the suppliers."

Camille nodded. "Makes sense. She got herself elected in a pretty conservative county. They'll expect a fair share of book throwing in exchange for them giving her some slack on her treatment center."

"Actually, the article said almost exactly that. I still can't believe she got elected over there."

"I can. Don't you think lots of the people there have seen their kids and friends and neighbors get addicted? Remember, if a young Black kid is on drugs, it's criminal. But put the same story in a small town of mostly white people and have one of their kids get hooked, and suddenly it's a disease and treatment is necessary."

"I guess so."

Camille refocused. "So, on your list, you're going to talk with Malika's sister, and then you'll track down what prison that doc is in so one of us can pay him a visit."

"And I'll figure out if Zhao owns a pharmacy over there."

"And if he does, it might be worth a chat with Rose to find out more about the doctor's drug charge."

Trish interrupted. "I have such a weird feeling that there's some connection between what happened to Charli and that doc."

"Well, you have that cop radar for sure."

"Okay, how about what you've learned?"

"We know that, by some crazy coincidence, Charli is in prison with the only person in the world who might know how we can find Zhao's computer. It was unbelievable to find out that Lizbeth killed the guy Brian was coaching with. And that the computer might have gone into the evidence room."

"Oh! Bad news about the computer and the evidence room."

"What?" Camille deflated.

"Turns out some dirty cop was running the evidence room and was selling electronics that got taken into custody. My guess is we'll never find that computer."

Camille didn't say anything.

"Not sure we want to let Charli know about that just yet."

"Well, I need to get busy and file a motion to reunite a former-prisoner mom with her kid. I promised Iris I'd help her get her daughter back, so that's my project for the upcoming week. I'm going to work with Sally on getting the statistics I need to hopefully convince a King County court commissioner that kids need their actual biological moms. Not their grandmas. Not appointed caregivers. Their actual moms."

"Good to keep in mind why we're doing this. Kids and moms. Moms and kids. What a fucked-up mess this whole criminal legal system is."

Camille finished off her smoothie. "I gotta get to the office. I'm ready to get into the ring on this one."

Trish stood up and hugged Camille. "I'm right there with you, my legal warrior. Let's do this!"

CHAPTER TWENTY

Trish headed out to Spring Lake Road to look for Malika's sister. After checking her GPS, she stopped in front of a long dirt driveway and took a minute to look, as always, for an escape route, just in case things didn't go as planned. Maybe through the small forgotten orchard off to the left. Trish made a mental note as she zipped up the Port Angeles basketball team hoodie Norma had given her and put on her beloved Seattle Storm baseball cap. She felt the familiar rush of adrenaline she always experienced before approaching a stranger who might be a potential witness, or at least a source of information for her investigation.

But just before taking a left toward the house, she spotted a woman at the crest of the hill beyond the driveway, working on a flat tire on an old Honda Civic. Trish grabbed the tiny binoculars out of her tattered backpack, took a few minutes to assess the situation, and pulled out her phone. She scrolled to the image of the yearbook picture of Malika's sister. *Yep. I'm in luck.* She shoved the binocs back into her pack and pulled ahead slowly.

"Need a hand?" she hollered through the open window on her passenger side.

The woman held up the pieces of a disassembled jack. "Any idea how to use this thing?" She was clearly trying to modulate her anger. "My fucking neighbor is trying some kind of DIY bathroom remodel." She pointed at the dilapidated faded-green house with an off-kilter porch that lurched to the left. "Fucking nails everywhere." She held up a three-inch long nail. "My boyfriend got a flat in almost this exact same place last week." She sat back on her haunches as Trish came around the back of her car.

"My dad wouldn't let me get my license until I showed him that I could change a tire." Trish smiled. "I got you."

"I'm Marlys." The woman held out her hand. "And I apologize for my language. I'm just so sick of this jerk." She cocked her head in the direction of the green shanty.

Trish got busy laying out the tools necessary to change the tire while Marlys leaned over her, hands on her knees, ready to help. "Thanks so much. My boyfriend is off fishing, so I'm hanging solo for a couple of weeks."

"No worries." Trish looked up at the tall Black woman in the metallic copper-colored parka and paused a moment, for effect. "Hey, you look familiar. Did you play basketball in high school here?"

The woman smiled. "Once an athlete in a small town, always an athlete in a small town." She shrugged. "They called me and my sisters the Franklin trio. We had such fun in high school. This place was basketball heaven for us."

"Franklin! So you must be Malika's sister. You look so much alike. That's why I thought I recognized you."

"You know Malika?"

"We played in a rec league in Seattle a few years back. She's a kick-ass point guard." Trish pulled the hubcap off.

"She sure was."

Trish took note of the past tense and stayed quiet, waiting for Marlys to continue.

"She had way more natural talent than I ever did. But I got the discipline gene, so it kinda balanced out." Marlys reached down and handed Trish the wrench. "Malika was born to play. She just walked out on the court and magic happened. Me? I had to work my ass off. But we made a good team. We pretty much read each other's minds."

"I hear ya. She had an uncanny ability to magically know where the ball would be, and bingo—there she was."

"I didn't know she played in Seattle."

"Just for fun. We had a blast."

"When did you last see Malika?" Marlys's question seemed sincere.

Trish didn't miss a beat. She had all the dates of Malika's comings and goings memorized. "I think it was about 2015. That's when she moved back here, right?"

Marlys nodded. And paused.

Trish knew she needed to tread carefully. "I really should have followed up with her. She seemed so out of sorts when she left. It felt pretty abrupt. Now that I'm here, I'd love to see her." She focused on Marlys's face, looking for a response.

Marlys looked directly into Trish's eyes for several seconds. It felt as if she was trying to figure out if Trish was trustworthy. "Did you know her baby? Daisy?"

Trish smiled. "She's adorable. Malika had her all trained up as a number one Seahawks fan. She had this sweet way of throwing her hands up in the air every time we made a touchdown."

Marlys laughed. "She sure did!"

"So, are they still around here?"

Marlys reached out and took Trish's hand. "I don't often talk about Malika, but since you two were obviously such good friends, I feel like I should let you know what happened to her. It's worse than one of those TV shows where a sister goes missing."

Trish's heart skipped a beat. Maybe the sister had some info on Willow's whereabouts. Or maybe there was bad news about Malika. The tire-changing operation came to a complete halt.

"I'm really sorry to have to tell you this."

Trish had started the investigation to find Willow, but at this point, she felt like she knew Malika and was almost as invested in finding her as she was in finding Willow.

"Malika got tangled up with her high school boyfriend. He was a nice guy in high school. Kind of a science nut. Then he got messed up on meth and became a first-class jerk." Marlys looked at the ground and then back up at Trish. "When he was high, which was most of the time, he beat Malika. Thankfully, she got Daisy out of there before she also became a victim of his crazy. He got Malika hooked on meth, and then he had her out with him, stealing shit to feed their habit. She ended up getting arrested."

This was a new wrinkle. Trish felt real tears welling up. "I can't believe it. Malika on meth?"

"And here's the saddest part. Her meth addiction kicked in even worse after her baby died in a fire at our parents' trailer."

Now the tears were flowing. The pain in Trish's heart made it feel like it was going to explode. "Are they sure? Are they sure Daisy was in the trailer?"

"You know about the fire?" Marlys looked surprised.

"No," Trish said quickly. "I know nothing about any fire here, but I was a volunteer firefighter for a while after college," she lied, "and the first thing they ask when there's a fire is whether all bodies have been identified. Was Daisy's body identified?"

Marlys's pause was nearly imperceptible. But she nodded woefully. "Yes. We know Daisy was there, and we lost her in the fire." Marlys turned away from Trish, bent down and picked up the detached tire, and rolled it toward her trunk. "It destroyed Malika. It really did."

Trish needed proof. She pushed gently. "Did the medical examiner confirm that Daisy was in the fire?"

Marlys glanced sideways at Trish and turned away. "Yes. Yes, he did." She kicked a rock off the shoulder of the road into the ditch.

Is she lying? There was no mention of a medical examiner identifying Willow in the news article. Something is off.

Trish caught herself. "I'm so sorry about the fire. Was anyone else hurt?"

Marlys had the distant look of someone who had suffered a personal tragedy and was tired of having to replay the scene over and over across the years. "Yes. We lost both of our parents. Our family will never recover. And adding the loss of Mom and Dad, first to meth and then to the fire, along with the loss of Daisy was just too much for Malika to bear."

Trish stood up so she could be face to face with Malika's sister. "I'm so very sorry. This is just awful."

"It was all because of that fucking oxy. My dad worked in the mill and fell off a machine. He hurt his back and got prescribed OxyContin. That was the beginning of the end of our family."

"What happened to your family is heartbreaking. I feel like anyone caught up in the whole oxy thing has been murdered by the drug company." Trish's outrage was real.

"You're absolutely right. My dad took the oxy for a year or so. Then, when the doctor stopped prescribing it, he turned to street drugs. He lost our family home, and my parents had to move into an abandoned trailer. And then he started making and selling meth right out of that rusty old piece of shit. If you would have told me when I was in high school that my dad would die a meth head, I'd have said you were crazy. But it happens. Even to a family like ours."

"It must have been terrifying to watch your dad sink into addiction."

"That's how he died. He was cooking meth, and he blew up their trailer. I'll never forgive that drug company. Or that doctor who, by the way, ended up in prison for selling heroin. That drug ruined so many lives. But a doctor, selling heroin? He seemed like such a nice guy. We couldn't believe it."

Trish perked up at the mention of the mysterious doctor. "Did you know him well, the doctor?"

"Played basketball with his daughter. He coached our community league when we were kids. I can't imagine what got into him. Maybe the money was too tempting."

"Did he ever apologize for prescribing the oxy?"

"Funny you should ask. He actually did. It seemed like, at one point, he figured out that he had been bamboozled by the drug company. I think that's when he tried to get Dad off it. But it was too late. Dr. Walters getting caught with heroin never made any sense to me."

"Any chance the doc was on oxy himself?" Trish was becoming fixated on this local doc selling heroin.

Marlys shook her head. "I don't think so. But who knows? Oxy is poison in so many ways."

"Right. Poison to the patients. Poison to the docs. Poison to the communities."

"Exactly."

Trish knelt down, placed the spare tire on the rim, and began tightening the lug nuts. "So where is Malika now?" She held her breath, hoping against hope that Marlys would point her in some helpful direction. Trish still wasn't completely convinced that Daisy had been in the trailer when it caught fire, so finding Malika was imperative.

Marlys shrugged. "She got arrested, and then qualified for this cool new drug-court treatment. And she did really well."

"That's awesome. Meth is nearly impossible to kick."

"Yeah. It really is." Marlys frowned. "Malika was getting her life back on track, and then Quinn got his claws back into her. Again. I can't imagine what made her keep going back to him. He actually was a sweet kid in high school, so maybe she was somehow holding out hope that the old Quinn was in there somewhere. But really, it was probably just too much for her, losing the baby at the same time as Mom and Dad. For whatever reason, she found some kind of solace in Quinn Hastings. I always wondered if she went back to punish herself for leaving Daisy at Mom's, knowing full well what was going on inside that rat trap."

Trish wondered for a minute if it seemed weird that she was asking so many questions, but Marlys seemed to want to process what had happened to her family. So Trish continued, staying cognizant of the fact that Marlys might suddenly cut her off.

"Why'd she take Daisy over there in the first place?" Trish's question was a bit tentative.

"Quinn was threatening to hurt Daisy, and while Malika seemed to be able to put up with him abusing her, she wouldn't tolerate him being around Daisy. So she asked Mom to watch her for a while. And Mom loved that little girl. Like, loved her to the moon and back."

"How long did Daisy stay with your folks?"

"She was there for several months."

"What about Malika?"

"She ended up in jail for the second time, that we knew of. But she couldn't post bail before her trial, so she sat there for months. And to tell you the truth, either my sister Monique or I could have posted bail. But honestly, we talked about it and decided that she'd just go back to Quinn, so we didn't want to help her get out."

"Then what happened?"

"Then she got sentenced to jail for something like ten months. Not prison, because her sentence wasn't a full year. I didn't know that. You don't go to prison if your sentence is shorter than a year. And I guess that kind of sucks because county jail has no programming at all, so it's in many ways actually worse than prison. People in and out all the time, no consistency."

"Did she get back in the drug-court program?"

"They didn't have any programs for relapses, which sucks because it's pretty common for people to have to go back into a program a few times. They just sent her to jail."

"Did you visit her in there?"

"We did at first, but then she told us to stop coming if we weren't going to post bail. But she finally got clean in spite of her awful situation."

"So, I take it she got out, what, like five years ago?"

Marlys nodded. "She did."

"What happened when she was released?"

"Well, this time she steered clear of Quinn by spending lots of time out by the ocean, running and hiking. Out at La Push. It's really rough terrain there."

"Where did she stay?"

"When she wasn't out in the woods or at the ocean, she stayed with a high school friend out near Neah Bay."

"Did she stay away from Quinn?"

"As far as I know, she did," Marlys said slowly.

"So, what happened next?"

"When spring arrived, she took off."

Trish's stomach fell. "She's gone?"

"She just took off."

"Any idea where she went?"

Marlys paused for a beat. "Um . . . not really. But she always liked the mountains, so it's possible that she's somewhere close to where she can hike."

"And she's been gone for five years? No word from her at all?"

Marlys shook her head. "She just needs to stay away from Quinn." She hesitated as though she was considering her options. "She thinks he killed Daisy, and in a way she's right. If he wasn't such a first-class asshole, Malika wouldn't have had to leave Daisy at Mom's and she'd still be with her."

It struck Trish that Marlys hadn't said that Daisy would still be alive. Something was missing here, and she was going to figure out what. She was relieved that she had a meeting scheduled with Rose tomorrow. And it looked like the agenda was growing by the minute. "So you think Malika might have taken off for the mountains?"

"Ya. And if she doesn't want to be found, she won't be." She took a breath. "At least not until she's good and ready."

CHAPTER TWENTY-ONE

Camille loved the view from her waterfront office. It was calming and exciting at the same time. Lake Union was an urban lake surrounded by houseboats and marinas, punctuated by small parks. And interspersed along the shorefront were boat-repair facilities that attracted all kinds of commercial vessels. Camille watched as a talented captain piloted the giant NOAA ship through the canal and toward the NOAA facility at the south end of the lake. She tried to remember what NOAA stood for—National Oceanic and Atmospheric . . . something. Then she pondered what kind of scientific research had taken place on the ship and imagined it out at sea conducting experiments in the icy cold and rough waters of the Northern Pacific. It looked so calm and at the same time unwieldy and out of place there in the lake.

Camille turned her attention to her own pile of scientific research, provided to her by Sally and Sam, with the help of their new research assistant, Iris. As a nurse, Camille had been trained that science was science. It might've rolled with the times and with the scientific evidence, but at its root, research was what society needed to rely on. So how come the science of addiction and the sociological studies about women and their children were treated as optional by the court system? Why did judges believe they could ignore research and insert their own subjective opinions into the lives of litigants and upend their families?

Was it that sociological research was somehow less respected? If there weren't test tubes and chemical reactions, was the research considered less reliable? She put down her papers and stared at the wake of the ship. Or maybe it was just that lawyers and judges were more used to reading legal cases and law review articles. It seemed to be way past time for the courts to meld together psychology, sociology, and the law, which was why it was essential to educate women like Iris, who had lived experience in the criminal legal and family law systems. But then again, putting family issues and issues of addiction and mental health into the legal system in the first place was questionable. The legal system was designed to be adversarial—not therapeutic. And beyond family law, the criminal legal system had always worked at cross purposes with strong families, mental health, and general medical care.

Camille pulled out one of the articles that would hopefully support her argument in court to reunite Iris and Abby. She grabbed her pink highlighter.

Within a couple of hours, her notepad was filled with bullet points, arrows, circled phrases, and stickies of every color imaginable along the sides of the paper. Oftentimes she had to strain to read her own notes when she was entrenched in a subject. And this time was no exception.

Her mother was exactly right. Men and women ended up in prison for entirely different reasons. And prisons were nowhere near gender responsive to their needs.

"You still here?" Lucia asked as she swept into Camille's office and stopped to gather up a scattering of dirty coffee cups. "Sally stopped in; can I bring her back?"

Camille looked up. "Did you know that children whose mothers are in prison are more negatively impacted than if their parent actually dies?"

Lucia took that as a yes, called Sally into the office, and sat on the arm of the purple leather couch. Sally entered, and Lucia quietly pointed at the matching chair.

"Hi, Sally," Camille said absentmindedly. "Listen to this." Camille picked up an article that looked like a rainbow had exploded on it. Highlights of every conceivable color filled the page. "The US incarcerates more women than any other country. And the gender differences between women and men in prison are staggering." She flipped down her glasses from atop her head. "Women generally do not end up in prison for committing violent crimes. Most of their crimes are property crimes related to economic conditions and addiction."

Sally jumped in. "And if a woman does commit a violent crime, it's almost always when they are forced to defend themselves. But when a woman is incarcerated for a self-defense crime, we still treat her just like a man who has committed a violent crime. The underlying reasons for the violent event are completely different. That's where gender-responsive programming should come in. It's time to provide women with treatment and programming that is targeted to their specific needs."

"Exactly." Lucia put her handful of cups on the coffee table and sank into the couch, obviously ready to watch a couple of highly educated pros engage in an interesting dialogue.

"And check this out." Camille pulled out another multicolor-highlighted article. "When men go to prison, usually their kids are cared for by the children's actual moms. So, when a father goes to prison, that man's children stay with their mom—who is typically their main care provider in the first place. So even though they miss and need their dad, they still live with their primary bonded parent. But when a mom goes to prison, their kids usually end up in either foster care or with a relative, so those children are deprived of security and a continued bond with their primary caregiver. You can see the dramatic difference in outcomes between children whose moms are in prison and those whose dads are in prison."

"So, kids with moms in prison are at higher risk than kids with dads in prison," Lucia confirmed.

"Yep," Sally said. "And only four percent of kids in foster care end up in adoptive homes. The rest end up in institutions, group homes, shelters, and all kinds of foster homes—most of which are subpar, to say the least."

"But why should any kid who has a loving mom end up in foster care in the first place?" Camille felt the familiar combination of anger and frustration welling up. "And even if a kid ends up in foster care, we can't just keep terminating their parents' rights because a mom is in prison. That kid will never get adopted and will, likely, end up being raised by the state."

"Well, those are the at-risk kids who fill the trauma-to-prison pipeline," Sally continued. "In public health, when we find a problem, our first step is to turn upstream and figure out the cause of the problem. It's not rocket science to figure out that people in prison are vastly more likely to have parents in prison. So, if we really want to make our communities safe, we need to find a way to keep parents connected with their kids—especially moms."

"Exactly." Camille read from another article. "'Of all minor children in the US, two point three percent have a parent in prison.'"

"What's the racial demographic breakdown?" Lucia was fully engaged.

Camille scrolled down the page with her forefinger. "Point nine percent of white kids have a parent in prison. Two point four percent of Hispanic kids, and six point seven percent of Black kids." She looked up. "No huge surprise there." She flipped the page. "And guess who is now addressing this crisis? *Sesame Street*! Did you know that there's now a *Sesame Street* character who has a parent in prison? They're trying to find a way to make these kids feel like they're not alone, so enter Alex the Muppet."

"I didn't know that, but it makes sense. It's an epidemic that no one seems to care about." Sally didn't need articles to quote. She had all the stats in her head. "And guess what happens to kids once they age out of foster care after prisons take them from their parents? By age twenty-three, less than fifty percent of former foster kids have a job. Twenty-five percent of former foster kids are homeless within five years of aging out of the system. And in that same five-year time period, over seventy-five percent of women who were foster children are pregnant. Eighty percent of the young men have been arrested, and sixty percent have been convicted of a crime. And only six percent have at least a two-year degree. Oh, and the national recidivism rate is forty-three percent." Sally took a breath. "This whole system needs to be overhauled. You lawyers need to get your shit together. Your court system is ruining families and children."

"Exactly. And how about this? Instead of caging women, how about we provide them treatment?" Camille held up another article. "This one's about a woman who witnessed her child being run over by a car, right in front of her in a grocery store parking lot. If that happened to me, I'd be admitted to some cushy psych ward—maybe forever. But since this happened to a poor woman, she didn't have access to psychological treatment, so she self-medicated with street drugs. And in order to pay for her habit, she started committing petty crimes, which led to more drugs, which led to bigger crimes. Which landed her in prison. All because she experienced every mother's nightmare. She saw her child killed. Right in front of her. So, of course, we send her to prison."

Camille threw down the article in disgust. And picked up another one. "This article talks about how men who go to prison blame all kinds of circumstances that got them there. But guess who women blame?"

"Themselves," Lucia said softly. "I saw it firsthand with my own eyes."

The three women looked at each other. That last point was huge. They let it sink in.

"Do you really think there's any chance that you can convince judges that these kids just need their moms?" Sally asked.

"I might have a fighting chance of completely upending the criminal–family law system if I can get a declaration from you or someone on your research committee. The more credentials, the better."

"Ha. I assume the most-highly-credentialed person on my dissertation committee is off limits—him being your lovely husband."

"Anyone else you can think of?"

"Not necessarily with his credentials, but I can get one of the research PhDs to help."

"Great. Thanks."

"I'll get right on it," Sally promised. "You really think you can get a judge or court commissioner to listen to you?"

Lucia stood up. "If anyone can, it's going to be Camille."

"Okey doke then, we'd better leave you alone. Looks like you have a brief to write."

CHAPTER TWENTY-TWO

Trish got up the next morning and did her usual routine: coffee, toast, and then ready for a quick run along the Port Angeles waterfront. Today was her meeting with Rose about Malika, the convicted doc, and now also the trailer fire. She glanced out the porthole over the galley and said a little prayer of thanks that it wasn't raining. Then she pulled on her fleece leggings and settled her yellow reflectorized headband over her ears. It was still a little dark, even at 8:00 a.m. She tied her shoes, scrambled up the four steep steps of the companionway, and pulled open the hatch to the cockpit, where she abruptly caught her breath.

Quinn Hastings was sprawled out on the cockpit bench, smoking a clove cigarette. He glared at her. "Camille Delaney? I knew I'd find you." His brown-toothed smile was a feeble attempt at flirtation.

Trish was nothing if not fast on her feet. "You looking for the chick I rent this boat from?"

Quinn looked confused.

"Not sure I can help you. Found this place on Airbnb. Pretty cool, isn't it?"

Quinn tried to look nonchalant. "Ya. But I'm not looking for her. I'm looking for you, babe." He spat at a duck paddling up next to the boat. "You free Saturday night?" His wink made Trish's stomach turn.

"Well, I'm flattered, but sorry, not interested. I have a boyfriend." Trish tried to keep her hands from trembling as she quickly clicked closed the padlock on the companionway. "I gotta go. I have to get in my run before my morning meeting." She pushed past him and hopped onto the dock. This wasn't going to be a jog. She broke into a full-on sprint. Quinn was just climbing off the boat when Trish reached the parking lot. She felt a wave of temporary relief but kept up her pace just in case. She ran along the waterfront, past the log yard next to the paper company. Just when she felt she could slow down a bit, an electric-blue late-model Ford F-150 flew past her. Quinn Hastings yelled something unintelligible out the window just before he turned left into a long greenbelt. Trish went on autopilot, snapping a shot of the license plate and looking around to check her escape route. Thankfully, it was apparently starting time at the mill, and there was a slow roll of trucks entering the parking lot. So Trish continued her run, relieved that Quinn seemed to be gone, at least for the moment.

When she reached the beach out on Ediz Hook, a long, thin spit across from the marina, she finally stopped to catch her breath and called Camille.

"Quinn Hastings knows your name."

"Huh?"

"I had a not-so-welcome guest this morning, sitting in the cockpit of *Sofia*."

"How'd he find you?"

"No idea, but he thought I was you."

"Well, shit."

"I told him I'm just renting the boat from you. Found it on Airbnb. So we better get an ad up on there for the rental. Then you can just close the calendar, since I've rented it for the winter."

"Got it. I'll tell Amy. How does that impact you now?"

"Not sure it does, but I think I need to up the pace of this investigation. He's creepy for sure, but I'm pretty sure he's harmless. And . . . he likes me."

"Gross. You sure you're okay? This is becoming a thing. You getting hit on by your potential witnesses."

"I'm fine."

"Any idea where he got my name?"

"He probably got it from the marina, or the boat registration. You're not that hard to find."

"What was he doing at the boat anyway?"

"As far as I can tell, I think he was there to ask me out."

"O-M-G. Seriously?"

"Part of my job. Turning away potential suitors."

"Be careful—your last so-called date with a witness landed you in the hospital over in Friday Harbor and almost got you killed."

"True that. Also, he drives a nearly new, big, blue Ford truck. I can't imagine how that dude can afford a rig like that. I'll run the plates and find out what's up."

"Well, that's weird. Let me know what you find out. Are you okay going back to the boat?"

"Yeah, but keep your phone on, just in case. And keep an extra eye out for anything weird over there. I don't think this guy is anywhere near smart enough to cause any real trouble. But just stay alert."

"Thanks to you helping us with online security, he wouldn't be able to find our houseboat, just my office."

"Still, you and your staff need to be careful. I'll send you a pic of him just in case."

"Okay. You meeting with Rose today?"

Trish looked at the clock on her phone. "Yeah. At ten. I better get going." She pulled her leg up to stretch her quad. "And by the way, any chance you can go visit the doc who got thrown in prison? I think it's going to be easier to get you inside as a lawyer than if I have to jump through all the hoops for a visit to the men's prison. And besides, I'm going to be kinda busy here, tracking down all the people who might know what happened to Malika. And I'm still not convinced that Willow was in that fire. I'll call you later to debrief."

"Okay. Stay safe!"

"Will do!"

Trish stuck her phone into the pocket of her leggings. Frustrated at having to cut her run short, she turned back toward town and slowed her pace a bit.

—

Amy was busy gathering the exhibits for Iris's motion when Camille arrived at the office.

"Once we get that filed, can you please help me figure out where some doctor who landed in prison is?"

"Gonna need more info." Amy smirked at her boss. "Like, maybe a name or something."

"Good point. I have it somewhere in my notes." Camille sat at her desk and began flipping through a purple pad. "It's here somewhere . . ."

"Okay, I gotta get this declaration signed by Iris. She's waiting on me. Let me know when you find the name and I'll have Lucia tell me how one goes about arranging a prison visit. That's beyond my pay grade."

"Oh! And one more thing. Can you put an ad up on Airbnb advertising *Sofia* for rent in the Port Angeles marina, and then block out all of the rental days, as though it's been rented?"

"What? You want to rent your boat? Really?"

"Of course not. I just want it to look like I do."

"Oka-a-a-y," Amy said slowly.

"As usual, some dude has the hots for Trish. He tracked her down, and she told him she's renting our boat. Long story."

"Apparently so. I'll see what I can do."

"Thanks! And I think I'll head over to PA in a couple of weeks, so can you clear my calendar for a few days? Sam's taking Gracie to his meeting in New York—kind of a father-daughter getaway."

"That's sweet. Will your trip to PA be after Iris's motion?"

"Yeah, after. Thanks."

Lucia popped her head into Camille's office. "You going to try to set up a legal visit at the prison?"

"I guess so. Any idea how to do that?"

"Yep. I'm on it. It might take a bit to get it scheduled."

"Jeez. Nothing is easy when it comes to DOC." Camille turned to boot up her laptop, to check her emails and address the growing list of clients waiting for her to respond to their litany of case-related requests.

———

The redbrick Port Angeles courthouse looked every bit the historical landmark that it was. Trish took the steps up to the entrance two at a time. The tall white pillars framed an impressive door located directly under the clock on the belfry. And since it was midwinter, the grass in front of the imposing building was an inexplicable shade of Pacific Northwest green.

The door was as heavy as Trish expected. She held it open for an elderly woman, who scrunched her eyes to look up at the security guard running the metal detector. The woman fumbled with her belongings and tried to put them in the plastic bin to go through the detector. Trish helped her place her oversize purse into the bin and waited as the woman tried to make it through. It took three tries with a very patient security guard to get all the woman's pockets emptied and to identify what she was carrying inside her bra. Turned out the detector didn't like the small jewelry box filled with her deceased husband's Mason pins.

"Okay, ma'am. Thanks for your patience. You're next." The guard smiled gratefully at Trish. "Are you here for a hearing? Can I help you find your courtroom? This place can be a little overwhelming for litigants."

Litigant? Dang. Trish had dressed in one of Gigi's suits to look like a lawyer—navy suit with a white shell under it, and a pair of tan low-heel Ferragamos. She was trying to blend in to the local scene, but quickly realized when she walked through the gaggle of lawyers mingling in the marble lobby that lawyers dressed differently here in PA. The women wore mismatched suits, sensible shoes, and suntan-colored hose, and the men had some version of a somewhat rumpled navy jacket over tan or gray slacks. And more sensible shoes. She wasn't exactly going to disappear into this crowd. Some of the lawyers actually stared at her as she ascended the staircase that led to another lobby under a spectacular yellow-and-green stained glass rotunda. *This place is gorgeous,* she thought as she scrolled the reader board, looking for the prosecutor's office.

Trish barely recognized the woman who welcomed her into a large office filled with weighty, dark furniture. Last time she had seen Rose, she was all decked out in fleece and tight jeans, with her frizzy hair heaped up on top of her head, tendrils flying out everywhere. Today, her hair was slicked back in a harsh ponytail, and she wore an all-black pantsuit with a hot-pink blouse.

Trish skipped the pleasantries. "Thanks so much for meeting with me. I know how busy you are, so I won't take up much of your time." Trish looked admiringly at the grouping of plaques on the wall, over an oversize credenza filled with pictures of Rose with various community and state leaders, mixed in with several of those etched-glass awards given out for all types of community service. This woman was a real pro. She had relationships with politicians from both sides of the aisle, which in the current climate was a serious accomplishment.

Rose waved her hand. "Don't mind the décor—I keep telling myself that one day I'll try to make this place look like something other than a 1980s partner's office at some big stuffy law firm. But people keep committing crimes, and addicts need treatment. And office design keeps falling to the end of my to-do list." She laughed. "And to be honest, you are a welcome interruption—any friend of Camille's, and especially of Camille's mom, is a friend of mine for sure." She pointed to a giant maroon leather chair in front of her desk. "Please. Have a seat." And then, rather than sitting behind her imposing mahogany desk, she came around and sat in the chair next to Trish. "You want a coffee?"

"Oh, no thanks, I'm good."

"So, how can I help?" Rose sat back and crossed her legs. Her petite profile belied the power of her elected office.

Trish got right to the point. "I have a few issues." She held up her index finger. "One, I'm curious about a fire that happened around five years ago." She added a finger. "And two, I'm wondering if you know a young woman named Malika Franklin—or could check on her record." Her third finger went up. "And three, I have some questions about a doctor you prosecuted on a drug charge a few years back."

"Okay. Shoot. What fire are you asking about?" Despite her staff hurrying in and out of her office to drop off and grab various piles of paperwork, Rose was one of those people who could laser focus on another person while ignoring everything going on around her.

"In 2015, there was a fire caused by a meth explosion. It was a trailer. A man and a woman were killed in the fire. Do you remember it?"

Rose nodded. "I do. It was out behind Hastings Auto Shop. Really sad case. They were a lovely family before they got hit by the opioid crisis. And I'm sorry to say that this was not the only fire we've had caused by meth explosions. Why do you ask?"

"As Camille told you, we're working on a cold case where a baby disappeared. We traced her here and then learned that she might have died in that trailer fire. But there's no evidence of anyone other than the man and woman being the victims. I'm hoping you might know more." Trish watched as Rose leaned forward, her eyes narrowing.

There was a long pause. Then Rose spoke. "This is very weird. I vividly recall a couple of middle-aged white guys in expensive suits who came to meet with me not long after that fire. They were really pushy. Asked all kinds of questions about whether we found the remains of a baby. I have no idea who they were or why they were so intent on this whole question about there being a baby in that fire."

Trish froze. "Wait. What? Tell me about them."

"There's not much to tell. They said they were investigators from Seattle and were quite insistent that we call back the arson team to see if a baby was in that fire. Which I didn't do, because there wasn't. Of that I'm certain. But now you're here asking the same question. What's up with this baby?"

It took a minute for it to sink in that there had been suits up here looking for Willow. Had Martin been following Malika and known the whereabouts of Willow—at least back then? Her mind was racing.

"So," Rose asked, "this baby. Who is she? And why is everyone looking for her? Maybe I can help?"

Trish considered her options. Since Rose was a close friend of Camille and Pella, she could surely be trusted. "The baby's name is Willow. She was kidnapped from the hospital at birth. Her mother was in prison when she was born. Still is. The mother's name is Charli Zhao, and her husband, Martin Zhao, took the baby from the hospital."

"Oh my God."

"Thing is, it's not his baby. It's his brother's baby." Trish looked at the clock on Rose's desk. "How much time do you have? I know you must be slammed."

"I blocked out thirty minutes."

"I talk fast." Trish gathered her thoughts. "The mom, Charli, is in prison at WCCW. Her twin sister is my partner. The baby's nanny, Malika Franklin, took the baby over here to get away from being under the control of Charli's ex, Martin Zhao. But from what you just told me, it seems that maybe Martin knew she was here—hence the suits from Seattle. Malika, the nanny, seems to have been a DV victim. She lived with a guy named Quinn Hastings. She took off after the baby, Willow, allegedly died in this fire. And at some point, she ended up in jail here for a drug-related charge. She was apparently in your diversion program, got clean, but relapsed and got arrested again. She couldn't afford bail, so she sat in jail forever, then got out and pretty much disappeared."

"Okay, I can have someone in my office look into it and see if we can locate her in our system." Rose looked at her watch. "We have a few minutes. What's your question about the doctor?"

"You remember prosecuting a local doc, Dr. Walters? He got caught with a bunch of heroin in his car." Trish looked at Rose expectantly.

"Of course. It's not often that one of our few town docs turns out to be a heroin dealer. And before that, he was prescribing oxy like it was candy."

"How did you know that?"

"This town is on the precipice of becoming like that little town in Appalachia in that book *Dopesick*. And a few of our town doctors got all wrapped up in the hype that oxy wasn't addictive, so they were prescribing it to lots of folks who were hurt on the job, out logging or in the paper mill. Then all hell broke loose, when it turned out that the drug company was lying and we all found out that oxy was addictive as hell. So, the docs were trapped with hundreds of addicted patients. This guy, Walters, was right in the middle of all of it. Really sad on one level. And really illegal on another, when he started selling heroin."

"Were you sure he was selling it?"

"He never admitted to it. In fact, he insisted that he'd been framed. But there was no evidence of who would have framed him, or why."

"Who did he say framed him?"

"He kept pointing the finger at the local pharmacy, but he had no evidence to support his claims."

"Let me ask a question. Did he have a change of heart about oxy before he got arrested?"

"Actually, yes. There were several patients who testified at his sentencing that he had cut them off from oxy when he discovered how addictive it was."

Trish knew she was running out of time with Rose. "I have lots of questions about that. But for now, any way you could tell me where he's incarcerated?"

"Sure, but now I'm dying to know what he has to do with this missing baby. Maybe we undercharged him? Did he kill a baby?"

"Oh, no. It's just that his situation is really similar to how my friend, Charli, got arrested. Her husband planted heroin in her trunk, and now she's serving a twelve-year sentence for a crime she didn't commit."

Rose was just about to say something when another assistant stuck her head in the door. "You wanted to be in Judge Carson's court for the arraignment of that guy who got all the press last week for smuggling fentanyl on the ferry from Canada. You have about three minutes to get down there. There are reporters everywhere."

"Oh shit. Gotta go." Rose barely said goodbye as she raced to follow her assistant through her outer office, and she quickly disappeared.

Trish reached into the fancy briefcase she had borrowed from Camille and pulled out her Nemo notepad to scratch some notes about Martin being more in the picture up here than they had considered. Then she dialed Camille.

"I have a really strong feeling that Martin Zhao was behind the doctor getting put away in that heroin bust," she told Camille without saying hello. "And as it now stands, I'm not convinced that Willow was in that fire. We have lots of work to do here."

"Got it. I cleared my calendar so I can come up after my motion to get Iris's daughter back."

"Good. I need an extra set of hands up here."

CHAPTER TWENTY-THREE

Family law motions court was nothing if not unique. Commissioners sat on the bench, day in and day out, and made life-changing decisions for parents and families and divorcing couples. The worn marble hallway outside the courtrooms was a slice of local life. Attorneys mingled with colleagues who would be their adversaries inside the courtroom just minutes later. And terrified litigants sat on long, ancient wooden benches, awaiting their fifteen minutes in front of the court commissioner that would likely change their lives in unforeseen and unexpected ways.

Camille located Iris standing alone, crying slightly, outside the elevators in the crowded lobby. "You ready? Let's go inside the courtroom and find a seat." She hugged Iris. "I got you," she whispered in her ear.

The courtrooms were just as crowded as the area outside. There were only two rows of benches for the lawyers and their clients, so finding a seat early was key. And having the opposing party in the same room could be destabilizing for most litigants. Camille could feel Iris tense as her mother stuck her head in the door, likely trying to figure out if she was in the right place. Camille reached for Iris's hand and gave it a squeeze.

"Don't look at her. Just focus on why we're here." Camille pulled out her notepad and the pages of motion papers for a last-minute review.

There were three hearings ahead of them, and Iris sat transfixed as the lawyers made their legal arguments, the parties looked shell-shocked and often cried, and then the commissioners made their rulings, which brought on more tears.

"This all happens so fast," Iris whispered to Camille.

"That's why we need to be well prepared. We only have a five-minute argument to explain that you need to be back with Abby. And remember, we're not asking to get you full custody yet, only visits."

Just then, the court clerk called their case, and Camille ushered Iris up to the podium and motioned for her to stand to her left.

"Ms. Delaney, this is your motion, you have five minutes." The commissioner had her paperwork in front of her, and Camille was happy to notice that there were several stickies along the sides, indicating the commissioner had read everything carefully.

"Thank you, Your Honor. As you know, the court may order adjustments to the residential aspects of a parenting plan under RCW 26.09.260 upon a showing of a substantial change in circumstances of either the parent or of the child, if the proposed modification is only a minor modification in the residential schedule that does not change the residence the child is scheduled to reside in the majority of the time and does not result in a schedule that exceeds ninety overnights per year in total, if the court finds that, at the time the petition for modification is filed, the parenting plan does not provide reasonable time with the parent with whom the child does not reside a majority of the time and, further, the court finds that it is in the best interests of the child to increase residential time.

"It is important to put this case into perspective, so I'll take a minute to give the court some context. Attached to Ms. Thomas's motion is a declaration from a professor at the prestigious University of Washington School of Nursing. In his declaration, the expert explains it is estimated there are approximately two million children with incarcerated parents in this country. Over seventy-five percent of all women in US prisons are mothers." Camille paused and looked at the commissioner, looking for a glint of compassion. Finding none, she continued. "Most of these women are incarcerated for drug and property offenses, often stemming from poverty and/or substance-use disorders, just like Ms. Thomas. And like most incarcerated mothers, Ms. Thomas was the primary caretaker of Abigail. It is undisputed that incarcerating a mother tears her child away from a vital source of support.

"Incarcerated women are often custodial parents, and when they are sent to prison, their absence has a profound effect on their children. These children are often the forgotten victims of the system, and this is now considered and analyzed by researchers as an epidemic in our society. Parental incarceration may affect children differently than other types of separation because of the stigma associated with prison and the unpredictable nature of the criminal legal system. The impacts of parental incarceration on children include psychological stress, antisocial behavior, academic suspension or expulsion, economic hardship, and criminal activity. Other known harms include feelings of social stigma and shame as well as trauma-related stress. These children have more mental health problems and elevated levels of anxiety, fear, loneliness, anger, and depression, less stability, lower educational achievement, impaired teacher-student relationships, and more problems with behavior, attention deficit, speech, language, and learning disabilities. They have problems getting enough sleep and maintaining a healthy diet and suffer significant mental and physical health problems later in life.

"And for mothers, reuniting with their children typically decreases their chances of being reincarcerated. And their risk of relapsing in their substance-use disorders is remarkably lessened if they are able to regain their children.

"Ms. Thomas was a model prisoner. She obtained her AA degree inside. She attended and even led substance-use-disorder recovery groups inside. She has been clean and sober for years, and to prove that, she has voluntarily supplied the court with UAs for the past six months. She has a good job and has been in total compliance with all terms of her probation.

"The existing parenting plan should be modified to remove all of the inconsistent requirements that are, quite frankly, impossible for her to complete because they are too costly, or are at odds with her criminal terms of release, or are otherwise irrelevant to her current situation. For example, she should not be ordered to complete an inpatient program for addiction since there is no evidence that she is currently addicted to anything.

"The only way to chip away at this epidemic is one child at a time. At least for now. And it is clearly in *this* child's best interest to be reunited with her mother. First in reunification therapy, and then beginning eight hours every Saturday and moving to every other weekend after a month. This should be the temporary plan while the case proceeds and the parties can get an evaluation by a guardian ad litem to determine a workable long-term parenting plan. Thank you, Your Honor."

The commissioner looked over her reading glasses at Iris's mother, who was there without a lawyer. "Ms. Smith, you have five minutes."

"It doesn't make any sense to put Abby back with her drug addict mother. She might as well have abandoned her own flesh and blood when she went off and got herself on those drugs. And who had to care for her kid while she was off in prison going to college?" She stuck her finger in her chest. "Me. That's who. I took her kid in. I been feeding her. I been taking her to the doctors. I have to pay for her food and other stuff, and it ain't cheap to raise a kid. I think the only reason she wants her back is to get the welfare money, which ain't all that much anyway. And"—she pointed at Iris—"she'll probably just hook up with another junkie and ignore the kid, and I'll have her back in my lap before you know it."

"Anything else, Ms. Smith?"

"I guess not. This is just ridiculous. Junkies shouldn't be mothers. That's all I got to say."

"Brief reply, Ms. Delaney?"

"What's missing from the grandmother's argument is any information at all about how this child is doing. This court has no idea what the situation is at her current home. Ms. Thomas has proven that her circumstances have changed dramatically since this order was entered. And there is no doubt that all the research shows that children who lose their mothers to incarceration do infinitely better if they are reunited with their mothers. Ms. Smith has provided no evidence that it is not in Abby's best interest to be reunited with her mother at the soonest possible opportunity."

The commissioner sat thoughtfully on the dais. "Ms. Delaney, I have to admit that when I first read the parenting plan in this case, I was leaning toward not reuniting this child with her mother. But Ms. Thomas"—she looked at Iris—"your path back to the community has been very impressive, and I do believe that you have given up your previous life of addiction. And for that, I congratulate you." She paused.

"This court finds that it is in this child's best interest to have the parenting plan modified."

Iris gasped and began to cry.

"And I will enter the mother's temporary order for reunification therapy, and a gradual increase of time while a guardian ad litem can investigate and make permanent recommendations to this court."

Camille squeezed Iris's hand and handed her a tissue while the commissioner signed the court orders.

"Good luck to you, Ms. Thomas." The commissioner actually smiled at Iris, then quickly looked to the bailiff, who handed her a stack of papers as she called the next case.

CHAPTER TWENTY-FOUR

The only way to find Willow at this point—if she was, in fact, alive—would be to track down Malika. Trish had decided to return to Marlys's place, to see if she would provide even a tiny clue about where Malika might be. So far, the only lead was that Malika might have taken off for the mountains five years ago. Trish looked off into the distance at the looming Olympic Mountains and considered her options. Her dad was an avid hiker and mountain climber, and she'd learned firsthand about the various mountain peaks in the state while dining on freeze-dried hiking food in front of a chilly campfire all throughout her childhood. It made sense that Malika would head up into Olympic National Park. It was close to PA, and she'd hiked and camped there as a kid. The park encompassed the better part of the Olympic Peninsula and was surrounded on three sides by water: the Pacific Ocean, the Strait of Juan de Fuca, and the Salish Sea. Most of the mountain range was inside the national park, with some of the steepest peaks in the country. And then there was the Hoh Rain Forest on the west side of the mountains, which received more rain than anywhere else in the contiguous United States. Trish hopped in her car to go see what else she could find out from Marlys. En route, she picked up her phone and dialed her dad.

"Hi, Dad! I have a quick question."

"Hi, hon. Just a minute. I'm up on the roof taking down the Christmas lights. Let me get down the ladder."

"Wait. Is Mom there? Are you alone? What the hell are you doing on the roof?"

"I'm fine. Putting you in my pocket for a minute. Hang on."

There was no reasoning with her dad. He simply refused to believe that he was getting older and that he might want to consider slowing down.

"Okay. All good now. What's up, hon?"

Trish had the kind of relationship with her dad that did not require pleasantries.

"I'm working a cold case, and I need to find a woman who took off into the Olympics about five years ago. If you wanted to disappear into those mountains, where would you go?"

"You mean she's living up there somewhere? Or just off hiking?"

"No idea." Trish paused. "Let's assume she was living up there somewhere."

"Well, if she needed a job, I'd start with the visitor centers. There are three in the park, but the most popular one is up at Hurricane Ridge."

"We went there when I was a kid, right?"

"Yep. Way before you got into backcountry camping with me. Some of the centers are only open in the summers, as I recall."

"Anything there year-round?"

"Try the visitor center or the wilderness information center."

"Are they all up in the mountains?"

"I think the main visitor center is down in Port Angeles. The Hurricane Ridge one is up in the mountains."

"I think I'll start there. And is there any specific place up in the park where someone might go if they wanted to disappear?"

Trish's dad didn't miss a beat. "I've always wanted to do the Skyline Ridge Trail. It's, like, fifty miles long, but it's not exactly remote. Some of the year, I hear, it's pretty overrun with hikers."

"Is there anything that would qualify as really challenging, so there might be fewer people there?"

"I'd say the Olympic National Park Traverse."

"What's that one?"

"It's something like a hundred miles of trails that are kind of patched together. It's very difficult and has some huge elevation gain."

175

"So, not for a novice?"

"I wouldn't say so. You need to deal with snow, steep passes, cold weather, and lots of solitude."

"Wow. Sounds amazing."

"There are raging glacier-fed rivers, rocky terrain, and probably some of the most beautiful scenery you'll ever see. And you will never see a sky as deep blue as you do high up in those mountains."

"How do people get supplies up there?"

Trish's dad laughed. "You eat what you can carry. Lots of freeze-dried stuff, day in and day out."

"Well, I guess it's possible she'd go and try something really challenging. She was recently sober and seemed to want to prove something to herself."

"You sure your person wanted to disappear, or maybe just hang out in the mountains? And if she took off a few years ago, not sure your looking around up there now is going to give you any useful info."

"Well, when you're working a cold case, you have to start somewhere. Lots of times, you find clues, or people who have useful information."

"I don't expect you'll find many people up there at this time of year. Are you sure you aren't on a wild-goose chase?"

"I really don't know. But I have to try. I think I'll head up to Hurricane Ridge and see what I can find out."

"Okay, my dear. I need to get back to my Christmas lights."

"Just promise me that you'll let Mom hold the ladder for you."

"You bet. Love you, baby." He hung up.

He was lying, of course. Trish looked at the phone and shook her head.

Trish spent the rest of the drive out to Marlys's trying to put herself into Malika's mindset. Where would she want to go to get away from Quinn Hastings once and for all? And to try to drown her sorrow and stay sober after losing her parents and Willow? It would depend on her level of fitness and experience in the mountains. That might be something Marlys could shed some light on. But what if she had Willow with her? That would put this whole mountain expedition in a new light. Trish pulled into Marlys's driveway and was pleased to see the familiar silver Honda parked in the carport, sporting a brand-new set of tires.

"Hey!" Marlys hollered as she came out on her front porch, holding a tiny dog with tight curly hair.

"So cute." Trish gushed over the pup.

"Cute, but crazy." Marlys tousled the dog's hair and put him inside, where he immediately tried to crash his way through the screen door. "He's a handful." She turned toward the door. "Stop!" she commanded. The dog ignored her and lunged at the screen again.

"Pretty sure no one is going to sneak into your place with that little guard dog on duty," Trish joked.

"Nice to see you again. What's up?" Marlys shut the door and sat on the front steps.

"You mentioned the other day that Malika took off for the mountains. I do some winter climbing and was thinking that, when I'm up in the mountains, I could ask around to see if anyone knows her."

Marlys was clearly skeptical. "It's been, like, five years. And she made it very clear that she didn't want us following her or trying to find her."

"Well"—Trish sat next to Marlys—"what do you think? You know her better than anyone. Where do you think she is?"

"Why do you ask? We've kinda decided to leave her be. And my sister is still mad at her."

"I'm a kind of amateur sleuth, and I do some mountain rescue, so my interest is piqued."

"I do miss her," Marlys said quietly.

"And I bet you'd rest easier if you knew where she was. I'd love to put your mind at ease."

"Our family did a lot of car camping when we were younger, and Malika always wanted to do more serious hiking. Even though our basketball schedule kept us busy every summer, she managed to get up into the mountains whenever she could. Her goal was to learn to mountain climb, and she even learned to rock climb. I'm pretty sure that, at one point, she was up in the mountains."

"Was she pretty fit?"

"I guess so. After she got out of jail, she spent lots of time running on the beach out at La Push. She seemed really focused on being outside and running. And I read somewhere that some people replace their drug addictions with things like marathon running or rock climbing, so it made sense to me that she became a fitness nut."

"Especially since she was an athlete. It must have come naturally."

Marlys nodded. "She was an athlete way before she was a drug addict. So that makes sense."

"I have a feeling I might be able to find her," Trish said with more certainty than she felt. "I'm going to head up to the park and ask around. I'll let you know if I find anything,"

"I have a good feeling about this." Marlys was suddenly optimistic.

"I'll do my best." Trish was just about to say goodbye when a tall Black woman decked out for cold weather jogged up the driveway. Trish turned to Marlys, who held out her arm and introduced Trish to her sister Monique.

"Monique James, meet Patrice . . ." Marlys paused. "Sorry, I don't know your last name."

"Swanson. Patrice Swanson." Trish strode up to the third Franklin sister and shook her hand. "Nice to meet you." Her salutation was sincere.

"You too." Monique seemed a bit hesitant.

Marlys took over. "Turns out Patrice knew Malika in Seattle and has a background in mountain rescue and wants to take on our missing sis as her new project."

Monique didn't look impressed. "Uh, she's been gone for five years. I watch enough real-crime drama to know that this is what they'd call a cold case." Not a flicker of enthusiasm for Trish's offer to find their missing sister. In fact, Trish detected a bit of a glare in Monique's eyes.

Marlys put her arm around Monique. "What's the harm? We need some kind of closure on this."

Monique returned the hug and kissed her sister on the forehead. "Look, she's gone. Let it go." She turned to Trish. "Nice to meet you, but our family has been through enough. You should leave."

Marlys ignored her sister. She looked at Trish, who felt like she'd inadvertently walked into the middle of a family feud.

"Malika loved the mountains. It was her happy place," Marlys announced in a voice that was an octave above normal conversation.

She was clearly trying to make a point with her sister. "Ever since high school, she'd go up hiking around Hurricane Ridge. She was fearless. By the time she graduated, she'd gotten some kind of numerical qualification for rock climbing. We had no idea what she was talking about, but apparently it was a big deal. She was very proud of herself."

"Enough. You should go." Monique was adamant. "This is too hard on Marlys."

"What's the harm in telling Patrice that we know Malika's been seen up in the park? I'm tired of pretending like we have no idea where Malika is."

Trish tried to ignore the explosion in her chest. *Finally. A lead.*

Monique flashed an angry look at her sister. "She doesn't want to be found. Let's just respect that."

Trish ignored Monique and focused on Marlys. "When was the last time someone saw her?" She held her breath.

Marlys physically turned away from her sister and directed her attention fully at Trish. "Right before Christmas. She was leading a group of women doing some kind of snow climbing, or hiking. It sounded like she was some kind of leader—maybe teaching the women."

"You mean this past Christmas? Like a month ago?" Trish tried to stay calm.

"I took it as a sign of our Christmas angel sending us a message." Marlys's voice was featherlight.

Monique softened just a little bit. "We have no idea if that was Malika. Just because someone saw a Black woman leading a climbing group, that doesn't mean it was Malika."

"I know it was her. I just do."

Trish imagined Marlys as a little girl stomping her feet in an effort to make something happen.

"Intuition is often right in these situations." Trish was trying to find some common ground for the sisters.

Monique was fuming and Marlys looked like she was going to cry.

Trish needed to end this conversation and get busy. She finally had a lead to follow. "I can't imagine what your family has been through. If you don't want me to look for Malika, I'll back off," she lied.

"Good." Monique's visage was menacing. "Please just leave our family alone."

Trish turned toward her car and began to walk away.

"She was up near the visitors' center at Hurricane Ridge!" Marlys hollered just as Trish was about to close her car door.

CHAPTER TWENTY-FIVE

Turned out it was complicated, but not impossible, for a lawyer to get an appointment with a prisoner. Still, it had been a couple of weeks since she had applied for the meeting. Camille ran through her questions for Dr. Walters as she passed the winery tasting rooms in the quiet Seattle-adjacent city of Woodinville and wound her way toward Monroe Correctional Complex, located about an hour northeast of Seattle in the foothills of the Cascade Mountains.

The men's prison in Washington was even more imposing than the women's. It was surrounded by serious-looking cement walls topped with rolls of barbed wire and had the kind of guard towers one would expect at a high-security prison. Camille parked in the large gravel parking lot and stood looking up at the two-story building, with its formal stairway leading to two heavy doors. The Monroe Correctional Complex sat on top of a treeless hill amid a heavily forested area just outside of the town of Monroe, which had become an exurb of Seattle as the city spread to the northeast. The snowy Cascade Mountains towered several miles up Highway 2 to the east. Camille knew to leave her purse, phone, and other personal items in her trunk. As she closed it, she took a minute to soak in the view of the mountains, knowing that for the next hour or so, she'd be stuck in some cramped attorney-client meeting room. Camille turned up the wide cement steps holding only her car keys, a legal pad, and a pen, hoping they'd let her bring in something to take notes.

The guards at Monroe were just about as friendly as those in the women's prison, but by now Camille was familiar with the cold shoulder. She silently went through the metal detector, then waited in a dark hallway, where a guard pointed to a window in the wall with a small opening like one would see in a bank. Through the darkened window, Camille saw a guard who was half a floor higher than where she stood. He gestured for her to stick her hand through the opening at the bottom of the window, which she did. He stamped her hand with some kind of invisible ink and pointed at another heavy door at the end of the short hallway. The men's prison was dark and scary, unlike the women's prison, which looked more like a brick one-level high school punctuated by metal fencing, barbed wire, and gates but which was also flooded with light and had several courtyards. Here, there was no effort to make the place look like anything other than a giant, hellish monstrosity.

She followed a guard outside. They were buzzed through a metal gate in a chain-link fence and across a cement area, then buzzed into a low building. The oppression of the men's prison was overwhelming. Camille reminded herself to breathe as she was ushered into a tiny room with a small metal table bolted to the floor. There were two metal chairs across the table from each other, also bolted to the floor. There were guards visible at a console just outside the doorway. Again, they were positioned about half a floor over the rest of the open area, giving the impression that they were looking down over their subjects.

Camille's escort pointed at a chair and then turned toward the guard area. "We'll keep an eye on you." He had the voice of a heavy smoker. "Hit that button here next to the desk if you need out." He left the door ajar as he exited, leaving her alone in the stuffy room with a filthy window that had apparently been put in the door so the guards could watch the legal visits. A small nod to prison safety. She wondered if anyone could even see through it.

Camille's assumption that her "client" would be along shortly was sadly mistaken. Were the guards just leaving her hanging there because they could? Or was there some kind of logistic problem with bringing the prisoner to a lawyer visit? Well, she figured it didn't matter what the reason was and settled in for the wait. The walls of the tiny room began to close in on her as the minutes turned to hours. There was nothing to read, nothing to look at. As she resigned herself to an interminable wait, she turned her back to the guards and began to meditate. It was the only thing she could think of to do in the harsh, silent space.

At nearly the three-hour mark, the door opened, and a guard pushed a handcuffed man in the familiar prison khakis and gray sweatshirt into the room. The guard said nothing, just closed the door loudly.

Camille stood to greet the doctor. He had clearly been a handsome man at one time, but now he looked haggard and exhausted.

"I'm Camille Delaney. Thanks very much for meeting with me, Doctor."

The doctor's smile was subtle. "No, I should thank you. I have no idea why you're here, but it's always nice to have a visitor."

He looked so worn down.

"Any idea how much time we have?" Camille asked.

The doctor shook his head. "It's been a very long time since I had a legal visit. I have no idea how these work."

"Okay, well, let's get down to business."

The doctor sat and leaned his elbows on the table awkwardly because of the handcuffs. "I gotta say, I'm very curious to hear why you're here."

"I'm working on a case that seems quite similar to yours."

"How can I help?"

"Do you know Martin Zhao?"

The doctor stared quizzically at Camille and slowly nodded his head. "I do . . ."

"I believe that Zhao was involved in my friend's arrest."

"Oxy, right? It always comes back to oxy."

"Yes, oxy. I understand you got sucked into the oxy mishegas several years back."

"I sure did. I went down hook, line, and sinker. And by the time I figured out what was going on, I had unintentionally addicted too many patients to count." His visage of hopelessness was melting away as they spoke. He seemed happy to have someone to talk with.

"So, does Zhao somehow fit into what happened to you?" Camille asked.

"He has absolutely everything to do with why I'm here. He owned the main pharmacy in Port Angeles. Once the town docs started prescribing the oxy, he did everything he could to keep it flowing. He even set up a clinic where they handed out oxy without even seeing the patients. It was a poorly camouflaged drug operation."

"It sounds like, at some point, you figured out what was going on."

"I'm ashamed to say that it took me way too long to understand the depth of what Zhao was up to. Once the information started coming out about how the drug company had hoodwinked the doctors, I tried to get my patients weaned off of it. But for most, it was too late. I'd see them every day lined up in front of Zhao's fake clinic. It was heartbreaking."

"Well, you must have done something to piss Zhao off, because I'm about ninety-nine percent certain that he planted those drugs in your car."

"You got that right. I was on the verge of blowing the lid on his whole operation when I got pulled over one night. I had finally figured out who at the DEA to get in touch with, and I had all the evidence to show what was going on. And *bam*, red lights in my rearview mirror, and here I am. I was, and continue to be, convinced that Zhao was behind the whole thing."

"Did your lawyer try to get the search thrown out?"

"Oh yes. We tried everything. But—and I don't mean to step on your lawyer toes here—but there's something very fucked up called 'exigent circumstances' that allows cops to search without a warrant."

Camille felt her pulse quickening. "Exactly what were the so-called exigent circumstances that allowed for the search?" She held her breath.

"Amber Alert."

The exact same MO as Charli's arrest. Camille felt faint. Maybe it was sitting in that stagnant room for the past several hours, or maybe it was the frustration of seeing how Martin Zhao had set up both Charli and Dr. Walters. "Can you explain what your understanding was of the alleged Amber Alert?"

The doctor clearly took note. "'Alleged' is spot on. Someone had apparently reported a missing kid who'd last been seen getting into a black Toyota Camry. They reported the kid had been taken from a local park by a stranger."

"And you coincidentally happened to drive a black Camry, I take it."

The doctor nodded. "Why exactly are you here?"

"Because the exact same thing happened to Zhao's wife, a good friend of mine, and she's doing twelve years in WCCW after her car was searched during an Amber Alert. They found a kilo of heroin and a gun under her seat—so she got a gun enhancement on her sentence."

"Holy shit. That's exactly what happened to me." He paused for a moment. "And Zhao's wife is in prison? On a drug charge? Are you kidding me?"

Camille nodded. "It's a long story, and one that I'll tell you about sometime. But for now, I need to know everything about your arrest."

"Are you saying he did the same thing to his own wife?"

"It's beginning to look like it."

"What an asshole."

"You don't have to convince me of that," Camille agreed.

"Okay, so what's next? Is there any way to get this in front of a judge? Can this reduce my sentence? And if we can prove this was a setup, I expect this could get Zhao's wife out as well." For the first time since they'd started talking, the doctor had a hopeful glint in his eyes.

"I honestly don't know, but that's exactly why I'm here. And I'm very persistent."

The doctor began to tear up. "I've tried to resign myself to my fate here. I work with the men, teaching in their GED program, and I try to keep busy. But there's no way to explain the utter hopelessness I feel. Some of the men have come from horrible circumstances, and I do feel sorry for what brought them here. But you put this many men into a hellhole like this, and things become violent quickly. Some days, it's all I can do to try and stay alive."

"I can't imagine." Camille wanted to reach out and touch her new friend, but prison rules were branded in her mind.

"What do we do now?" he asked.

"Give me the name of your lawyer."

"Nichole. Robert Nichole. Do you know him?"

"I don't know any lawyers in Port Angeles."

"He's from Seattle. My dad insisted I hire a big-gun lawyer from the city."

"Oh! Is he a really, really tall dude?"

"Yep! That's him. He's like six nine or something."

"I know who he is. Do you stay in touch with him?"

"I haven't in a long time, but I can contact him, if that would be helpful."

"Do you still have the evidence about Zhao? About his running a drug ring, and an illegal clinic?"

"I sure do. My dad should have everything. And I think Robert would have it too."

Camille leaned over the table. "Is there anything you need in here, Doctor? I can see what I can do to get money on your commissary account. Or is there anything else you need?"

The doctor smiled. "That's very nice of you to ask. I'm okay. My parents keep my commissary account full, and I have everything I can get here inside. But lots of the guys have nothing. No one to send money. There's a nonprofit that sends books inside, so if you feel like letting your friends know, I'm sure they'd really appreciate some donations. The men really like to read, and it's almost impossible to raise money to help men in prison. And to be totally truthful, when they're in my GED class, they're actually very humble and appreciative. Their lives are just so messed up, they often can't stay calm and on track."

"What's the nonprofit?"

"Books Behind Bars."

"I'd be happy to get the word out." Camille stood. "I need to get back to my office now. I'm really glad to have met you. And I promise I'll do whatever I can do to help you, Doctor."

The doctor stood. "It's Henry. Please call me Henry."

"You can count on me, Henry." Camille waved at the guards, who were surprisingly responsive. One of them was at the door within a minute. She turned to Henry. "You have my word. I'll be back."

The doctor waved at her with his cuffed hands. "Thanks so much for coming."

The door clanged closed behind her.

CHAPTER TWENTY-SIX

The visitor center at Hurricane Ridge was only open on weekends in the winter, so Trish had to wait until Saturday to head out to see what she could learn about Malika. The center was about twenty miles south of Port Angeles, up in the jagged Olympic Mountains.

The weather was pleasantly nice for a January day, and Trish flipped on her aviator sunglasses, opened her window, and blasted her Brandi Carlile playlist on the stereo. It'd been a while since she'd been in the mountains, and she began to realize how much she missed hiking. At the chorus of "Broken Horses," she sang her heart out with Brandi.

The sky was an indescribable shade of blue, and the snow was almost blinding. Trish could feel the tension leaving her shoulders as the evergreen trees waved their arms, welcoming her back.

"Where are you, Willow?!" she shouted to no one in particular.

The visitor center was vaguely familiar. Trish's dad had reminded her that they'd been there together years ago. She felt like dancing as she approached the ranger at the information desk. On the way up, she'd decided how to play the next few minutes.

"Hi, there. I'm looking for an old friend who leads women's hiking groups up here. Does that ring a bell?"

The ranger pointed to a rack of brochures on the wall. "Nope. But there are lots of hiking groups that leave stuff here for novices." He gave Trish a blank look, sizing her up. "And there are some groups that lead more rigorous hikes, and some do climbing groups. If your friend leads groups here in the park, I'd start over there."

Trish hadn't considered that Malika might actually be running some kind of business leading hiking groups, so she spent a few minutes perusing the colorful trifold marketing materials carefully placed on the wall in a plastic stand. Nothing jumped out at her.

"My friend. She's Black," she said somewhat more loudly than she meant to.

The ranger quickly looked up from his computer. He paused and shrugged.

Trish wasn't going to give up easily. She pulled her phone out and showed the ranger the picture of Malika. "Could you just take a look, please? A friend said she saw her up here around Christmas."

The ranger shook his head. "Sorry, ma'am." He didn't even pretend to look at the picture.

Trish persisted. "I can't imagine there are very many Black women leading climbing groups up here."

"This is a big park; one thousand four hundred and forty-two square miles, to be exact. There's no way to know every climbing group up here." He turned back to his computer.

"Well, if I leave you my contact info, would you please let me know if you think of something that might help me find her?" She pulled out her Nemo notepad and wrote her name and number on a corner of a sheet of paper, ripped it off, and put it on the desk.

The ranger didn't look up. As Trish walked around the corner, he crumpled up the paper and threw it in the trash.

He knows her.

At noon, the sun was high in the sky, and Trish looked out over the breathtaking scene. *Might as well take a little hike as long as I'm up here in the clear air.*

The switchback trail up to Klahhane Ridge was exhausting but exhilarating. Trish couldn't wait to tell her dad she'd taken a day off to do some hiking. The views were incomparable. Trish felt a new surge of enthusiasm for her investigation. She was increasingly convinced that Malika could be found somewhere up or near the park. Marlys had confirmed that she'd been seen around Christmas, and the ranger had fallen for one of her oldest tricks. Give a witness your contact—if they throw it away, they usually know something they're not telling you. But what about Willow? It didn't seem like anyone could live off the grid with a child Willow's age. Or maybe Malika had created a life for her and Willow out here somewhere. If Willow was even still alive.

Just ahead of Trish were two women walking at a quick pace as though their goal was to get their heart rates up, not just to enjoy nature. Trish moved quickly to catch up with them and hollered hello from about six feet behind them. To Trish's surprise the women appeared to be in their midsixties—but man, were they fit.

The taller, skinny woman waved at Trish. "Hey! It's not often we find someone as crazy as us to be hiking this ridge in the winter!"

Her friend laughed. "True!"

"Actually, I haven't been up here since I was in high school, when my dad took me camping in the park here."

"Well, welcome back. You can't find a more spectacular place to spend a sunny Saturday here on the peninsula." The shorter woman, with a long gray ponytail, waved her arm as if to introduce Trish to the wilderness surrounding them.

Trish walked in lockstep with the speedy women. "You two are moving right along!"

"Dick Van Dyke says it best: keep moving!" The tall skinny woman pointed to herself. "I'm Ginny, and this is Birdie."

"Patrice."

"What brings you back to the mountains on this gorgeous day, Patrice?"

Trish decided to just get down to business. "Actually, I have a friend who leads women's groups up here in the park, and I'm trying to find her."

Ginny turned to Birdie. "There are several women's hiking groups out of PA. We come from Sequim, but we have lots of hiking friends in PA."

Birdie chimed in. "But the big place for hiking groups is in the Staircase area. There are some nice beginner hikes there, and I've seen a few women's groups. Some of the ladies didn't even know how to pitch a tent. It's so nice to see the women taking that on and learning to be independent in the mountains."

"Have you ever seen a tall Black woman leading a hiking group up here?"

The two women looked at each other. Trish noted their hesitation. Birdie spoke first. "Nope. Doesn't sound familiar."

Ginny glanced at Birdie. "Me neither," she said, almost too quickly.

"I'll try Staircase. Maybe someone down there will have seen her."

"You know, maybe Staircase isn't the place to start your search." Ginny sounded authoritative. "I'd try Madison Falls Trail. It's closer to PA, and more women's groups hike there."

"Good point. Start with Madison Falls," Birdie agreed swiftly.

They know more than they're saying. Trish grabbed her notebook out of her daypack and used the other half of the paper she'd given the ranger to write down her contact info. "Could you hang on to my contact info and let me know if you hear anything about a tall Black woman leading women's groups up here?"

Ginny reached out slowly. "Of course."

"Yes, of course," Birdie echoed.

As they walked around a bend in the trail, Trish spotted a large rock and said, "I think I'll sit here for a bit and drink in the scenery. It was very nice to meet you both. And now I'm even more inspired to get back to the mountains more often!"

Trish watched as Ginny wadded up her contact info and shoved it into her back pocket as the two women turned to the steep grade below them. In a minute they were gone.

What was that all about? There's no way those two don't know Malika. Them and the ranger. Why all the secrecy? Trish climbed up on a huge boulder and pulled a PowerBar out of her pocket to enjoy her last hour up in paradise, which of course reminded her of her favorite Brandi Carlile song. She took a deep breath and belted out the last lines of "You and Me on the Rock" into the wild.

CHAPTER TWENTY-SEVEN

The drive back to Port Angeles was about a half hour. Trish blasted the stereo as she drove down the twisty, curvy road. She barely noticed the phone vibrating on the seat next to her.

"Damn." She missed the call. It was Johnny Jenkins. She told her phone to call him back.

"Hey. I got something for you."

Trish took a drink of water. "What's up?"

"Jing is back!"

"What? Are you kidding me? She's been gone since around when Malika took off, right? Have you spoken with her?"

"Yeah. That fancy condo's been sitting empty since she left. Must be nice to be rich. Then she reappears and it's like she'd never been gone. She was so gracious when I welcomed her back. She's really a lovely lady. No idea where she took off to. But she's for sure more engaged than before. Yesterday she asked me about the Seahawks score, which was unusual for her. She used to be pleasantly tight lipped around me."

"Any idea where she's been?"

"Nope. But one thing I did notice is that she seems way more clearheaded."

"Well, didn't you say that she was recovering from surgery when Malika was there?"

"Yeah, but it's not just that. She's tracking better. Something is different."

"You told me that she was strung out on oxy. Maybe she got off of it?"

"Maybe . . ." Johnny sounded thoughtful.

"Okay, let's think about this. I feel like I need to get down there and talk with her. She might know something. Any ideas about how we can make that happen?"

"She's become a bit of a fitness buff. She said doing the hip rehab turned her on to yoga, which she does every day here in the gym, downstairs in the condo complex. Maybe you can run into her down there?"

"That could work. Can you get me in there? Like, tomorrow?"

"I don't see why not. Like I said, she's a chatterbox these days. She'd probably love to have someone to talk to while she does her yoga and weight routine."

Trish got practical. "Does she have a time of day she usually hits the gym?"

"Yep, I usually see her come down midmorning. If you show up around eight, you'll probably catch her sometime in the next hour or two."

"Okay. I need to run by the boat and grab some stuff. I can probably catch a six p.m. ferry back to Seattle tonight so I can get over to Bellevue bright and early."

"Boat? What boat?" Johnny was curious. "I might need to go into the private eye biz."

"I'll explain later. Gotta go, see you tomorrow morning."

She dialed Camille. "How'd it go at the prison?"

"Oh my God. That poor doctor. He got Zhao'd just like Charli did."

"'Zhao' is a verb now?" Trish laughed. "I like it."

"Does Amber Alert sound familiar?"

"Holy crap. Seriously?"

"Yep. Henry—that's the doc—was closing in on Martin's illegal drug operation. Just like Charli said, Martin was selling heroin and other illegal drugs to all the folks whose docs were refusing them more oxy. And listen to this: he even opened a clinic in PA where he hired some kind of providers to prescribe oxy basically without even evaluating the patients. He's got the whole town on oxy lockdown."

"I bet he's doing it in other towns as well."

"Probably. But we're getting plenty of evidence on this one. I think we're close to being able to take this all to the prosecutors. I spoke with my old pal Trent Conway, the King County prosecutor in Seattle, to find out what it will take for him to file a motion to set aside Charli's conviction."

"And I bet he told you that we're going to need a witness who can confirm all this circumstantial evidence."

"Pretty much. But he's definitely open to further discussions. Funny thing is that he was also one of my mom's students in crim law at SU Law."

"Your mom pops up at the most opportune times."

"Yeah. He mentioned that he appreciated her relentless pursuit of truthful and honest convictions. If this isn't one, he's willing to reopen it." Camille added hopefully, "All we need is evidence of the actual planting of the drugs. And somehow that doesn't seem like it's going to be very easy. I have a meeting with him this afternoon—fingers crossed."

Trish could feel Camille's frustration. She changed the subject. "Guess who I'm going to meet with tomorrow?"

"The witness who can tie this whole thing together?"

"Who knows? Sometimes evidence shows up in the least-expected places," Trish said. "Johnny just called and told me that Jing is back at the condo. I'm going over there tomorrow morning to see if I can talk with her."

"Wow. Any idea where she's been?"

"Nope. But Johnny says she's more lucid than she was when Malika and Willow were there. She was really suffering after her hip surgery, and fully on the oxy. Maybe she's weaned off it. Hopefully, I'll find out more tomorrow."

"Okay, and I think I'm going to pop up to PA this week." Camille added, "Sam has a conference in New York, and he's been planning to take Gracie along with him for a father-daughter getaway. I'll ask Gigi if Libby and Angela can stay with her for a few days. I really want to talk with Rose after I meet with Trent, and hopefully we'll have some good news and we can let her know what we're working on."

"Cool. When can you be here?"

"I have a court hearing tomorrow morning. If Gigi agrees to watch the girls, I can be there late tomorrow afternoon."

"Perfect. How about we meet up on the ferry from Seattle. I think there's a two p.m. boat. I will hopefully have talked with Jing by then and have some info."

"Okay. Let's be in touch midday tomorrow."

"Wait a sec—don't hang up," Trish commanded. "You know how to bowl?"

"Um . . . no. Why do you ask?"

"Robin invited me to a women's bowling league! I haven't bowled in years. Sounds like a good way to blow off some steam and get to know some of the local women."

"Bowling? Really?" Camille was less than thrilled.

"According to Robin, it's a huge monthly event for the women in the PA area. Rose is gonna be there."

"On second thought, can't imagine anything I'd rather do on a weekday night than bowling in Port Angeles. Amy's calling. Gotta run. See you tomorrow."

CHAPTER TWENTY-EIGHT

The gym in the Braeburn was impressive not just for its size, but for the fact that it was surprisingly well equipped. *I guess you get what you pay for.* Trish sat on a bench and grabbed a couple of thirty-pound weights and began doing a set of shoulder presses, keeping her eye on the door.

After about thirty minutes, a couple in their midsixties strode up to the stair-climbing machines and turned on the wall-mounted TV. There was nothing Trish hated more than the sound of a TV in a gym—but on second thought, it would likely drown out her hoped-for conversation with Jing.

As she moved on to the heavier weights for leg presses, her phone lit up with a text: *Incoming!* It was Johnny. She positioned herself so she could see the doorway.

Jing was exactly as described. Very tiny, and even in leggings and a T-shirt, there was a sense of glamour mixed with an intangible bit of power. Even if she wasn't there specifically to meet Jing, Trish would have headed over to her like a magnet.

The man on the stair-climber said something to Jing that Trish couldn't hear, and Jing responded with something between a laugh and a sweet giggle. As she got closer to Trish, Trish could see a bevy of gold necklaces hidden under Jing's light-pink T-shirt, and her ears sparkled with a row of what were probably actual diamonds and jewels. Pretty big ones. Her thick gold bracelet was surrounded by several gold chains on her wrist, and at least one narrow diamond chain. Not exactly what you'd see on someone who was about to engage in a strenuous workout.

Jing began by doing some hip flexor stretches, followed by some shoulder and back stretches. And then she sat on the mat, legs extended, and bent her torso over so that her head was very nearly touching her knees. On the second rep, her head easily touched her knees. *Very impressive.*

Trish placed her weights gently on the floor and went over to Jing. "Wow. You're so flexible. How long did it take you to touch your head to your knees?"

The petite woman smiled slyly. "One year. Physical therapy." Her accent was pronounced. "I work very hard. I have excellent physical therapist."

"You sure do." Trish's admiration was genuine.

"And very good yoga fitness instructor."

Jing continued her stretching seated on the floor, one leg over the other as she twisted around so her torso was nearly facing the wall behind her. Trish sat and followed Jing's lead.

"Very nice." Jing directed Trish almost harshly, "Sit up more straight, tuck your chin."

Trish held back a laugh. It wasn't often that anyone offered her instructions in the gym. She was accustomed to being the teacher, not the student. Still, Jing had a presence about her that pretty much demanded compliance.

"How's this?" Trish sat up tall and twisted her torso.

"Many more better." Jing sat cross-legged and somehow managed to get up without touching the floor with her hands.

"Nicely done." Trish stood in the same manner as Jing had.

They spent the next several minutes with Jing leading Trish in a series of complex stretching and yoga-inspired fitness moves.

After a three-minute plank, Jing sat back on her haunches. "You do not live here. Why you are here?" Her eyes narrowed and pierced through Trish.

There was something about Jing that made Trish feel like she'd known her forever. This wasn't the time to engage in small talk and her typical PI spiel. "You're right, I don't."

"So what you want?" Jing extended her neck so that her face seemed to be reaching for Trish.

Trish glanced around to see if anyone else was still in the gym and was relieved to see that the stair-climbing couple was wiping down the equipment and turning off the big TV. She paused as the couple gathered their water bottles and towels and exited the room.

Jing raised an eyebrow as if to say *I'm waiting . . .*

Here goes. "I'm a friend of Johnny's, and I'm looking for Malika. I'm hoping you can help me."

Jing sat down on the mat by crossing her legs and lowering herself easily down to a cross-legged seated position. She put her elbow on her knee, cradling her chin in her hand.

Trish was mesmerized.

Jing knew how to command attention. She waited for several minutes before she spoke.

"You know where I been?" She didn't wait for an answer. "I been in rehab." She looked around the gym and lowered her voice. "Drugs rehab."

Well, that explained Johnny's comment about her seeming to be more clearheaded.

Surprised by Jing's forthrightness, Trish hesitated. *So, let's get it all out on the table.*

"Drug rehab?" It was all she could think of to say while she considered her next move.

Jing got right to the point. "My son. He got me on the drugs after my hip operation. Lots of drugs. He owns pharmacies."

"You sure look good now." Trish meant it.

"Ya, but that rehab was hell. If you never take that oxy, don't ever start."

"Well, it must've been really hard to get off those drugs. So, congratulations."

"You not here to talk about my drugs. You looking for Malika."

Trish nodded.

"You know what? She was on the drugs too. And we both had to get off the drugs." She leaned forward. "Both of us," she whispered loudly.

"You were in treatment with Malika?"

"No. Not together at treatment, but we both had to get off the drugs." Jing narrowed her gaze and jutted out her chin. "And we both did."

"Do you know where Malika is now?" Trish tried to modulate her breathing.

"No."

Trish felt the blood drain from her face.

"But I talk with her." Jing paused. "Sometimes."

Trish felt like she was on a roller coaster, up one minute and down the next. "But you don't know where she is?"

"I don't ask. But I send her money. She is very poor girl."

"Where do you send the money?"

"I send money on the Venmo." Jing smiled.

"How'd you get in touch with her?"

"She text me."

"How long ago?"

Jing pulled back. "Why you ask so many questions?"

"I used to be a detective. Now I'm an investigator. I help families find their loved ones sometimes."

Jing twisted her mouth sideways. "Doesn't make any sense. Her sister know how to reach her." She stood up as if to leave.

Her sister knows where she is?

"Are you sure her family knows where she is?"

"Not her family. Her one sister."

"Do you know which sister?"

"The one she have a big fight with."

"Any idea what they were fighting about?" Trish asked.

"I don't ask. But Malika tell me she never want to see her sister again. Ever."

Probably Monique. That might explain why she was so dead set against me looking for Malika up in the mountains.

Trish tried to gather her thoughts.

"Why you really looking for her?" Jing persisted.

Nothing to lose at this point. Jing is nobody's fool.

"Well, I'm actually looking for Willo—I mean, Ju," she stammered.

"Ju? She gone. We can't find her. I look already."

"You looked for her?"

Jing nodded. "Yes. But no one can find her."

Trish gingerly sat down next to Jing. She spoke softly. "Can you tell me how you looked for her?"

Jing's imposing demeanor was cracking. "I hire private detective. Just like you. He cannot find Ju." She began to cry. "They said Ju die in a fire. But I do not believe. So, I hire man to go find her. He no good. Did not find my Ju."

Trish remembered Rose telling her about the suits from Seattle who descended on PA not long after the fire. *It wasn't Martin. It was Jing.*

Jing continued. "My brother. He help me. He own big freighter ship company. He have lots of money. He love Ju very much."

"So the PI believed that Ju died in the fire?"

"PI man didn't work very hard. I bet you are much smarter than him. We should hire woman. We are much smarter. And don't ever give up."

Trish smiled.

"That man give up."

"Sounds about right."

Jing leaned over conspiratorially. "Now what we do?"

Trish took charge of the conversation. "Why do you think she didn't die in the fire?"

"No body found." Jing's voice returned to the subtle power she held.

"Yeah, I know." Suddenly this little powerhouse felt like a colleague. "I've spent a good deal of time up in PA, and I'm not convinced that Ju died in that fire either."

"I hire you now. You find her."

"I'm already on the case. You don't need to hire me."

"Well, I am here to help. I need to find Ju."

"Okay, do you have a few minutes more to talk? I have some questions."

"This pretty much all I do these days. Work out in gym. Do yoga. Play mah-jongg. Getting boring."

Trish held out her hand. "Well, welcome to Team Ju."

Jing reached out her thin hand and gave Trish a high five. "What you want to know?" She was all business.

"When did you first hear from Malika?"

"She text me a few years ago. Say she get out of jail. Jail! Malika in jail! So awful."

"Why was she in jail?"

"Drugs. Oxy. And stealing stuff."

"Probably to support her drug habit," Trish added.

"Rich people. Like me? We get on the drugs and we go to rehab. I never arrested." She sounded like she was spitting the words out of her mouth. "Poor girl like Malika? She go to jail."

It wasn't often that Trish was left speechless, but she was getting pulled under Jing's spell. The last thing she'd expected was for Jing to be lecturing her on inequalities of the criminal legal system.

"Before she go to jail, she get into some kind of public treatment at the jail system. But then she get out and back on the oxy." Jing looked seriously at Trish. "She have a very bad boyfriend. He get her back on the drugs. She get arrested for a second time and go to jail."

"I met the boyfriend." Trish couldn't stop the words from falling out of her mouth. She hadn't planned to disclose this much to Jing during their first meeting. But there she was, opening up to her new colleague, almost as if she couldn't help herself.

"Bad. Right?"

"Yes. Very bad." Trish thought better of telling Jing exactly how bad that asshat was to Malika and Ju. She redirected the conversation back to Willow.

"Does Malika think Ju died in the fire?"

Jing nodded. "She tell me Ju died. I don't believe it."

"Do you think Malika believes it?"

"Says so. I not so sure. But she seem very sad."

"Any chance Ju is still with Malika?"

Jing hesitated. "I am not sure. Malika is very secret. But if she is, I need to find her."

"How often do you talk with her?"

"At first I do not talk. I text only. My son, he was very in my business."

Trish let the comment about the son go for the moment. "Do you save the texts?" That would almost be too good to be true.

"No way. My son. He is very nosy. I keep Malika private."

"Why?"

"He hate Malika. Really hate her. He is trying to find her. He wants Ju."

Trish knew that Jing was holding back, but for now, it didn't matter that Martin hated Malika. And of course he wanted Ju. "When did you two last text?"

"Maybe before Christmas," Jing said thoughtfully.

"Just texting to say happy holidays?"

"She have a charity now. She help other women get off the drugs."

Trish perked up. "Do you know the name of the charity?"

Jing nodded. "Yes. Now instead of me give money to Malika, I give to her charity."

This is golden!

"Do you have the name?"

"Something like climbing women. Can't remember exactly."

"Can you look it up on your Venmo?"

"I get scared that my son find out I'm Venmoing money, so I cancel my Venmo and I gave money on my credit card."

"Great. So let's look it up on your card."

"I stopped on the credit card because my son get into my card. He did not find the money was going to Malika, but I get scared, so I cancel that card and now I just give cash to her friend who picks it up from me. Like I tell you, she is very secret."

Getting closer.

"Is there a way I could find that friend?"

"We wait until Malika calls me."

"I thought you two only text."

"Malika very afraid of my son. He is very scary to her. Now she will never answer my text because she's never sure it's me. Now she only call me on her phone. Calls it a burner phone."

"Did you ever tell Malika that you won't send money unless she tells you where Ju is?"

"No."

"Why not?"

"Because I am afraid she will disappear and I will no longer have any chance to find Ju."

CHAPTER TWENTY-NINE

The King County Courthouse took up a full city block halfway between the financial district and the stadiums in downtown Seattle. In the past decade, the area around the courthouse had progressively been overtaken by life on the streets. Homeless people mingled around the dilapidated bus stop in front of the courthouse doors. And the litigants, lawyers, and jurors stood nervously in the long line snaking out of the entryway and down the block. The wait to get through security often involved having to step over or avoid contact with individuals suffering the ravages of addiction. The looks on the faces of the people with the familiar tags of jurors told a story of their shock and disbelief that there was an active drug trade going on in such proximity to where justice was supposed to be served.

Camille hurried up the hill and crossed the street to the city building where there was another security line—this one on the basement level, where one could usually breeze through security fairly quickly—and in any event, it was warm and dry. She joked with the security guards as she passed her backpack through the X-ray machine and took off into the underground tunnel that landed her on the first floor of the courthouse, where she stood in the sea of jurors and litigants in the high-ceilinged lobby. Getting in an elevator just after the lunch break was always a challenge. Her longtime strategy was to ignore the bank of twelve elevators circling the lobby and just choose a few and wait for one of them. Running to and fro between elevator banks had always proved futile.

Once she'd made it upstairs, Trent Conway, one of the most senior of the deputy prosecutors in King County, stood to greet her when she walked into his office. "It's been a while, my friend."

Camille smiled. "Last time we saw each other was in Judge McIntyre's courtroom, when you showed up just in time to arrest my fave defendant."

Trent laughed. "That was classic for sure." He pointed at a fake leather chair in his cramped office.

As Camille was making her way between the piles of paper neatly stacked on the floor of the office, she commented, "When I have more time, I gotta tell you about the doc you arrested. Crazy story." She sat. "But our time is limited, so that will have to wait."

Trent pulled out his phone and looked at the screen. "I have about twenty minutes. You want to talk about a motion to get some friend of yours out of WCCW?"

"Yep. She was set up, and I'm getting close to being able to prove it."

Trent smiled. "I know that no lawyer daughter of Pella Rallis would want to hear how difficult it is to prevail on a CR 7 motion. But that said, I'm all ears—just for you." He made an exaggerated gesture of putting down his phone. "Talk to me."

"Okay. My friend was busted for having a trunkload of heroin."

"Well, that sucks."

"And a gun under her seat."

"Well, that likely got her a nice fat gun enhancement on her sentence."

"Her husband turns out to be a drug dealer . . ."

"Camille, this isn't a first for the department. Wives get busted for running drugs for their husbands all the time. You gotta give me more than that."

"Hang on, I'm getting to that." Camille continued quickly. "Her husband is a pharmacist who owns a string of pharmacies where he hands out oxy pills by the thousands. And now he's expanded into selling illegal drugs. Heroin, meth, and more recently, fentanyl."

"Go on . . ."

"My friend discovered what was going on and was about to turn him in when she coincidentally got arrested, as did her boyfriend, who happens to be the dealer's brother."

"Oh, what a tangled web we weave. Why is nothing ever straightforward in the world of criminals?" Trent asked no one in particular. "Tell me about the arrest."

"She got pulled over, and the cop told her he could search her trunk because her car matched one that had just been called in as an Amber Alert."

"Well, that's a clever one."

"Yeah, they faked the exigent circumstances that allow for a cop to search the car, which would obviously be illegal otherwise."

"Exactly. So I'm not sure how I can helpfully respond to a CR 7 motion, if that's all you got."

"What if we could prove that the Amber Alert was falsely reported?"

"Not good enough. What else you got?"

"He did this same thing to a doc over in Clallam County when the doc was about to turn in the same dealer. See a pattern here?"

"I do, but my kick-ass crim law prof, Ms. Pella Rallis, taught me that in order to overturn a conviction, we need something called evidence. You might remember that whole concept from the bar exam."

"I know. I'm working on it. I just need to know what evidence would be helpful."

"Oh, I dunno. Maybe, like, a witness?"

"Very funny."

"Or a confession from the guy who planted the drugs?" Trent shrugged.

"Even funnier."

"Hey, counsel, I'm not saying we won't work with you and evaluate the evidence once you find something we can work with. I'm just saying that, so far, I haven't heard anything that helps your friend in any meaningful way."

"You know Rose Adams?"

"Of course! I love Rose. Always brought a fair fight to the courtroom. But I haven't seen her in years. Whatever happened to her?"

"You won't believe this—she's the new Clallam County prosecutor!"

"Finally saw the light and left the dark side," Trent joked.

"Actually, she's doing some very progressive stuff over there. Lots of her defendants are going into diversion programs."

"Good for her." Trent nodded with approval. "No need to clog up our already overflowing jails and prisons with addicts who just need treatment. Unless they persist in committing more crimes to feed their habits."

"If I bring both of you evidence, can you work together to get these two innocent people out?"

"I can't say for sure until I see what you've got, but I'm open to it."

Camille stood. "I gotta head out to catch a ferry. All I need is to bring you a witness, right?"

"Well, that would at least be a good start." Trent walked around his desk and shook Camille's hand. "Tell your mom I said hi. She was the best prof I ever had, and honestly, I don't think I'd be where I am today without her encouragement."

Camille gave Trent a thumbs-up and hurried down the hallway toward the elevator bank. After three full elevators passed her by, she pushed into the marble stairwell and ran down the five flights. A witness? How the hell was she ever going to find one of those?

—

Trish was already hunkered down on her laptop in the fifth row of the port side of the ferry, which had become their regular meetup place on the huge boat. Camille plopped down next to her in her business suit and the sneakers she'd changed into in the car.

Trish looked up. "I talked with Jing."

"And?"

Trish smiled. "So close, yet so far. She's been in touch with Malika." She leaned back in her seat. "But she doesn't know where she is. *And* she thinks Willow is still alive but has no evidence to prove it."

"Oh my God."

Trish nodded. "Jing's been in rehab and is off the oxy. She hired a private investigator and seems very intent on finding Willow." She paused. "And as an aside, she's a buff little yoga-fitness diva with a personality to match. She's actually super cool. How about you? Any luck with Trent?"

"About what you'd expect. He's open to a motion, but without evidence, we're sunk. It's clearly not enough to just show that both Charli and the doc were framed by Martin."

"Both of them did motions about the searches, right?"

"Yeah, but it's not illegal to search a car if there's a possibility that a kidnapped kid might be in the trunk. That's the whole point of an Amber Alert. Cops can do lots of things that would otherwise be illegal so long as there are exigent circumstances."

"I know, but this is so frustrating. I'm going to see if there's any way to find out who called in an Amber Alert when Charli was arrested."

"Don't you think it's too late?"

"I have no fucking clue, but we need to do something to get Charli home."

"Any chance at all that we can find a witness?"

"Snowball's chance in hell."

The two longtime friends looked at each other, each wishing that the other would magically find the evidence they needed.

Trish interrupted the silence. "Oh, and I met two women up on Hurricane Ridge who I think probably know where Malika is."

"Seriously?"

"Yeah, and the ranger up at the visitors' center also might have some information. I need to find a way to befriend some of them. Everyone denies knowing anything about her. But to be honest, a lone Black woman up in the park teaching hiking and climbing would be unusual enough that people are going to know about her."

"So, what's next?"

"The hiking women were from some women's group over in Sequim. I might need to consider joining a hiking group this week. I need to get to know them. Build trust. I'm pretty sure they know something."

"What about the ranger—any follow-up with him?"

"I'm considering my options," Trish said as she looked off at the roiling waves out the ferry window.

Camille pulled her laptop out of her backpack and booted it up so she could answer the rapidly growing list of emails from Amy and her clients, who were all getting a little cranky that they hadn't heard from their lawyer lately. She began responding to them one by one.

"Bingo!" Trish held up her hands as though declaring a touchdown. "Secretary of State website says that the company that owns the pharmacy in PA is the chain owned by Zhao."

"Now we're getting somewhere."

CHAPTER THIRTY

Whatever Camille had expected at a women's bowling night, this wasn't it. Admittedly, she hadn't actually been in a bowling alley since college, but still. Bowling seemed to be almost an afterthought at this place. There was a long bar that ran almost the entire length of the wall behind the twelve bowling lanes. And between the lanes and the bar were tables and booths for diners and bar patrons. Each booth had its own little electronic jukebox, and the entire place was filled with some kind of laser-light show that pulsed along with the live all-woman country-western band on a huge stage to the right of the lanes. The place was filled with women drinking and laughing and intermittently bowling. Some of the tables had been pushed together to hold plates of apps, pitchers of beer, and a few open bottles of wine. There was hardly a place to sit in the packed venue.

Camille and Trish turned in their boots for new-looking pink bowling shoes, complete with lights that blinked when they walked.

"You're gonna bowl?" Trish poked at her friend.

"Hell no, but who could pass up these rad shoes with flashing lights?" Camille swept her hand downward to show off her new footwear.

As they mingled over to the bar to order drinks, Rose waved at them from lane seven just before she planted herself into a classic bowling pose and swung the ball straight down the lane for a strike. She pivoted and high-fived the bench of partying women as another got up and grabbed what looked like her own customized ball from the ball return. Rose slapped her opponent on the rear end, in a poorly disguised effort to throw her off her game. Camille and Trish looked on approvingly as Rose's opponent slid on one foot and one knee and willed her ball to the left. Two pins were left standing, which the woman dispensed with quickly once her ball returned to her.

Rose grabbed her beer and came over to greet her two friends.

"You're a pretty serious bowler," Camille commented.

Rose laughed. "You grow up in PA, you learn how to bowl. It was pretty much our only legal entertainment when I was in high school. I was captain of the high school bowling team." She pulled back her leather jacket and exposed a well-worn T-shirt from her time at PA High.

"Very nice." Trish's admiration showed.

"You bowl?" Rose asked.

"Haven't bowled in a while," Trish responded as she fingered a marbled-yellow bowling ball.

Rose looked up at the electronic leaderboard. "You're in luck, we just finished this round." She leaned over the computerized player list and asked Trish how to spell her name.

Camille offered, "T—"

Trish quickly interrupted. "It's Patrice. P-A-T-R-I-C-E." She gave Camille a quirky smile.

"You're up!" Rose turned to the women on the bench, who were comparing their crazy bowling manicures, and introduced them to Trish. "Ladies, Patrice here is taking my spot for a bit." She turned expectantly to Camille and laughed knowingly as Camille declined to take a spot on the team.

The bowlers stood, and each introduced themselves to Trish. And then Camille watched in astonishment as Trish bowled a strike, ending in a pose that looked like it could have been on the cover of a bowling magazine.

Rose clapped approvingly. "Nice form!"

Trish grinned widely.

"I had no idea," Camille yelled over the music.

Trish shrugged and winked and sat next to her new bowling partners, who each offered a funny multipart handshake ending in a fist bump.

Camille looked around the room at the women of all ages and likely differing political beliefs and socioeconomic status and marveled at the camaraderie of the disparate crowd. Across the room, she spotted Robin sitting with a bunch of women all wearing green-and-white T-shirts with the Port Angeles High logo. Teachers, most likely. Camille waved wildly at her friend, who ran over to give Camille a hug.

"What on earth? Has hell frozen over? Camille Delaney at a country-western bowling bash?"

Camille laughed. "Stranger things have happened. This place is very cool. I might even take up bowling." She filled a short plastic glass with white wine from the table loaded with drinks and food and popped a cheesy jalapeño in her mouth. "Yum."

"Okay, this is too much. Now you're eating bowling food." Robin shook her finger at Camille. "This might not be organic, you know."

Camille faked spitting out the app and then opened her mouth to show Robin that she'd eaten the whole thing in one gulp.

Robin looked at Rose. "You have no idea what you're creating right here. City slicker lawyer raves about the culinary delights at the bitchin' bowling bash!"

Rose laughed and pulled Camille over to introduce her to some of the lawyers on her legal team at the prosecutor's office.

"This is my friend and the daughter of the best damn crim law prof on the West Coast," Rose yelled. "Meet Camille Delaney."

The group of very young lawyers raised their glasses in a toast. "Welcome!"

Rose sat and pulled a chair over for Camille and prodded a young woman to move over a bit. "Sorry, Sheila."

The young woman moved her chair to let Camille fit in.

"Sheila, meet my friend Camille. Her mother was my best-ever law school prof." Rose turned to Camille. "Sheila is one of my assistants and is about to take the LSAT. She's going to be a great lawyer someday."

Camille smiled. "We can use more lawyers like Rose, that's for sure. Good luck on your LSAT!"

Rose changed the subject. "Not that I want to mar this event with business, but how's your cold case coming along?"

Camille wiped her fingers with a magenta-and-white paper napkin. "We're getting a bit closer to finding Malika, the woman who might either have the missing baby or might at least know where she is. So that's good."

"Must be a big relief for that little girl's family."

"Actually, I think I told you that her mother is in WCCW. And I think we may have found a way to get her out on a CR 7 motion."

"What? You're filing a Rule 7 motion?"

"You know CR 7 allows for the overturning of a verdict when justice requires it."

"And when was the last time you saw that maneuver actually work?"

"I'm no criminal lawyer. But as far as I can tell, it's the only hope for wrongfully convicted people, so I might have to file one." She paused. "As soon as I get more evidence."

"What county?"

"King."

"Thank God. I can't imagine how the public would respond to a court granting a CR 7 motion here in Clallam County."

"Thanks for the vote of confidence." Camille smiled.

Rose put down her beer. "You're taking on a huge uphill battle, my friend. You know Conway will oppose whatever you file."

"I assumed he would."

Rose moved closer to Camille as if getting ready to tell her a secret. Her voice lowered an octave. "Okay, now that I've done my best to warn you not to even attempt this flier of a motion, the former defense lawyer in me is dying to know what you have up your sleeve."

Camille scooted closer. "I think Trish told you that we were looking for that doc that you sent to Monroe for the trunkful of heroin?" Her tone was conspiratorial.

Rose nodded. "That one wasn't hard to remember. A nice guy. No priors. Ends up going down for heroin. Didn't ever seem to add up to me."

"Do you remember that the search happened because of an Amber Alert?"

Rose paused and thought for a minute. "Not really. But it sounds familiar."

"Well, it turns out that that's exactly why our friend Charli's car got searched. Amber Alert. And then a trunk full of heroin."

"And?"

"And both of them were about to turn in a guy who's running a barely legal oxy ring and then branched out into heroin and whatever else he can foist off on folks around here."

"Jesus. You have evidence?"

"We're working on it."

Rose put her arms on the table and put her head down like a kid in school who'd gotten in trouble. She looked up. "Just tell me that you're not going to jump in to represent the doctor and file a Rule 7 motion up here."

"I think I have my hands full over in King County." Camille was beginning to feel the weight of what she was taking on. "But if I find evidence that exculpates the doctor, I'll for sure share it with his legal team."

"Well, shit. I kinda like this job, and there's no way I'm going to officially cooperate with a CR 7 motion on this flimsy story."

"I know, I know," Camille said quickly. "I'm gonna come up with something good."

"Good. You're gonna need something pretty impressive to share with the doc's lawyer if you expect my office not to vigorously oppose overturning a sentence on a guy that the community thinks was poisoning us with a shit ton of heroin."

The two women were silent for a moment, when the band stopped playing.

"Okay, ladies!" the lead singer in sequined blue jeans yelled to silence the crowd. "Quiet!" She stuck two fingers in her mouth and let loose a piercing whistle.

The women shushed each other. One started snapping her fingers, and before long, the entire room was filled with laughing women who were clicking their fingers in rhythm. The lead singer let loose a short melody and danced in time with the finger clicking and motioned for the woman on the drums to join in.

The room quieted.

"As you all know, each month here at the bash, we choose a non-profit to support with our vast financial resources."

The crowd laughed. And one woman hollered, "Yeah, a bunch of millionaires right here!"

The lead singer pointed at the heckler. "You know as well as I do that the majority of charity donations come from folks like us."

More clapping and a few choruses of "Yes!"

"Might be because those of us who live real lives know what it's like to go without. Or to have a friend or family member become addicted." She raised a hand. "We've been there, haven't we, ladies?"

More audience appreciation.

"Tonight we're raising money for an awesome program created especially for women who are coming out the other side of addiction or domestic violence, which I believe lots of us know a thing or two about."

The audience erupted in finger clicking.

"Please give your attention to Ginny Christopher. She's from the Women Who Hike group over in Sequim." The singer handed the mic to a tall skinny woman with long wavy gray hair. "Ginny, tell us about the org we're supporting tonight!"

Ginny seemed a bit nervous as she held the mic. "Can y'all hear me?"

The audience gave her a thumbs-up.

"I'm a member of a women's hiking group over in Sequim. Well, we have several members over here in PA as well." She looked over the crowd and pointed at a few other gray-haired women, laughing and holding up their glasses.

Ginny continued. "The organization we're raising money for tonight is a bit unusual. It's very private and confidential." She paused. "You see, it's for women who've gotten hooked on drugs then ended up in jail or prison, which as we all know is the last place someone with addiction belongs."

The women murmured among themselves.

"I won't ask for a show of hands, because this oxy epidemic is personal to so many of us here on the peninsula. But I, for one, have a son who ended up in jail for oxy, and it took several years for him to finally get sober."

The audience clapped.

"Our friend who runs this program was herself a victim of DV, and she became an addict and ended up in jail at least twice. The second time was after a relapse, and that's when she finally got clean. And when she got out—clean and sober—she took up climbing and hiking. Now she teaches hiking to women who've been in jail or prison or who have conquered addiction. And she even teaches them some rock climbing techniques. And a few times a year, they all gather for family camp with their kids. The next one is in June, so we'll be looking for donations of kids' fleece and other warm clothes, as well as sleeping bags that are kid friendly."

Several women hooted. Some clapped, and others raised a hand in solidarity, kind of like a gospel meeting.

"The thing is, many of the participants are also victims of DV, and so the entire program is run from a confidential location. And whenever we donate, or even drop off climbing equipment or other gear, we do so through a third party so no one can find the women involved in the program."

The room had gotten very quiet.

"I can't emphasize enough the importance of keeping this confidential. This is the first time we've tried a public fundraiser, and I told the director of the program that she could trust all you ladies to keep this quiet. I know that people will probably talk about the program, but we will do everything in our power to keep the location of this work private. So please don't ask if you can volunteer or otherwise become involved, because you can't." Ginny looked around the silent room and then raised her voice. "But you can donate! And we'll come around with Squares for credit card donations, and if you have cash, we have cans set up with volunteers around the room.

"All of your money will go to supplying the program with what's needed to teach the women how to replace their addiction to substances with a new appreciation—not exactly an addiction, but close—to a lifetime of enjoying and understanding the wilderness. I know most of us who live here spend at least some time out in the park. And it's time we made that experience available to everyone, especially those who have lost their personal freedom for some period of time due to addiction and family violence." She stopped and took a deep breath. "Please donate generously to Mountain Pathways!"

Camille was taking it all in—the pieces were beginning to fall together. She turned to Rose with hope in her voice. "I need to know more about this org."

Rose leaned over and whispered, "It's all very hush-hush. No one really knows much about the org, or its leader. I guess that's what makes it all so mysterious. I'd—"

Rose didn't finish her sentence as Trish appeared out of nowhere and grabbed Camille by the arm. "Sorry to interrupt." She pulled Camille from the table. "I need to talk to Camille. It's an emergency."

Camille looked quizzically at Rose. "I'll be right back." She almost glared at Trish, who was proceeding to drag her across the room and out the front door. The twosome stood outside in the frigid night.

Pulling away, Camille asked, "What the hell was that back in there? You physically dragged me away from that group of lawyers I'm schmoozing up so they'll be more open to our CR 7 motion."

Trish pointed back inside. "That organization they're raising money for? I'm ninety percent certain that's Malika."

Camille lowered her voice. "I was just wondering about that."

"The woman on the stage, she's one of the women I met up in the park—and it matches what Jing told me about Malika and some nonprofit."

"It figures. And Malika's sister told you that Malika is leading women's groups up in the park, right?"

Trish nodded and closed her eyes for a second. "How many former addicts who are DV victims do you think are teaching hiking to recovering women in Olympic National Park?" Trish asked as a man in a dark-green puffy coat with some kind of official-looking patch on the shoulder hurried through the door of the bowling alley.

Trish hid behind Camille as the man walked out, and one of the volunteers yelled after him.

"Thanks, Fritz! We'll never tell your wife you were at our bowling night!"

The man laughed. "Thanks for doing this, ladies!"

"Thank you for your donation!"

The man got in his truck, which was idling where he'd double-parked in front of the alley.

Trish caught her breath. "That guy? He's the ranger from the park."

The truck stopped right in front of Trish and Camille, and the ranger stuck his head out the window. "You were the one asking questions up at the park the other day, weren't you?"

"I'm just looking for my friend," Trish answered.

"You need to just leave it. She doesn't want to be found. Go back to the big city." He put the truck in gear and spun the wheels as he drove out of the crowded parking lot.

CHAPTER THIRTY-ONE

Coffee and smoothies in a sailboat cockpit on a cold, sunny January morning was about as good as it got. Camille and Trish were all bundled up, watching the sunrise reflecting on the snowy Olympic Mountains.

"She's up there somewhere. I'm positive." Trish held up her coffee cup in a toast to Malika. "And I gotta hand it to her. She's done a pretty great job of keeping herself mysteriously private."

Camille was deep in thought. "You know . . ." She paused. "Something struck me about the program she may be running up there."

"What's that?"

"Her participants seem to be mostly women who've served time."

Trish nodded.

"One thing I've learned from my legal clinic—and to be honest, from Lucia—is that the women at WCCW become very attached to each other. The women coming home form a very tight sisterhood, even though sometimes one of the conditions of their probation is that they aren't supposed to have contact with 'felons.'" Camille made air quotes around the word.

Trish smiled and stood up, nearly knocking over the smoothie on the bench next to her. "And you think one of those women will know where Malika is. Brilliant!"

"You know, Lucia is pretty much the go-to person for women getting out. She's constantly directing women to programs and helping them find jobs and housing."

"Bam! Lucia! Right under our noses the whole time!"

Camille grabbed her phone and hit the FaceTime button, grinning broadly when Lucia's face filled the screen.

Lucia yawned. "It seems pretty early for a social call. What's up?" She squinted as she reached for her thick glasses.

"You know everyone." Camille launched right in. "I mean all the women coming home from prison."

"I'm not sure I'd say I know everyone. But yeah, I sure have lots of girlfriends who've recently come home. Why do you ask?"

Trish hovered over Camille's shoulder. "You ever heard of a woman over on the peninsula who teaches hiking or climbing groups?"

"Why do you ask?" Lucia's pullback was barely perceptible.

Camille put her hand on Trish's knee, nonverbally communicating to her to slow down.

"Do you know anything about some kind of women's climbing group over here? Does that sound at all familiar to you?" Camille asked.

"Yeah," Lucia answered slowly and waited.

"Do you know the group leader?"

"No. That program is kept really quiet. The women there are mostly DV victims, and the whole point of the program is to keep it very confidential."

"Understood." Camille looked at Trish off camera and mouthed, "Now what?"

Trish leaned in. "We think it may be Malika leading that group— we might be very close to finding Willow. How would we go about getting in touch with the group leader to see if it's Malika?"

Lucia was silent for a moment. And then she spoke hesitatingly. "I actually don't personally know how to reach the leader. If you promise on your life that you won't tell anyone, I'll tell you what little I know."

Camille's and Trish's affirmations were somber.

"Okay. First of all, I had no idea that it might be Malika who's running the program. No one knows her real name. We all call her Frankie. And the only way to reach her is via Lizbeth. She sets up all the meetings through her sister, who was a victim of the guy who Lizbeth killed. You remember Lizbeth's story?"

Camille and Trish nodded.

"If you want to find Frankie, you'll need to go down and talk with Lizbeth—in person. She for sure won't talk about this on JPay or on the phone. All the prison calls are recorded."

"So how does she run an org if they can't communicate about it?"

"Our network is pretty amazing. We have some people, like Lizbeth's sis, who meet up with the women in the visitors' room and get the word out on both the inside and outside."

"It's like there's a whole parallel world out there that those of us who have never engaged in the criminal legal system know nothing about."

"Exactly. And we go to great lengths to keep it that way. Trust is huge in our community."

"I can't tell you how much we appreciate your help with this." Camille's gratitude was obvious.

"Just please don't tell anyone that you have any idea who Frankie is. From what I understand there's some guy with lots of money and influence who's looking for her, and we sisters stick together to protect her however we can." Lucia's ferocity came through FaceTime as though she were in the cockpit next to them. "I have a Pilates class in twenty minutes. I gotta get going. I take it you're gonna head to WCCW shortly." It was more of a statement than a question.

"Like, today." Camille stood up and downed the last of her coffee. "I'll be in touch. And, Lucia?"

"Yeah?"

"Thank you." Camille kissed her two fingers and pressed them against the screen.

Lucia responded with a firm look and put her index finger on her lips in a *shh* movement before ending the call.

Camille and Trish looked at each other and spoke in unison. "Martin."

CHAPTER THIRTY-TWO

Trish picked up the scrap of paper that Camille had scrawled a quick goodbye note on and smiled as she crumpled it up and put it in the trash. Her afternoon run had reinvigorated her, and she synced her phone with her minispeaker and turned on the shower, which was about half the size of a telephone booth. The pieces of the investigation were starting to come together.

All cleaned up and ready to get busy, she opened the skinny bathroom door into the salon and stopped short. The faint odor of clove cigarettes wafted through the cabin. Trish looked around for anything she could use as a weapon and seized on the fire extinguisher clipped to the wall. As she grabbed for it, a rough hand circled her wrist. Quinn Hastings pulled her out of the bathroom and shoved her down on the banquette.

"Now what?" Trish made herself sound exasperated.

"Now you gotta help me." Quinn almost looked sincere.

"I ain't helping you. You broke into my place, scared the shit outta me." She pointed at the companionway. "Get out."

Quinn positioned himself between Trish and the only exit. "Here's the deal. I need help finding the bitch who owns this boat."

"I'm renting this place. I don't know the owner."

"I think you do."

Trish crossed her arms. "Nope."

"Look, my boss is getting outta control. He's looking for some Black lady he saw on a video security camera. I'm somehow supposed to find her."

They must have been caught on the store security video that night at the pharmacy when Quinn was stocking shelves. "What the hell would I know about some video footage?"

"Look, you seem cool, and you might not know much about this, but my boss got ahold of the name Camille Delaney from a credit card receipt at the pharmacy where I work. He saw her on the security system video. She was there with some Black woman and a kid, and he's looking for them."

Trish shrugged. "I can't help you. I don't know any Black woman with a kid around here."

"Well, Camille Delaney is the woman who was at the store, and she's the owner of this boat, so . . ."

"So, what?"

"So he thinks she might show up here, and he wants me to wait for her."

Oh shit.

"My boss checked her out. He knows she drives a Ford Explorer, and she's a lawyer from Seattle. Stuff like that."

Trish decided to play along. "What's in it for me if I help you?"

Quinn smiled. "Attagirl. My boss is rich. And I mean really rich. He bought me that Airstream you saw the other day."

"Nice guy."

"He owns a bunch of pharmacies and rakes in big bucks. I bet he'd be happy to throw some dough your way if you'd help him find your landlord."

"Okay. Maybe you should find out how much before I decide to help you."

"I can offer you five K."

"Ten."

"I'll see what I can do." Quinn smiled.

"Tell me why he's so hot to find her."

"Well, I was working at the pharmacy and noticed a Black woman who looked a lot like his ex-wife, who's in prison."

"How do you know what his ex looks like?"

"He has her mug shot on a bulletin board in his office. It's almost covered up by other papers, but I noticed it because it seemed weird to me."

"So how does this connect to my landlord?"

"I called him from the pharmacy. Thought maybe the ex had gotten out of prison and he might want to know."

Trish took it in. "And . . ."

"And he got all torqued up and started asking questions about the kid with her. I told him it was a little girl. Some kind of mixed race. Turns out he was looking for his missing kid, and he thinks it was his kid with what turned out to be his ex's twin sister. After that call, I never heard anything more until now."

"That's weird." It was all Trish could think of to say.

"He thinks Delaney can lead him to the kid."

Trish was quiet for a few seconds as she thought through her next move. Her phone was on the counter in the galley. If she could distract Quinn for a minute, maybe she could make a run for it.

"If you're gonna just wait around here, you might as well have a seat. You hungry?"

"I could eat."

"Okay, well, I gotta get into the galley to get you some food. Sit over there." She pointed at the banquette that was opposite the exit. If he'd just move, she could probably get off the boat more quickly than he'd be able to get up and catch her.

Quinn's phone rang. "Yeah." He mouthed to Trish, "My boss."

"Okay, where's she at?" He held his phone and opened the Maps app. "Okay, I see it. On my way." He picked up his navy-blue backpack and threw it over his shoulder.

"What's up?"

Quinn picked up Trish's phone. "He found her. I gotta get to work." He opened the hatch.

"My phone!" Trish got up to grab it from him.

Quinn pushed her back. "Sorry. The boss thinks you're in on this. Me, I'm not so sure. But he says I gotta lock you in here so you can't tell the lady lawyer that we're coming for her." He looked around the cabin and pulled the radio off the wall and, with it, all the wiring. "Nice boat.

Sorry about that." He climbed up the narrow steps and slid the hatch open.

Trish grabbed Quinn by the leg, and he kicked her hard, causing her to fall back onto the wood floor.

"I hate to do this. But boss's orders." He held up her phone, and she watched as he hurled it about twenty feet into the steel-gray water. "I already jammed the forward hatch, and now I gotta lock you in here. Sorry. You're gonna be stuck here for a while. I gotta go shut down the lawyer."

Trish got up and tried to reach Quinn as he closed the hatch to the boat. She heard the combination lock click and listened as he jumped off the boat onto the dock. He knocked on the hull as he left. "See ya!" he yelled.

Trish ran to the bow and tried the forward hatch with no luck. She looked out at the fog just lifting to expose the empty marina and hit the wall hard with her fist. "Goddamn it!" She opened the small porthole and began yelling.

—

So much for the unexpected sunny January days. Camille hung up the phone after spending an hour driving in the increasing rain and talking with Amy, going over upcoming motion hearings on a handful of clients. She'd told Amy she'd only be gone for a couple of days, but that had morphed into almost a week, and clients were getting restless. Tomorrow she'd head back to the city, she promised. Camille dialed Trish for about the tenth time, and it went directly to voice mail. She left another message telling Trish to call her and that she was going to stop on her way back and have dinner with Robin before heading back to Seattle. They had a lot of catching up to do. Robin's stepmother was running a program for women and kids over on San Juan Island, and Camille was anxious to hear about the data Gloria had been collecting with the help of Sally Berwyn, the PhD nursing student, along with her new intern, Iris Thomas.

To Camille's dismay, Robin had suggested a raucous BBQ joint to meet up at. And it was as noisy as Camille had expected it would be on a Friday night. No heart-to-heart chats at this place. *Oh well, at least the food got great reviews.*

Camille and Robin spent the meal catching up on family gossip, the girls' latest antics, and Robin's ongoing search for the perfect man, which explained the choice of dining establishments. The owner of the BBQ joint was recently divorced and had reached the top of Robin's list of eligible bachelors in Clallam County. In fact, she went back to the buffet three times in an effort to grab his attention. Camille was disappointed but not surprised that there'd been no time to get caught up on Gloria's island program. However, she'd known Robin since she was a kid, and her quest for the love of her life had been ongoing for decades.

The two women hugged in the misty rain out in the crowded parking lot. Camille hopped in her car, turned up the defroster, and took off down the highway toward the marina.

It wasn't long before she saw red flashing lights in her rearview mirror. Dang. She looked at her speedometer and figured she'd probably been speeding. She pulled over onto the shoulder and rummaged in her purse for her license.

"Step out of the car, ma'am." The flashlight in her face almost blinded her.

"I beg your pardon?" Camille held out her license.

"Out of the car!" The cop wasn't fooling around.

Maybe they think I'm drunk.

"Okay, I'm getting out." Camille was a bit impatient and thankful that she'd not had any wine at dinner.

"Hands on the car." Another flashlight shone in her face.

"Wait." She faced the cops.

One of them grabbed her by the arm and twisted her onto the car.

"Am I under arrest?" The lawyer in her took over.

"No, ma'am. We just need to check your car." A flashlight circled around inside the car. And one of the cops reached into the car and took the keys out of the ignition. He headed for the liftgate door on the back of her SUV.

"Hold on! I'm a lawyer, and you have no probable cause to search my car!" she said over her shoulder as she held her hands on the roof of her car.

The cop popped the door open.

"Stop! I have no idea what you're looking for, but you do not have my permission to search my car."

"Amber Alert, ma'am."

The blood rushed from Camille's head. She stumbled and struggled to maintain her balance. "What Amber Alert?" *Oh my God.*

She couldn't see the cop's face behind his bright flashlight. "A kid was just reported taken by someone in a blue Ford Explorer. You may remember from law school that we can search your car in exigent circumstances." He pointed at his partner. "Blue Ford Explorer?" And pointed at Camille's car. "Blue Ford Explorer." Camille tried to calm herself as the cop gave her a smarmy smile.

He walked to the back of her car.

Camille looked over the shoulder of the cop as he swiped his flashlight around her trunk. "Okay, you can see that there's no kid in there. Please let me go along my way."

The cop reached into the trunk and pulled out a navy-blue backpack. "What's this?"

Camille knew there had been no backpack in her trunk when she left the prison. "Leave it," she demanded. "You looked for a missing child. She is not in this car. You have no probable cause to open that backpack."

The cop ignored her and unzipped the backpack, emptying the contents onto the side of the road at her feet. Camille felt the bile creeping up her throat as she watched them open up a large baggie filled with gold and dark-gray pills.

The cop grabbed a pill and held it up to his partner. First the gray one: "'OP' on one side, and '80' on the other." He pulled out a gold pill. "OP 40."

"Got us a shitload of oxy right here."

His partner grabbed Camille and cranked her hands behind her back. "You have the right to remain silent. Anything you say can and will be used against you in a court of law. You have the right to an attorney. If you can't afford an attorney, one will be appointed for you."

Camille focused her full attention on every detail of what was happening. She knew that a legal case often rose and fell on the defendant's memory of what transpired during a search. She looked carefully to ensure that both cops had their body cameras on and rolling. Martin Zhao wasn't going to take her down without a helluva fight.

The ride to the police station left Camille in a fog. Booking. Fingerprints. Mug shot. It seemed like everything was happening to someone else. The actions of the two cops illegally opening the backpack were seared in Camille's brain. But this was a small town, and who knew which side the cops were on. Martin Zhao clearly wasn't playing around.

After being completely humiliated, Camille was finally given access to a phone. Trish hadn't been answering, and Camille didn't want to freak out Gigi. Sam would lose his shit, and besides, he was in New York. Camille dialed Lucia.

"What's up, boss?"

"Listen carefully. I've been arrested in Port Angeles. Call my friend Shoba Desai. She's a defense attorney. Tell her I need her in Port Angeles ASAP. And if she can't get here, I need a good referral. They just did a totally illegal search of my car and found a pile of oxy."

"Oh my God. Are you okay?"

"Actually, I have no idea. It's all a blur. And see if you can find Trish. She's not answering her phone."

"Jesus Christ. You got set up, just like Charli?"

"Looks like it. Please hurry and get me a lawyer over here as quick as you can. I think my phone time is up. I'm counting on you."

The holding cell in the Clallam County jail wasn't exactly a hotbed of activity. Camille sat on a bench with a young woman who'd been arrested for a DUI. She looked like she was about to throw up all over her lime-green minidress. Camille leaned back on the cold wall and began to organize her thoughts for her motion to dismiss her case for an illegal search. Friday night. She wondered if they had judges on duty over the weekend or if she'd be stuck in jail until Monday. She squeezed her eyes shut to keep from crying.

CHAPTER THIRTY-THREE

Camille was shocked but not totally surprised to see her mother standing at the counsel table right there in Clallam County, deep in conversation with Camille's friend and lawyer, Shoba Desai. Pella Rallis owned any room she entered. She'd always been that way. And today was no exception. Pella was dressed in a smart gray suit that matched her long silver hair. She winked at Camille, who sat in the jury box with three other people who'd been arrested over the weekend. Pella shot her daughter an air kiss.

How her mother had gotten there from her island in Greece in less than thirty-six hours was a mystery to Camille, but her gratitude and love for her mother filled her up in a way that was hard to describe.

Before long, the mingling lawyers around counsel table parted to allow Rose to enter. She reached out for Pella's hand and tried to look professional, but her fondness for her mentor was obvious. Camille caught Rose's eye and held up her handcuffed hands, tilting her head as if to say *Really?*

Rose looked genuinely at a loss. She leaned over and huddled with the deputy prosecutor as the bailiff boomed out, "All rise!"

The courtroom stood up in unison as an overweight, older judge strode up to his perch on the bench. "Please be seated." He reached out to the bailiff, who handed him a stack of paperwork.

"Let's get started." He looked over his half glasses at Camille and her fellow defendants waiting in the jury box. "State of Washington versus Camille Delaney."

Camille stood and felt a gush of love for her mother as she jumped up and introduced herself to the judge. "Pella Rallis for Ms. Delaney, Your Honor."

Shoba waited for a second and added, "And Shoba Desai here on behalf of Ms. Delany as well, Your Honor."

The judge looked curiously at Camille. "Two big-city lawyers up here on our Monday-morning calendar." He nearly rolled his eyes. "How do you plead, Ms. Delaney?"

Camille's voice was clear and certain. "Not guilty, Your Honor."

The judge stuck his nose in the paperwork. Without looking up, he asked the prosecutor, "Bail?"

The young prosecutor with the slicked-back hair stood. Then Rose stepped ahead of him. "We ask that Ms. Delaney be released on her own recognizance."

"Really?" The judge looked surprised. "There was a lot of OxyContin in that baggie, counsel."

"Ms. Delaney is a well-respected member of the bar. We have no concerns about her reliability."

The judge whipped out his pen and signed the paperwork with a flourish. "You happy, Ms. Adams?"

Rose ignored the sarcasm. "Thank you, Your Honor."

Camille got up and let the courtroom officer guide her by the arm back to the booking area for processing. She kissed the air toward her mother just before the door closed behind her.

CHAPTER THIRTY-FOUR

Having an in with the prosecutor had its advantages. While Rose wasn't about to go light on a defendant, she could at least expedite the discovery that Pella and Shoba had asked for. The next day, Trish, Camille, Shoba, and Pella sat around the large monitor in Camille's office and downloaded the body cam footage. While they waited for it to load, Trish regaled them with the story of her latest run-in with Quinn Hastings and how he'd locked her in the boat for the better part of the day. Given Camille's circumstances, Trish tried to make light of her brief imprisonment.

"Well, maybe there's a silver lining to your Quinn situation," Pella mused. "Imagine if Camille had come back to the boat. There's no telling what could have happened. He sounds pretty unstable."

"True," Trish agreed. "He was for sure intent on finding Camille."

"Okay. Let's do this." Shoba hit Play.

It was tempting to just close her eyes and let her lawyers review the recording that could very well change Camille's life forever. The voices of the two cops made her feel nauseated. Pella took charge.

"Stop. Rewind."

The women leaned forward.

Pella pointed at the backpack. "There were no exigent circumstances that justify them searching that backpack."

Camille sighed. "That's what I told them."

The recording moved slowly forward at Pella's instruction.

Lucia stood in the doorway and positioned herself to see over the lawyers' shoulders as they watched the recording of the cop lifting the backpack out of the trunk. Camille's voice could be heard over the gravelly voice of the cop telling them loudly that she did not authorize them to open the backpack. Pella shot her daughter a professorial look. "Perfect defendant. You tell 'em!"

As the two defense lawyers scratched on their notepads, Trish yelled, "Stop!"

Camille hit the Stop button.

"Rewind." Now Trish was in charge. "Can we zoom in?"

Camille moved aside so Trish was in control of the computer. She rewound and played a few seconds, twice.

"What?" Camille asked.

Trish pointed. "Watch carefully as they take the backpack."

The women focused intently on the screen.

"See? See there?" Trish pointed. "That pack of cigarettes. How does this thing zoom?" She fidgeted with the buttons until she got the cigarette pack to fill the screen. "Those are clove cigarettes. They call them kreteks. They're not sold in the US."

"Okay, so . . . ," Camille wondered aloud. "How does this help us?"

"Those are what Quinn Hastings smokes. I'll bet you a trip to Hawaii that his fingerprints are on that pack." She rewound the recording and put her face right up to the screen, almost touching it. "He just happens to work at a pharmacy owned by Martin Zhao. He also told me that Martin saw that video of Gigi and Gracie at the pharmacy, and he apparently thinks Gracie is Willow."

"Wait. What?" Camille was starting to feel dizzy. Was it from not eating, or just from having her life turned upside down? "Why would he think that?"

"Seven-year-old mixed-race girl with Gigi. I can see how that might set Martin off on a wild-goose chase," Trish commented.

"That's why he's coming after you. He thinks you know where Willow is," Shoba added.

"Not sure that having me arrested was the best move if he wants me to tell him where Willow is."

"Well, maybe he's willing to trade you for Quinn, if in fact it was Quinn who planted the drugs," Trish said. "Wouldn't surprise me at all if he double-crosses his accomplice."

"If those are Quinn's clove cigarettes that were found in Camille's trunk," Shoba mused, "then he has lots to be worried about. Let's get him to flip on Martin."

Trish picked up the storyline. "Well, he's obviously the one who planted the drugs. I don't expect he'd have the good sense to understand an Amber Alert, so he probably didn't know that the cops can only search the open space where a child could be hidden. He just dumped his backpack in the trunk and took off." Trish turned to the legal team. "We need to get prints off this cigarette pack and the backpack too. You lawyers need to work your magic so we can get the prints."

"The car's still in impound, and I'm sure the backpack is in the evidence room," Shoba stated. "I'll ask the prosecutor for an inspection, but I need to be there when they do it."

"Actually, I'm not so sure we need those prints before we approach Quinn. He knows full well that he planted that backpack in the trunk," Trish stated flatly.

"This Quinn Hastings. What do we know about him?" Shoba flipped to a clean sheet on her yellow legal pad.

Trish stood up and stretched. "We know that he was a science nerd in high school. They say he was a nice kid, but he got mixed up with meth or something that turned him pretty violent. He was Malika's boyfriend, and he was an abusive asshole to her. He's clearly still using, but I'm not sure what. I saw him snorting some powder the first day I met him. He went from being just kinda creepy to being almost maniacally cruel. It was really abrupt, now that I think back on it."

Shoba nodded. "Probably meth. It makes people crazy. And often violent. And they'll do most anything for their next fix."

"So, if Martin is supplying Quinn with his drug of choice, Quinn is likely to do Martin's bidding, right?" Camille asked.

"Exactly," Shoba responded. "But I thought you all said that Martin is mostly selling oxy."

"Apparently he's branched out into street drugs. Especially now that the docs are getting wise to how addictive oxy really is, Martin's clientele is looking for street drugs. He also has a clinic of some kind that just hands out oxy scripts," Trish explained.

"Not sure how we get Quinn to turn on his source." Camille was thinking out loud.

"Oh, he'll turn on him once he realizes that he's going down for planting drugs on someone in furtherance of a crime," Shoba explained. "And that evidence will be very interesting to the prosecutors who convicted Charli and the doctor. They're way more interested in the person who's highest up on the chain, and that would be Martin Zhao."

While the women had been brainstorming what Martin's endgame was, Pella had been intently focused on her laptop. "Okay. I just emailed you all a draft of our motion to dismiss all charges against Camille based on an illegal search." Her eyes darted from woman to woman. "We have one job here right now—to get the charges dropped. Then we can turn to the why behind this whole mess."

Each woman dutifully turned to their laptop and waited for Pella's motion to appear in their email.

Pella continued. "Next up will be to draft a motion to inspect the contents of the car trunk. But that evidence will go more toward getting Charli and maybe even the doctor out of prison based on the obvious setup." She looked up. "That would be a CR 7 motion, and those are a bear—almost impossible to prevail on one of those."

"Unlike the rest of this crew, I've never seen you with your lawyer hat on, Pella. You're pretty intense." Trish's respect was clear.

"There's a reason Professor Rallis was voted best prof at SU Law so many times." Shoba smiled. "I never thought in my wildest dreams that I'd one day be cocounsel with her."

Pella looked at the team. "That's very nice, Ms. Desai, but right now we need to put one hundred percent of our time and attention on getting these charges dismissed. This is my daughter we're talking about here." She closed her laptop and threw down her half glasses. "I'm quite confident that we can win on this illegal-search issue. But every good lawyer has a backup plan, and ours is to turn Quinn Hastings into our witness, to show that he was working with Martin to set up Camille, and maybe even Charli and the doc. Just like you said, every prosecutor likes to go up the chain and charge the kingpin. Quinn Hastings is just an underling in this scheme. But why did Martin plant drugs on his own wife and the doctor?" Pella looked around the group.

Camille chimed in. "Charli and her boyfriend, who is Willow's dad, discovered that Martin was running an illegal drug ring out of the pharmacy they ran together. When Charli and Brian discovered it, Martin had drugs planted on them, and off they went to prison. Same for the doctor. When he threatened to expose Martin's drug ring, he found himself on the wrong end of an Amber Alert, just like Charli and me."

"So what does Willow have to do with all of this?" Pella asked.

"Charli had Martin's laptop that had all of the evidence of his illegal business dealings on it. He kidnapped Willow out of the hospital to hold her hostage so that Charli would never turn his computer in to the authorities. But what he doesn't know is that Charli and Brian don't even have the laptop because it ended up getting taken into evidence in a completely unrelated crime. So, not only are we looking for Willow, but we're also looking for that laptop, which is clearly a long shot. But crazier things have happened."

Pella was getting up to speed. "And this Malika that you guys are looking for may know where Willow is, right?"

Trish nodded. "Malika was Willow's nanny, and Malika was the last person we've been able to identify that might know where Willow is. And we think we may be getting close to at least finding Malika. In fact, right before this arrest happened, we learned that a woman matching Malika's description may be running a hiking group for DV victims and former addicts. But the location is secret."

"It sounds like you have a strong lead on where you might find her," Pella noted.

"We do."

Camille turned to Lucia, who had been hovering around the edges of the meeting. "Can you please let Lizbeth know I'm heading her way?" She looked at her watch. "Sam is still in New York with Gracie for a few more days, and Angela and Libby have been hanging out at Gigi's. I'll grab Sam's car and head down to the prison right now. I can get there in time for the evening classes and meetings. I'll pop into the recovery group meeting and find Lizbeth."

Pella smiled at her daughter. "You'll need to catch me up on the cast of characters." She paused. "And I assume that, for now, we're not telling Sam about this whole shit show, right?"

"It'd completely freak him out. And he's presenting a huge paper at the meeting—let's not throw him off his game. He has a huge grant riding on this research. All of this can wait until his return."

"And what about Martin thinking Gracie is Willow? Will he be looking for her here?" Pella asked.

"Good point," Camille noted. "For sure he won't find her in New York, so we've got a few days to figure out our next steps."

"Oh, how I wish I could go along with you to the women's prison. I haven't been down there in years." Pella crossed her arms wistfully.

"You'd need to get clearance." Camille hugged her mom and turned to gather her paperwork, which she handed to Lucia in exchange for her camel coat. She grabbed her backpack. "It'll be good for me to do something other than sit here and worry. I gotta go."

"Clearance? I have top security clearance from the US government."

Camille froze and looked at her mother, waiting on some kind of explanation.

"You have no idea what goes on over there in the migrant camps. I'm working on some very secret stuff with an agency that you would recognize. But if I tell you, I'd have to kill you." She winked.

Camille stood in the doorway for an extra second, wondering what else her mother was doing that she had no idea about. Then she blew a kiss at the team and swept out of the office.

CHAPTER THIRTY-FIVE

It wasn't lost on Camille that she herself was just one unconstitutional search and seizure motion from being stuck on the wrong side of the now-familiar barbed wire. The prison had become less and less intimidating as the months had passed, and she'd gotten to know the women inside. But today she felt the chill of knowing that women landed here for all kinds of reasons, even fake drug charges, like Charli. She could have conceivably been next, if Quinn Hastings hadn't been so ignorant as to how an Amber Alert actually worked. She tried to shut out visions of herself in khaki and gray as she waited for the guards to buzz her through the cyclone-fence gate. It all seemed like an illusion, the difference between inside and outside. *Why do we lock up so many women in this country?*

The women were just taking their seats in the recovery group when Camille walked in. Jessica Kensington shot Camille a wide smile. "I heard you might be joining us tonight." She got as close to Camille as possible without violating prison rules. "I'm glad to see you."

Camille returned the smile and scanned the room. "Actually, I'm looking for Lizbeth," she said as Lizbeth walked through the door. Camille waved, and Lizbeth ignored everyone in the room except Camille and hurried over. The twosome huddled at the back of the room while Jessica greeted the women in the group as they settled in.

Lizbeth took the lead. "What's going on?"

"We're getting very close to finding Malika."

"Tell me more." Lizbeth had clearly dealt with having her hopes dashed in the past.

"I need your help, Tru." Camille locked eyes with Lizbeth. It was the first time Camille had used Lizbeth's prison name.

"What do you need?" Her curiosity was piqued.

"We've learned about a woman by the name of Frankie, who leads women's hiking and climbing groups up in the Olympic Mountains, and we understand that you may know how to find her."

Lizbeth looked sharply at Camille. "What does Frankie have to do with finding Malika?"

"We think Frankie *is* Malika."

Camille paused to let that sink in.

Lizbeth was silent, doing some kind of mental calculations as she chewed her fingernail.

"Tell me what you know about Frankie." Camille's demeanor had switched from friend to lawyer about to undertake a rigorous cross-examination.

"First, you need to tell me why you think Frankie may be Malika," Lizbeth responded in kind to Camille's lawyerly aggression.

Camille softened. "Trish learned from Malika's sister that Malika has been running some kind of program up in the mountains for women in recovery. And when Trish dug into it, she got the cold shoulder from a handful of people who seemed to know more than they were letting on. They tried to wave Trish off her investigation. She figured out that there's a woman who matches Malika's description who has been seen leading groups up in the Olympics. And then, we ended up at a big fundraiser for a women's climbing group that focuses on teaching hiking and climbing to women who are in recovery and coming out of prison. And Malika's last name is Franklin, so calling herself Frankie makes sense." She paused. "Does any of this sound familiar?"

"Sounds plausible." Lizbeth had on a poker face.

Camille continued. "Here's what we know. Willow was last known to be in Malika's care." She skipped over the whole trailer-fire incident. There was no need to freak Lizbeth out until they had more information about whether Willow was ever in the fire anyway. "We know that Malika ended up back in PA with a baby, who everyone assumed was her daughter. She lived with her boyfriend, who is no gem. She ended up addicted to oxy, did some time in jail, was in and out of a treatment program, relapsed and was back in jail, where she finally got sober. Then she took off for the mountains. After that, the trail goes cold."

Lizbeth appeared to be weighing her options.

"Tell me about Frankie," Camille urged.

"Frankie is an amazing person who beat a very serious addiction to oxy. And she got away from her abuser. Now she runs a program out in the mountains for women who are in recovery and often are also DV victims. The program is highly confidential, and no one knows where it is or when the hikes take place, except my sister."

"Wait. Your sis knows Malika?"

"Maybe . . ." Lizbeth's voice trailed off as she looked lost in thought.

"I need to figure out how to get ahold of Frankie and see if she's Malika." Camille was firm.

Lizbeth stepped back and folded her arms. She waited a minute to speak. "Okay. Maybe you're on the right track. I'll get you in touch with Frankie. But you gotta swear not to tell anyone that you know where she is. Or who she is, especially if you're right about her."

"You have my word." Camille was deadly serious.

"Here's the thing. I don't know exactly what Frankie's hiding from, but there's some guy who wants to find her. He's powerful. And rich. And he has guys out looking for her. We have a kind of underground system to help keep women safe from abusers. I don't get the impression that the guy looking for her abused her, but she's terrified of him. In spite of her fear for her own personal safety, she's become a leader in the movement of women in recovery, even while this dude is chasing around after her for reasons none of us fully understand."

"If Malika knows where Willow is, and it sounds like she might, then Charli's ex, Martin, is going to be desperate to find her. I'll bet you a million dollars that she's hiding from him."

"You might be right." Lizbeth turned to face the front of the room. "Hey, Jessica, can you help us back here for a minute?"

"Hang on," Jessica responded. She pivoted and addressed the group as they finished reorganizing their chairs into a circle. "Linny, can you please gather the homework and start the sharing circle? I need to talk with Camille here. She's the lawyer who runs the family law clinic." A scattering of women snapped their fingers in Camille's direction, and

Camille realized that many of her legal clinic clients were in the group right in front of her. She held up her hand in a high five. A short, heavy-set Black woman got up and collected the papers.

Lizbeth addressed Jessica. "Red, we got an issue to discuss. Camille is looking to get introduced to Frankie."

The look on Jessica's face was hard for Camille to read, but it caught her off guard a bit.

"Actually, to be fully transparent," Camille said, "we think Frankie might be the woman who was Willow's nanny. Her name was Malika. We believe that she took Willow over to the peninsula to get her away from Charli's ex. We know for sure that she and Willow lived in PA for a while, but then the trail went cold." Camille looked for some kind of recognition from her former adversary. "We're hopeful that Frankie may be the nanny, Malika—Malika Franklin—hence maybe the nick-name Frankie. We know that Malika recovered from addiction and was in and out of jail for a period of time. Then she took off. Her sisters think she went up into Olympic National Park to disappear. The tim-ing seems to line up with the little I've heard about Frankie, so it would be awesome for Charli if it turns out to be a valid lead."

"Does Charli know this?" Jessica asked.

"Not yet. We told her we were getting close, but we don't want to get her hopes up if this is another dead end. She's had so many disap-pointments in trying to find Willow. But, for sure, if this seems to be positive, we'll be here in a hot minute to tell her the good news."

"Look, Camille, I know and trust you, and I'm sure you have the best intentions in the world." Jessica looked Camille straight in the eye. "But the women working with Frankie are mostly fresh out of prison, where they have worked hard for their sobriety. And many of them have been victimized in ways you can't imagine. Their safety is Frankie's number one concern."

Camille caught her breath. "Wait. You know Frankie?"

Lizbeth leaned in. "Like I told you, no one inside knows Frankie. But we all know of her. She's a bit of a legend around here."

Jessica was more serious than Camille had ever seen her, including the day she got arrested in the courthouse. "I've only been in for a mat-ter of months, but in that time, I've seen women leave this prison. And as you know, those of us inside manage to stay pretty closely in touch with our sisters who've gotten out. Now that I'm leading the recovery group, I stay updated on the status of my former group members after they're released, and Frankie is changing their lives with her innovative program. We cannot risk her being exposed." Jessica looked at Lizbeth, who nodded subtly. "Frankie is running from someone—we don't know exactly who—but if he gets wind of her location, our sisters on the outside will lose their lifeline."

"I understand." Camille felt like she was being let in on a secret of monumental proportions. "And I was just telling Tru that I believe that the person Frankie is running from is Charli's ex. He's desperate to find Charli's baby."

Lizbeth jumped in. "It makes sense that if Frankie is, in fact, Malika, Martin Zhao would stop at nothing to find her if he believed she could lead him to Charli's baby."

Jessica looked Lizbeth squarely in the eye. "Tru, if we get Camille in touch with your sister and something goes wrong and Frankie is outed, that will be the end of her program. She'll take off, and I'm not sure we'll ever see her again."

Lizbeth nodded solemnly and turned to Camille. "The women in Frankie's program are not only DV survivors, but they've kicked addiction and come out the other side. And many of them are risking getting sent back here because they're hanging out with their sisters who are also survivors of prison, so they may be violating their terms of probation by looking to each other for support. Frankie did jail time, not prison, so she doesn't have a felony. But most of the other women do, and they're prohibited from hanging out together, even though they're each other's very best supports."

"What a monumentally fucked-up system." Camille rolled her eyes. "We send trauma victims to prison, and then when many of them find solace in the sisterhood inside, where they work together to overcome their challenges, we tell them that they must walk alone on the outside without the main sources of their support. Seriously?"

"Yes," Jessica agreed. "It's fucked up for sure. But those women have a lot at risk, so if we put you in touch with Lizbeth's sister, you'll need to follow her instructions to the letter. She knows how to keep the women safe. You can't be followed, you can't bring your phone, and you shouldn't even try to figure out where you are when you go up the forest service roads."

"Understood."

Lizbeth looked at Jessica. Jessica nodded slowly. "I say we set a meeting."

"Agreed." Lizbeth was all business.

"Thank you." Camille's voice was barely a whisper.

Lizbeth took charge. "Okay, here's the sitch. You remember I told you that the reason I'm here is because that asshole coach was attacking my baby sis, right?"

Camille nodded.

"Well, as it turns out, the coach's wife, Talulla, was maybe the most victimized of everyone in this whole ungodly catastrophe. That guy raped and sodomized her regularly. He beat the crap out of her, and at times he locked her in the basement for weeks. Somehow she managed to stay alive, and she and my sis, Isabel, met at my trial and became friends. So now they're working together to support the work that Frankie is doing."

"I'm curious—how did they hook up with Frankie?" Camille asked.

"Isabel and Talulla were working at a women's DV shelter together. So, when I learned that many of our WCCW sisters were getting involved in some trauma recovery hiking group and really finding value there, I told Isabel about it. Then she and Talulla reached out to Frankie through some of our sisters from here. They and Frankie hit it off, and by that time, Isabel and Talulla had learned a lot about how to fundraise and run a DV program, so the three of them decided to formalize Frankie's program a bit. It's been amazing to see the successes of the women. And for me, it's been especially cool to see my little sis take on this big challenge and create a program that's so unique in that it's entirely confidential."

"How soon can I go meet with them?" Camille didn't want to waste any time.

Lizbeth shrugged. "Probably in the next day or so. I think the team is working on supplies for early spring hiking, so I'm pretty sure Frankie isn't holding classes this month."

"I gotta go take over this recovery meeting." Jessica stopped as she headed for the front of the room. "We're trusting you, Camille. Don't screw this up."

CHAPTER THIRTY-SIX

The women at WCCW worked fast. Within a few days, Camille was on her way to the parking lot at the base of the trail leading to the Staircase, where she would put herself into Isabel's hands for the trip up to Frankie's hiding place somewhere in the park.

A slightly younger version of Lizbeth was waiting in a bright, albeit well worn, red Jeep with the engine running. Camille parked and grabbed her puffy coat and a fleece hat. She'd decided to change out her leather gloves for something warmer and pulled on her down sailing gloves. Even the deep breaths she took didn't calm her nerves. She might be an hour away from braiding together all the disparate pieces of what had happened to Willow.

Isabel waved Camille over to her car. "I'm Isabel." She couldn't have been more serious. "You don't have your cell phone, right?"

Camille pointed at her car. "It's in my glove box."

Isabel shook her head. "Well, let's hope no one breaks into your car. The glove box is the first place they look after they crash open your window when you park at a trailhead. But it's winter, so . . ."

Camille shuddered. She felt like she was in a murder-mystery movie. Despite it being midday, the gray sky made it feel like it was dusk, which wasn't all that unusual for winter in the Pacific Northwest. She stood still, waiting for Isabel to instruct her on the next steps.

"Hop in."

Camille complied, grateful to be inside the warm car. "Thanks for your willingness to take me to meet with Frankie."

Not even a smile. "I hear you're a friend of a friend of Frankie's. But I gotta tell you, it's pretty unusual for her to ever meet with anyone except for the women who come up here to hike with her. You understand that you are not to tell anyone where Frankie is, right? Many of the women she hikes and climbs with are in some kind of confidentiality program. That keeps their abusers away from them. Other women don't want anyone to know where they are because some of them have testified against big-time drug dealers, and others just want the peace of mind to know that they're finally free of addiction and they don't want their former using friends to find them."

Camille nodded. "Got it."

Isabel spun her tires as she took off up a forest service road that wound through twists and turns up into the mountains. They drove through a surging stream and up and over a tall muddy bank. Then off the road and across a brown winter field of dead grass and back onto another forest service road. There was no way Camille could ever have retraced this obstacle course even if she'd wanted to. The next road was so filled with potholes that she had to hold on to the brace bar on top of the Jeep to keep from bouncing out. At one point, they drove over a sapling that had come down across the road.

Isabel finally slowed down and turned to Camille. "Even if you could find your way back up here, it wouldn't matter. Frankie moves her camp about every two weeks. And sometimes she just comes down and stays in town, but that's unpredictable, and we're never sure when she'll show up and when she'll leave."

Camille took Isabel's opening of a conversation as an opportunity to try to better understand the program. "So, you and Talulla run the logistics and bring the participants up into the mountains to learn to hike and climb?"

"Pretty much. All of us are survivors of either DV, assault, or addiction. And we've all learned that being out in the wilderness is not only good for the soul, but it's healthy and it gives us time to think and meditate and most of all to realize that we can do hard things. Hanging out with Frankie is not just physically intense, but it's very emotionally intense, so most people try to stay up here for a week or two at a time, if they can manage taking the time away from work or kids. And if not, we just stay as long as we can, even if it's just a weekend."

"It's an amazing program you all have created up here." Camille's appreciation was sincere.

Isabel stopped abruptly and turned off the engine. "Okay, we hike up from here."

Camille caught her breath. Here she was, somewhere up in the mountains with no way to communicate with the outside world. She considered for a moment that maybe this wasn't the smartest thing she'd ever done, then decided to surrender to the moment. There really wasn't any other choice.

Isabel pointed at two well-placed rocks that stood at the edge of the clearing. Behind them was a narrow trail with overhanging brush Isabel easily ducked under. "This way."

The trail zigged and zagged for about ten minutes and landed the twosome at the edge of a breathtakingly clear sapphire-blue mountain lake. A short scramble across some giant rocks led to a campsite where a tall Black woman was hunched over a fire, boiling water in a metal teapot, steam billowing up into nothingness, her back to them as she filled a small espresso pot.

"I make a mean espresso." She stood and grinned broadly at Camille as she handed her a metal coffee cup.

Malika. Hot damn.

Without missing a beat, Camille held out her cup. "Thanks. I could use something hot to drink."

Frankie turned to Isabel. "Thanks so much for bringing our new friend up here. I think we're good now."

"Cool. I gotta get back and finish that inventory. See you tomorrow." Isabel turned and scrambled across the rocks.

"Tomorrow?" Camille didn't try to stop the words from spilling out.

Frankie smiled. "The only way you can get a real idea of our work is to spend a night up here under the stars." She looked up at a sliver of blue sky. "Looks like these clouds are going to clear up shortly."

"I wasn't actually prepared for an overnight visit." Camille wasn't sure what else to say.

Frankie waved her off. "You're gonna love it. Isabel will let Lizbeth know that you're here for the night, and she'll let your people know."

Recognizing that she had no other option, Camille sat on a flat rock in front of the fire and cupped her hands around the hot mug. She spent a few minutes taking in the spectacular scene. "It's gorgeous here." She drained half her coffee.

"It gets dark early this time of year." Frankie stood up. "You're gonna need to get a little taste of what we do with the women. Our first order of business is to take a nice silent hike around the lake." She took Camille's cup and sized up her attire. "Not the best hiking shoes, but they'll do." She rummaged in her tent and handed Camille a down vest. "Put this on under your jacket and you should be fine."

Camille did as she was told, captivated by the confident leadership that oozed from this woman.

"Okay. This is what we call a walking meditation. Be very mindful of everything you see and hear and feel. It's mad quiet up here, so be alert for bird songs and maybe even some frogs." She pointed out at the lake. "Just wait until tonight. The frogs are glorious."

There really wasn't much to do other than play along. And besides, who could complain about taking a hike around a serene mountain lake?

"Let's go. No talking. Just listen and feel." Frankie put her finger over her lips softly.

About a quarter of the way around the lake, Camille noticed that all her senses were on alert. The hues of nature were striking—all shades of blue and green punctuated by various pops of brown and gray. The sounds of the birds and the rustling of the breeze in the dead winter foliage sounded like a melody. And the cold air had become welcoming rather than something to resist.

Intermittently, Frankie would stop and hold her hands up in the air as if in a gesture of celebratory prayer or some kind of yoga pose. At one point, she stopped and began a series of full body stretches, which she silently invited Camille to mimic. Camille's self-consciousness began to dissolve as she followed Frankie—stretching, twirling, and walking as if they were performing some kind of ballet for an invisible audience watching from the rocky shore.

As they danced along the path, the unmistakable sound of rushing water got louder and louder. Frankie climbed over a group of downed trees that had become silver logs and pushed aside a stand of bushes to expose a small waterfall. She sat on one of the logs. Camille did the same. It was hard to tell how long they stayed there lost in the mist, enveloped by the sound of water. Then, as Frankie led Camille out of the small wooded area and to the shore of the lake, the clouds began to part. Camille almost gasped at the deep color of the sky, which was framed by evergreens, with snowcapped mountains hovering on the horizon.

Frankie moved more quickly over the last quarter of the lake. At times she danced and spun, and other times she bent down to crawl or roll on the grass. It was a class in free-form movement. When they were almost back at camp, Frankie looked up at a tree that appeared to be reaching out over the lake and gestured Camille to follow her. Before she knew it, Camille was climbing up a leafless deciduous tree right behind Frankie. When they were about twelve feet off the water, Frankie grabbed a limb and began to hang, and then to swing freely.

Camille watched her new friend with a twinge of envy. *Imagine being so unencumbered that you can spend your days swinging from a tree out over a mountain lake.*

After a few minutes, the twosome made their way down the tree and back onto solid ground. Frankie looked at Camille expectantly and took off running at a full sprint for the campsite. Camille did her best to keep up, but ended up a minute or so behind Frankie, who was sitting by the dying embers, hands on her knees, catching her breath.

Camille sat.

Frankie looked up at her. "So, what did you get?"

"Get?"

"What was your experience of our silent hike?"

Camille hesitated, not sure if she was safe to fully engage. She was, after all, actually kind of working at the moment, even if it was in a rather unconventional location.

Frankie read her mind. "I know this probably seems weird to you. But this is how we build trust. We may think we know something about each other, but do we really?"

"You have a point."

"Okay. I'll go first." Frankie was clearly comfortable with vulnerability. "I'm a little wary of you. You think you've found Malika. And in a way you have."

Camille held her breath. This was the first acknowledgment of the fact that Frankie was Malika, and it just dropped into the conversation so naturally.

"I may once have been Malika. I may once have been in active addiction. I may once have been an abused woman. I may have been in jail. But now, right here, today, I am a survivor. I am strong. I am capable. I am a leader. I am Frankie."

"Your participants are very lucky to have your leadership."

Frankie ignored Camille's comment. "How about you? Who are you right now?"

Camille shrugged. "I guess I'm a little nervous. I've never been much of a camper, and I have no idea what to expect up here with you. I guess I'd say I'm confused."

"Okay, let's go with that. What could possibly be confusing about the color of the sky? Or the sound of the silence? Or climbing a tree? Or having a good fast run?"

Camille pondered for a moment. "You're right. I'm not confused. I'm feeling free."

Frankie nodded. "Free. That's good. Free from what?"

Camille was getting the hang of it. "Free . . . free from expectations and responsibilities."

"Freedom. That's a big feeling, isn't it?" Frankie poked at the embers and threw on some kindling.

The women were silent for a few minutes.

"So, in service of and furtherance of your experience of freedom, why exactly are you here?"

Frankie had completely flipped the script. Camille was here to gain information from Frankie, and Frankie was somehow empowering her to reframe the whole investigation.

"Freedom," Camille said and paused. "In furtherance of freedom. I'd say I'm here to free my friend Charli of the shackles that keep her in limbo worrying and wondering where her daughter is. She needs to be freed of the terror of not knowing."

"I can help Charli with that." Frankie got up and opened a well-stocked cooler and began opening baggies of fresh veggies and grimaced when she realized that the bag of brown rice was nearly empty. She poured what was left of the rice into a cast-iron skillet and filled it with bottled water and placed it on the fire.

Camille reminded herself to breathe.

"I know you're curious about how I got from being a high school basketball star to a nanny, to a drug addict, to a trauma survivor, to a leadership recovery coach."

Camille nodded. "You have no idea how many people are curious to know what brought you here."

"Well." Frankie handed Camille a bottle of kombucha. "I can tell you a bit about how I got here, but what I won't tell you is what happened to baby Daisy. That's for me to tell only one person. And that person is Charli herself."

Camille felt her heart flutter. While it seemed reasonable that Frankie wanted to speak directly to Charli, it was more than a little disappointing that she would not return from this little mountain soiree with any real answers, except that they had for sure found Malika—which, in and of itself, was actually a big win. She began to let herself relax into the moment.

"This dish takes about a half hour, so let's catch a nice meditation while it cooks," Frankie suggested.

Camille was liking Frankie more and more. She lived entirely in the present moment and didn't seem to have a care in the world about what anyone else thought of her. And, having no phone, no distractions, no kids, no clients, and no legal motions to think about for the next twelve or so hours, Camille settled on her fireside rock.

Frankie stirred the bubbling concoction of rice and chopped veggies and sprinkled in a handful of walnuts along with a small bag of spices.

"You remind me of my mom." Camille smiled.

"Sometime I'd like to learn more about your mom." Frankie took a deep breath through her nose and exhaled loudly through her mouth with a sound between a buzz and an om.

"I have a feeling you two will become fast friends." Camille looked up at the deep-blue sky and closed her eyes.

CHAPTER THIRTY-SEVEN

Sometimes magic happens. And this was one of those times. For reasons no one could exactly explain, the DOC immediately approved the request for Frankie to be allowed to visit WCCW. It had been only a couple of days since Camille had spent what she had come to feel had been a transformational twenty-four hours with Frankie, and here she was in the parking lot of the prison, listening to Enya on her earbuds while Gigi and Trish held hands in silence. They kept their eyes on the road, waiting for Isabel's dusty red Jeep to appear.

The three women slowly got out of the car as Isabel parked right next to them. Frankie sat straight up in the passenger seat, looking like a cross between royalty and a guru. Her face was unreadable. Camille waited as Frankie slowly unbuckled her seat belt and opened the car door. There was something mindful about her. And to Camille, she looked a bit out of place away from her beloved wilderness. Camille stopped to take in all that was Frankie—her purple velvet blazer, a crisp white button-down tucked into her jeans, and purple cowboy boots. Camille was suddenly self-conscious of her standard all-black attire. But since she was Seattle through and through, it was fitting.

Should she hug Frankie? Shake her hand? Camille felt prickly, as though she were in the presence of a celebrity. She waited for Frankie to make the first move.

Frankie's smile was almost angelic. She graciously shook hands as she was introduced to Trish and Gigi, and then took Camille's hand as though she were a little girl wanting to be led across the parking lot. Gigi and Trish took the hint and followed behind.

Hand in hand, Camille walked Frankie up to the reception desk and watched in amazement as the guard actually smiled and welcomed Frankie to the prison.

Do they know who she is, or is it just Frankie's way of creating magic wherever she goes?

No matter. The women went through the metal detector, and for the first time ever, the wait to enter through the glass doors was only seconds. Frankie moved as though she was in a walking meditation, looking ahead. But at the same time it was almost as if she wasn't seeing anything but whatever was exactly in front of her.

Another guard smiled directly at Frankie, who looked at him as if she felt sorry for his penance as a prison guard. *Surreal,* thought Camille.

The vacuity of the prison visiting room struck Camille more emphatically than usual, now that Frankie had entered. She felt like she was part of an entourage as she organized five chairs around the metal table.

For the first time, Frankie spoke. "I'll meet with Charli over there." She pointed to the table along the bank of floor-to-ceiling windows overlooking a handful of outdoor tables, farthest from the ever-present vending machines. "Alone."

Camille, Gigi, and Trish looked at each other. Gigi took the lead. "Of course. This is between you and Charli." She got up and moved the extra chairs.

"Thanks for understanding. I have known this day would come and have played it out a million times in my head. I've never been so ready to meet someone. I hope I can stay centered enough to answer all of Charli's questions." Frankie began to tear up.

First she's some kind of guru, and then she's like a nervous teenager.

As Gigi placed the two chairs across from each other at the chosen table, Charli appeared and looked expectantly at Frankie, who stood and shot Charli a deeply authentic look of knowing.

Frankie's mysterious aura dissolved as she waited for Charli to cross the room. The two women sat down, looking like sisters who'd known each other forever.

———

Charli spoke first. "Thank you so much for coming. I'm a nervous wreck." Her voice was shaky.

"Me too." Frankie leaned over the table toward Charli. "Let me say first that I don't know exactly where Daisy is, but I can for sure point you in the right direction."

Charli began to cry. She wasn't going to correct Frankie and say her daughter's name was actually Willow. *Who cares?*

"I'm going to tell you a bit about Daisy's journey and mine, and then we can come up with a plan, okay?"

Charli nodded through her tears.

"Okay. First of all, when I met Daisy, her name was Ju. Her grandma Jing had named her Ju."

Charli's heart felt like it was opening. Just as she'd thought, Jing had taken Willow. That was good news.

"But there was always something amiss in that household. Jing had to have some kind of hip surgery, and before I knew it, she ended up getting hooked on oxy. You familiar with oxy?"

Charli nodded. "My ex and I owned a chain of pharmacies, and he ended up becoming an illegal oxy supplier, so I know it well."

"Makes sense, because that asshole kept shoveling her full of oxy. He thought he was duping me by putting it in these fancy little glass pill bottles so no one would know what she was on. He really didn't give me much credit."

"Trish told me that Jing went to rehab and finally got off the oxy."

Now it was Frankie's turn to tear up. "I think of Jing often. For a few years, we talked intermittently, and she helped me so much by sending money. But she couldn't communicate with me because her son was all over her phone and tech. And then it became hard to keep in touch with all that was going on. I'm so relieved she's off the pills."

"I know how it is to recover from an oxy addiction. So many of the women here are in the struggle. And it's deep. And hard."

"It's beyond hard. But we're getting ahead of ourselves."

"Okay, go on." Charli was sitting on her hands, unconsciously rocking back and forth.

"So, you probably know that I took off to try and save Daisy from these weird guys who seemed to be way too interested in her. They were like mean-ass security guards watching over both Jing and Daisy. But not me. In fact, they acted as though I didn't even exist. Which turned out to work in my favor."

"I hear you took Willow home to Port Angeles."

"Willow? Is that her real name?" Frankie said it again softly. "Willow. Such a perfect name for her. One of my favorite climbing trees in the park is a willow."

Charli nodded tearfully.

"Okay, I'll call her Willow then. So, Willow and I ended up in Port Angeles. And I'm not proud to say this, but we landed back at my high school boyfriend's place. Even before I took off the first time, my boyfriend had changed in ways I couldn't imagine. He was a good guy back in high school, but over time, he turned really controlling and sometimes mean when we were together. He was early on in what turned out to be a pretty serious addiction. And by the time we got back to PA, he had totally gone down the rabbit hole. But I went back to him anyway. And before I knew it, I ended up circling the drain right along with him. With meth, it happens very fast."

"I'm so sorry that happened to you."

"Yeah, well, it brought me to where I am today, which is something I'm very proud of." Frankie paused. "But back to Daisy—I mean Willow. So, as Quinn became more abusive to me and even threatened Willow, I decided to get her out of our place. And by that time my mom was totally in love with her, so she offered to have Willow come and stay with her, which I was so very grateful for."

Charli felt faint. "Was your mom good to her?"

"Beyond good. Willow adored her nonny. But by then, the whole oxy situation was getting out of hand. My own dad had been prescribed oxy for an on-the-job injury, and he got addicted. And one thing led to another, and he ended up cooking meth and caused a fatal explosion in their trailer. Both of my parents died in the fire."

Charli shook her head in disbelief. "Oh my God, I'm so sorry."

"We were a good family. Me'n my sisters were basketball stars on our high school team, and my parents never missed even one game.

They were the best. I never in my wildest dreams would have thought my dad would die as a drug addict. It was too much to take in."

"And . . . Willow?"

"By an amazing stroke of luck, she was at my sister's the day of the fire. But . . ." Frankie stopped and started to full-on cry.

Grateful that the no-physical-contact rule didn't apply in the visiting room, Charli reached over and gently put her hand over Frankie's.

"I am working very hard to forgive my sister Monique for what happened next."

Charli held her breath.

Frankie began to cry softly. "They told me that Daisy died in the fire." She closed her eyes and tried to pull herself out of the abyss. "And I went down fast. It was all meth, all the time. I was lost."

"What kind of a sister does that?"

"Looking back, which I do often, I think they wanted to keep Daisy away from Quinn, who, like I said, had become a wildly violent drug addict. So, even though I struggle to fully understand what they did, I can feel their concern. But back when it happened, I was in such a dark place, I felt like I'd never come out. I loved Daisy like she was my own baby by that time. And all my friends just assumed that she was mine, so everyone was devastated."

"Except your sisters, right?"

Frankie wiped her nose with the back of her hand and swallowed, making a gulping sound. "My sister Monique runs a day care in her house, so she somehow managed to keep Daisy's whereabouts a secret from everyone. I don't know exactly how she did it, but maybe it was for the best. We'll never know. I was going downhill fast, but like I said, when they told me that Daisy died, I fell hard into the drug scene."

Charli tried to imagine Frankie's dive into addiction and wondered how she had gotten to where she was now.

"I was in and out of jail a few times. My sisters wouldn't bail me out, which made me hate them at the time. But now, looking back on it, it probably saved my life. I got into a diversion program, but then I relapsed, and the program wasn't all that forgiving. The last time I got out, I committed to sobriety. For some people, hitting rock bottom, like getting tangled up in the legal system, helps them make life-changing decisions. But no one knows how to actually kick the addiction. What really worked for me was using the skills I learned in the diversion pro-gram, even though I had to do it all on my own. Those skills, combined with my unstoppable commitment to my health and well-being, are what saved my life once and for all." She paused. "The last time I was in jail, after my sisters abandoned me, I got clean and sober and made the decision to stay away from Quinn. So I moved in with a high school friend over in La Push, and her sister's daughter was in Monique's day care in PA. And one thing led to another, and I discovered that Daisy was alive and living with Monique!"

Charli tried to imagine how that must have felt, but she came up short. She was speechless.

"It didn't take me long to come up with a plan to bust Daisy out of Monique's place."

"And . . ."

"And I went in like Rambo. Doors flew open, Monique was scream-ing. I grabbed her cell phone and threw it as far as I could out the front door. And then I don't even remember how I got upstairs to Daisy, but next thing I knew, Daisy and I were in Monique's garage. And all of Monique's camping gear caught my eye, and I started throwing every-thing I could find into the back of my friend Johnny's old red Jeep that he lent me when I took off from Seattle rather abruptly. Tents, sleeping bags, camp stoves—it was like being in an REI with an empty cart. I was on-fire mad. Monique was in shock or something. And besides, I'd taken her phone, so all she could do was watch me load up my car. She even had dried hiking food and bottled water on the shelves. Her washing machine is out in her garage, so I pulled everything out of the dryer and into the dirty laundry basket, hoping that some of Daisy's clothes would be in the pile, and took off."

"Where'd you take Willow?"

"We made our way up into Olympic National Park and found an out-of-the-way campsite, where we stayed for a few days while I got organized. Turns out I was right to grab the laundry. There were enough clothes for her to have something warm to wear. It gets cold up there at night."

"Okay, so where did you go next?" Charli felt the flush of hopefulness.

"We spent the summer camping all around the park."

Charli waited with her eyes closed.

"One day, Daisy woke up with a horrible earache. I tried home remedies, none of which worked, so I had a friend—hikers are the nicest people—take us down out of the mountains to the clinic in PA. And that's where I lost her."

Charli took a sharp breath.

"I tried to get her care, but since I had no ID and I couldn't prove that she was my daughter, they called CPS and took her into the system." Frankie's quiet crying quickly turned to sobs. "I lost her. I lost your daughter. But we can probably find her now that we know who her mother is." Frankie squeezed Charli's hand. She spoke softly and confidently. "I heard about you around the campfire a few months ago from a woman who'd just come home from prison. I did some research, and we can have her dependency file opened so you can find her."

Charli leaned over the table and put her head on her arms. She didn't even try to stop the tears.

Frankie waited as long as it took. Her regal bearing returned slowly. "Let's talk about you for a minute," she said gently. "How'd you end up here? I've heard bits and pieces of your story, but I'd like to hear it directly from you."

Charli focused through her tears. "You probably already know that I got set up by my ex. We own a chain of pharmacies, and I discovered that he was running an illegal drug ring. But when I tried to shut him down, he planted a bag of heroin in my car and had me arrested. And he put a handgun under my seat, which I later learned makes for a longer sentence." She paused. "There's something called an Amber Alert, and it lets cops search your car without a warrant because there might be a kidnapped kid in your trunk. That's the short version."

"The same thing that happened to Camille, right? She told me all about it at our campout last week."

"Yeah. But thankfully, she can probably get the search thrown out because they opened a backpack in her trunk, which was illegal because they could see that there wasn't a kid in the trunk. So that made it an illegal search without a warrant."

"But those are almost identical setups, right?" Frankie asked.

"Yep. I wish I had been that lucky. The guy who put the drugs in Camille's car just chucked the backpack in there. Not me. Whoever did it was smarter than that."

"Camille says she thinks it was my old boyfriend, Quinn Hastings, who set her up. Any chance he was the one who planted the drugs in your car?"

Charli perked up. "I have no idea, but it's a great question."

Frankie focused on Charli. "Tell me about your pharmacy empire. I know Quinn pretty well. If he was the one who put the drugs in your car, I might be able to convince him to come forward, especially since his prints are likely all over the evidence in Camille's case and the prosecutor will be full of questions for him."

"Well, it happened in Seattle, not PA, so I'm not sure it could have been Quinn."

"What year?" Frankie's voice was sharp.

"2013."

Frankie was silent. "Me'n Quinn moved to Seattle right after high school, in 2012."

Charli caught Frankie's eyes. The look that passed between them was everything.

"And . . ." Frankie stopped for a moment. "We were students at Bellevue College. Quinn was studying to become a pharmacist. What was the name of your pharmacies?"

"The first few were in the Seattle area so we called them Cascade, after the mountain range. Why? Do you know them?"

"Well, Quinn got a job at some pharmacy near the college, and not long after that, he dropped out and left me, to go back to PA. Was right around the time he got involved in drugs."

"And you think there's a chance that Quinn was working for my ex, Martin?"

Frankie nodded. "It's looking like that may be the case. I know exactly where that store was because I took him and picked him up sometimes. We only had one car between us."

"Where was it?" Charli tried, unsuccessfully, to quell the butterflies in her chest.

"Out by Crossroads."

"Was it close to Uwajimaya?"

"Yeah, right across the street."

"Oh my God, I bet that was our third store. We called it Cascade Three." Charli grabbed the table to steady herself. "I can't believe this." She let loose the tears. "This might be huge."

A minute or two passed as the women sat in silence, taking in what had just happened.

"Okay, let's gather the team now." Frankie waved at the threesome sitting across the room. They nearly ran over the other visitors to get to Charli and Frankie.

Trish was the first to speak. "So, do we know where Willow is?"

Frankie took charge. "We know where to look, and I'll fill you all in when we leave here. But for now, my goal is to get Charli out of here, and I think I may have a plan."

Charli glanced at her sister. Gigi stared back in disbelief. "We're all ears."

"I have spent the past several years avoiding Quinn Hastings. I've been living in and around Olympic National Park most of that time. But before that, I hiked the entire Pacific Crest Trail solo. That's where I decided that my life's work would be to support women coming out of jail and prison in their sobriety and help them to find the strength to stay away from their abusers. Quinn was my abuser."

The women were rapt.

"Now I need to speak with him. I'm going to need to find a safe place. As I understand it, he's likely going down for planting oxy in Camille's car—assuming you guys can show that his fingerprints are on that pack of cigarettes."

Trish interrupted. "But what does that have to do with Charli's conviction?"

"I'm pretty sure Quinn planted that heroin in Charli's car. And if he did, he needs to come clean about it." Frankie was insistent.

Trish looked puzzled. "But Charli went down in King County, and Quinn's in PA—"

Frankie interjected, "We lived in Bellevue for a couple of years after high school, and Quinn was studying pharmacy at Bellevue College."

The women held their collective breath.

"Me'n Quinn lived there when Charli was set up. And it looks like Quinn was working at one of Martin and Charli's pharmacies while he was in school."

Trish interrupted the palpable silence. "And you think we can get him to come clean about his part in this mess?"

Frankie nodded. "I'm gonna try."

"Why would he do that?" Charli asked.

Camille spoke for the first time. "Because the prosecutor isn't interested in the person who planted the drugs. The prosecutor wants the kingpin. That would be Martin Zhao. And we know that Martin's still dealing, so Frankie wants to flip Quinn on Martin."

"I swore that I would never set sight on Quinn Hastings again. But the only way we'll get you out of here is if we can convince him to flip, and I'm pretty sure I'm the only person who can make that happen."

The women around the table were silent.

Frankie spoke. "I need to get him alone someplace. But not in my park. That's my refuge. I don't want his energy anywhere near my life there. And he's gonna detox once we've got him away, so it needs to be close enough to medical care but still isolated. Somewhere with minimal services, and wilderness. It's time for Quinn to find himself."

"How do we get him to go with us?" Trish asked.

"I have a very strong feeling that if you tell him you're taking him to me, he'll go more than willingly."

"You two were high school sweethearts, right?"

Frankie looked at Camille. "That's one way of putting it. He's into me in a weird way that's hard to explain. First he's all warm and fuzzy, then he loses his shit. And when he got on the oxy and later the meth, he turned into some kind of monster. He was awful." She stopped abruptly. "He'll come."

Trish redirected the conversation. "So, where do we take him?"

"How about the San Juans?" Camille offered. "One of the small, isolated islands. You can be very remote but not necessarily far from medical services in a pinch."

Frankie nodded. "Might be exactly perfect. I just need to get him where he can't get ahold of any drugs. And an island sounds like it would fit the bill, because there'd be no way for him to escape."

"Have an idea as to which island?" Trish asked Camille, who had spent the better part of the summers sailing around the San Juan and Gulf Islands and parts farther north.

Camille considered the options. "I'm thinking James Island. It's about seven miles over the water from Anacortes, where there's a great hospital. But the only way you can get there is by boat, because it's just a tiny little island with a few campsites and a dock. And no one will be there at this time of year." She turned to Frankie. "It might be pretty cold, and probably windy. And there are no cabins there. You'd need a tent. But that sounds rough." She reconsidered. "Would you rather have a cabin? I think there are some island parks with cabins. I can check."

"No, not really. I have mad foul- and cold-weather gear. Cold, unfriendly weather is the perfect backdrop for a good detox. As long as it's not pouring rain, I can make a campfire." She looked around the table. "Anyone know the weather report for the next few days?"

"Not sure, but the weather in the islands can be different than the city because it's in a rain shadow," Camille responded. "We can check when we get in the car."

Gigi leaned in. "What else do you need? And how will we get him there?"

"We'll need a boat, or will the water taxi drop them off there?" Trish asked.

"Well . . ." Camille smiled. "We do have a sailboat."

"We do indeed." Trish winked at her friend. "Are you suggesting we grab Quinn and sail him across the strait and drop him and Frankie off?"

Camille nodded. "Why not?" She glanced at Frankie. "You don't get seasick, do you?"

"I think I'm about to find out."

CHAPTER THIRTY-EIGHT

A few days later, the red Jeep and the blue Ford Explorer pulled up, caravan style, in front of Talulla's place, in a sleepy neighborhood in Port Townsend, about an hour east of Port Angeles. The plan was for Frankie to grab all the gear she'd need for a few nights on a cold and windy island in February.

The last few days had been so full of emotion, and the anticipation of what was to come was palpable. Trish exited the car and opened the gate of the white picket fence. She turned to Gigi, who was still sitting in the car. "You want to get out and say hi?"

Gigi shook her head. "I'll wait here." She blew her nose. "I'm a nervous mess."

"I understand," Trish replied. "Camille and I can help Frankie pack up." She cocked her head toward Frankie, who was already at the front door. "She's gonna need some serious gear for a couple of days on a remote island in the winter." She looked at Camille expectantly.

"Exactly." Camille reached for her puffy coat and turned to Gigi. "You stay here. No need to get out. We won't be long."

"You okay?" Trish held Gigi's hand and kissed it.

Gigi winked at her partner. "I'm good. I just need a few minutes alone."

"Okay, we'll be quick."

Frankie was already in the garage filling a long duffel bag with a tent, sleeping bags, and all kinds of camping gear to get her through a few days off the grid. An older woman with a head of fluffy peach-tinged pink hair stood in the garage in lavender sweatpants, a green down vest over a baby blue hoodie, and a pair of Uggs. The wrinkles on her face gave her an aura of wisdom rather than age. She was drinking coffee from a huge cup with some writing, mostly worn off, on the side.

"You must be Talulla," Trish said as she reached out to shake the woman's hand.

The woman put her cup on the giant top-loading freezer and shooed away Trish's outstretched hand and leaned in for a friendly hug. Her voice was low and raspy—as if she'd smoked a thousand cigarettes in her day. "I was waitin' to meet all you gals." She put her hands on her hips and watched Frankie throwing together her gear. "Where ya headed, hon?"

"Heading up to the San Juans for a short camping trip. It's complicated to explain. I should be back midweek." Frankie opened the freezer and rummaged around, throwing various frozen packages of food onto the cement floor of the garage.

Talulla bent down and opened a fifty-pound bag of brown rice and filled a gallon baggie. "Don't forget the rice again." It looked like a standing joke between the logistics person and the team leader.

Frankie pecked Talulla on the cheek. "When have I ever forgotten to pack the rice?"

Talulla shrugged playfully. "Oh, I dunno, maybe last weekend? And why on earth are you going camping in the islands in February? It's a different kind of cold up there. Wet. And windy."

Frankie sat down cross-legged on the floor of the garage and began ripping open a box of energy bars and threw the bars into her duffel. Then she gestured to Camille to pull down a bigger box off the shelf and asked her to put a handful of freeze-dried meals and some packs of walnuts into the bag. Frankie looked up at her. "They have potable water over on that island?"

Camille opened her phone and googled James Island Marine State Park. "Checking."

Just as Frankie was zipping up her duffels, Gigi tentatively poked her head into the garage.

Talulla stepped forward, as though she was accustomed to strange women showing up at any time of night or day. "Here for ya, hon. How can I help?"

"She's with us." Trish picked her way over the mess of camping and climbing gear that covered the garage floor. "You okay?" Her voice was warm and filled with love.

"I just wanted to use the bathroom if I could." Gigi was uncharacteristically meek. She looked exhausted.

"You bet. I'm Mama Talulla, by the way." She shot Gigi a big smile. "Welcome to our headquarters."

"Nice to meet you, Mama." Gigi hugged herself as if she were cold, or maybe just a little insecure.

Talulla pointed Gigi into the house. "Right past my so-called office, which some of you might call my kitchen table. Down the hall on the left."

Gigi disappeared into the house, and in moments let out a scream—it didn't sound fearful, but then again, it didn't sound like she was happy either. "Trish! Get in here!"

Trish was on her feet in a flash and inside the kitchen, followed by the other three women, who found Gigi sitting at Talulla's desk chair— her hands clutching a laptop in a death grip. She was uttering "Oh my God, oh my God, oh my God" over and over.

Trish knelt in front of Gigi and looked up at her. Gigi's eyes were filled with tears, and she ignored Trish and locked onto Talulla. "Where did you get this computer?" Her voice was strong and almost accusatory.

"Calm down, hon, it's just some old workhorse. I've had it forever. Damn thing just won't quit."

Gigi was almost fondling the laptop. It was as though only she and Talulla were in the room. Gigi was almost in a trance. "Your husband was a high school coach, right?"

Talulla nodded. "Tru killed that asshole with her bare hands. Well, it helped that she had a baseball bat handy. And please don't call him my husband. We call him the decedent." She dropped her voice. "Why do you ask?"

"And my sister's boyfriend, Brian, worked for your . . . the decedent, right?"

Talulla nodded again, completely unaware of the connection that both Camille and Trish were making between Gigi and the computer she was now holding like a baby in her arms. "Ya, his assistant coach was Brian something." Her voice trailed off.

Gigi continued, just to be sure. "All of your husband's, I mean, the decedent's stuff was confiscated when they arrested Tru, right?"

"It was."

"And it looks like somehow you got the stuff out of evidence, right?"

"They called me and asked if I wanted all his crap. And to be honest, I was broke and I needed anything and everything I could get my hands on while I waited for the life insurance money."

By now both Camille and Trish were tearing up. Trish was rubbing Gigi's knee, and Camille was leaning against the refrigerator, feeling like she was in a dream.

Gigi held up the computer so Trish and Camille could see the array of UW tennis team stickers strewn haphazardly across the closed laptop, all surrounding a worn-out sticker of Lucy limply holding a tennis racket. "I think I'm going to faint."

Talulla and Frankie knew when to wait to be let in on a secret.

Hope filled Gigi's voice as she asked, "Did you ever wipe the memory of this computer?"

"I wouldn't know a computer memory if it hit me in the head." Talulla laughed. "I did have some kid break into this old thing a very long time ago, just so I could use it. And all I do is use it for emails and keeping lists and stuff in Word. I don't know how to use any of the programs."

Gigi closed her eyes as if she were praying and asked, "Was there another part to this computer, a black box with a wire that plugged into it? That would be a hard drive."

"Oh dear, I have no idea. But if there was, it might be around here somewhere." Talulla pointed into the garage. "I got more boxes than I can count, and that doesn't even include the boxes in the basement."

Trish got up and addressed Talulla. "It looks like this is likely Charli's old computer. Charli is Gigi's sister, and she is in WCCW on a drug charge. The charge came out of a discovery she and her boyfriend, Brian, made about her husband running a drug ring out of his pharmacy. Charli downloaded the evidence onto her computer. Brian hid the computer in the locker room in some box of climbing equipment, and before he could go and get it back, he was arrested. It looks like Charli's computer was inadvertently taken into evidence when Tru killed your husband. Gigi thinks this is that computer, and it could well help us get Charli out of prison."

"Lordy, lordy, you have no idea how many times I wanted to pitch that old machine into the Sound, but it just kept on working—for the most part. What do we do now?"

"I'd say we start rummaging through those boxes you mentioned." Trish waved her hand toward the garage.

Frankie took in the scene. "Okay, so if we add this computer data to the testimony we're hoping to get from Quinn, that should go a long way toward the motion you're planning to file to get Charli out, right?"

"That's the plan," Camille confirmed.

Frankie turned to Gigi. "You okay staying here with Talulla and Lizbeth's sister, Isabel, to look through the boxes for that hard drive? Me'n Camille need to get Quinn up to that island, and since I don't know how to sail, I'm assuming that we'll need Trish as first mate, correct?"

Trish put her head on Gigi's knees and looked up at her. "Frankie's right. I need to go with Camille. We'll need to set sail at the crack of dawn to get across the strait before dark. And I think I'll go pay our pal Quinn a visit this afternoon. Gotta entice him to come for an early-morning sail."

Trish pulled out her phone. "Over here." She gestured to Frankie. "I'll need some proof that you'll be there in the morning." She paused. "I know you're not keen on having photos taken. I'll delete this as soon as we have Quinn with us out on the strait."

Frankie leaned over Trish's shoulder and smiled for a selfie. "I'm trusting you." She winked.

Gigi's energy had changed entirely. The moping ended, and her natural spark reappeared. "I'm good. I'll stay here with Talulla as long as someone can watch the girls back at home. I've had Angela and Libby at my place while Camille's been running up and down the peninsula this past couple of weeks."

Camille looked at her watch. "Sam and Gracie are landing at six tonight. I'll text Angela and Sam and tell them that the girls should plan to stay at our place this weekend. I already told Sam I was taking the boat back to Friday Harbor on Saturday, so he's not expecting me home until Monday."

"Perfect." Gigi turned to Talulla and pointed to the boxes lining the garage. "Do we start here?"

Talulla pulled a big box off the shelves and ripped off the packing tape. "Let's do this."

CHAPTER THIRTY-NINE

The look on Quinn's face when he saw Trish at his door was hard to interpret. Shock? Or maybe hopefulness? After all, he'd been trying to convince her to go out with him ever since they met.

"Hey." He was clearly trying to sound casual.

"Hey." Trish didn't want to scare him away. "Got a smoke?" she teased.

His smile was flirtatious. "I do." He nodded.

"I forgive you for locking me in the boat. But it was a bit of an asshole move."

"Boss's orders. I knew you'd get out once the marina security guard came by."

"I did." Trish sized him up. He didn't appear to be loaded. Yet.

Quinn held out a pack of kreteks.

Trish took one and waited for him to light it. "So, you're probably wondering why I'm here."

"Where are my manners—you want to come inside?"

"No thanks. I'm here with a crazy message from a friend of yours."

Quinn crossed his arms and leaned against the doorjamb. "This oughta be good." He seemed curious but cautious.

Trish held up her phone to show him the picture of her and Frankie. "I found our friend Malika, and she wanted me to ask you to come see her. Says you two have quite a history."

Quinn leaned out the door and snatched the phone from Trish's outstretched hand.

"What the fuck? Where is she?" Quinn looked almost desperate.

"She wants to see you."

"I thought she was dead or something." Quinn's mantle of coolness dropped away. "I finally gave up looking for her. Someone said she died out on a trail in the desert or something."

Trish almost felt sorry for Quinn in that moment. "No idea about where she's been. I told you—we played basketball together back in Seattle. I just reconnected with her, and somehow the conversation turned to our old boyfriends and she mentioned you."

"Tell her to come out here. I'll meet her here anytime." Quinn's words came fast.

They'd anticipated this. "She says it's too painful. Her baby died out here. I can see why she'd want to steer clear of this place."

Quinn nodded, appearing somewhat relieved that Trish seemed to have valid information about Malika.

"I get it. She freaked out after her kid died. Took off, was in and out of jail, then I lost track of her."

"Well, she's gonna be on that boat tomorrow morning at seven thirty, and she wants to see you. She's heading out not long after that, so if you want to see her, be on time."

"Why tomorrow? Where is she now?" There was a tone of urgency in his voice.

"Not there. No idea where she is. Your old girlfriend is a little mysterious."

"Okay, okay, I'll be there. Seven thirty?"

"Yep. Don't be late, or you might miss her."

Trish dropped the fragrant cigarette in the gravel and ground it out. Quinn seemed frozen in place. He didn't move from his doorway as Trish pulled out of the long driveway.

CHAPTER FORTY

As planned, Trish had dropped off Camille and Gigi at the grocery store while she paid Quinn a visit. They caught up at the coffee shop next door, then headed back to the boat.

When Camille saw her mom in the faint gray light of impending dusk, huddled in the cockpit of *Sofia*, snuggled up in a down sleeping bag, she was flooded with feelings of apprehension combined with thankfulness. Every time Camille saw her mother, she had a reaction. Sometimes deep love. Sometimes frustration that she didn't get more time with her. Sometimes jealousy that she often felt like she took second place to her mother's commitment to her beloved asylum refugees. And sometimes just plain awe at everything her mother was and had become.

Without thinking, she broke into a full run. "Mom!" she yelled. And then her sensibilities took over. "What on earth are you doing? It's freezing out here."

Pella shot her daughter a sly smile and pulled out a handful of sleeping bag warmers. "Technology is everything, my darling." She squeezed a warmer in her arms. "I need to take back a boatload of these for my people. It's cold like this over there, and they have nothing. These are amazing."

Always focused on her "people." Camille wished for a moment she could be one of her mother's "people." Pella reached out for a hug without moving from her perch on the cockpit bench, and Camille leaned down and nearly threw herself into the safety of her mother's arms.

"I'm so scared, Mom." Camille let loose the cascade of tears that had been building up since her arrest.

Pella held her daughter and kissed her gently on the top of her head, then pulled her back so she could look her in the eyes. The two women barely noticed Trish and Frankie standing on the dock, waiting respectfully for the mother-daughter magic to play out.

Camille lived for these moments with her mom. They were few and far between. Her mom put one hand under Camille's chin and, without letting her gaze leave Camille's, pulled a legal pleading out of her backpack with the other. She gingerly handed the pleading to her daughter and illuminated it with her cell phone.

Camille had no glasses, and besides, she wouldn't have been able to read through her tears. "What is it?"

Pella leaned back to take in her daughter. Her voice was bold. "Charges dismissed." Her matter-of-fact demeanor belied the excitement and relief written all over her face.

"Wait, what?!" Camille collapsed back into her mother's arms. "My charges? Dismissed?" She couldn't breathe. "But the oral argument is next Tuesday."

"Well, looks like we have a free afternoon now." Pella held up her hand to high-five her daughter, who was still taking it all in. Camille held on to her mother's hand and enveloped her in a huge hug.

The tears began to flow as the mother-daughter duo disentangled themselves.

"Charges dismissed!" Camille hollered down the dock to Trish, who was pushing a dock cart filled with canvas grocery bags.

"What?! What charges?"

"My fucking badass mother got my charges dismissed!" It was finally beginning to sink in.

Trish's earsplitting whistle echoed off the water in the nearly empty marina. She abandoned the bags and bolted on board, where she grabbed Camille and did a little happy dance. "Un-fucking-believable!"

"Oh jeez. Where are my manners?" Camille wiped her face with the back of her hand and turned to Frankie, who was standing patiently on the dock. She held out her hand and assisted Frankie to board the gently rocking boat. "Mom, this is my friend Frankie."

Pella held up her arms from what now felt like her throne. Frankie leaned over and placed a kiss on Pella's cheek. "Camille was right, I do think we'll be good friends." Frankie turned to take in the pinkening sky. "Your energy is something special," she said as she pivoted back to face Pella. "I'm glad to know you."

"Likewise, my dear." Pella's response was clearly heartfelt.

Camille turned to Frankie. "My mom just got my charges dismissed for the illegal search of my car." She looked directly at her mother. "How on earth—"

"Well, I just couldn't wait," Pella interrupted. "I just had to pop over here and have a little chat with my favorite student, Rose." She dropped her voice. "Don't tell Trent that Rose is my favorite—we need to keep him on the hook for later. Hopefully," she added.

"What? You met with the prosecutor?" Her mother broke every preconception Camille had about being a lawyer.

Pella shrugged her shoulders. "Sometimes you just want to drop by and visit an old friend with a nice hot chai tea."

"You can do that in the criminal law world?"

Pella nodded. "Someone had to let her know that there was no reason for her to waste prosecutor time on a losing motion. Funny thing is that my motion had gone into the system, and Rose had no idea we'd even filed it." She laughed. "We had a nice visit. I haven't had a Socratic dialogue in quite some time. But after I dragged her through a piercing analysis of the intricacies of the Fourth Amendment, we landed together on the only sensible result. You can't proceed to trial on an unconstitutional search. I even offered to come and school the local police on this."

"Of course you did." Camille felt the tension lift from her.

"Well, ladies, she declined my offer, and you could tell she was one pissed-off prosecutor. Very, very unhappy with her law enforcement team. As well she should be." Pella paused. "Any chance the cops were in on this? It's just so wrong to do this kind of search. They had to know it wouldn't stick."

"No idea." Camille had obviously considered the possibility that a crooked cop had been involved here. "It happens, for sure."

Pella interrupted. "And that's not all." She leaned forward as though she were about to share a secret. "Those cigarettes?" She leaned back and threw her hands in the air. "Quinn Hastings all over them. And the backpack as well. Just our luck that he'd been fingerprinted back during an old drug bust." She rubbed her hands together and turned to Trish. "Brilliant catch. Rose is very interested in talking to your pal Quinn. We had a very robust discussion about the importance of going up the chain. It's not the lowly addict who should be prosecuted—it's the person up at the top who is using these broken people for their own financial gain."

"Wow, Mom. Rose is willing to talk with Quinn to flip him on Martin?"

"She sure is. Any chance he'll do it?"

Frankie chimed in. "He will if I can get to him and help him understand what'll happen if he doesn't."

"Okey doke, then. Looks like you ladies have your work cut out for you." Pella smiled. "I'm grateful to just be here with you amazing warriors. I must be honest, when Camille told me what you all were up to, I had to work hard to hold the vision of a successful outcome. Now it sounds like a plan is uncovering itself to you ladies. Nicely done."

Trish hopped onto the dock and handed a bag of groceries to Camille, then checked the mooring lines were securely cleated.

Frankie clung to the heavy stays holding up the mast as she carefully moved up toward the bow of the boat. When she got to the bowsprit, she sat down gently and crossed her legs. The glow of the sky reflected off the water, encasing Frankie in a pink beam of light. Camille could see her new friend's back expanding and contracting with deep breaths. It was as if nothing else existed in the world for Frankie. Pella pointed at her and nodded approvingly. She turned back to Camille and Trish and held up both arms in a salutation to the sunset, then put her hand in Camille's, squeezed it, and copied Frankie's deep breathing. Soon the three women in the cockpit were in a kind of eyes-open meditation, taking in the last drips of the sunset.

Sometimes the five or ten minutes after the actual winter sunset brought the most spectacular of skies. And then things went dark quickly. When the lights of the marina came on, the spell was broken, and Pella stood up, still inside her sleeping bag. "What do you all eat around here? I'm starving."

Thankful that they'd stopped at the grocery in Port Townsend, Camille unlocked the new lock on the hatch and took the bag of groceries and climbed down into the galley.

"What's for dinner?" Trish's voice caught Camille by surprise.

Camille rummaged around in the canvas grocery bag and pulled out a bottle of wine and uncorked it as Trish took the plastic marine-style wineglasses off the shelf and began pouring.

"It's Friday-night pasta!" Camille announced as she took out the heirloom tomatoes she'd been surprised to see at the local grocery. She pulled out the pot and filled it with water as Trish held up her glass in a toast.

"To the best damn lawyer in the world!" Camille beat Trish to the toast.

Frankie held up her bottle of half-drunk kombucha. "Pretty sure we have two kick-ass lawyers here. But this one's for you, Pella!" She got up, clinked her bottle with their wineglasses, and joined the twosome in the kitchen.

Trish and Frankie busied themselves finding bowls, flatware, and napkins to set the table, as Camille toasted the pine nuts, sliced the kalamatas and tomatoes, and then washed the arugula while Pella opened the goat cheese and parmesan.

Placing the one-pot dinner on the table, Camille sat in wonderment at her good fortune. "I'm not a prayer, but I do want to give thanks for my incredible mom here, who just saved my ass from a lengthy prison sentence." She leaned over and placed a big kiss on her mother's cheek.

Pella took over. "I do think it's appropriate under the circumstances for us to each offer a word of thanks for something that's important to us." She held up her glass of wine and looked each woman directly in the eye. "I could not be more proud of each of you." They each took a sip of their drink.

Trish went next. "What happened today was more than just a lucky break. It was magic, plain and simple." She looked at Pella. "Wait till we tell you about our day." She toasted and took a sip.

"Frankie?" Pella raised an eyebrow. "How about you?"

When it came to the aura of vibrational royalty, Camille noted, Frankie gave Pella a run for her money. It was glorious to watch the two changemakers sharing space.

After about thirty seconds, Frankie spoke. "Let's all just close our eyes and feel the rocking of the boat. And smell the delicious food. And bask in these new friendships." She closed her eyes and said, "Today was the day I've known was coming for the past five years. I am just thankful that I was able to be present with Charli and offer her unrelenting hope that she finds her beloved daughter. I take this mantle seriously. I will do whatever needs to be done to serve Charli and Willow and to ensure that they are reunited."

Camille handed Frankie the bowl of pasta. "We're so grateful to have you on our team, Frankie."

"The women inside need advocates like you and your team, who're working hard on the outside to humanize the struggles of the women and tell their stories."

Camille turned to her mother. "Do you think we can ever get Tru out of prison? She killed her abuser when she found him assaulting her younger sister."

"That's a complicated one. Ever since I've been working in the criminal law arena, there have been rumblings about passing what used to be called a battered women's defense. That would mean that a woman who kills her abuser can put on evidence of her own abuse at the hands of her abuser to argue a kind of self-defense. But every time we try to legislate it, we lose. My hope is that, as more women get into office, there might be more of an understanding of this kind of complicated relationship. And better yet, we need women in office that have dealt with personal trauma. That's something that can't easily be understood by those who haven't suffered that kind of hell."

Camille nodded. "The problem is that our government is not set up for ordinary citizens to become legislators. Who can just walk away from their jobs and family for three months or so every year to go to their state capital? Rich white men. Or even rich women, that's who. Women who have come up through these traumatic situations just don't have the resources to become politicians. They need to work and take care of their families, and so their voices and experiences are never heard in the halls of power."

"So . . . ," Trish said thoughtfully. "I never even thought of this. We'll have a hard time changing these kinds of laws because no one in office really understands the dynamic."

"Exactly." Pella pointed her fork at Trish.

"Well," Frankie added, "I work closely with these women, and I could see some of them having the passion to run for office. They're hella smart, but for sure they would never have the income or resources to take three months off each year. This is really screwed up. How can we change the laws when the people making the laws can't possibly understand what would work to solve these thorny issues? This is fascinating. And really frustrating."

Camille looked at her friends. Anytime her mother was at a table, the conversation turned to something life changing. And provocative. And important.

The discussion was interrupted by a text from Lucia advising Camille to check her email. The text ended with a smiley emoji. Camille grabbed her laptop and logged on.

While the email was loading, Frankie stood and grabbed her jacket. "I gotta get out of here. If Quinn shows up tonight, it's best that I'm not here. I'll head over to Ginny's to spend the night."

Trish spoke up. "If you see a bright-blue truck up there, come right back—that's Quinn's rig."

"Got it." Frankie paused and looked each woman in the eye. "The next few days are going to be intense for me. I hope I can get some rest."

Camille hugged Frankie without saying a word, and Frankie climbed up the companionway into the black night.

Camille turned her attention to her email. "Oh my God." She looked up. "Mom, take a look at this."

Pella leaned over to read Lucia's email.

Surprise, surprise. Hope this helps! I contacted my friend Zara, who is the director of the Innocence Project in Seattle, and asked if she'd send me a brief they used to successfully get an innocent person released. And voilà! Here it is! I got so excited about using this brief that I even took a stab at drafting the facts section. I learned from Zara that the legal section is the same for most motions, but we have to add the facts of our specific case. So, she's been helping me with a draft motion.

Pella flipped her glasses down off the top of her head. "Open it up!"

"I knew Lucia was a bit of a jailhouse lawyer, but I had no idea that she was this interested in the intricacies of the law."

The two women read silently for several minutes. And as they scrolled down the last page, Pella commented, "This girl belongs in law school. This is a brilliant start of a Rule 7 legal brief."

Camille was stunned. "It's amazing that Lucia did this with no formal legal training. I'm speechless." She pulled out her phone and waited for Lucia to come on the line.

Without even saying hello, Lucia said, "Was it stupid of me to even try to write a legal brief that's this complicated?"

"Absolutely not. It's really, really good." Camille hit the Speaker button. "My mom is here and wants to offer her admiration as well. As a former law professor, she's notorious for being stingy with compliments, especially when it comes to legal writing."

Pella took the phone from Camille's hand. "I know nothing about your background, my dear, but I do know legal talent when I see it. I am strongly encouraging you to consider law school, Lucia."

Just like Pella to get right to the point.

"She's right, Lucia. You are exactly what the legal profession needs. You're smart, and you have experience in the criminal legal system."

Pella looked quizzically at Camille, who pointed to the phone.

Before Camille could say anything, Lucia spoke forcefully. "I know I belong in the law. You may remember that I wrote probably close to a hundred briefs when I was in prison."

Pella's eyebrows shot up, and Camille put her hand on her mother's shoulder.

"I even drafted a few motions to open a dependency proceeding, so I'm working on one to open up Willow's dependency. I should have it done by tomorrow. That'll hopefully allow you all to open the records to find out where Willow went after Malika lost her to CPS. I reached out to the civil legal aid clinic, and they sent me some samples to follow."

"What? You know how to open a dependency proceeding?"

"Well, I wouldn't say I know how, but I definitely drafted a few of these when I was in prison, working in the law library with Tru. It's pretty common for the women inside to lose their children to the CPS system, so when they were ready for release, sometimes Tru would help them file those motions."

"Well, shit. I have no idea how to file this kind of motion. It never occurred to me to ask Tru," Camille noted.

"Tru's a badass. She's been lawyering inside of prison for years." Lucia's voice was filled with admiration. "We could all learn a lot from her. I sure did."

"All the more reason we need to get you to law school." Camille's commitment to seeing Lucia as a licensed lawyer was growing by the minute. It was becoming obvious that the best lawyers would be ones who had direct experience in the system.

"I figured that there would be no chance that the bar association would let me sit for the bar, so I kinda tabled my dreams. That's why I work in a law office. It's as close as I think I'll ever come to being a real lawyer."

Pella took charge of the conversation. "Actually, your having been impacted by the criminal legal system is exactly why we need you in the profession. Who knows better the problems—but more importantly the solutions—to the whole issue of mass incarceration than someone like you?"

"But I don't want to go through all the trouble of taking the LSAT, going to school, and working my ass off, only to find out that they won't let me practice law. Those law school loans are big and serious. I'd need some kind of certainty before I commit to take on all that debt."

Camille looked at her mom. "You must know someone at the law school that can help Lucia work through this, right?"

Pella waved her hand. "Of course I do. As soon as I'm back in Seattle, I'll pop over and speak with the dean. I can't imagine that she won't reassure us that Lucia can sit for the bar. What's the point of a law school that promotes social justice if it won't include and support students who have been directly impacted by the criminal legal system?"

"But what about the bar association?" Camille asked.

"I am going to figure this out," Pella said with authority. "Lucia, my mission at this point in my life is to find young women with potential and help them step into positions of power. I got you."

It was clear that Lucia was crying lightly on the other end of the phone. "Oh my God. Thank you so much, both of you. If there's any way I can become a lawyer, I'm all in. I left behind so many women who need serious legal help. And, no offense, Camille, but it would be awesome if one of us from inside could come in and provide legal services. And that would also show the others that it's possible to succeed on the outside."

"My mom is right. We got you. We'll make this happen. If I were you, I'd hop online and order an LSAT study book today."

"Too late—I've been studying for the LSAT for months. I just didn't think it would ever be possible to actually go to law school."

Camille and Pella exchanged smiles.

"I better get going," Lucia said hurriedly. "I have an LSAT study session early tomorrow morning."

"Lucia?" Camille's voice was stern.

"Yes?"

"Thank you for this brief. And thank Zara at the Innocence Project. This is going to save us, like, a week of legal research and drafting."

"She's exactly right." Pella spoke loudly into the phone. "And tell Zara hello for me. Haven't seen her in years."

"I will."

Lucia hung up as Camille downloaded the brief onto her laptop so they could get busy editing it to best fit the facts of their case.

—

After a quick call with Sam to be sure everyone was home safely, Camille and her mom cozied up in the V berth with a couple of cups of hot chamomile tea.

"I think you should argue the CR 7 motion to get Charli out of prison once we have the evidence gathered," Camille told her mom.

"Why on earth would you say that?"

"I've never argued a criminal motion before, and you're the crim law diva of the group."

"You've argued hundreds of family law and tort case motions, my dear. You can do this."

Camille tried to identify why she was so hesitant to argue the motion that might get Charli out of prison. "I think the stakes here are too high for me to do this as my first crim law motion."

"Tell me more."

Ever the law professor, her mom asked question after question, when what Camille wanted was answers. Or maybe just agreement that she was right about her insecurities.

"The stakes in family law are high." Pella looked over her steaming tea at Camille. "In family law, you have the future of children and families in your hands. What do you think is different here?"

"Because it's someone's personal liberty. That's huge. How do you do it? Immigration is similar: you are freeing people from the horrifying conditions of those camps. If you lose, your client gets sent back to likely death, or has to stay in unspeakable conditions." Camille looked up at the ceiling to gather her thoughts, thinking about how to answer her mother's questions. "It's a little terrifying to know that if I do something wrong, Charli might get stuck in that hellhole for years."

"Isn't that why she needs you?"

"What do you mean?"

"People facing prison, or life in an internment camp, or deportation, need someone who believes deep in their bones that they deserve to be released. This isn't some kind of game, like other areas of the law where only money is at stake."

"I know—that's why you should argue it. There are lives on the line. Charli's life, to be exact."

"Let's talk about the law. We all know how messed up the system is. Don't you think that things would have turned out much differently in our society if we exercised compassion instead of punishment?" Pella's question was straightforward.

"Of course."

"Well, when we come from a place of compassion and love for the person who has ended up inside a prison, we make the strongest arguments. And the judge will feel your passion and your need to have the right outcome."

"The judge would get the same vibe from you; you ooze confidence and competence. And besides, the judge may well be one of your former students, or at least have read one of your essays or your research."

"This confidence and competence you say I ooze. Do you think I was born with it?" Pella paused. "No, I earned it in the many courtrooms where I've argued. If the evidence comes together as you anticipate, with Quinn's confession and the data on the computer, Charli's case should be winnable."

"Easy for you to say."

"But my question for you is, what's next? There are many women inside that need your help. There will be clemency motions, sentence reduction motions, and the work to find a better solution to imprisoning people with substance-use disorders is overwhelming. You can't shy away from a court hearing if you are going to support this community of women and men who need a badass lawyer to help them. You must start somewhere." Pella was firm.

"What if I lose?"

"You can't think that way if you want to play in this arena. What's that Roosevelt quote about getting in the arena—something about the credit going to the person who's in the arena getting dirty and sweaty and bloody? The one who fights valiantly, and if he fails, he does so by daring greatly. I don't remember the exact words, but the point is that if you want to change the world, you need to take some serious risks for the mission you believe in."

Camille was quiet.

"And I've watched you from afar. You believe in the women inside. You believe that they shouldn't be there. You believe that there is a better way to help mothers and women who struggle with addiction. And if you're serious about this, you need to get into the arena. This is your work. Not mine. I'm here to support you in any way I can. But this is not my work anymore. My work is on Lesvos. My work is fighting for refugees. My work is also finding women like you and teaching them everything I know so they can be justice warriors. This is your moment in time. You need to do this yourself."

Pella's decision had been made.

Camille kissed her mother on the cheek, put her tea on the shelf, and turned out the light, hoping that she would finally get a good night's sleep now that her charges had been dismissed.

"Mom?"

"Yes?"

"Then how come you drafted and were going to argue the motion to get my charges dismissed?"

"Because it's you. And my passion would have been palpable. That's why."

"Mom?"

"Yes?"

"Thank you."

"I love you."

"I love you too. G'night."

CHAPTER FORTY-ONE

Frankie was nothing if not timely. Exactly as planned, in the darkness of predawn, she appeared alongside the boat, with a large dock cart brimming with duffel bags in various colors.

Trish was heading up to the cockpit for Frankie to hand her the gear when her phone began to vibrate. She held it up to show Camille and Pella Gigi's movie-star grin, flashing on her screen. "Any luck finding the hard drive? I'm putting you on speaker, hon—the team's here."

Gigi was almost yelling. "I think we found it! We were down in Talulla's basement all night, but I think we found it! But we can't get it to turn on."

"Did you plug it in?"

"We tried but can't get it to work. Oh my God. This thing has to work. We're so close." The panic in Gigi's voice filled the cabin.

"One step at a time." Trish held steady.

"We can take it to a computer store in town and see if they can get it to work."

"No, hold up. We need a forensic computer person to do this so it'll stand up in court." Trish looked at the lawyers, who nodded in unison.

"Oh my God. Where do we find a forensic computer person in Port Townsend? This can't wait." Gigi's tears were clear through the phone.

"I have a computer forensic guy in Seattle. His name is Alex. I'm going to call him." Camille pulled out her phone and took it into the V berth so she could hear over Gigi's heated conversation with Trish.

"Hurry!" Gigi almost wailed.

Trish's PI demeanor took over. "Hang on, do you know Charli's password? Even if we can get it turned on, we'll need her password to open Excel."

Gigi was silent on the other end of the line. Then she said, "JPay is down today. They're not sure when it'll be back up."

"Okay, can you get down to the prison and ask Charli?" Trish asked.

"I need to wait for the next family visit time." Gigi was on the verge of panic. "I can't just pop down there today."

"Okay." Trish tried to calm Gigi. "Camille has a forensic computer person. Let's start there."

"But we need the password . . ."

"We do, and we'll find a way to get it. Don't worry. We got this."

"Don't Camille and Pella need this for their motion?"

"They do, but there's no deadline. We can file it when we're ready."

Camille reappeared from the V berth. "Thank God my friend Alex is an early riser. He says he can help. He's in Seattle, so you need to get that drive over to him. Can Talulla take you?" Camille spoke loudly to be heard on speakerphone across the small cabin.

"I think so, I'll ask." Gigi was beginning to calm down.

"Good. Camille will text you Alex's contact info." Trish looked expectantly at Camille, who was in the process of doing just that.

"I let him know that you'll be in touch today."

"Okay-I-gotta-go." It came out all as one word before Gigi hung up.

—

Camille took her coffee cup up into the cockpit, where she turned on the engine to warm it up, while Trish shooed Frankie down into the cabin so Quinn wouldn't see her when he arrived. She handed Camille Frankie's gear, which Camille threw down into the cabin for Frankie to stow.

Just as the sun was coming up, Quinn appeared. "Hey! Where's Malika?"

Camille noticed that Quinn was wearing a clean pair of Carhartts and a decent-looking fleece under a newish down jacket. It was an obvious attempt to look good for his old girlfriend.

Trish stood on the edge of the boat, hanging on a sturdy stay that held the mast in place. "I told you she'd be here."

Quinn nearly flew onto the heavy boat and landed clumsily in the cockpit. "Where is she?" His look portrayed a developing suspicion.

"I'm down here." Frankie's voice was muffled by the buffeting wind.

Quinn jerked his head in the direction of the companionway. "You're serious? She's really here?"

Camille felt a pang of sympathy for what was in store for the woeful addict over the next few days. "Hang on . . ." She held up her hand to stop Quinn from bombing down into the cabin. Per the plan, she told Quinn, "Hope you don't mind. We're heading out for a morning sail."

Quinn shrugged. "Sure, why not? A sunrise sail with my old flame." He smiled as Trish untied the lines of the boat and threw them to Quinn. Camille stepped away from the companionway to make room for him. He handed the lines back to Trish before knocking gingerly on the companionway door as he hopped hopefully down into the cabin. Camille threw the boat into reverse and motored down the fairway of the marina out toward open water. There was just a sliver of fiery-orange sun breaking through a narrow slit in the black clouds of dawn.

Camille couldn't hear what was transpiring down below, but she could clearly see that Quinn and Frankie were engaged in a solemn conversation at the dinette. Her mother was curled up in the V berth with her laptop, working on their legal brief, but within eyeline and earshot of Frankie and Quinn.

It was oddly comforting for Camille to see the familiar red boat carrying another freighter pilot as it came out of the silvery mist, heading in the same direction as they were. She reached her hand up and waved slowly and dramatically. The captain of the pilot boat returned the wave as it pulled away into the mist ahead of them. If anything went wrong in the next half hour or so, the pilot boat would be close by. She turned her attention to Trish as they trimmed the sails and took a GPS heading toward the south tip of Lopez Island. It would be six hours and twenty-five miles over what was looking like pretty treacherous waters, as expected in February.

"So?" Camille asked Frankie as she climbed back into the cockpit, leaving Quinn down below looking a bit gray.

"So, I told him that I'd learned that he'd been identified as the one who put the oxy in your car." She paused. "By the way, he has no idea that you're Camille, and I think we should just leave it at that."

Camille and Trish agreed.

"Then I told him that he's likely going down for planting drugs in Charli's car too. He thinks Zhao is turning on him, which is a good place for him to be right now. He's scared. I told him I asked my friends"—she pointed—"that would be you, to help me get him away so he doesn't get arrested. Just like we planned."

Trish joined the conversation. "Think he'll flip on Zhao?"

"I do. I just need to get him alone for a bit."

"He have any drugs on him?" Trish asked.

"Probably, but he'll either run out or we'll confiscate them soon. Right now, he's mostly freaked out because he gets seasick." Frankie laughed.

"Oh dear, it's going to be a bit of a rocky ride across the strait today." Camille feigned concern. "So sorry, Quinn."

"You have anything for seasickness?" Frankie asked.

Camille considered her options. "Do you want me to? Not sure I'm feeling super sympathetic to the guy who almost had me put in prison."

"Okay, then, I'm hearing that's a no."

Camille shrugged and tightened the winch, which caused the heavy boat to heel over—the water lapping the very edge of the cockpit. She laughed into the wind.

The farther they got from land, the bigger the waves became. Even though the boat was a heavy oceangoing vessel, it shook violently as it attacked the intimidating swells. Frankie, who said she'd never sailed before, was beaming as the boat climbed the big waves and crashed down the other side.

Camille recalled her first sailing instructor, Captain Carol, saying that there are two kinds of sailors: those who carefully avoid heavy seas, and those who relish a wild and rocky ride, with saltwater spray penetrating their pores. Camille was the latter. Sam, not so much. So as the wind picked up, she happily reefed the mainsail and loosened her knees so she was riding the seas, as though she were on an untethered bronco.

Before long, Quinn was up in the cockpit, looking pale. He threw himself at the rail, where he began retching. The women looked on flatly.

"What the fuck. Turn this thing around. You're gonna get us all killed out here!" It wasn't clear if Quinn's temper was heating up because he'd just snorted some meth or if the seasickness was making him crabby. He pulled his vial of white powder out of his front pocket. And cursed.

The women all watched as he tentatively moved toward the companionway, clearly trying to decide whether he should risk going down below to snort the powder or risk it being blown away if he tried it in the cockpit. He decided to go below and give it a try.

But he forgot that Pella was down in the cabin, and as soon as he shook the powder into his hand, Pella executed a kickboxing maneuver that would make a WWE pro smile. Despite the pitching boat, she managed to hit Quinn's hand with her foot and let loose a deep guffaw as the powder sprayed across the cabin.

"Your mother is a serious badass." Frankie was transfixed. "Honest to God. If I hadn't seen it with my own eyes, I wouldn't believe it."

Meanwhile, Quinn was laid out on the floor of the cabin. He was too seasick to get up, or maybe starting to withdraw. Either way, things could get ugly, Camille thought. She smiled as her mother picked her way over Quinn and held on to the handles of the ladder as she pulled herself up into the cockpit.

Frankie held out a hand to help Pella find a seat as Camille and Trish focused on the direction of the wind and the waves. They were so big the crew found themselves looking up as they climbed them and then down as they crashed over the crest with a loud boom that shook the entire boat.

Frankie shouted into the wind, "I had no idea sailing was this crazy!" Her grip on the side of the cockpit was strong. "This is insane!" she yelled as the green water of a giant wave covered the entire bow of the boat.

The plan to restrain Quinn somehow in the cabin seemed unnecessary, as he was barely able to stand up at this point. Camille shrugged and pointed down into the cabin. "Leave him?" She shouted to be heard over the wailing wind.

Trish shot her a thumbs-up, and Frankie nodded in agreement. "He ain't going anywhere."

Pella faced the sea spray and inhaled deeply as the sun momentarily broke through the clouds, turning the water into an indescribable shimmering mass of greenish blue. The whitecaps took on a whole new look as the sun reflected on them. "Nothing like a stormy sail to make you feel alive," she said loudly.

Just as the women settled in for the rocky ride, a freighter appeared in the mist off to the west. "Here we go!" Camille pointed at the red pilot boat bravely coming alongside the freighter in what appeared to be about ten-foot seas. It was a miraculous ballet played out by the captain of the pilot boat and the freighter captain, who fearlessly grabbed the ladder and hoisted himself up—climbing up the fifty feet to the freighter deck as the ladder tried to blow itself off its hull attachments in the strong wind.

The crews of both boats exchanged waves, and the pilot boat circled them widely as if to say goodbye and good luck.

For the next several hours, the women were mostly quiet. Camille and Trish were laser focused on the water and the sails, while Frankie watched the entire dance between Camille and Trish play out. They rarely spoke, but it was clear that they each knew what the other was thinking. Pella, meanwhile, kept an eye on Quinn, who had found a spot on the floor of the cabin where he could wedge himself between the dinette table and the banquette. No one could hear him, but it looked like he was letting loose some major moaning.

It was dusk when the boat slipped out of the windy strait and behind the south tip of Lopez Island. Cabbage Point, at last. Trish and Camille let out a sigh almost simultaneously as they entered the somewhat calmer water of the San Juan Islands. Camille nudged Frankie and pointed at the south tip of Decatur Island, to the northeast of the tip of Lopez. "Right around the point from those white cliffs is James Island. Looks like you'll be there just as it gets dark. You gonna be okay?"

Frankie nodded. "Way less windy on the lee side of the island for sure. I can put up my tent in the pitch dark if need be." She looked at Trish and Camille. "You two are a couple of kick-ass sailors. That was crazy today."

"A wild ride, for sure." Camille changed the subject. "You have dry clothes to change into, right?"

"No camper goes out into the wilds in February without a few changes of clothes. I'm good. And I have some stuff for Quinn to change into too."

Camille pointed to the helm and motioned for Frankie to take over, which Frankie enthusiastically did as Camille climbed up to loosen the reef in the sails.

When Lopez Pass was on their beam and the water had become considerably calmer, Trish went down and grabbed a bag of misshapen, smashed-up sandwiches. It had been way too pitchy out there to eat, and the team was famished. They quickly polished off the food as James Island came into view and the sun began to set to the southwest over the Olympic Mountains.

Frankie pointed. "Thanks for keeping Quinn away from my mountain hideout. I just couldn't stomach him even stepping foot in my haven up there."

Pella looked dreamily at the setting sun. "No matter where you go, the sunset reminds us of the beauty of life on this planet." She drank in the unique bluish-gold-gray sky that was emblematic of a true Pacific Northwest winter sunset. "I forgot how magnificent the sunsets are here this time of year. Isn't it gorgeous?"

They all paused and took a few minutes to soak in the beauty of the jagged mountains off in the distance as the colors of the sky became deeper and more dramatic. The reflection off the water was spectacular. And then the color dissipated, and the sky went black.

"Not much nautical twilight in February." Camille sighed.

The searchlight on the mast was essential as Camille eased the boat onto the small dock on the west side of James Island. On either side, the island rose to rocky prominences, as was common in the San Juan Islands. Trish hopped off and tied up the boat. Frankie began handing up her camping supplies to Pella, who handed them to Camille, who offloaded them onto the dock next to Trish. In about five minutes, Frankie was ushering Quinn off the boat. She held him by the arm and walked him to the rocky shore while Trish shuttled the gear up and away from the rocky shoreline. When Frankie reached the shore, she reached into Quinn's pocket and pulled out his phone, which she promptly threw as far as she could into the dark water. *What goes around comes around.* Quinn could barely walk, so he was almost too out of it to care. His legs buckled as he hit solid land, and he began retching.

Frankie was almost loving in her tone. "Better get ready, my friend, it's gonna be a hellish few days of this."

Quinn rolled his eyes and looked like he wanted to grab her, but he fell back onto the rocks and moaned.

"You need help pitching your tent?" Trish asked.

Frankie shook her head. "Nope. I'm good. I got my phone all charged up and a few battery backups as well. You guys are going to be, what? An hour away?"

"We'll stay over in Davis Bay tonight. It's about five minutes away. Then we'll be in Friday Harbor, and if you need us, I'll borrow a Zodiac and we can be here in twenty or thirty minutes."

Frankie put her hands on her hips and took in her surroundings. Thankfully, the clouds were parting, and the full moon lit up the jagged shoreline enough for her to get her bearings and find the campsite.

"Okay, we're all good here!" She waved to the team on the boat. "I'll let you know if we need anything!"

Trish looked at Camille, who gave her a thumbs-up, indicating to cast off. Camille revved the engine, and the threesome headed off toward the west side of Decatur Head, where the well-sheltered Davis Bay would hopefully provide them with a restful night's sleep.

CHAPTER FORTY-TWO

It had been a long night for Quinn. Detoxing off meth was not for the faint of heart. But he'd hung in there for the first twelve hours. By morning, he seemed to be building trust with Frankie.

"How the hell did you get off this shit?" He groaned as another wave of nausea took hold of him.

Frankie's presence was strong and steady. "You have to want it. Really, really want it."

Quinn pulled the sleeping bag tight around himself and shivered uncontrollably. "I have no fucking clue what I want." He didn't have the energy to get violent; rather, he curled up in a ball and began to cry.

Frankie moved close and rubbed his back. "Let me tell you about a guy I once knew who was super smart and was on his way to living his dream of being a pharmacist."

Quinn opened one eye and tried the deep-breathing exercise Frankie had taught him during the chill of the night.

"My boyfriend, Quinn, he'd seen firsthand the damage done by people in our community who'd gotten hooked on oxy. And he was all about going after the pharmacy companies—as a pharmacist who would fight back."

Quinn lifted his head for a moment before it flopped back. The tears started.

Frankie continued. "My boyfriend was kind and quirky. And even though his mom and dad were sometimes mean, and they drank way too much, he loved them. And he stuck up for them, even when they kicked him out when he was only fifteen."

The tears turned to sobs as Frankie put a cold cloth on Quinn's forehead. She sat comfortably in the quiet, stuffy tent, listening to the waves lap on the rocks and the birdsong alerting the world to the upcoming day.

Quinn pulled himself up and reached for the thick zipper. Frankie watched him struggle to exit the tent as the wind buffeted the door flap. He stumbled out into the stormy morning and whipped his head around. His anger took hold, and he stuck his head back into the tent.

"Get me the hell off this fucking island!"

Frankie threw on her waterproof gear and zipped the tent behind her. She took a few long strides and stood face to face with Quinn, where she seemed to be processing his anger as if it were her own. When he backed up, she stepped closer to him. He turned and began to walk away. And then spun around. He was beginning to sweat, and his face was twitching. He opened his mouth to say something, but instead he stomped off.

As Quinn scrambled down the steep hill to the water's edge, he either tripped or just plain fell down into the mud, where he lay, pounding the tangle of mossy exposed tree roots with his fists. He began to vomit. Over and over.

Frankie sat a few feet away on a flat-topped rock and began to sing "Amazing Grace." Her voice was clear.

Quinn pulled himself up to his knees but couldn't steady himself enough to get up. He collapsed into a child's pose and clenched his hands, and as he hit the ground over and over, tiny droplets of mud began to fly until he was ensconced in a brown cloud thrown around by the wind.

Frankie continued to sing.

"Shut the fuck up!" The whistling wind filtered Quinn's voice. He tried, in vain, to stand, but his legs weren't having it. He finally collapsed in a fit of tears. "Get me outta here . . ." It sounded like a whispered prayer.

Frankie sat humming for many minutes, maybe almost half an hour, as Quinn moaned and retched in the rain, which was quickly turning into puddles around him.

When Quinn finally rolled onto his back, exhausted, his unfocused eyes looking up toward the canopy of evergreens above them, Frankie moved toward him and held up a plastic bottle of Gatorade. "My old boyfriend, the pharmacy student, taught me to always keep hydrated when I was playing basketball. He knew the importance of electrolytes."

Quinn didn't move, but Frankie considered—and took a calculated risk—by putting the bottle next to him, knowing he could easily turn it into a lethal projectile. She put the bottle down gently and sat on her haunches so she could run if necessary.

Quinn barely noticed. At one point, he sat up and leaned back against a giant rock. It wasn't clear to Frankie if Quinn even knew how cold and wet he was. She tightened the hood of her Gore-Tex jacket around her face and began to take deep, slow, rhythmic breaths.

The rain picked up, and the pair sat solemnly, Frankie in a meditative state and Quinn in and out of alertness, sipping intermittently on the Gatorade, until he seemed to pass out.

Without taking her eyes off her patient, Frankie crept up several feet of steep hill to the cooler and took out a PowerBar. She grabbed a Mylar thermal blanket, unfolded it, and placed it over Quinn—after checking his pulse, just to be sure.

As the rain turned to mist, Frankie unpacked her camp stove and heated some water for coffee and instant oatmeal. The peacefulness of the small island in the light drizzle overtook her, and she settled in to listen to the waves gurgling across the rocky beach while Quinn snored loudly.

Wintertime in the Pacific Northwest was a palette of all shades of gray punctuated by some occasional blue and deep green. It was often impossible to determine the time of day because the entire landscape melded into the sameness. Colorless. Windy. Misty. Never quite light. Frankie loved every minute of being out in it. She reflected on the past few days and closed her eyes, imagining her anticipated reunification with her beloved Daisy. Or Willow. "Where are you?" she whispered.

Frankie's moment of reverie came to an abrupt halt as Quinn collided into her daydream.

"Coffee." It wasn't a question.

Frankie held her breath as Quinn seized the pot of hot water. Another possible weapon if he became volatile.

He snatched a metal cup from the rock where Frankie had set up a makeshift kitchen and looked expectantly at Frankie. There was an inkling of a long-forgotten smile somewhere on his face.

A glimmer of the old Quinn. "Here." She held up the french press. "Coffee's in here, just add water." She pointed at the cooler. "I figured you still like coffee with your cream and sugar." She smirked. "In there." She stayed cool in hopes of being a calming force on him.

"I feel like shit."

Frankie affirmed him with her eyes. "I know you do."

"And I'm a wet, freezing mess." He wiped his face with his sleeve.

Frankie got up mindfully and pulled a roll of clothes out of a duffel bag. "Here you go. Throw your dirty stuff in this bag." She handed him a black plastic garbage bag.

Without saying a word, Quinn undid his belt and stripped down. Shivering, he pulled on the dry clean clothes, talking as he did so. "Why the hell are you here? And why did you kidnap me to this shitty little island? It's fucking freezing here." He zipped up the fleece hoodie. "And where the hell have you even been?" He hovered over Frankie, who handed him an unwrapped energy bar and waited as he doubled over with some kind of stomach cramp. "Goddamn it. You have to be out of your fucking mind to be out here alone with an asshole like me."

"Not really. I care about you. And if you're ready, I'm here to help you get clean."

"Do I have a choice right now?" There was an edge to Quinn's voice.

"Nope. Not right now. But you'll be off this island soon, and then it's up to you." Frankie took a spoonful of oatmeal. "The first twenty-four hours are usually the worst. Then it comes and goes in waves intensely for several days, and then less crazy for a few weeks, getting better as time passes."

The sweat was breaking out again on Quinn's face. He closed his eyes and wrapped his arms around himself, shivering. "Oh my God. Make it stop." He groaned and rocked back and forth.

"I had to do this in jail." Frankie swept her arm around the campsite and wilderness beyond. "At least you're here. With someone who cares."

A look of desperation overtook Quinn's face. "Why the hell would you even say you care about me? I treated you like shit. And your baby. I'm dangerous, especially to you."

"You are not dangerous. And you did not treat me like shit."

Quinn looked at Frankie sideways. "Huh?" He doubled over again.

"Quinn on meth treated everyone like shit. Mostly himself." Frankie locked eyes with Quinn. "One thing I've learned over the past few years is that we all go through iterations of ourselves. But who we are deep down is always there. Trauma makes us do crazy things." She looked out over the calming water in the small bay below their campsite. "And we are not our trauma."

The look of suspicion on Quinn's face began to melt. And the tears welled up.

"I saw a TED Talk by a guy who represents people on death row. And he says that we are all better than the worst thing we've ever done. You are not an asshole. You did some asshole things." She laughed. "Lots of asshole things."

Quinn listened.

"I forgive you, Quinn. You're an addict. I'm an addict. And I forgive you."

"So, what's next?" He glanced around the campsite. "What if I do decide to get sober? I wouldn't know where to start."

"What do you mean?"

"My life is meth. Has been for a long time. All my friends are addicts. And I make my money selling to them."

"What about your pharmacy job?"

"If we're in some kind of truth-telling thing here, I can tell you that my boss is a huge kingpin in the meth, heroin, and fentanyl business. And he's partnered up with docs who dole out bogus prescriptions to people who were once hurting but now are just addicts. And when those addicts can no longer get prescriptions, they often turn to heroin—which of course my boss also sells."

Frankie leaned in. "Which brings us to why we're here."

"Huh?" Quinn took a gulp of coffee.

"Like I told you, I brought you here to try and save your ass from going down for a big-time drug deal."

"Well, shit. I was hoping we were here to rekindle our high school romance." He almost smiled until another chill overtook him.

"Listen to me carefully." Frankie paused for effect and waited for the burst of wind to die down. "You put a bag of pills in my friend's car a few weeks ago. Don't try to deny it, your prints are all over the bag, and you left a pack of cigarettes in the trunk as well. Kreteks. That pack has your prints all over it too. The woman you planted the drugs on is a pretty well-known lawyer, and she got the charges dismissed because of a bogus search of her car."

Quinn was quiet.

"The thing is that the same thing happened to a very good friend of the lawyer's. Only that time it was a bag of heroin planted in her car. And a gun. Your boss has it out for both of these women. You planted drugs in both cars, and the one in Bellevue went down for a really long time because of the gun enhancement to her sentence."

Quinn shook his head. "I didn't do it."

"Yes. Yes, you did, Quinn. They have your prints on both cases," she lied, knowing full well that there would be no way to get any prints from Charli's case.

Frankie got up and turned on the camp stove again. She pulled out some freeze-dried vegetarian stew, put it in a bowl, added water, and stirred. "Look, Quinn, that woman you took down in Bellevue is actually Daisy's mom. I never told you this, but I was Daisy's nanny in Bellevue, and through a bunch of strange circumstances, I ended up running away with her to PA to keep her safe from her dad, who was holding her hostage so his wife wouldn't turn him in for running an illegal drug empire. That dude is your boss. He took down his own wife. And now that he knows that we have your prints on the drug bags, he's going to come after you. You're the only one who can take him down. To put it bluntly, your life is in danger. So now, it's up to you. Who's going to take who down? It's just a waiting game now."

Quinn was rapt. It was hard to read him, but from the look on his face, he was worried.

"But he'll have me killed if I turn on him. I'm serious, he's a scary dude. I overheard him once talking about how he put a contract out on some private investigator over in China. He thought killing someone was a big joke."

"Well, I need to get my friend, Daisy's mom, out of WCCW. So I'mma need you to sign something where you admit that you planted the drugs as ordered by your boss. If you don't do that, then you are going down for putting the drugs in the lawyer's car, and Daisy's mom's car too. It's checkmate, my friend. And that's why you're here." Frankie stirred the boiling pot. "It's up to you, but if it were me, I'd put that asshole right in prison, where he belongs."

Quinn was considering his options, fidgeting as the shakes began to take control of his body. "I feel like hell. Do we really have to be having this conversation right now?"

"Yep. Yep, we do. You are here on this remote little island specifically to keep you away from the prosecutor, who has issued a warrant for your arrest. The clock is ticking."

Quinn leaned over, his head in his hands. "I'm gonna puke." He shot up and placed his hands against the nearest tree and vomited. "You brought me here knowing I'd be sick as hell. Did you even think to bring something to help me through this?" His anger was brewing.

"You gotta do this alone. No one can do it for you. I work with lots of women who have left a life of addiction. You can do this—if you want to."

"Want? What do I want? How the hell can I even answer that question when I'm all fucked up like this?" Quinn wiped his face and roughly opened the tent and fell inside, curling up in the fetal position as Frankie looked on. She got up, put a blanket over him, zipped him inside, and then dished herself some stew as dusk fell.

CHAPTER FORTY-THREE

It was all law, all the time as they sat in the cluttered sailboat cabin, moored in its home slip in Friday Harbor on San Juan Island. Mother and daughter were deep into the intricacies of the Fourth Amendment when the phone rang.

"Alex!" Camille squealed, and she hit the green button on her phone. "Hey! Did you breach the hard drive?"

"We got in." His voice was flat.

Somehow tech geeks never seemed to fully embrace the idea of expressing joy when their genius landed in a way that changed someone's life.

"Well, good." Camille tried to contain herself. "That's good." She high-fived in the direction of her mother and put the call on speaker.

Pella leaned across her laptop to hear the conversation.

Alex was midsentence: ". . . need the password now."

"Okay. Okay. So, the hard drive is alive, but you can't get the data without a password, right?"

"Affirmative."

"Is Gigi there?"

"Yeah."

"Let me talk to her, please."

The phone rustled.

"Gigi, can you go down to WCCW and get the password? Even if JPay is up and running, they check the messages, and I don't think we want to take any chances with this password—DOC is all up in the women's email."

"Agreed. But I can't just show up at the prison. I need to wait for the next family visit day." The tension in Gigi's voice came clearly over the phone. "That's next Saturday. We can't wait that long."

"Well, I'm stuck in Friday Harbor, waiting on Frankie and Quinn . . ."

Both women were silent.

"I got it!" Camille felt the adrenaline surging. "I can call Viyja—she teaches at WCCW and goes in a couple of times a week. Can you at least ask Charli if she can go to Viyja's class?"

"You mean the stats class? I think she's in that class!"

"Perfect. I gotta go. Stand by."

It wasn't hard to track down Viyja and obtain her help in procuring the password. In fact, she was going inside that evening, so the timing was excellent. Camille and her mother returned to coauthoring the legal brief that might get Charli released. Their discussion focused on the legal question of whether a confession from Quinn could have been discovered before Charli's trial by the exercise of due diligence. A heated discussion ensued, such that Camille nearly didn't hear her phone ringing.

"It's Frankie."

Pella shot Camille a look of concern. "That's either really good or really bad."

"Frankie? You okay?"

"Um . . . I'm good, but Quinn, not so much. I need you guys over here—stat."

"Huh?" Camille stood, looking around the cabin for her foul-weather gear. "What's up?"

"He fell. Hit his head. He was so dehydrated that he lost his balance on the slippery rocks. He's out cold. And bleeding." Frankie was remarkably calm. "I have a pretty good first aid kit, but he's hurt pretty bad. I have access to plenty of ice-cold water, so I'm kind of icing it, but it's a bloody mess. He probably has a bad concussion—or worse."

Camille shook Trish, who was doing the crossword puzzle with her earbuds in. "We gotta go. Now!"

Trish sat up. "Where we going?"

"Quinn's hurt. We need to go pick him up and get him to the hospital."

"Well, at least we know Willcox won't be on call." Trish winked as she threw on her gear.

"Frankie? You still there?"

"Yep. When can you be here? We're on the rocks by the dock facing Decatur Head. That's where he slipped. What a shit show."

"The boat next to us has a fancy Zodiac that they let us use in the summer—I checked when we arrived, and it still has the key under the seat. We can get there in about fifteen or twenty minutes."

"Okay, well, please get going. I need you guys now." The request was clearly urgent.

Pella stood up and stretched. "Where's my rain jacket?"

"You really want to go out in this weather, Mom?"

"Of course I do. I probably have better emergency field-medical skills than you guys, I help out in the migrant camps with Médecins Sans Frontières all the time."

"You do recall that I was an ER nurse in my first career, right?"

"I do, and I bet you did most of your care in a hospital, with all the accoutrements afforded medical science, yes?"

Camille nodded as she pulled on her rain pants. "I did."

"Well, I'm here to tell you that field medicine is a bit different. We'll make a good team." Pella pulled the fleece cap down over her ears with a flourish. "Let's split."

Trish laughed at the mother-daughter duo bumping into each other as they reached for the ladder up the companionway, where Trish stood silhouetted against the kaleidoscope of gray haze. "Hope we can get back by dark."

"Good point." Camille checked the mooring lines on *Sofia*.

Pella shooed away Camille's attempt to help her off the boat. "Go see if you can start that little Zodiac." Pella pointed at the serious-looking orange inflatable boat with the huge engine that was waiting for them across the dock, which Trish had already boarded. She was rummaging under the seat to find the key.

"Bingo!" Trish held up a key attached to a floatable key chain.

"Fire her up!" Camille yelled as she unwrapped the lines from the cleats.

The three women stood, still staring at each other as the engine sputtered briefly and came to life.

Pella held Camille's hand as she put one foot on the boat while pushing off the dock with the other.

Leaving the marina, Trish hit the power, and off they went, ignoring the speed limit posted on buoys all around the harbor. No one was there at this time of year anyway.

Each woman found a handle to grasp, and they faced the frigid sea spray as they flew across the choppy water of San Juan Channel and through Upright Channel, skimming along Lopez Island, past the empty ferry landing and over to Thatcher Pass. The sun broke through and reflected on Mount Baker hovering on the northeast horizon.

Thankfully, Frankie had a bright-red rain jacket. Camille could see her waving them in from the beach. Quinn was flat on his back, looking lifeless.

Camille panicked and shouted into her mother's ear, "If Quinn has some kind of serious head injury, we can't use him as our witness to get Charli out. Shit!"

Pella pushed a gray tendril back from her face. "Well, let's just hope that this is nothing more than a concussion, or less."

Trish hopped out as the boat bumped up against the dock. Bowline in hand, she cleated it and waited for Pella to throw her the stern line. "Got it!"

Camille grabbed the giant first aid kit, and the trio ran full steam up the floating dock, holding hands to keep their balance as it rocked in the waves.

Thankful that the sun chose to reappear and throw some warmth onto the isolated beach, Camille reached way back into the recesses of her memory to her days as an ER nurse and knelt down to examine Quinn, who was limp on the rocks. She pulled a flashlight out of her pocket and flashed it in his eyes to see if his pupils reacted to the light. If they didn't, it would be a sign of possible brain damage. Next, she palpated along his limbs, feeling for broken bones, and then pulled back the dressing on his head to examine the wound. She looked up at Frankie. "That's a nasty laceration there. He's going to need stitches. Has he been conscious at all?"

"He comes out of it for a few seconds on and off," Frankie reported.

"Well, his pulse is good, and his pupils are reacting." She looked down at the patient. "The bleeding seems to have stopped, but the issue is whether he might have a back injury. I think we need to call the medics to put him on a backboard."

Trish pulled out her phone and dialed, then spoke authoritatively to dispatch. She turned to the team. "They're right over in Friday Harbor. They'll be here in twenty minutes."

Frankie kicked a rock down the beach. "Shit. I shoulda just called the medics myself. Now we're losing time."

"You did an awesome job dressing that wound and keeping him safe and dry. He's going to be fine, as long as he didn't sustain a neck injury or some kind of brain damage." Camille put her arm around Frankie.

Trish knelt down and lifted Quinn's arm gently. "He's pretty limp. Should we try to rouse him?"

"I don't think so. It's probably better that he not get agitated," Pella said.

Camille hunched down next to her mom. "I hate to make this all about us—or rather, Charli—but this isn't looking all that good for our motion. How do we get a statement from him if he doesn't come out of this soon?"

Pella shook her head solemnly. "This sucks. In so many ways." She rearranged herself so that she was sitting cross-legged next to Quinn, holding his wrist to keep a feel of his pulse.

The minutes felt more like hours before the emergency police vessel screamed around Fauntleroy Point and headed straight for the beach. Trish ran out to catch the lines, and the medics hustled up the dock holding a big locker of medical supplies between them, one on each handle. The captain had a backboard held up over his head and used it to keep his equilibrium on the unstable dock.

"Who knows this guy, and what happened?" The medic skipped the pleasantries.

Frankie squatted down next to the medic, who was putting on a blood pressure cuff and checking Quinn's pulse. "Thirty-year-old male. Medical history significant for meth addiction, and maybe fentanyl. He slipped on the rocks right here and hit his head about an hour ago. Hasn't regained consciousness except for a few eye rolls. Last ate about two hours ago and has been drinking Gatorade most recently." Frankie was clearly well schooled in dealing with medical events in the wilderness. "He's detoxing right now, so he could probably use at least an IV."

The medics were one step ahead of her. The IV was up and running and they were rapidly chatting with dispatch and likely the local ER doc. Within a few minutes, they had Quinn loaded onto the backboard and were picking their way across the rocky terrain with him.

Camille wasn't sure if her surging tears were for Quinn or for the likelihood of getting Charli out slipping away. She wrapped her arm around her mom and put her head on her shoulder. "Goddamn it."

Pella stroked her daughter's salty hair and kissed her on the top of her head.

Frankie turned and began carefully climbing back up the narrow path toward her campsite, with Trish following right behind.

Camille took a deep breath. "So, now what? We have no Quinn to testify. And we may or may not have a hard drive with Martin's business dealings on it."

"We'll think of something." Pella took Camille by the hand, and together they climbed up to the campsite.

Frankie was obviously an expert at disassembling her campsite. She whipped through pulling down the tent and shoving it and the stakes into a medium-size pouch. Sleeping bags similarly went into pouches, and the garbage bag of Quinn's wet clothes was thrown halfway down the path. Trish gathered the cooking supplies, while Camille and Pella organized the cooler and together walked it down the path. They were casting off in a matter of minutes. This time, they were going with the wind, so it wasn't as cold and wet. No one spoke until they reached the dock in Friday Harbor.

"So close, yet so far," Camille lamented, barely loud enough to be heard as she climbed into the cockpit of *Sofia*.

Camp gear covered the floor of the cabin. No one had the energy to put anything away or make sense of the chaos. Camille dialed the local pizza place and then poured a round of wine for everyone except Frankie.

"I can't believe it!" Camille sat down hard on the banquette. "What are the chances we can get a statement from Quinn now?" The question was rhetorical.

Frankie reached for her phone. "Will this help?" Her smile was sly.

Quinn's voice engulfed the foursome. "Yes, I agree to be videoed. And I swear under penalty of perjury that my statement is true and correct. My name is Quinn Fredrick Hastings, and my address is 1970 Fruitport Road. I am of sound mind and body and am over eighteen and able to testify truthfully." He was reading off a scrap of paper.

Camille and Pella locked onto each other. "Are you fucking kidding me?"

Frankie shushed them.

"In the fall of 2013, my boss, Martin Zhao, directed me to put a kilo of heroin into a silver Audi convertible, and I did so. At my boss's direction, I also put a gun under the driver's seat. And then I followed Martin Zhao's direction to call 9-1-1 and reported that my son had been abducted from a park by someone in a silver Audi. This was untrue and I know this was intended to cause an Amber Alert. And I understood that this was meant to cause the arrest of the owner of the car. At the time I didn't know who the driver was, but I did understand from Mr. Zhao that the driver was arrested as a result of the Amber Alert and was sent to prison. In return, he gave me a brand-new Airstream trailer. Then in 2015, Martin Zhao directed me to put a kilo of heroin into the trunk of a black Camry belonging to Dr. Henry Walters. I did so. I also planted a handgun under his seat. And like before, at the direction of Martin Zhao, I called in an Amber Alert for a missing child that had been abducted by someone in a black Camry. I understood that the reason for this was to cause Dr. Walters to be arrested, which he was. Zhao bought me a blue Ford F-150 truck. Then, this past month, it happened again. My boss, Martin Zhao, directed me to put a baggie filled with lots of oxy into the back of a Ford Explorer. This time, I felt a little guilty, so I put my backpack in there so maybe they wouldn't arrest the woman, who I believed was a friend of a woman I was trying to date. I understood that the police can't search a backpack during an Amber Alert. So then I called in another Amber Alert, and as expected, she got arrested too. But I understand that my plan actually worked, and she got her charges dismissed. I did all of these things at the direction of Martin Zhao. He was my drug dealer, and I am aware that he runs a very big illegal drug operation out of his pharmacies, and even out in the back parking lots. I will tell you that if you go to his pharmacy in

PA—Port Angeles—on a Thursday around six p.m., you will probably find him paying off his dealers right there in his parking lot out behind his pharmacy. He'll probably have several baggies of heroin, meth, oxy, and fentanyl, which is the new drug everyone's getting hooked on. He'll be handing them off to the dealers for them to sell. I'll write up a list of the guys who will probably be there. This is Quinn Hastings, and this is all the honest truth."

CHAPTER FORTY-FOUR

The comfort of being all cozied up in the cabin of her sailboat law-yering alongside her mother overtook Camille, as she watched Pella performing a set of deep squats while Camille practiced her oral argument to overturn Charli's conviction.

Pella held up her hand from her position, her butt hovering a few inches off the floor. "You need a citation for that last point."

Camille grabbed a lime-green sticky and posted it on her notepad. "Got it."

"Continue." Pella had lapsed back into her role as a law professor.

Camille closed her eyes to refocus before launching back into the intricacies of constitutional law.

Pella stood up from her squat and nodded as Camille's argument reached its crescendo. Pella raised her hands as if she were conducting an orchestra, one hand facing up and raising toward the ceiling as she motioned with her other hand as if she was beckoning her daughter closer. From Camille's perspective, it was a dream come true. She'd been in the audience countless times for her mother's speeches in Seattle, New York, London, and across the world. She'd watched her mother argue in courts around the globe, including The Hague. But until this moment, her mother had been too busy saving the world to have the time or energy to actually coach her own daughter. To say Camille was nervous was for sure an understatement.

"And so, Your Honor, court, pursuant to CR 7.8(b)(2) and RCW 10.73.100 (1), Ms. Zhao respectfully requests that the court vacate her judgment and grant her a new trial, because there is newly discovered evidence which, by due diligence, could not have been discovered in time for a new trial pursuant to CR 7.5." Camille collapsed back on the banquette, tears welling up in her eyes.

Trish clapped softly. "Nicely done, counsel."

Pella was less effusive. "Okey doke, let's dig deeper into our weakest legal issues. We can polish this up quite a bit." She grabbed her glasses and her laptop.

Camille was getting a crash course on why her mother's students had so many ruthless yet loving pet names for her. She took a minute to swallow her disappointment and gather her thoughts while her computer booted up.

Camille's ringing cell phone punctuated the silence. "Viyja!" Trish hollered to the team as she picked up. "This is Trish on Camille's phone."

Camille and her mother held their breath, staring at Trish.

"Okay, just a sec." Trish looked up at her compatriots. "Viyja got the password!" She grabbed her Nemo notepad. "Okay, ready." She laughed as she scratched the coveted password on a clean page. "Let me say this back—capital *b*, *u*, dollar sign, plus sign, *e*, *d*, hashtag, number one. So, the password is 'Busted#1.'" She smiled at Camille and Pella, who were giggling and holding hands. "Thanks, Viyja! You're the *best*!"

Trish held Camille's phone up to Camille's face to open it up. She scrolled through the contacts until she found Alex. "Hi, Alex. It's Trish. We got the password. Call us back ASAP!" She clicked the phone off and held it to her chest. "Do we need to get something from Charli to attach to the motion, explaining the spreadsheets and other data on the hard drive?"

Camille nodded. "I'm going to go down tomorrow, assuming we have information from the hard drive for her to explain."

"Good." Trish stared at the phone as if willing Alex to respond. "Maybe he didn't recognize your number. I'm going to text him."

Pella looked up from her laptop. "Lucia just sent a draft motion to open up Willow's dependency action."

"And?" Camille asked.

AMANDA DUBOIS

Pella was silent for a few minutes, and then she began her scholarly nod. The pace of her nodding picked up as she read. "This is really good. Won't need much editing at all." She continued to read. Then she looked up, took off her glasses, and paused. "My only hesitation in filing this is that sometimes the dependency judges aren't keen on allowing kids to stay in the foster care system if their mom is in prison. They'd rather terminate the mother's rights and hope someone adopts the child."

Trish chimed in. "Yeah, Camille told us that we could open the dependency and find Willow, and then the court could actually refuse to reunite Willow and Charli. And one thing we don't want is to rock the boat."

"Exactly. We see this all the time. The court could very well terminate Charli's parental rights because it's unlikely that she'll get out of prison while Willow is still young enough to benefit from a relationship with her mother," Pella advised.

"What kind of crazy bullshit is this?" Trish yelled.

"Oh my God. You have a point," Camille almost whispered. "You are exactly right. I have several moms in my legal clinic who are in the process of having their rights terminated because the judges say they can't be a parent from prison. They'd rather put the kids up for adoption—which of course is ridiculous, because most people looking to adopt prefer babies, and these kids are of all ages, so of course they all end up in foster care. It's beyond fucked up."

"When I was doing legislative work on behalf of women in prison many years ago, the legislators were clueless." Pella looked both Trish and Camille straight in the eye. "Which takes us back to our conversation about why we need impacted people in the legislature. The people who were there when I was working on this issue thought kids were better off without parents or in permanent foster homes, rather than reuniting with their mothers. It was awful."

Camille leaned on the table, her chin cradled in her hands. "Do you think we should hold off filing this dependency case until we find out if they decide to release Charli?"

"I'm wondering that exact thing," Pella mused.

"Well, how about we file it and see what happens at the CR 7 motion. If we lose, God forbid, we can decide if we want to withdraw the dependency motion," Camille suggested.

"Sadly, I think that has to be our strategy," Pella agreed.

Trish spoke up. "Can we just not tell Gigi and Charli about this new wrinkle? They've been through hell, and I'd hate to freak them out."

"Agreed," Pella and Camille said in unison as Alex's name popped up on Camille's phone.

"Well?" Camille skipped the niceties.

"Definitely two sets of books here. Just as you expected. This thing is filled with spreadsheets with two tabs. I'd say it looks like whoever designed the spreadsheets had one tab showing what was being used for the tax man and one showing what was really going on."

"Well, this will help with any statute of limitations. I'm pretty sure there's no statute for fraud, so even if we can't nail him on the whole Charli situation, this one might stand."

"You're the lawyer. I'm just a tech geek trying to help."

Finally, it was all coming together.

CHAPTER FORTY-FIVE

When a life was on the line, everything about being in a courthouse could feel constricting. The dirty marble halls. The worn wooden pews. The ancient light-and-dark-brown-checkerboard linoleum floors of the courtrooms. The shabby metal coat racks with mismatched hangers. The imposing benches where the judges make life-changing decisions. Camille felt that constriction right down to her tight knee-length skirt and her pointy-toed high heels. Her jacket felt tight, and her silk blouse barely breathed in the stuffy room. Her mother, on the other hand, looked like she had been born in a courtroom. Within minutes of introducing herself to the bailiff, they were comparing recipes for the perfect cosmopolitan. Pella was regaling the court staff with the colorful details of eating at beach-side restaurants on Lesvos just feet away from where the chefs were cleaning freshly caught octopus and hanging their tentacles on a line across the entrance to the dining area. Or the perfect place to enjoy a well-earned cocktail after a grueling day in the oppressive refugee camps. Pella had a way of making the yin and yang of life between the terrifying squalor of the camps and the lively community life on Lesvos somehow make sense.

Meanwhile, Amy and Lucia were working with the court tech team to hook up a large monitor so Camille could play the video of Quinn for the judge. Camille knew that the court would already have reviewed the video, but it was so powerful that she wanted to play it on the record in open court.

Camille closed her eyes for a few seconds to get focused on her notes. When she opened them, the first thing she saw was Charli dressed in black slacks and a sky-blue lightweight cable-knit sweater being led into the courtroom in handcuffs. Charli looked as constrained as Camille felt. An Academy Award–winning performance would be required for Camille to communicate a sense of confidence to Charli. She plastered on a smile, and as soon as the guard removed the handcuffs, Camille hugged Charli and then held out the chair next to her at counsel table.

Gigi and Trish sat stoically in the front pew, holding hands. Gigi blew Charli a kiss and held up her hands as if she were saying a prayer. Charli mimicked her twin's prayer motion and tried unsuccessfully to hold back her tears.

Camille was mesmerized by her mother. Where Camille felt like a cement statue, Pella exuded the fluidity of a ballerina. Where Camille felt her throat tighten, Pella's thick Greek accent filled the room. Where Camille clung to her notes, Pella's confidence and gravitas needed no written reminders.

Just as Charli was getting settled in, Trent Conway made his entrance. Tall, blond, and square shouldered, in a navy-blue suit with a red-striped tie. A young associate raced in behind him, pulling a rolling briefcase. Trent ambled over to Camille's table and nodded at Charli first.

"Trent, this is Charli Zhao," Camille said as she stood to shake Trent's hand.

Trent was friendly, but standoffish. "Nice to meet you, Ms. Zhao." He turned to Camille. "Good luck, counsel."

The two legal warriors shook hands.

Trent turned his attention to the bench as the young man who'd followed him into the courtroom unpacked his briefcase. "Professor Rallis!" Trent's voice boomed with authenticity. "What a happy surprise. What brings you to this hallowed courtroom?" Trent moved toward Pella and then clearly thought better of giving her a hug.

"The astonishingly bad lawyering that put Ms. Zhao in prison brings me here, Mr. Conway." Pella paused and held out her hand, almost like a queen would. "You know, Trent, you'll be dismissing this case as soon as the judge rules." She tipped her head to the side and winked. "This one has 'loser' written all over it."

Trent laughed. "Well, let's not get ahead of ourselves."

Pella nodded. "Judge Perez was an excellent student—I am quite confident that he'll order a new trial." She put her hands on her hips. "And I'm quite confident that there is no way you're going to trial with Mr. Hastings as a witness."

"Is he out of the hospital yet? Not so sure he'll be much of a witness if he's in a coma." Trent shrugged almost playfully.

Camille shuddered; here she was about to argue her first CR 7.5 motion, and her mother was cashing in on her status as everyone's favorite law professor to psych out the competition. She leaned over and whispered to Charli, "My mom, using every trick in the book to gain the upper hand."

Charli smiled nervously as her eyes darted around the room, taking in all the nuances of the colloquy between the lawyers and court staff, as the tech team finished the sound check on the monitor.

The tech caught the bailiff's eye and gave him two thumbs up. "Good to go here—you ready, Howie?"

The bailiff stood and addressed the courtroom. "I'll go get the judge."

Camille's mouth went dry. She grabbed her water bottle.

Just as the bailiff went to get the judge, a junior prosecutor stuck her head in the door and gestured to Trent.

"Give me a minute, Howie. I need to deal with a bit of an emergency."

"No problem," the bailiff responded as Trent whisked out of the courtroom.

Camille felt like Trent was icing her, as if she were about to kick a game-winning field goal and he just called a time-out. She shuffled her papers and took a few deep breaths.

"Hold up." The bailiff held up his hand. "Can I help you?" He addressed the back of the courtroom.

"We're good here, thanks for asking."

Camille's heart skipped a beat as she recognized Frankie's voice. She twisted around in her swivel chair and almost fell backward as she bolted up.

"Hey, all." Frankie was clearly enjoying the commotion as she pushed Quinn Hastings into the courtroom in a squeaky wheelchair. Quinn had a huge bandage around his cleanly shaved head.

Quinn was obviously not as comfortable as Frankie was, to be the center of attention. He held up his hand in a weak wave. "Hey," he said softly to the bailiff, who had kindly gotten up to help move a chair out of the way for the wheelchair.

Camille looked up and said to no one in particular, "They're with me." She gathered her wits and blew a subtle air kiss to Frankie as Pella stood and gestured the two of them over to their side of the courtroom.

The bailiff helped Frankie park the chair in the aisle toward the back of the courtroom behind Camille's counsel table. "You okay here, sir?" he asked Quinn.

"Yeah. Thanks, man." Quinn gave the bailiff a fist bump.

Back at his station on the lower bench, the bailiff looked at the large clock hanging over the jury box. "Tsk, tsk, the judge likes to start on time," he jokingly admonished the courtroom.

"Sorry about that." Trent rushed back to his table, oblivious to the recent scramble over the wheelchair.

Within seconds, the tall dark-haired judge hurried in from his chambers and jogged up to the bench, his black robe flapping behind him.

"All rise!" The bailiff pounded the gavel.

"Please be seated." Judge Perez looked over his heavy black glasses at both counsel tables. "Good afternoon, counsel. And Ms. Zhao." He leaned forward and squinted. "Professor Rallis? How nice—and surprising—to see you." He peered quizzically at Pella, who had staked out the bench right behind her daughter's counsel table.

When she stood to address the court, Pella somehow managed to completely own the room just by the way she comported herself. "Judge Perez, it's a pleasure and an honor to be here in your courtroom. I was delighted to see your name on the door when I arrived." She paused for effect, knowing the judge was dying to know why she was there. "I'm just here today as an observer to support my daughter, Ms. Delaney, who is representing Ms. Zhao."

The judge bounced back in his chair. "Okay, Ms. Zhao, you've brought the A team here today to support you." He addressed Pella. "I'd love to catch up and hear all about your asylum work over in Greece. But first things first." He addressed Camille and Trent. "Are we ready, counsel?"

Camille stood. "Yes, Your Honor."

Trent looked like he was trying not to use his size as some kind of advantage over the table of women on his left. "The state is ready, Your Honor."

The judge looked at Camille. "Counsel, this is your motion."

Camille froze, just for a second.

The judge looked at Camille. "You need a minute, counsel?"

"No," she said a bit too loudly. "No, I'm good." She took a breath and launched into the argument she'd practiced what seemed like a hundred times. Suddenly her notes were irrelevant.

"Under CR 7.8(b)(2), a court may grant relief from judgment for newly discovered evidence which, by due diligence, could not have been discovered in time to move for a new trial under Rule 7.5." Camille was laser focused on the judge, who was listening intently. "Ms. Zhao's CR 7.8 motion is timely because there is an exception to the one-year time limit set forth in RCW 10.73.090 and 10.73.100 (1). This exception applies to allow a collateral attack on a conviction when the claim is based on newly discovered evidence. The evidence presented by Ms. Zhao creates a substantial showing that Ms. Zhao is entitled to relief."

Camille's voice resonated throughout the courtroom.

"This newly discovered evidence would have dramatically altered the strength of the state's case and would have probably changed the outcome of the trial."

Camille moved from behind the counsel table and stood in the center of the room, right in front of the bench, her purple legal pad long forgotten.

"The state charged Ms. Zhao with possession of heroin with a firearm enhancement for having a gun under her seat. And in order for a conviction to be valid, the state must prove that she had the mens rea—or guilty state of mind—for the act of possessing a controlled substance and a firearm." Camille paused. "But if Mr. Hastings had testified at trial that it was he who put the drugs in the trunk of Ms. Zhao's car, and it was he who hid the gun under her seat, and if the hard drive had been available to be admitted into evidence, there's no way the jury would have convicted Ms. Zhao."

Camille turned to the monitor set up in the middle of the courtroom and tried not to trip over the tangle of wires snaking up to where the bailiff had plugged in the equipment. No thought had been given to audiovisual aids when the courthouse was built in the early 1900s. Camille angled the screen so it was in the direct line of sight of the judge. She addressed the bailiff. "Can you please play the video?"

"Objection, Your Honor." It was the first time Trent Conway had spoken.

The judge turned his attention to the prosecutor. "Mr. Conway?"

"Hearsay, Your Honor. This is an out-of-court statement offered for the truth of the matter."

Camille and her mother had rehearsed the response. "Your Honor, this is sworn testimony. And this is a hearing, not a trial. The court only needs to decide this issue as a matter of law."

"But there is no opportunity for this pivotal witness to be cross-examined. That's the whole reason why hearsay is not allowed." Trent was firm.

"Ms. Delaney?" The judge looked as though he was leaning toward sustaining the objection.

Thinking quickly on her feet, Camille looked behind her to where Quinn was slouched down in his wheelchair. "No problem, Your Honor. If Mr. Conway wants to cross-examine Mr. Hastings, he's here in the courtroom." She pointed to Quinn and turned to the judge. "If you'd like to swear him in, I can put on direct testimony right now."

Trent scanned the courtroom.

Quinn held up his hand as if waiting to be sworn in.

Trent leaned up against his counsel table, a look of defeat passing swiftly across his face before he found his bearings. He was clearly not expecting the fellow in the squeaky wheelchair to be the key witness.

The judge looked at Trent. "Well, that would seem to take care of your hearsay objection, counsel."

Trent shrugged and sat down hard in his chair.

The judge gestured with his forefinger for Quinn to come forward. "Mr. Hastings?"

Quinn nodded and looked up at Frankie, who had hopped up to push the wheelchair to the witness box. But she was stymied by the morass of wires stretched between the bench and the monitor.

The judge turned to the bailiff. "Can you unplug some of these so Mr. Hastings can come up near the microphone at the witness stand?"

The bailiff and clerk jostled to unplug the various cords, and within minutes a pathway had been cleared.

The judge addressed Quinn. "Mr. Hastings, it's not necessary for you to take the witness stand. We just need you to be able to speak into the microphone from your wheelchair in order to make a record."

Frankie and Camille juggled the wheelchair up near the witness stand, while Trent and his sidekick whispered furiously at their table.

Camille owned the courtroom in that minute. "Your Honor, could you please swear in the witness?" Her voice was crystal clear and powerful.

The judge stood. "Mr. Hastings, please raise your right hand."

Quinn complied; he closed his eyes for a second, then opened them to look directly at the judge.

"Do you swear or affirm that your testimony will be the truth?"

"I do."

"Thank you, Your Honor." Camille didn't want to look like she was hovering over Quinn, so she sat down at counsel table and leaned forward. "Mr. Hastings, can you tell the court what you know about the drugs found in Ms. Zhao's car on March first, 2013?"

"Yes, I can."

Trent rose. "Your Honor, this witness should be warned of his Fifth Amendment right not to incriminate himself." His junior prosecutor smirked at Camille and rolled his eyes before giving her a flagrantly sarcastic smile.

The judge nodded. "Good point." He spoke directly to Quinn, "Mr. Hastings, you have the right not to testify to information and evidence that could incriminate you. Do you understand that the evidence you may be asked to testify to may, in fact, prove to incriminate you?"

Quinn looked at Camille. He wasn't exactly panicking. Yet.

"Your Honor." The entire courtroom turned to Pella, who was walking up toward the bench. It was deadly quiet.

"Ms. Rallis?" The judge was clearly curious.

"Pella Rallis. I am making my appearance as counsel for Mr. Quinn."

Quinn looked over at Pella and whispered, "Thank you."

"Hold up." Trent was back on his feet.

"What's the problem now, counsel?" The judge leaned forward, his chin in his hands. He took off his glasses and put them on the bench.

Pella walked up to the witness stand. "I need a few minutes with my client, Your Honor. Could we have a five-minute recess?"

The judge stood. "That seems like a very good plan. We'll be back in five minutes."

The entire courtroom stood as the judge exited the courtroom.

Trent was glued to his legal pad as Pella and Camille huddled up at Camille's table.

Pella whispered to Camille, "The statute of limitations on drug possession has long passed. There's no way they can charge Quinn for this."

"Well, we need to tell Quinn. He's really on the spot up there," Camille whispered back.

Pella strode up to Quinn and knelt next to him and spoke quietly but firmly. "Okay, here's the deal. The statute of limitations will prevent the state from charging you with a crime that happened seven years ago. And even if they could, they'd need physical evidence to support the charge, and the drugs are long gone."

"Well, actually, even if they could charge me, I'm ready to take responsibility for my actions. I put an innocent woman in prison when I was lost in my addiction. It's my fault she's been taken from her kid. I'll testify no matter what."

Frankie, who'd been lingering over Quinn during the short recess, put her hand on his shoulder and leaned over and kissed him on the cheek. "You made it through hell, and now you are officially back, my brother."

Quinn began to tear up just as the bailiff called the courtroom to order. "All rise."

The judge took his chair. "Well, Ms. Rallis?"

Pella was in her groove. "Your Honor, Mr. Hastings is prepared to testify."

"Counsel?" The judge looked expectantly at Camille. "You may continue your direct examination."

Camille cleared her table of all notes and spoke directly to Quinn. "Mr. Hastings, please tell the court what you know about the drugs in Ms. Zhao's car." She quickly added, "And the gun."

Quinn leaned awkwardly toward the microphone. "I was working for a guy named Martin Zhao. He was a pharmacist. And he owned many pharmacies. I now know that Ms. Zhao, the woman we're here trying to get out of prison, was his wife." He looked at Charli, who was beginning to tear up. Then Quinn turned to the judge. "Can I just say to Your Honor that I'm so very sorry for what I did. It's all my fault that Ms. Zhao has been in prison all this time—"

The judge interjected. "I'm sure you regret your actions. But right now, we need for you to clearly tell the court what you did."

Quinn continued. "I didn't know exactly why, but for some reason, my boss wanted me to put a kilo of heroin into the trunk of a silver Audi convertible." He looked up at the judge. "I was an addict at the time, and my boss, Martin Zhao, was supplying me with unlimited meth, and he was paying me way more than you'd ever pay a pharmacy clerk, which is what my job supposedly was." Quinn paused. "I'm really sorry for what I did, Charli."

Camille tried not to be distracted by her mother and Trish whispering at counsel table. She turned to Quinn. "You need to address the court, please, Mr. Hastings."

"Oh, sorry." He looked up at the judge.

"What did you do after you put the heroin in the car trunk?" Camille asked.

"I put a handgun under the driver's seat of the car."

"How did you get into the car?"

"Zhao gave me the keys."

"What did you do after you put the heroin in the trunk and the gun under the seat?"

"My boss told me to leave the car where it was parked and wait until the woman got in the car."

"Did you know the woman?"

"No, not then, but I do now."

"And who was the woman who got into the car?"

"It was Charli Zhao."

"Is Ms. Zhao here in the courtroom?"

Quinn pointed. "Right there."

Camille nodded. "What did you do next?"

"I followed my boss's instructions and called 9-1-1 to report that my kid had just been abducted by a Black woman in a silver Audi."

"And was that true?"

"Of course not."

"Then why did you do it?"

"Drugs. Money. And the threat of being set up on a drug charge." Quinn looked up at the judge. "That guy Zhao is a scary dude."

"Did Mr. Zhao give you anything else in return for you putting the drugs and the gun in the car?"

"An Airstream trailer."

"Thank you, Mr. Hastings. I have no further questions." Camille felt Charli reach under the table and squeeze her hand.

"Mr. Conway? Do you have any questions for this witness?" the judge inquired.

"A few."

"Your witness, Mr. Conway."

Trent stood and then reconsidered the image of a tall prosecutor grilling a guy with a bandaged head in a wheelchair. He sat back down. "Mr. Hastings, isn't it true that you recently sustained a head injury?"

"Yes."

"And isn't it possible that the head injury impacted your memory?"

"Maybe, but I for sure remember the events I just talked about."

"And isn't it true that you were a drug addict when you allegedly put the drugs in Ms. Zhao's car?"

"I for sure was an addict then, but I'm clean now."

"Now, isn't it true that you have a personal relationship with friends of Ms. Zhao?"

"Like who?"

"Well, during the court's recess, it sure looked like you have some kind of relationship with the entire team over there at Ms. Zhao's table. I take it you all are friends?"

Camille followed Trent's gaze over to her gallery of friends and noticed that Trish wasn't in the pew.

"I've recently become acquainted with Camille and Charli."

"But wouldn't it be convenient if, say, someone like you came forward to take the blame for a crime that happened many years ago?"

"You mean I'd just lie and say I did it?"

"Yeah, that's exactly what I mean."

"I wouldn't do that, man."

"So you say." Trent turned his back on Quinn and said over his shoulder, "I have no more questions for Mr. Hastings."

Camille shot up. "Mr. Hastings. Since the time you put the drugs and the gun into Ms. Zhao's car, have you ever done anything similar to anyone else?"

"Yes."

"Tell the court why you did this to others."

"My boss's instructions."

"What did Mr. Zhao tell you to do?"

"Objection, hearsay. And relevance."

The judge looked expectantly at Camille. "Counsel?"

"It's not being offered for the truth of the matter. It's being offered to show why he took an action. And if you can give me a little latitude, I'll show the court the relevance."

"Very well, objection overruled as to hearsay. And if you can make this relevant, the court will allow it."

Camille looked at Quinn. "Tell us about any other times you put drugs into anyone else's car."

"Well, there was a doctor in PA—that's Port Angeles."

"What happened that time?"

"Pretty much the same thing. I put the drugs into his trunk and a gun under his seat too."

"And why did you do that?"

"My boss paid me to do it. And gave me drugs."

"Anything else?"

"Yeah. A new truck."

"What did you do after you put the drugs and gun into his car?"

"Same thing. I waited for him to get in his car and called in an Amber Alert. I said my kid got kidnapped by a guy in a car that matched the car the doctor drove. I think it was a black Camry."

"Do you know what happened to the doctor?"

Quinn wiped away a tear as he faced the reality of what he'd done. "I was an addict. I didn't really think about what would happen to the people I set up."

"We understand you were in your addiction, but can you please tell the court what came of the doctor?"

"He's doing time at Monroe."

"He was convicted?"

"Yes." Quinn's voice had become a whisper.

"Mr. Hastings, you need to speak up so the microphone picks up your testimony," the judge directed the witness.

Quinn cleared his throat and spoke into the microphone. "Yes, Dr. Walters was convicted."

"Do you have knowledge of more recent crimes here in the Seattle area?"

"Yep. Zhao is still running a big drug operation out of his store over in Bellevue."

"Do you have personal knowledge of that operation?"

"I do."

"And was there another time where you put drugs into the trunk of a car over in Port Angeles?" Camille was on a roll.

Pella stood up. "I'm going to advise my client not to testify as to any more recent incidents based on his Fifth Amendment right."

Camille looked knowingly at her mother. "I'll withdraw the question. I have no more questions for this witness. Thank you, Mr. Hastings."

"Mr. Conway?" The judge was riveted.

"Mr. Hastings, do you have any proof that this mystery doctor actually exists?"

"What do you mean?"

"I mean, how do we know there's a doctor in prison in Monroe that you allegedly caused to be convicted."

"I honestly don't know how you go about finding a prisoner."

"I have no more questions for this witness." Trent's sidekick could barely contain his grin. But he quickly composed himself when his boss shot him a scathing look and a subtle shake of the head, as if to admonish him for showing such blatant emotion.

"Ms. Delaney, do you have any more witnesses?"

Camille was about to rest her case when her mother piped up. "Yes, counsel for Ms. Zhao has one more witness."

Camille looked curiously at her mother and went over to huddle with her at the table.

"Call Trish. She has the docket for Dr. Walters, and the list of prisoners at Monroe," Pella whispered. "You got this." She winked and handed Camille a stack of papers.

"Ms. Zhao calls Patricia Seaholm," Camille said loudly as she scanned the documents her mother had just handed her.

Trish bolted up and took the witness stand as though she'd done so a hundred times—which she clearly had back in her cop days.

"Ms. Seaholm, can you please tell the court your education and training?"

"Sure. I attended the police academy in 2003 and worked as a police officer and a detective for Seattle Police Department for ten years. Now I'm a private investigator."

"And in your capacity as a police officer and detective, did you ever obtain court records?"

"I did."

"Did you obtain court records from Clallam County for a conviction of a Dr. Henry Walters?"

"I did."

"When did you obtain the records?"

"About ten minutes ago."

"How did you get those records?"

"I got them off the clerk's website for the Clallam County Court."

Camille handed the clerk one of the documents Trish had just obtained. "Can you please mark this as exhibit one?" She turned and handed Trent a copy, then handed the clerk a copy to hand up to the judge. She gave Trish the official copy that the clerk had marked. "Can you please identify this document?"

Trish held the papers and looked at the judge. "Exhibit one is a copy of the judgment and sentence for Dr. Walters. He was convicted of possession of a kilo of heroin and having a gun under the driver's seat of his car."

"I offer exhibit one." Camille was surprised at the clarity of her voice.

"No objection." Trent had lost a bit of his bravado.

Camille handed another document to the clerk and had it marked as exhibit two. After giving copies to Trent and the judge, she handed it to Trish. "And what is this?"

"This is a list of prisoners currently in Monroe Prison."

"Is Henry Walters on that list?"

"He is."

"I offer exhibit two."

"No objection."

"Ms. Zhao rests her case."

"Does the prosecution have any evidence or witnesses to call?" the judge asked.

"No, Your Honor."

"Thank you, counsel." The judge scribbled some notes and looked back up. "Ms. Zhao, I do believe that there is new evidence that, had it been presented at trial, could have changed the outcome of your case." He looked at Trent. "In fact, it seems possible that there may not have even been a trial if Mr. Hastings had come forward sooner." He looked at Quinn for an uncomfortable period of time. "I'm granting your motion, Ms. Delaney."

Charli clutched Camille and sobbed.

Gigi bolted up and shouted, "Oh my God! Thank you, Your Honor!" She jumped up and ran to her sister.

It was all hugs and tears and thank-yous as Trent leaned over and shook Camille's hand. "Nice job. I'm going to recommend that the charges be dropped, so a new trial won't be necessary."

Pella stood back so Camille could savor her first criminal law triumph.

Trent continued. "I'd like to interview Mr. Hastings as soon as possible to see how we might be able to move forward against Martin Zhao. The statute has run on these older crimes, but it looks like Quinn has some information about more current activities that sound like felonies to me. And we'll be referring the whole tax fraud issue to the feds." He turned to Pella. "Will you be continuing to represent Mr. Hastings?"

"No. One unexpected cameo appearance in court is enough for me today." Pella laughed.

Without thinking, Camille blurted out. "His lawyer is Shoba. Shoba Desai." She hoped Shoba would be game. "But let me give her a call first."

Trent winked. "Gotcha. She probably needs to know who Mr. Hastings is and why you just volunteered her to jump into this mess of a case."

Camille smiled. "Exactly!"

"Okey doke, I'll call you tomorrow and see how your client can help bring her ex to justice." Trent strode over to Pella. "I'd really like to catch up over coffee. Maybe you and me and Judge Perez can meet up before you leave town."

"I'd love that, Mr. Conway." Pella was graceful in victory.

Camille hung back in the courtroom as her crew filed out into the long, dingy marble hallway. Getting Charli's conviction overturned was just the first step in bringing a drug-dealing kingpin to justice. The surge of adrenaline caught her by surprise as she pulled open the heavy oak door leading out into the fracas in the corridor.

She pulled out her phone and waited for Amy to answer. "We won! Let's confirm the hearing for the motion to open Willow's dependency file now!" She was so excited that she clicked off just as Amy and Lucia started whooping it up in the background.

CHAPTER FORTY-SIX

It only took a few days to process Charli out of the prison, so there wasn't much time to plan a big welcome-home party. But then again, Charli really didn't want a bunch of people around for her first couple of weeks out.

Gigi's white brick house stood geometrically centered on a small rise of green grass in the Wedgwood neighborhood of Seattle. The windows and black shutters were mirror images on either side of the deep-red front door. To complete the look, there were identical topiaries to both the right and left of the small entry porch.

Trish had taken it upon herself to throw up some mismatched holiday lights, which drew a stark contrast to the purposefulness of the architecture. The plentiful streamers and balloons tied to the railings shouted a well-deserved "Welcome home."

Camille waited for Sam to hand her the canvas bags of groceries they'd just picked up at Pike Place Market. It would only be the best for Charli's first lunch at home. The oily peppered smoked salmon from their favorite fishmonger. A huge piece of fresh king salmon. Greens, greens, and more greens—there weren't many fresh veggies in prison. Gorgeous heirloom tomatoes. Fresh basil. Fresh garlic. Wild rice. And frozen organic raspberries and raspberry vinegar for the sauce. A few baguettes from the French bakery, along with some fresh, locally sourced butter. Some creamy goat cheese and a chunk of Beecher's cheddar alongside a slice of Point Reyes blue. And panzanella crackers speckled with rosemary. Gigi was in charge of dessert, so Camille expected there would be chocolate involved. Lots of chocolate.

The house was buzzing with laughter and music. Charli and Gigi were holding hands with Gracie and dancing to Taylor Swift. Angela and Kaitlin were creating fabulous table centerpieces with lilies and white roses and more than a little ribbon. Libby was setting the table with the good china—white bone with silver rims.

Camille and Sam pulled out the cache of groceries and began to organize them on the huge marble kitchen island. Camille lost no time in ripping open the package of crackers, which she smeared with a hunk of blue cheese and promptly popped into Charli's open mouth as Charli clapped in time with the music and watched Gracie hop up onto the coffee table and wiggle her butt.

Pella was struggling to figure out how to work the fancy standing wine opener on the cabinet where the bar equipment was displayed. "Forget it!" She laughed and pulled out a corkscrew, clipped off the metal strip, and professionally twisted the cork out of the bottle of Sancerre. She poured an inch into a crystal glass and savored the first sip. "Oh my gosh. This is lovely." She closed her eyes and swished another sip around in her mouth. "Wow."

Camille handed a nicely appointed charcuterie board of cheeses and smoked salmon to Libby, who placed it closest to Charli. "I bet there was no Beecher's cheese when you were in prison. You gotta try this." She ceremoniously handed Charli a good-size chunk of the white cheddar.

"Oh my God!" Charli said through a mouthful of cheese. Then she put the rest of the chunk down. "This is so rich, I'm not sure I can eat it all. I was warned to ease into regular food after eating that prison crap for so many years."

Pella held up her wineglass in a toast. "Here's to one of my star students, Deputy Prosecutor Trent Conway. He's already charged Martin here in King County, and after Quinn's statement, Rose is right behind him over there in Clallam County!"

"When did you talk with him?" Camille's smile was a mile wide. "What great news! Last I heard, they were still interviewing witnesses."

Pella winked coyly. "Remember that lunch I promised Judge Perez and Trent in court the other day? I didn't want them to slow-walk this, because Zhao is definitely a flight risk. They were able to get preliminary charges filed so they could take his passport. But there will likely be superseding indictments coming soon."

Charli looked taken aback. "Did they take both of his passports? He has a Taiwanese one as well as US."

"That's an excellent question. I don't know that Trent and Rose are aware of his dual citizenship. I'll call them in the morning to be sure."

"If that asshole gets away . . ." Trish looked concerned.

"Maybe we should call Trent now," Camille suggested.

"I can do that," Pella offered. "In fact, I'll text him." She pulled out her phone and got busy.

"Martin'll do anything to avoid getting tangled up in the legal system." Charli was dead serious.

Pella looked up from her phone. "He has an autoreply that he's in court." She looked at the clock. "Court recesses at 4:30, so I expect he'll ping me in an hour or so. I told him it's urgent."

Gracie stood on the coffee table. "Attention! Attention!"

Everyone shushed each other.

"Yes, Miss Gracie?" Gigi said formally.

"If lunch isn't ready for a little while, I think we should take Auntie Charli for a walk on the trail so she can see my new scooter that Gigi got me."

"Oh, to be seven." Camille laughed. "Did you want to say anything about welcoming Auntie Charli home?"

Gracie shot her mom an exasperated look. "That's what the dancing was for," she said affirmatively, as though any idiot should know that. "We did our welcome dance. Now we need a welcome scooter ride." She had her hands on her hips and her chin thrust forward as she cocked her head back and forth. "I have a new scooter!" she said in singsong. "Let's go check it out! It has flashing lights!"

"I'm in!" Charli grabbed Gracie by the hand and led her to the back door. "Where's this fancy new scooter?"

"Wait up! I am not letting my sis out of my sight." Gigi handed Charli a puffy coat and pulled on one herself as Camille threw Gracie her bright-turquoise ski jacket.

"Lunch will be ready in about half an hour, so don't go too far!"

"We'll just head down the Burke-Gilman Trail," Gigi said, referencing the old railroad line that had been converted into an urban path that wound its way from the Hiram M. Chittenden Locks close to Puget Sound in Ballard. It went for about thirty miles past the University of Washington and through residential neighborhoods, up to Woodinville, where the local wineries had their showrooms.

"Sounds divine. I haven't been able to walk for any distance other than around the prison yard. I'd love to revisit the trail. I biked up the Burke to the university during grad school when I lived in Fremont. Let's go!"

Gracie took the twin sisters by the hand and led them to the garage, where two scooters were parked next to each other. "Why did you get two?"

Gigi smiled. "You're about to meet your cousin, Willow, and I thought it would be fun for you to have matching scooters."

"Okay." Gracie knitted her brow. "But I get the blue one, okay?"

"Well, I'm sure Willow will love either color, so it looks like it's blue for Gracie!" Charli couldn't stop hugging her sister. Her arm was firmly planted around Gigi's shoulder.

"Let's go!" Gracie took off, lights flashing and streamers flying from the handles as she pushed with one foot and the scooter made a buzzing sound.

The Burke-Gilman Trail was a cement pathway, wide enough for opposing streams of bike and pedestrian traffic to flow easily. Lunch-hour joggers dodged and wove their way through the parents and kids on their bikes, and the serious bikers, all decked out in their spandex, hollered "Right!" or "Left!" as they sped up behind the walkers. It was a chaotic kind of urban harmony. And to further confuse matters, the trail cut behind the houses in the neighborhood, so it was punctuated by crosswalks where it crossed local streets. Those crossings were well known to the locals. But on occasion, there would be some close calls as kids on bikes or runners raced out in front of cars, assuming they'd stop—which they usually did, just in the nick of time. But still, most parents found themselves hollering at their kids to stop at the crosswalks as the kids rode ahead, leaving their parents in their wake.

"Gracie, stop up ahead!" Gigi yelled as Gracie dutifully pulled aside at the crosswalk to let an adult biker speed past her.

"You should slow down!" Gracie hollered sternly at the woman in flashy black-and-red biker gear. "You can get hit in this crosswalk!"

The biker stood up to pedal faster and disappeared around the bend up ahead.

Gracie looked both ways, then nodded. "It's okay, we can cross." She kicked forward on her scooter and zipped off down the path. Gigi and Charli picked up the pace so they could keep Gracie in their sight. Just as they rounded a slight curve in the path, Gigi saw a big black Suburban across the next crosswalk about fifty feet ahead. Gracie was heading directly at the car, at which point Gigi yelled to catch Gracie's attention.

"Slow down! Watch out for that black car!"

And then everything seemed to happen in slow motion. A tall figure hopped out of the Suburban. He grabbed Gracie off the scooter and whipped around to glare at Gigi and Charli. "I better not ever see you in a courtroom again, bitch!" Martin Zhao stood his ground, with Gracie screaming and kicking in his arms. Then, in an instant, he was gone. Gigi raced to catch the license plate number, but the place where the plate should have been was empty. Charli started screaming for help.

"Call the police!" Gigi screamed to no one, since the pathway was suddenly empty of other pedestrians and bikers. "Fuck! Where is my fucking phone?!" She felt her pockets. "Goddamn it, I left my phone plugged in at the house." She turned and ran full speed back toward her place, about four blocks away, with Charli right on her heels. On the second block, a biker stopped to help and gave Gigi her phone.

Gigi dialed 9-1-1. "My name is Dr. Gigi Roberts from the University of Washington. I'm at the crosswalk where the Burke crosses Princeton Avenue Northeast. A child was just abducted from the Burke-Gilman Trail. She was with me. The kidnapper is Martin Zhao. He's driving a big black Suburban with no license plates. This was a targeted abduction. Please send out an Amber Alert!"

Dispatch had been listening carefully. "We're sending officers out now. Where exactly was the child taken from?"

"I just told you! We're on the Burke. We were crossing Princeton Avenue, and Zhao, the kidnapper, was waiting for the child at the crosswalk."

"Is this some kind of child-custody matter?"

"No. No! It's complicated, but he is about to be charged with a serious drug crime, and he is using this abduction to intimidate the star witness against him."

Gigi had kept running while talking on the phone, with the biker whose phone she was using following close behind. She ran up her front steps and into her living room.

"He took Gracie! Martin just kidnapped Gracie! Right off the trail! I'm on with dispatch now!" She collapsed as Trish ran to hold her up.

Camille, Sam, and the girls stood in shock until Camille gathered her wits and dialed Trent Conway.

Trish grabbed her own phone and dialed her former police partner, who had just been promoted to chief of the Seattle Police. The kitchen had become a war room. It was all hands on deck. No one had time to cry. The phones were buzzing.

Trish stated the obvious. "The first forty-eight hours are critical. But this case is a bit different. Gracie won't be hurt. She's his bargaining chip."

Sam chimed in. "Why the hell would Martin Zhao kidnap Gracie?"

Gigi looked at him softly. "I think he saw me'n Charli with a Black seven-year-old and assumed she's Willow. I'm so deeply sorry. We'll get her back to you. I promise. We can outsmart Martin Zhao any day of the week."

CHAPTER FORTY-SEVEN

Gracie awoke on full alert. She looked around curiously at the small room, where she found herself on a narrow bed that seemed to be connected to a wall. There were two small round brass-lined windows clasped shut with some kind of locking mechanism. The polished wood walls were filled with books, and there was a small built-in desk opposite her. Looking to her left, she noticed a small Asian woman with several sparkly earrings in each ear, sitting crisscross applesauce with her eyes closed. Gracie remained quiet, wondering what to do. She looked to her right, where she saw a chubby Asian man staring at his phone. It looked like he was playing a video game.

For the first time since she awakened, she noticed the deep pulse of the engines and the familiar rocking of being on a boat. She perked up and tried to see out one of the windows, which she now recognized as a porthole—just like her parents' sailboat windows, but fancier. She craned her neck without getting up. She didn't want anyone to know she was awake until she figured out where she was.

From behind her, the woman spoke. Gracie recognized Chinese, but only caught the word "time." The man grunted. Gracie froze.

The woman must have noticed Gracie's stiffening and got up and knelt in front of her. She recognized the word "grandma" and that the woman was calling her Ju.

"My name is Gracie," Gracie said in Chinese.

The woman looked into Gracie's eyes, and tears began to run down her face. She spoke softly and slowly in Chinese, but Gracie only knew a few words. One of them was "love."

Totally confused, Gracie started to cry. "What's your name?" she asked the woman in Chinese.

The woman responded, "Grandma."

Tired of trying to show off her Chinese, Gracie switched to English. "You are not my grandma. Who are you? Where am I? Where's my mom?"

Apparently, Gracie's escalating voice shook the man out of his video game trance, and he looked up.

The woman barked orders at the guy in Chinese, and he stuck his head out the door. Gracie recognized the words "food" and "water" and "hungry." The man closed and locked the door, putting the key into his pocket.

The woman came over and sat next to Gracie. She put her hand on Gracie's leg. "We on a very big boat. A ship. You going to be okay. I take care of you."

Gracie took in the seriousness of her situation and began to sob. "I don't want you to take care of me. I want my mom!" she shouted.

The woman quietly rubbed Gracie's back for several minutes. Gracie rocked back and forth with the barely perceptible movement of the ship. She caught her breath when someone knocked loudly on the thick wooden door, and the woman talked to the man at the door like she was giving him orders.

The table that rolled in looked like the tables that had brought dinner to her and her dad when they were in New York, at the big fancy hotel. She temporarily forgot her predicament and sat up to see what was under the silver covers on the food.

The woman pushed the man aside and lifted the dish covers. The room filled with the aroma of food. Gracie realized she was, in fact, pretty hungry, so she didn't fuss when the woman wheeled the table up to Gracie's perch on the bunk. The man nearly pushed the woman aside to grab the pot of tea and some kind of sticky buns. Gracie watched with interest as the woman pushed him back and turned to Gracie.

Gracie picked up the chopsticks and took a taste of the noodles. She smiled for the first time as she looked slyly at the woman who was hovering over her.

"The cooks on my brother ships are best!" The woman winked.

The man returned to his video game.

"What's your real name?" Gracie asked the woman as soon as she slurped the mouthful of noodles down.

"Well, you call me Auntie Jing now. But soon you calling me Grandma."

Gracie shrugged and shook her head. "I already have two really good grandmas. I mean really, really good ones. I don't need another one." She took another bite of noodles and hung her face over the bowl so as not to splash the sauce on her sweatshirt. She was quiet as she took several more bites. Then she looked seriously at the woman called Jing.

"Why am I on this ship? Where are we going? And when can I go home?" The questions spilled out, one over another.

Jing dropped her voice. "I get you off this ship and back home. I promise. But I need you help me." She looked serious.

"I'm a good helper." Gracie's tone mirrored Jing's in volume. "Why are we whispering?"

Jing paused, pointed at the man. "Shh," she said as she considered her next steps.

Gracie raised her eyebrows expectantly.

"Okay. Here the problem." Jing moved closer to Gracie and spoke quietly. "That man not want us get out of this room."

Gracie leaned in. "Why? You said this is your brother's boat. Why would he want to keep you locked in here?"

Jing ignored the obviously excellent question and pointed at the chubby guy. "His job to take us on this ship and not let us off. And they took my phone."

"You mean he's kidnapping us?" Gracie was all business. "Your own brother?"

"I don't know kidnapping. But that man watching us all the time."

"That sounds like kidnapping. Where is this ship taking us?"

Jing changed the subject. "We need get that guy phone. Then I call for help. Get us off this ship."

Gracie nodded. "You mean steal his phone? Like, at nighttime, when he's asleep?"

"I think sooner than night. Before ship get too far in the ocean."

"Okay. I'm a good helper. What should I do?"

Jing looked around the small stateroom. "I not sure."

"We could hit him in the head," Gracie offered helpfully.

"Not sure we can do that. But you right, you a good helper."

Gracie smiled. "I told you so."

"You sure did." Jing turned her attention to the duffel bag on the floor, where she rummaged around for her purse.

Gracie watched as Jing pulled out a small glass jar with flowers on top. It reminded her of the collection of old glass perfume bottles her great-grandma Taylor had on her dresser. Jing opened it and spilled several pills into her hand.

Jing turned her back on the man, who was still transfixed by his video game. She hunched over so he wouldn't see what she was doing if he happened to snap out of it. She grabbed a spoon off the wheeled table and crushed the pills.

Gracie glanced at the man with her eyes. "Are we going to poison him?" she whispered.

Jing shook her head. "No, but these very strong pills, and they make him very sleepy. Then I get his phone and call for help."

Gracie nodded silently.

Jing balanced the spoon on the table and took Gracie's hands in hers. "I going to make mess, and when that man get up to help, you put this"—she pointed to the powdered pills—"in his sticky bun and tea. Okay? You do that?"

Gracie studied the shelf next to the man, where he had put his food and tea. Her eyes traced a path between her bunk and the chair where the man was sitting. She looked at Jing and gave her a thumbs-up.

Jing smiled. "I count on you."

Gracie held up her fist for a fist bump. "Okay. I can help with this. I'm really fast."

"Fast good, but careful better." Jing added very slowly, "It very important this pill in his food and tea."

"I'm ready." Gracie took the spoon and put her hand over the powder so it wouldn't spill.

Jing counted. "One. Two. Three." And she got up and pushed the tray off the table gently.

The man looked up, and Jing snapped at him in Chinese. She pointed at the tiny door that led into the bathroom as she barked orders. Jing dropped to the floor and began to pick up the broken glass from the water pitcher as the guy ran to the bathroom. Jing pointed at the shelf and nodded at Gracie.

Gracie was at the shelf in a flash. She quickly and carefully put the powder on the sticky bun and pushed it in for good measure. Then she put the rest into the teapot and into the cup of tea that was half-empty. She stood on the man's chair as though she were trying to avoid the broken glass, while Jing and the man chattered angrily in Chinese as they picked up glass and mopped up the mess on the floor with bath towels.

As soon as the bulk of the mess was soaked up, the man opened the door and yelled for help. In a minute, a younger man came in with a mop and took over. The man almost smiled at Gracie as he lifted her off the chair and placed her gently on her bunk. Then he returned to his video game.

The cleanup helper left, and the man took a minute to pull out his key and lock the door from the inside. Jing took a paper and pen off the desk and brought it to Gracie.

"You know little Chinese?"

Gracie smiled. "I'm number one in my class in Chinese. I know lots of words," she bragged.

"We write together now." She cocked her head at the man, who was shoving the sticky bun in his mouth as though he hadn't eaten all day.

Gracie whispered, "You want to draw characters until he falls asleep, right?"

Jing smiled and nodded and wrote "big boat" in Chinese.

"Big boat!" Gracie said in Chinese, so excited that she forgot to whisper.

The man looked up at her and narrowed his eyes. He returned his attention to his phone and seemed to be texting as he looked up at Gracie.

Jing put her finger over her lips in a *shh* motion.

Gracie whispered, "Big boat."

Jing nodded.

"Small window," Gracie whispered.

Jing winked at her.

"Blue car."

"You very good Chinese." Jing looked proud.

Gracie beamed and gave Jing a high five.

They kept up the game while watching their captor, whose eyes were drooping just a bit.

Suddenly his phone rang. He spoke rapidly in Chinese, then turned to Jing and spoke sharply. Gracie recognized the words "son" and "phone."

Jing turned to Gracie and whispered, "I need to go. Just few minutes. I be right back, I promise." She squeezed Gracie's hand. "You okay?"

Gracie bit her lip and nodded, turning her gaze from Jing to the man and back.

The door opened, and a tall Asian man grabbed Jing by her arm and roughly pulled her out of the cabin. It seemed like they knew each other, by the way she was screaming at him and him at her. Then Gracie realized that he was the one who had grabbed her and brought her to this ship. What was this guy doing with her new friend Jing? And why was he being so mean to her?

After the man fell asleep, Gracie quietly climbed down and picked up the phone that had dropped from his hand. Then she went back to practicing her Chinese characters. She might need to know these now that she was surrounded by Chinese people.

After filling the page, Gracie looked up and noticed that her guard was snoring loudly. Should she call or text? A call might wake the guard, so she decided to text. Once her mom and dad knew where she was, they'd come get her for sure. But where exactly was she? She stood up on the bunk and looked out the window and recognized one of those red boats that drop off pilots onto the big ships.

Holding her breath, she focused on the phone and was dismayed to realize that the letters and numbers were all Chinese characters. Her heart began to race. Her mom wouldn't recognize Chinese words if she texted them. She sat in consternation for half a minute until she came up with a plan.

Standing back on the bunk, she took a video of the small red boat that was pulling up alongside the ship in the gray light of dusk. Then she dialed Libby and sent the video. As soon as it appeared to have been sent, she texted in Chinese, *Red boat—red boat—red boat.* And then her name in Chinese. And she waited.

CHAPTER FORTY-EIGHT

"Mom! Dad!" Libby tore into Gigi's living room.

"Shh! Trish is about to call the police chief." Sam gestured a swatting motion to Libby.

"It's Gracie! She's on a big ship! Out on the strait! I know it's her!" She held up her phone. "It's *Gracie!*" she screamed.

Sam leaned over to look at Libby's phone. "This is in Chinese. What does it say?" Sam asked impatiently.

Libby's words tripped over each other. "It says 'Red boat, red boat, red boat.' And 'Gracie'! And here's the video." Libby paused while the group surrounded her as she held up her phone. It was a wobbly clip taken out of a porthole. The camera had captured a red pilot boat churning rapidly toward the camera's location. Camille immediately recognized the backdrop of the Olympic Mountains towering over the marina at Port Angeles just before sunset.

"It's a pilot boat out of Port Angeles. Whoever took this is high up over the water. It looks like it's taken from a freighter," Camille said with certainty.

Sam nodded in agreement. "And how do you know this is from Gracie?"

"See these characters?" Libby pointed at the text. "It says 'Gracie' in Chinese. She's on a ship! See the red boat? We just saw that same boat when we were sailing with Mom. Gracie was with us!"

Camille nodded and hugged Libby by the shoulder. "When we were crossing the strait from Friday Harbor to Port Angeles in December, Gracie and Libby were working on their Chinese and practicing saying 'red boat.'" Camille's voice tightened. "She's trying to tell us where she is!"

"That's a pilot boat there for sure." Sam held the phone up to Camille, who stared at it intently. "How the hell did she end up on a freighter heading for open water?" Sam demanded of no one in particular.

Trish flew into action. "I'm calling the police chief." She waited for a beat. "Hey, Kim, I think we found her. Looks like she's on a ship heading out the Strait of Juan de Fuca! I'm not sure how far US jurisdiction goes off the coast, but right now she's in Washington, or maybe Canada. We need to get law enforcement out there!" She cradled her phone against her ear as she texted the video to her old partner. "I'm texting you the video we just got from Gracie. And here's her message. I hope you have access to a Chinese interpreter!"

"On it," the chief responded over speakerphone. "I'll get a team out on the water over there."

"Like now!" Camille shouted.

Trish batted away Camille's words with her hand, to focus on her conversation. "The video shows a pilot boat out of PA approaching the boat, so they're probably right off the coast of PA now." Trish sounded like a cop.

Camille began to gather her purse and their jackets. "Let's go!" She turned to Libby. "Find out when the next ferry is out of Edmonds. It's just a little over an hour to PA from Kingston." Then she directed Gigi, Charli, Frankie, Pella, and Trish to follow them.

"We're right behind you." Gigi quickly put away the perishable food while Charli pulled together their jackets.

"I'll wait here," Pella offered. "Someone should be available here in town."

"Thanks, Mom." Camille kissed her mother's cheek and blasted out the door.

As soon as they hit the freeway in the U District in Seattle, Camille dialed Rose. "Hey, it's Camille. We have a huge emergency up there."

"Up where?"

"PA!"

"How can I help?" Rose obviously noted the urgency in Camille's tone.

"Our foster daughter just got kidnapped—there's an Amber Alert out." The irony didn't escape Camille.

"Any idea where she is? And really, what is up with you and your friends and the Amber Alerts?"

Camille ignored the attempt at humor. "Our daughter, Grace, is on a ship of some kind—probably a freighter—heading out the Strait of Juan de Fuca. She was kidnapped here in Seattle and just called us from the ship."

"Holy shit." Rose was in full law enforcement mode. "I'm going to merge our police chief. Hang on." She clicked off for a moment. "Camille, you there?"

"Yep."

"Nic! You there?"

"I am. What's up?" Cops all had the same voice when they were on duty.

"I have my friend Camille on the line. Her daughter was kidnapped and is on a freighter heading west out toward the Pacific in the strait."

"We're already on it. I just spoke with Chief Kelley in Seattle. Because it's offshore, she called in the FBI. They have a team heading over there now. We're standing by as well. Gotta get there before they hit international waters. Those freighters move fast."

"Do we need a search warrant?" Rose was always a lawyer first.

"The feds already have one, and they have Judge Chambers on call, just in case."

Camille noted the respect between these two—it was clear they had worked together often. She spoke up. "This is Camille Delaney, Gracie's foster mother. I can't tell you how much we appreciate your department's prompt action."

"Happy to oblige, ma'am. And you might want to thank Chief Kelley—some friend of hers put this at the top of her priority list tonight."

"Oh my gosh! Thanks so much!" Camille felt a brief sense of relief as she hung up the phone.

It was about thirty minutes to the small waterfront village of Edmonds, about fifteen miles north of Seattle, where the car ferries sail across the Sound to Kingston on the Olympic Peninsula. And thankfully the ferry line wasn't an issue that evening. While they waited, Camille's phone rang.

"You hung up on me." It was Rose.

"Sorry, I thought we were done."

"I know you've been busy getting ready for your friend to come home from prison, but I wanted to catch you up on the whole Martin Zhao thing."

"I'm all ears! I just learned that Trent Conway referred the case to the feds for tax fraud. So, what's up over there?"

"I couldn't tell you about the ongoing investigation we initiated after Quinn Hastings spilled on Zhao."

"Investigation?"

"Oh yeah. Now that our local police know how not to screw up an arrest . . ."

Camille laughed at the reference to her unconstitutional search.

Rose continued. "We got them to take down Zhao. He was dealing right behind his pharmacy, just like Quinn said."

"Oh my God. Seriously? Okay if I merge Trish in here? She's with Gigi and Charli, and Frankie, Quinn's old girlfriend."

"Sure, it's about to hit the press up here anyway. The secret is out."

Camille clicked on Trish's number and hit Merge. "I have Rose on the line. They busted Martin!"

Trish didn't miss a beat. "Did he make bail?"

Rose and Trish clearly spoke the same language. Camille said, "He did. Rose charged him. He's going down."

"Finally!" Charli's voice could be heard in the background.

"Well, that explains why he was in Seattle. He kidnapped Gracie while he was out on bail."

"Zhao is the one who kidnapped your daughter?"

"Didn't I mention that when we first spoke?"

"No. You just said she'd been kidnapped."

"And now she's on a freighter headed out to sea . . ."

Camille stopped midsentence when Trish interrupted.

"Holy shit. Hang on a sec. I need to look at my notes." The line was quiet. "Okay, now I remember—when I talked with Jing in the gym that day, she told me that her brother owns a freighter company. I'll bet you a million dollars that Jing and Gracie are on one of her brother's freighters."

Rose didn't miss a beat. "Do we know which freighter company he owns?"

Camille chimed in. "Well, we know it's probably a Taiwanese company, and it's pretty easy to identify what freighter was off the coast of PA about forty-five minutes ago." She looked at Sam, who was booting up a navigation app that identified ships anywhere in the Salish Sea. "Give us a second." She turned to Sam. "Which of those ships is Taiwanese?"

"*Guangzhou*, and it's about halfway from PA to the coast." Sam spoke loud enough for Rose to hear.

"Pretty sure the feds are on it, but I'll let them know, just in case."

Trish's voice conveyed a sense of urgency. "Hey, do you know where Zhao is? My guess is that he may be accompanying his mom and Willow on that ship."

"Crap." Rose paused. "Why do you say that?"

"Just makes logical sense. First, despite Conway taking his passport, Zhao has dual citizenship, so he still has his Taiwanese passport. He kidnaps who he thinks is Charli's long-lost daughter and hops on his uncle's freighter, where he and Gracie can both hide out. Nice play, if he's trying to hush Charli and Quinn from testifying against him." Trish nodded at her own hypothesis. "And if I remember correctly, if they're heading to Taiwan—they're not a signatory to the Hague Convention, so we can't extradite him."

"I need to let the feds know." Rose was focused.

Trish was anxious to get off the phone. "I'm going to call my friend Dave Kimball. He's a special agent, and I think PA is probably part of his territory. Let's hang up and check back in ten minutes."

"'Kay, I'm on it." Rose hung up.

Camille waited for Trish's name to show up on her phone while she and Sam stayed locked on the image of the small icon on the navigation app as it made its way west down the Strait of Juan de Fuca toward the Pacific Ocean.

"These guys need to hurry . . ." Sam spoke softly but firmly. "It's less than an hour to open water."

Camille answered Trish before it even rang. "Did you reach him?"

"He's on the line, hang on . . . Kimball, you there?"

"I am." His voice was steady and strong.

Trish took over. "My friend Camille Delaney's daughter Gracie was abducted from Seattle and is on a freighter headed for open water in the Pacific. Any chance you're in the loop in this case?"

"In the loop, in a manner of speaking. How 'bout on a coast guard helicopter about two knots east of said freighter?" Kimball was speaking loudly to be heard over the background noise.

"Really?"

"Really. And I'd love to chat, but I should probably put my full concentration on getting this kid home safely. These joint operations take some serious attention out here."

"Hang on," Trish shouted.

"Make it quick."

"You involved in a bust in PA recently? DEA nabbed a drug kingpin by the name of Martin Zhao. You know about that one?"

"I do, but really, Seaholm, I need to focus on one thing at a time. They're about to lower me from a helicopter at dusk onto the deck of a moving freighter, and it's a little intense here at the moment."

"Okay, I'll make this quick. I think there's a good chance that Zhao might be on that freighter."

"Hold up! What?"

"The kid you're about to rescue—Zhao thinks the girl is his wife's daughter. It was Zhao who kidnapped her a couple of hours ago."

"Jeez, Seaholm, nothing is simple with you."

"Yeah. The Zhao drug bust and the kidnapping are totally entangled."

"What makes you think Zhao is on that boat?"

"It's mostly just a hunch, but it makes sense that he'd try to hop a ride on a freighter to get out of the country."

"We have his passport. He won't get far."

"Not so fast. He's got dual citizenship, so I'm ninety-nine percent certain that he's traveling under a Taiwanese passport, if he even needs one at all. And his uncle owns that freighter line. They're headed back to their home port of Taiwan, which is not a signatory to the Hague Convention, so he'll be out of your reach."

"If you're right, we're going to need backup."

"Yes, you will. Zhao is pretty well connected, and he has a big operation. I'd assume that if he's on that freighter, he has some bad dudes accompanying him."

"You sure about this?"

"I'm sure he kidnapped Gracie—his ex-wife saw him plain as day. And I'm sure he's not keen on the idea of spending decades in prison, so it wouldn't surprise me if he tried to hitch a ride on one of his uncle's huge cargo ships, where it'd be easy for him to slip out of the country unnoticed."

"Okay, sounds like this goes beyond our shores. I'm calling in backup from Homeland Security. Gotta go."

CHAPTER FORTY-NINE

It seemed like forever since the big mean Asian guy had dragged the screaming Jing out of the cabin. Gracie had taken to alternating between watching the man snoring and looking out the porthole. Even though it was almost dark, she could tell that it looked like the San Juan Islands, where her parents took the family sailing during the summer. She considered sending another text, because there was no sign of anyone coming to rescue her. Then she noticed a line of helicopters with giant searchlights flying around the ship. She couldn't see exactly what they were doing, but it seemed like a good thing.

She drew a sharp breath when someone began banging on the door. The guy who had the keys was still sleeping and didn't seem to hear it. Gracie wondered what to do. Should she get the keys from him? She couldn't make up her mind.

The door banging had turned into shouting out in the hallway, and the banging turned urgent and louder. Gracie grabbed the phone she had placed back into the sleeping guy's hand. If someone got into the room and took her out, she'd at least have the phone. She hid it in her sweatshirt pocket and impulsively took the keys from the guy and threw them up onto the top bookshelf. Then she climbed up on the desk to see out the window.

Before long, the ship's engines changed pitch, and it felt like it was slowing down.

The yelling in Chinese out in the hall was replaced by deep boom-ing voices. "FBI! Stop where you are!"

Gracie heard scuffling out in the hallway, and the serious voices sounded like they were getting farther away. But they didn't stop yell-ing. And the yelling was really loud. "Hands up!" And louder: "Let me see your hands!"

The guy in Gracie's room snored in spurts; he was oblivious to the scene outside the door.

More footsteps running down the corridor. By now the ship was almost still in the water. Gracie held her breath, wondering when they'd come and rescue her. Then it dawned on her. How would they know where she was on the giant ship? She glanced around the room and picked up Jing's bright-red scarf. Biting her lip, she pulled out the phone and texted Libby again.

Red flag window. Red flag window.

Putting down the phone, Gracie opened the small porthole and stuck the red scarf halfway out the window, then closed it on the fabric so it wouldn't blow away. Libby was smart. She'd know what to do.

———

"Mom! Gracie texted again!"

Camille twisted around in her seat as the family car was pulling onto the ferry. "What's she saying?"

"'Red flag window.' What does that mean?"

"No idea, but let's tell Kimball. Maybe he can make sense of it."

Camille called Trish and asked her to text her FBI pal.

"Maybe she's putting a red flag in her window," Libby mused.

Camille closed her eyes and held her breath. "Let's hope so."

"She's a smart kid," Sam chimed in. "She knows she's on a huge ship and it might be hard to find her. It's a brilliant move, really." He'd barely turned off the car before Camille bolted for Trish and Gigi's car, right behind them on the ferry. The freezing spray whipped up by the wind startled her as she ran across the cold metal deck.

Camille waited impatiently for Trish to roll down her window, then stuck her head into the passenger space. "If Sam's right and Gracie stuck a flag out her window, how will they see it in the dark?"

Trish smiled. "That whole ship is lit up like it's on a movie set right around now. The coast guard has serious searchlights on their copters, and by now there's probably a phalanx of coast guard vessels heading that way with some serious wattage. If there's a red flag, they'll see it. Kimball texted me that they'd be on the lookout. But their first order of business is to find Zhao so he can't hurt her."

Now that the ferry was underway, the wind and spray created a curtain of mist around the cars. "Get in here," Trish ordered Camille. "Your hair will freeze into ice out there."

Camille complied and squeezed into the back seat. "Sam says it looks like the ship's stopped moving, so that's good, right?"

Trish nodded. "These multiagency busts are highly orchestrated. This is for sure not their first rodeo. These guys are well trained in maritime boarding operations. When I was on the force, we sometimes supported their practice runs boarding ferries out on the Sound. It was an incredible dance between the feds, the coast guard, and Homeland Security. They know exactly what they're doing. Now that they're aboard, they'll find Gracie."

—

Gracie was torn. Should she open the door and try to escape? Or were there more bad guys out there? She pressed her ear against the door and tried to decipher the Chinese being yelled up and down the corridor outside. Within minutes, the bossy police-like voices took over.

"Everyone down!"

The response was frantic Chinese. Then some guy screamed "Gun!" in Chinese. That caused more yelling and banging around, with the police shouting in English and the other men frantically chattering in Chinese. But as far as she could tell, the whole idea of a gun got their attention. Suddenly, the sound of Chinese was overtaken by a woman's voice in English. It was Jing, and she was telling the police that she would translate.

Thereafter, it was police telling everyone to stay on the floor with their hands on their backs in English, followed by Jing translating. But before she could finish, it sounded like the police grabbed her and took her down the hall while she screamed, "Let me go!"

Gracie stepped away from the door, deciding to wait it out for the cops to rescue her, when someone grabbed her from behind and pushed her to the floor. To her horror, she was face to face with the sleeping guard. He spat in her face and pulled her across the floor by her feet, despite her desperate calls for help. The guy was actually sitting right on her, which made it really hard to breathe. He pulled her hands together and put his belt around them so she couldn't move them. She began to cry.

"Let me go!"

The guy grunted and shoved her face into the floor as he looked around, trying to figure out his next move. He groped his pockets for his phone and came up empty handed. Gracie wiggled herself on the floor so he wouldn't find his phone in her pocket. His breathing was heavy and his face was red. Maybe those pills were still working—he didn't seem to know what to do next, so he sat back and closed his eyes for a second.

"Gracie!" It was a man's voice. "Gracie—are you in there?"

The guy glanced toward the door and then back at Gracie, and put his hand over her mouth as she tried to yell for help.

"Shit. Check again. This should be the stateroom." The man outside sounded really mad.

He banged on the door. And Gracie wiggled in vain to get away.

This time it was a fist pounding even harder on the door. "Open up! FBI!"

That seemed positive.

Then silence.

Gracie could feel her heart beating fast. She took several deep breaths to calm herself while she looked around the room, planning her escape—just in case the guy moved enough for her to get out from under him.

The crash of an axe splintering the door startled both Gracie and the guard. He scrambled to grab her, but she kicked him in his groin and bit his hand just as a tall man in a navy-blue jacket pushed his way into the small room. The guard guy tried to choke Gracie, but she kept kicking him until the tall guy pulled her away.

"It's okay, Gracie, I'm here to take you home to your family."

Gracie was either too scared or too excited to cry. "I knew you'd rescue me," she said matter-of-factly. Then she turned to watch two other men in matching navy-blue jackets jump on the guy who had been guarding her.

"My name is Dave, and I'm a friend of Trish and your mom's."

Gracie noticed she was starting to shake.

Dave took off his jacket and put it over her shoulders as he unwrapped the belt from around her wrists before picking her up. He stopped at the door that had been destroyed by the axe. He tried the handle. It was locked.

Gracie pointed up at the top bookshelf. "I threw the key up there so that guy couldn't open the door."

Dave smiled. "That was very smart." He put Gracie down and climbed up on the bunk so he could reach the shelf. He felt around blindly, then winked at Gracie. "Got it!"

"Can we get out of here now?"

Dave put the key in the lock and slowly opened the door. Before he left the room, he stuck his head out into the hallway and shouted, "All clear?"

Another man's voice responded. "Clear! The crew is on the bridge, and we have Zhao and his entourage in custody, along with his mother."

"Okay, Gracie, hold tight around my neck. We're going to climb down some pretty steep stairs to get you out of here."

Gracie nodded seriously and squeezed the man's neck. Maybe even a little bit too tight.

Climbing down the steps of the freighter as it was turning around to head the other way gave Gracie a flash of dizziness. And when they reached the flat surface of the freighter Gracie let out a little "Whoop!" This might have gone from the worst day to the best night. There in the spotlight right below them was a red pilot boat heading their way. "Do I get to go on that pilot boat?" she asked her new friend Dave.

"Actually, you're going to be on an even cooler boat. See that coast guard ship down there? The one with the flashing blue lights?"

"My sister Libby is going to freak out, even if it's just a coast guard boat. I hope it goes as fast as a real red boat!" Gracie smiled widely. "Am I going now?"

"As soon as it gets close to the ship, we'll hoist you down onto the boat." Dave pointed at a basket with all kinds of straps. "See that? You get to ride in it all the way down to that boat."

Dave held Gracie by the back of her jacket as she looked down over the side of the ship at the red-and-white boat bobbing in the brightness of the giant searchlights below.

"Here." He handed her a neon-orange life vest. "Put this on."

Gracie backed away from the rail of the ship and tussled into the vest as a group of guys in matching navy-blue windbreakers with big yellow letters on their backs gathered around her. They waited until she had adjusted the vest, then directed her to lie down in the basket hooked by thick lines and cables to a hoist centered on the massive deck. For the first time, it dawned on Gracie that she was going to be lifted up in the air and over the side down to the waiting boat. Were the shakes from the cold or the idea of dangling over the water in the still, dark night?

She looked up at her new friend Dave as one of the men clipped all kinds of belts over her to keep her in the basket. "Is this thing safe?"

"You bet it is!"

Gracie narrowed her eyes. "Well, if it's so safe, maybe you can hop on for a ride down with me."

Dave looked at the men surrounding the basket and shrugged. "Any problem with me hitching a ride along with Miss Gracie?"

The men looked at each other. "I won't tell the captain if you guys won't." One guy laughed.

"Okey doke, then." Dave carefully placed one foot on either side of the basket and tightened his life vest. Grabbing the thick cable with one hand, he used the other to give a thumbs-up to the operator of the hoist. "You ready, Gracie?"

Gracie bit her lip and nodded. All she could see was the starry dark sky above her as the noise of the engine punctuated the blackness. A little jiggle, and they were lifted up off the deck and slowly swung out over the open water toward the pulsing blue lights far below.

Sensing Gracie's mounting fear, Dave began chatting. "You know, in the FBI, we have to learn how to jump out of airplanes, and this is even a little bit scarier—so you get the bravery award! Look at you, just having fun, hanging out over the water with me."

Gracie mustered up a smile. Then she closed her eyes as the basket swayed back and forth as it began lowering toward the boat far below. Her tummy did a little flip.

"Wait till you tell your friends how cool it was to be way up here, floating in a basket."

Gracie lifted her head and tried to see the boat, but all she could see were stars that were gradually being obliterated by the mist coming up from the water as the pair slowly descended.

We must be getting close to the boat, Gracie surmised as the lights got brighter and she could hear men barking orders below her. Dave was directing them as the basket continued to lower.

Suddenly, there was a jolt. Something had grabbed on to the basket and was pulling it sharply.

"Hang on, Gracie! We're almost there!" Dave was smiling widely. "You did it!" He shot her a thumbs-up.

The basket lurched to the left as it was pulled over so it could land on the deck of the boat.

Gracie gritted her teeth and held her breath as several men in uniforms yanked the basket to the deck and immediately started yelling commands at each other to disconnect the giant cable from the basket. One guy jumped on and pulled himself up to disconnect the basket from the cable, while several others stabilized the basket on the deck. Once the straps were unclasped, Gracie was finally able to sit up and take a look at her surroundings.

She got right to the point. "Is this just like the red boat?"

"Well"—Dave smiled—"it's a red boat, but not sure it's exactly the same as *the* red boat."

"Can I call my mom and dad? Am I going home now?" She peered inside the cabin. "Can I sit next to the captain?"

Dave was one step ahead of her. "Here's your mom and dad." He held out the cell phone.

"Mom 'n' Dad! I'm on a red-and-white boat! It's just a coast guard boat, so not as cool as a real red boat. And I got to swing down here on a basket. And my friend Dave climbed on the basket with me. And I had to fight a bad guy. And I practiced my Chinese with a nice lady, but now I'm not so sure she's nice since she knows the guy who kidnapped me. But she really didn't seem to like him—so maybe she's okay."

All she could hear on the other end of the phone was what sounded like her mom crying and her dad telling her he loved her.

CHAPTER FIFTY

Camille had mostly fond memories of her time at the law office of Whitfield, Bahr, and Moses, where she had practiced divorce law for the Seattle elite. But her cozy office in Fremont had become more her style than the icy-white marble décor of the high-rise where she and Charli now stood, looking out the two-story-high windows facing the giant silhouette of Mount Rainer, which towered over the two stadiums just south of downtown.

Camille and Charli stood up to greet Camille's former law partner Jothy Bahr as he took the stairs down to the lobby two at a time.

Camille air-kissed Jothy's cheek and held out her arm toward Charli in a gesture of introduction. "Jothy, meet my friend Charli Zhao."

The two shook hands briefly before Jothy turned to usher them up the stairs and into the inner sanctum. Camille was pleased that he was directing them to his personal office rather than one of the austere conference rooms off the reception area on the floor below. It was a sign of collegiality and friendship that he chose to conduct the meeting in his office.

Several of the staff greeted Camille by name and asked about the girls. Just because the place looked like a soulless modern museum with well-lit original art lining the walls of the public spaces didn't mean that the people at the firm were not warm and friendly. Camille stopped at a few cubicles and admired pictures of babies and grandchildren—and a couple of puppies.

Jothy had the corner office, which looked down over the expansive view of Elliott Bay, with the familiar white-and-green ferries cutting through the whitecaps to the islands and peninsula on the west side of Puget Sound. The ever-present Olympic Mountains tore a jagged streak on the horizon. Camille caught her breath as she considered for a moment how much her life had changed since she had left the firm only a couple of years ago. The shadow of the mountain range brought back memories of the transformative twenty-four hours she had shared with Frankie. Nope. She wouldn't trade her life now for her spacious old sky-high office. Absolutely not.

"Earth to Camille . . ." Jothy teased his friend out of her momentary trance.

"Sorry, I . . . I forgot how spectacular this view is." It wasn't actually a lie, but it certainly wasn't what she had on her mind.

Jothy motioned for the women to sit in his matching modern gray chairs. "Camille tells me you're ready to file for divorce. I'm here to help," he said as he sat in the chair opposite Charli.

A thin man with a pink bow tie popped his head in the office and said, "Sorry to interrupt. Camille, you want your regular? Green tea, no sweetener?"

"Thanks, Marco."

He looked at Charli. "And for you?"

"I'll have the same, thanks." She turned to Camille. "You pretty much know everyone here, don't you?"

Camille smiled. "I spent lots of years right down the hall."

Jothy picked up a light-blue pad and a Montblanc pen. "And we'd take her back in a heartbeat," he said sincerely.

"Okay with you, Charli, if I just jump in here?" Camille changed the subject.

"Please do—I'm not exactly sure what all is relevant," Charli said.

Camille continued. "Charli has a helluva story to tell, which you'll no doubt learn more about as the case unfolds. But here are the highlights. Charli and her husband, Martin Zhao, own a chain of pharmacies."

Jothy jotted down notes.

"About eight years ago, Charli, who has an MBA and was the CFO, realized that something was amiss with the accounting. One thing led to another, and she figured out that Martin was running two sets of books."

Jothy looked up from his pad, his eyes wide and his eyebrows raised. "You sure about that?"

Charli nodded.

Camille continued. "Zhao had gotten caught up in the OxyContin craze and was supplying oxy way beyond what was medically appropriate, if you get my drift. The guy was basically running an illegal drug operation through his pharmacies."

"And you had evidence?" Jothy asked Charli.

"Oh yes. And by that time, I was having an affair with his brother, Brian." She paused. "You're a divorce lawyer, I'm sure you've heard this a million times, so I won't dwell on the facts of the affair. Suffice it to say that Brian and I delved into the books and decided to turn Martin in for his illegal operation—I didn't want to get blamed for it because I was the CFO."

"Seems reasonable." Jothy turned back to his note-taking as Marco reappeared with the tea.

Camille smiled at Marco and took over the narrative. "But Martin beat them to it. He had a bunch of heroin planted in each of their cars, and both Charli and Brian got arrested for possession with intent to distribute. Worse yet, he planted a gun in Charli's car, so she got a gun enhancement to her sentence."

"Jesus. And heroin? Where'd he get heroin?"

"By that time, Martin realized that once people got hooked on oxy, it was a quick step to other street drugs, and so he got himself a side gig selling heroin. Right behind his pharmacies. He had pharmacy techs dealing drugs and cut them in on the split."

Jothy leaned forward and looked at Charli. "This is an insane story. I assume you managed to beat the rap by turning him in?"

Charli shook her head. "Nope. I just got out of prison, where I spent the past seven years."

Jothy flopped back in his chair. "Holy crap, that's awful!" He learned forward. "You okay?"

"I am now, thanks."

"How about your boyfriend, Martin's brother, right?"

"He's still in Monroe Prison."

Jothy was silent.

"But his sentence is almost over, so he'll be home really soon."

Camille got them back on track. "You're not going to believe this. We got Charli's conviction overturned on a CR 7.8 motion."

"A CR 7.8 motion? Those are nearly impossible to win. Who argued it?"

Camille pointed at her chest with her thumb. "That'd be me . . ."

"Holy shit, Camille. That's a long way from the divorce world, floating up here in the clouds. You seriously argued a crim law motion?"

Camille appreciated the recognition. "Crazy, right?" Jothy's reaction reminded her of why she had been so freaked out in court that day. "Actually, my mom helped me prepare."

Charli interrupted. "Your friend Camille was amazing. She looked exactly like Pella Rallis's daughter up there, arguing a CR 7 motion."

"Okay. I always knew you were a fearless trial advocate, but wow. I'm not sure I would have been so brave." Jothy paused. "But then again, my mom isn't Pella Rallis, so there's that. How'd they finally arrest Zhao?" Jothy was spellbound by the story. "Is he in custody?"

"He is now. He was out on bail when he tried to make a run for it. The feds got him while he was trying to escape to his mother's home country of Taiwan. The evidence was tight. We found Zhao's old computer, and Charli spent the past couple of weeks with the feds, explaining the double set of books. It has tax fraud written all over it. I expect they'll be charging him soon. But what sealed the deal is that law enforcement set up a sting operation where they caught him redhanded with a huge bag of fentanyl and meth right behind his pharmacy. Oh! And he did it to me too."

"He did what?"

"Planted drugs in my car, almost got me thrown in prison. But the guy who tried to set me up left the drugs in the backpack so when they opened it during an Amber Alert search, it was illegal."

"Jeez, Camille . . ."

"I know, right? He's done for. I bet you know Rose Adams. She's now the prosecutor over in Port Angeles."

"You're kidding. She was the queen of the defense bar for years."

"Yeah, there's a story there too, but she's getting ready to heap a shitload of charges on Zhao, and my bet is he pleas out. And then there'll be federal tax fraud charges coming soon."

"Well, divorcing him certainly seems prudent."

Charli got serious. "I understand a bit about community property, and as I understand it, I'm entitled to half of the value of the pharmacies as well as our penthouse and beach house on Lopez Island. Also, last I checked, we have a substantial stock portfolio."

"Well, I'm not sure about his restitution, but you should be able to get your half." Jothy turned on his divorce mode.

Camille chimed in. "Actually, restitution isn't the main problem. It's civil forfeiture. The state can take drug money from a convicted dealer. But Trent Conway tells me that they'll probably just take his liquid assets if they can prove that the money was obtained illegally. He said they wouldn't go after the real estate or the business because it's hard to prove that they were bought with drug money."

"So," Jothy said thoughtfully, "maybe we just have Charli move a chunk of the liquid assets to live on, but leave enough for the state. Then we get her the illiquid assets in the divorce and give him the remaining cash, and let the state do what it wants with it?"

"Exactly what I was thinking."

Charli changed the subject. "And here's the thing: Camille is going to team up with a trial lawyer friend to file suit against Martin on behalf of a bunch of women I did time with and several of their friends, who were all damaged by him shilling out oxy without proper prescriptions."

"Nice play." Jothy nodded at Camille.

"And most of the money that I get in the divorce, I'm going to use to fund halfway houses and my friend Frankie's women's recovery group. So, let's squeeze as much money as we can out of that asshole. And if I can get the business in the divorce, I can also use the profits to fund my nonprofit. As the former CFO, I know that can be a lucrative business—even if we do it all legally." She smiled.

Jothy was speechless. It was clear he wasn't accustomed to having a wealthy client seeking to clean out her spouse so she could give most of the money away.

Charli added, "Do you think I need to start a nonprofit?"

"It'd probably make sense from a tax-planning perspective. We have some business lawyers here at the firm who do some nonprofit work. We can get them involved as needed."

"Camille emailed me your questionnaire, which I just filled out and emailed to Peg, your paralegal. It has a comprehensive list of all our assets. I know you'll probably have to get the pharmacies valued, and the condo and vacation place, so I'd like to get those started as soon as possible." Charli was all business. "Oh, and can you get this filed right away? I'd love to get it served on him before he goes to prison." Charli smiled slyly.

Camille looked at her watch. "We'd better get going. I have an argument in dependency court right after lunch. We're about to find out where Charli's long-lost daughter ended up after she was taken into the foster care system."

Charli nodded nervously. "It's a big day."

CHAPTER FIFTY-ONE

Dependency court was unlike any other part of the judicial system in King County. The lawyers on either side enjoyed long-standing relationships with each other, and the collegiality was noticeable. Camille felt like a fish out of water as she worked her way through the throng of lawyers, laughing and shouting over at each other about pending cases. Worried parents and grandparents mingled in the crowd, seeming shell-shocked to even be in this court, where the future of their parental rights was on the line.

The court staff knew everyone on a first-name basis, and they were wrangling lawyers and litigants whose cases were set to be heard that afternoon. Several pairs of lawyers huddled on the old benches, negotiating deals with families that would allow them to avoid a hearing.

"Anyone here on the Zhao matter?" a short bespectacled court clerk hollered above the din.

Camille raised her hand, but her response was drowned out by the crowd. "Over here!" she yelled louder.

The clerk headed over. "You're fifth up on the docket." She leaned in. "Have you spoken with the prosecutor yet?"

Camille shook her head. "No. Should I?"

The clerk shrugged her shoulders. "Up to you, but most of these cases settle out here in the hallway." She pointed at the groups of lawyers hashing out settlement details.

"Okay. Who's the prosecutor on this case?"

The clerk looked at the file. "Over there." The clerk gestured. "Hey, Jason, you're on Zhao, right?"

Jason looked like he had just stepped out of a tattoo parlor—he was inked all the way up to his face. "I think so." He juggled his files. "Yep! I am."

"I have opposing counsel here." The clerk looked at the stack of pleadings in her hand. "Camille Delaney."

"Be right over!" he shouted. "And nice to meet you, Camille."

Camille was bewildered by the way things rolled in dependency court. "You too." She waved and turned to look quizzically at Charli. "This, down here, is a whole new world to me."

Charli leaned up against Camille. "You think they'll tell us anything about Willow here in court?"

"I'm not sure. The motion has been filed, and there was really no response from the prosecutor, so I expect we'll get some kind of order that allows us to obtain the file."

"Sorry, I should have called you before this hearing," Jason said breathlessly after weaving his way down the hallway. "The state doesn't oppose your motion."

Camille smiled. "Thanks much. I'm new to this area of practice—I'm just here as a favor to my friend Ms. Zhao."

Jason nodded. "I figured it was something like that. I haven't seen you around before, and most everyone here is pretty much a regular."

"So I gathered."

"Anyway, here's your file." He handed Camille a file folder. "We'll send you an electronic copy, but since most people are anxious to get the info, we print out the allowable info about the foster children for the parents' review."

"Thanks so much." Camille held the file as though it was the crown jewels. "How do we get the order signed off on by the judge?"

Jason lifted the file carefully from Camille and pulled out a signed court order. "It's right here. These hearings are mostly administrative, so the court just signs all uncontested orders every morning."

"So, what are the next steps?" Camille asked.

"Well, you'll reach out to the department with this order, and they'll retrieve the child from her temporary placement and return her to the mother."

Charli spoke for the first time. "That's it? When do I get Willow back?" Tears were welling up.

"Shouldn't take more than a day or so."

"Jason! You got the Dennison order?" the clerk hollered.

Jason riffled through his case files. "Just a sec!" He turned to Charli. "Good luck, Ms. Zhao." He pulled a file out and waved it in the air. "I'll be over in a sec!"

"Thank you so much." Charli shook Jason's hand before he disappeared into the sea of lawyers and litigants.

Camille gestured toward a spot on one of the crowded benches. "Let's sit."

Charli looked like she was barely aware of where she was as Camille pulled her gently by the hand over to the bench.

"You ready?" She looked Charli directly in the eye.

Charli nodded silently through her tears. Her hands shook as she took the file from Camille. Then she closed her eyes and bowed her head in prayer. Camille rubbed her back gently.

Charli took a deep breath and opened the file as Camille looked over her shoulder.

Name: Gracie

Age: Seven

Race: Black/Mixed

Location: Seattle

"Oh my God." Charli looked, wide eyed, at Camille. "Oh my God."

She turned the page, where Gracie smiled at them. It was her school picture from last year.

The two women were alone in the sea of anguished parents surrounding them. Speechless. Then the tears started to flow. Camille couldn't breathe. She cradled her head in her hands. Charli put her head on Camille's shoulder, and the two women embraced, sobbing.

After a couple of minutes that felt like an hour, Camille clapped her hand over her mouth. "Oh my God. Oh my God . . ."

"Thank you. Thank you. Thank you." Charli held Camille's face in both hands.

Camille tried to stop her sobbing by taking deep breaths, but the tears wouldn't stop. She shook her head in disbelief and hugged herself.

"Gracie," she said softly. Then she looked up at Charli, who was also trying to stop her gasping sobs.

The two women grabbed each other's hands and sat staring at each other.

Charli spoke first. "I will never take her away from you. There has to be a way to do this together."

"You're her mom. She needs you." Camille wiped away her tears.

"Well, so are you. And she needs you too." Charli tried to clean the mascara off Camille's face with her thumb.

"What do we do now?" Camille, for once, seemed out of ideas.

"We find a way to tell Gracie that she has two moms. And I'll do whatever I can to figure out how we can raise her together. She has sisters and fabulous parents. We'll make this work."

Camille collapsed back against the marble wall. "Thank you," she whispered.

The two women sat holding hands, eyes closed for several minutes.

"You ready?" Camille turned her head to look at Charli.

Charli nodded. "I'm not sure I can even stand up."

"Me neither." Camille took a deep, shaky breath and noticed the hallway had, for the most part, emptied out. Court was in session, and most of the deals had been cut. She stood and held her hand out to help Charli up. "I'm sorry if I made this all about me. You've waited for seven years for this moment."

"I'm just overwhelmed and happy to know that Willow has been so well loved and cared for all these years, especially after all we learned about her first year or so over in PA with Frankie."

Camille ushered Charli toward the exit. "I have no idea how I'm going to tell Sam and the girls."

"I guess we just tell them that your family got a little unexpectedly bigger," Charli offered gently.

Camille grabbed Charli's hand and squeezed it as they walked down the busy sidewalk. "I can't imagine anyone I'd rather add to my family."

EPILOGUE

Charli stood at the end of the long modern glass table in the oversize dining room overlooking the churning waters of the Strait of Juan de Fuca, the ever-present Olympic Mountain range twenty-five miles off in the distance, imposing itself over the lavender mist on the strait. That mountain range had almost become a part of the family for the group gathered around the table.

"I'm so glad you could all be here for the inaugural meeting of the board of directors of the Unshackled Fund." Charli gestured toward the sixteen-foot-tall windows. "I haven't been at our Lopez Island get-away out here on Flint Beach since I went down. And to be honest, I was hesitant to even come here. But filling this place with the people I love most in the world gives me hope for the future."

Camille looked around the table at her fellow board members. Frankie and Talulla sat arm in arm, smiling widely, while Lizbeth's sister, Isabel, pulled a notebook out of her backpack and offered to be the board secretary. It seemed like Gigi hadn't left Charli's side since she arrived.

Rose was the first to speak. She looked directly at Quinn, who had just come out of inpatient rehab, and then turned to Charli. "I just want to say that I'm really honored that you invited me to participate in this project. I gotta be real: in my wildest dreams, I never thought I'd be here sitting next to this guy." She smiled at Quinn. "The bravery that recovering addicts bring to this work is staggering to me, and I just want to acknowledge those of you who've made it through the dark night of addiction. And"—she smiled at Charli—"thank you so much for asking me to serve on your board."

Sally spoke next. "My job here is to keep alive the memories of all those who have perished at the hands of the pharmaceutical industry, especially from oxy. I'm here in memory of my sister, Kitt." She looked skyward. "Love you, sis. May your death serve to inspire a system of healing and harm reduction so the other families will never have to experience the loss that ours did." She kissed two fingers and shot the energy up into the heavens.

Camille leaned over and rubbed Sally's back. "Exactly. That's exactly why we're here. Thanks for sharing your sister's story with us. Her life will create second chances for many addicts and their families."

"I gotta weigh in here before I start blubbering." Quinn put his elbows on the table and leaned forward, his chin in his hands. "The amount of grace and forgiveness I experience from everyone here at this table will be on my heart for the rest of my life." He wiped away a tear. "I know I harmed many, many people, not the least of which are right here in this room. I don't know how you all have gotten to a place in your lives where you can give assholes like me a second chance. But I will never, ever let you down." He squeezed his eyes shut to try to quell the tears. "I promise, I will make amends for the harm I've caused."

Frankie got up and walked over to hug Quinn. "I love you, my brother, and I'll always be here for you."

Quinn didn't even try to stop the tears at this point.

The room was silent for a few minutes, then Charli took charge of the meeting.

"I would like to call to order the first ever meeting of the board of directors of the Unshackled Fund. One thing I learned in prison is that there are just as many invisible shackles that hold us back as the ones they put on me when I was in labor." She paused and looked around the table and then at the giant screen on the wall, where Pella's face beamed from her apartment across the world on Lesvos. "And it shouldn't take a trip to prison for women to learn how to unlock those self-imposed shackles."

Camille waited as Charli's statement sank in, and then she spoke. "You all know that my friend Gloria is doing some work over on San

Juan Island with formerly incarcerated women. I spoke with her this week, and she's offered to help us in any way she can."

Sally chimed in. "Gloria is a force. We can all learn a lot from her."

"This world needs more collaboration. When powerful women band together, there's no stopping us." Gigi's statement was met with finger clicking around the table.

Charli didn't wipe away the tears that were streaking down her cheeks. "I would like to remind everyone that the reason we are all here is to make sure that each and every woman coming out of prison here in Western Washington—and, hopefully soon, across the state—has a place to live and a way to get their children back. And partnering with orgs like Gloria's is the best possible way to launch this project." She waited for a beat. "So, that's why I'm donating almost all of the money I receive in my divorce settlement, which will be several million dollars, to this cause. And then I can continue to fund it from the profits of my *legal* pharmacy chain. My goal is to fund existing organizations already doing this work, and to create halfway houses for the women coming home. We'll also pay for family law legal services, and to give each and every one of our clients an opportunity to get up in the mountains with Frankie. We will also offer supportive coaching to help the women stay drug-free."

"I have something to add." Camille's voice pierced the quiet room. "You all know that I'm teaming up with an old trial lawyer friend to represent a growing group of women who have suffered serious life-changing damages due to the actions of Martin Zhao. His unconscionable violations of almost every standard of care for a pharmacist and a pharmacy have wreaked havoc on more lives than we can probably ever count." She turned and looked at the big screen. "One thing I learned from my mom is that our lives need to matter. We need to leverage every bit of privilege that we have to make a difference. So, with that in mind, I'll be donating most of my fees for processing this lawsuit to the Unshackled Fund."

Charli interrupted. "Oh my gosh! Really?"

Camille nodded. "The way I look at it, you get half of the community assets in the divorce, and then I'll clean out whatever's left and whatever we can squeeze out of the insurance company in this lawsuit. That asshat won't have a pot to piss in—if and when he ever gets out of

prison." She met Rose's gaze. "As lawyers we don't often get an opportunity to prevent a wrong—we mostly end up doing damage control
for the messes people, and society, create. I'm sure Rose joins in my
gratitude for being able to use our legal skills to actually intervene and
make things right again."

Rose didn't look away from Camille. "You are exactly right. The law
has gotten so focused on punishment and retaliation, when it should
be about rehabilitation. I'm not saying that people shouldn't be pun-
ished, or somehow bear the consequences of their actions. But putting
trauma survivors into cages with no access to treatment does absolutely
nothing to protect society from the disease of addiction and trauma.
People who are trying to survive heartbreaking childhoods, and sexual
violence, and poor medical care after an injury—which are the leading precursors of addiction—need treatment and care, not prison in its
current form." She stopped for a moment. "I know this is the last thing
you would expect to hear from a prosecutor, but I've seen what happened to Quinn and Frankie play out over and over again in the courtroom, as a defense lawyer and now as a prosecutor. And even though
Frankie went through our diversion program, it wasn't enough because
there was no ongoing program for those who inevitably relapse. Don't
get me wrong—it's a good start. But there's lots of work to do. And
Quinn had absolutely no help from any local or state agency. Taxpayers
just have no heart to fund these kinds of programs. So, until the state
finds its way to drastically increase its funding of these programs, it's
up to nonprofits and private funding to help people in recovery, which
is no way to transform a broken system. So I just want to say thank you
from the bottom of my heart to anyone who commits to funding this
work. You all are true angels from heaven."

It was Frankie's turn. "As you all know, I'm a self-taught healer. No
one had the grace to help me when I relapsed. I appreciate the diversion program, but once I was out of that program, no one gave my life
a second thought. It was nature, the mountains, and my own deep will
to heal that got me back from the brink of hell. I have no idea how I'm
going to do it, but I'm going to find a way to train other recovering
addicts and trauma survivors to join me in my work. And it's time for
me to come out of hiding and celebrate this work, not just hang out
up in the mountains in my secret hideaway." She paused. "Especially

now that I don't have to look over my shoulder for Martin Zhao." She grinned widely.

"I wanna be your first student apprentice." Isabel was laser focused on Frankie. "You have no idea how long I've waited to hear you say this. I've watched you for years, and all I want to do is follow in your footsteps."

"And now you'll have all the funding you need to expand your program as you find and train other leaders." Gigi began to clap lightly. "This is just awesome."

Quinn waited for a pause in the conversation. "Well, don't forget the men. We get addicted too. And man, do we ruin lives. Oxy and meth make anyone violent—we need love and forgiveness too."

Camille nodded. "Absolutely, and once we get this women's program up and running, nothing is stopping us from expanding to create programs for men."

"That would be awesome." Quinn was visibly grateful. He took a breath and continued. "You all might know that I was on track to becoming a pharmacist when I got waylaid by meth." He paused and looked around the table, stopping to lock eyes with Frankie. "I've decided that I'm going to apply for the PhD program in clinical psychology at the U, where I want to study the science behind addiction." He looked at Sally. "And I'm hoping you can help me find my way through the bureaucracy over there. I have a 4.0 GPA from undergrad. Before my wild ride on meth." Quinn smiled weakly.

Frankie closed her eyes and smiled widely.

"Actually," Sally responded, "grad schools are looking for students like you. They want people with lived experience to engage in scholarship that makes a difference in the community."

"God bless you, Quinn. There are so many good ideas around this table, but you going back to school to help others is beyond special." Charli crossed her hands, palms over her chest. "I have deep gratitude for each and every one of you. And it occurs to me, as I look around this table, that each of us has a ripple effect that we don't often even think about. I expect, as we team up for this project, that ripple effect will increase by a magnitude that none of us would be able to accomplish on our own. So, I just want to thank all of you for your willingness to use your considerable experience and brilliance to bring mothers and their children back together, which in turn will heal society in ways we probably can't even imagine." She took a deep breath as she made eye contact with each person around the table. The team sat in silence for several seconds, taking in the enormity of the task ahead.

After a pause, Charli opened her laptop. "I'd say our first order of business is to get a budget from Frankie and her team so we can get that program funded ASAP. Then our second step is to fund a family law clinic that can go inside the prison and work with the women. The reunification of moms and kids is our number one priority." She looked at Camille. "I know you have a crazy-busy law practice, but I'm hoping you'll find time to lead this initiative. I've already reached out to the family law clinic at the Seattle University law school, and the director is thrilled to offer students to help with this effort. They just need a lawyer to be in charge." Charli scrunched up her shoulders and shot Camille a coy smile. "So . . ."

As if on cue, Gracie buzzed into the room. "Mom-two! I love this place! Me 'n' Dad-two found a whole bucket of oysters right there on the beach!"

The tall Asian man right behind Gracie laughed. "Hey, you! Don't drip seawater all over the floor!" He winked at the group sitting around the table as Gracie pulled an oyster out of her bucket and showed it off.

"Dad-two says we can fry these up for dinner!"

Jing popped in just behind Gracie and Brian. "How the meeting going?" Her gaze was intense. "I been thinking. I like to teach yoga to the women come out of prison." She cocked her head. "I take time away from Gracie to help the women. It best for everyone."

Brian hugged his mom. And looked at Charli. "Brilliant. Mom was just working us through a yoga routine down on the beach." He faked rubbing his lower back and laughed. "I feel like a human pretzel. The prison gym can't hold a candle to yoga with Jing Zhao." He laughed.

Gracie leaned down and put her hands on the floor, butt high in the air, and said something in Chinese. "That's 'downward dog' in Chinese," she said from her upside-down perch while Jing moved Gracie's hands into the proper position.

"You do like this." Jing got on the floor next to Gracie and demonstrated.

Gracie shouted at Pella on the big screen, "Hey, Yia Yia, look at me! Now I have two yoga grandmas!"

The warmth of Pella's smile permeated the room. "You're so lucky to have a Seattle grandma now!"

Gracie, still upside down, nodded her head wildly. "I know! At first I told my new grandma that I already had enough grandmas. But I was wrong. Now I got three! And this one is really cool!"

Charli went over and hugged her beau, who was still holding the bucket of freshly picked oysters—the aroma of salt water filling the room. "Now, here's something neither of us ever thought we'd dine on again. This is a long way from prison food." She kissed his cheek and looked at her friends. "It looks like Gracie ruined my surprise for our mystery dinner guest." She laughed. "Everyone. Meet my guy—Brian! And his mom, Jing. He just got released last week and has been decompressing here with me and Gracie—who's been splitting time between us and Camille and Sam, et al." She looked at Camille. "How many other moms are out there, aching for just this moment?"

Now it was Camille's turn to cry.

"You can make this happen." Charli looked up at Camille while she hugged Gracie. "Over and over and over. We're just one of many. We need you to train new lawyers to reunite moms and their kids. And teach the judges the importance of ending this whole trauma-to-prison pipeline." Her voice went up an octave. "We need you."

"You had me at reuniting moms and their kids." Camille's smile came from someplace deep in her heart. This would be a huge part of her life's work. "I am one hundred percent in." She looked over Brian's shoulder at Sam, who was leaning against the doorjamb, taking in the room full of warriors. "One hundred percent."

Sam smiled back and blew her a kiss.

AUTHOR'S NOTE

It's my deepest hope that this story has inspired you to join in the spirit of Camille and the gang in supporting programs that help mothers reunite with their children after prison. Research shows that we can minimize the risk we create in our communities when the criminal legal system separates moms and kids. Knowing this—after I wrote the last scene in this book—I decided to start a charitable fund that supports many programs like the ones in my story. I'm calling it the **Unshackled Fund**. As you know, all the proceeds from my books go to organizations and people doing this work—so just by purchasing this book you've already made a difference. And for that I thank you from the bottom of my heart. But if you're like me, now that you know, it'll be hard to turn your back on these moms and kids. And so, I'm hoping that you'll do more. Please visit AmandaDuBois.com to learn how you can join me in solving this important issue in our communities.

—Amanda DuBois

ACKNOWLEDGMENTS

Over the years, I've had the great privilege of becoming friends with many, many women who served time in prison. And boy, have they taught me a lot. Several of these friends helped to bring this story to life. Here's a huge thanks to all of you, especially Deb Sheehan, the program manager at Freedom Education Project Puget Sound (provides college classes in the women's prison in Washington); Carolyn Presnell, the program director at Weld Seattle (works with people returning home from prison and those recovering from addiction to discover a new sense of belonging and becoming); and Cynthia Brady, substance abuse counselor; and an extra thank-you to my very special friend Ivy Woolf Turk, founder of Project Liberation in NYC (provides a paradigm-shifting personal-development platform for women across all stages of criminal justice involvement). Ivy's also a certified life coach.

There are other women who've taught me about their lives as moms in prison, and who inspired me to write this story. They're important to me, and I want to acknowledge them here: Ginny Burton, Kristi O'Brien, Michelle McClendon, and Carolina Landa.

And I couldn't have written this book without the help of my friends who are national experts in their fields. Thanks to all of you!

Pella Rallis and Sally Berwyn couldn't have spouted all those stats if I hadn't had the help of two women: Emily Salisbury, PhD—director, Utah Criminal Justice Center, and associate professor of social work at the University of Utah. Emily is the national expert on criminal needs assessments designed to address the needs of justice-involved women. And Regina LaBelle, JD—distinguished scholar and initiative director, Georgetown University, and former Obama-Biden official. Regina's scholarship focuses on pursuing addiction policies rooted in science and evidence and driven by compassion.

When my friend Kim Bogucki, retired Seattle Police Department detective and cofounder of the If Project, read my manuscript, you can bet her red pen came out to fix the cop scenes. Thanks, Kim!

As a family law lawyer, I can write a family law court scene with ease. But for the record-vacate hearing, I needed to call in an expert! Thanks, Lara Zarowsky, JD, executive and policy director at Washington Innocence Project. And for the criminal-procedure stuff, I needed criminal lawyers on speed dial—thank you, Corrie Boseman, JD, and Robert Flennaugh, JD.

Thanks also to Gary Ernsdorff, JD, and Candice Duclos, JD, at the King County prosecutor's office—division of civil forfeiture—with a special shout-out to Leesa Manion, King County prosecutor, for introducing us!

When I was writing the scene with Frankie and Camille in the mountains, my friend Chris Poulos, JD, just happened to post a picture of a hike he was taking—and it quickly became the cover art for the book. Chris has overcome addiction and a prison sentence and is now a national leader in changing the lives of people in prison. He's also a lawyer, a mountain-rescue volunteer, and an amazing photographer.

No book gets created without early readers—thanks so much, Heidi Bateman, Cathy Cooper, and Julie Fisher Cummings!

And, most importantly, a huge thank-you to Shelli Ardnt and Jenny Mothershead, who are currently incarcerated at WCCW and took the time to read the manuscript to make sure it accurately reflected their experience inside the prison.

ABOUT THE AUTHOR

Amanda DuBois worked as a labor and delivery nurse before becoming a lawyer. She has practiced in the areas of medical malpractice and family law. She founded the DuBois Levias Law Group in Seattle, Washington, where she is actively engaged in litigation; and Civil Survival, an organization that teaches advocacy skills to formerly incarcerated individuals. Amanda serves on several boards that support social justice and women's issues. Her most recent passion is funding her Full Circle Scholarship, which provides tuition assistance at her alma mater, Seattle University School of Law. This scholarship is specifically granted to students whose lives have been impacted by the criminal legal system. All the author's profits from your book purchase will be donated to the Full Circle Scholarship or to individuals or organizations that promote social justice issues. This is the third novel in the Camille Delaney Mystery series.

READ ALL THE BOOKS IN THE

CAMILLE DELANEY MYSTERY

SERIES!

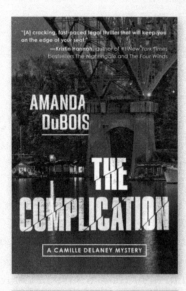
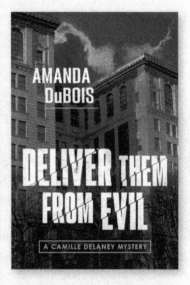
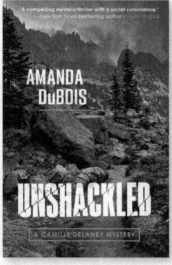

Printed in the USA
CPSIA information can be obtained
at www.ICGtesting.com
JSHW060539201124
73813JS00002B/2